CHAOS
REIGNING

CHAOS REIGNING

A NOVEL

JESSIE MIHALIK

HARPER Voyager
An Imprint of HarperCollins*Publishers*

CHAOS REIGNING. Copyright © 2020 by Jessie Mihalik. All rights reserved. Printed in the United States of America. No part of this book may be used or reproduced in any manner whatsoever without written permission except in the case of brief quotations embodied in critical articles and reviews. For information, address HarperCollins Publishers, 195 Broadway, New York, NY 10007.

HarperCollins books may be purchased for educational, business, or sales promotional use. For information, please email the Special Markets Department at SPsales@harpercollins.com.

Harper Voyager and design are trademarks of HarperCollins Publishers LLC.

FIRST EDITION

Designed by Paula Russell Szafranski

Library of Congress Cataloging-in-Publication Data has been applied for.

ISBN 978-0-06-280242-2

20 21 22 23 24 LSC 10 9 8 7 6 5 4 3 2 1

To Dustin. Without you, I'd be lost.
I love you.

ACKNOWLEDGMENTS

Welcome to the third and final book in the Consortium Rebellion Trilogy! I can hardly believe it's been three books already. Thank you so much to everyone who made it possible, including the readers who celebrated each book with me. I hope you enjoy this one, too.

A book takes a team to produce, and I'd like to thank the following people for helping me get this one out into the world.

Thanks to Sarah E. Younger, my agent extraordinaire. Without you, there would be no trilogy. I'm so delighted we get to work together!

Thanks to Tessa Woodward, my incredible editor, whose insightful comments helped this book become far better. Thanks to the entire team at Harper Voyager, including Elle Keck, Kayleigh Webb, Imani Gary, and everyone else who helped make this book a reality. You really are the best team in the business!

Thanks to Patrick Ferguson, Tracy Smith, and Whitney Bates for always being willing to read my early drafts and give feedback, as well as for putting up with me when I'm on deadline!

ACKNOWLEDGMENTS

Thanks to Ilona, Gordon, Bree, and Donna for all of the help, support, industry advice, cheerleading, and general awesomeness. You all are the best and I appreciate your help so much!

And last but not least, my deepest love and gratitude to my husband, Dustin, who supported my writing dream from the very beginning and made this book—and all of the others—possible. Without his love and support, I wouldn't be where I am today. Dustin, you're the best husband anyone could ask for, and I am so, so lucky to have you. I love you!

CHAOS REIGNING

The wineglass shattered in my hand, slicing deep into my palm and fingers. Red blood welled, but bitter disappointment overshadowed the physical pain.

Stupid, stupid girl. The silent words echoed in my father's voice.

I should not have checked my com at the party, but communication from my brother Benedict was scarce, and I couldn't resist. *Mistake.* Benedict's latest war update painted a bleak picture, and I'd stopped paying attention just long enough to break the glass.

I'd been doing *so well*, but there would be no hiding this, not with blood dripping down my arm. I glanced around. I'd stepped out into the garden, away from the rest of the party, but the twilight shadows were not deep enough for me to slip away entirely. Susan, my bodyguard, watched over me from the patio, and it was only thanks to the angle that she hadn't noticed the injury already.

There was nothing for it.

With a sigh, I tripped on the air and fell into the grass,

landing with a yell. Glass shards sliced deeper and I didn't have to fake the next pained groan.

"Lady Catarina, are you all right?" Susan shouted, her voice full of concern. She was the first to notice, as expected, despite the distance between us. After Ferdinand's disappearance, House von Hasenberg family members were now assigned bodyguards at all times.

Footsteps approached, and I sat up, cradling my bloody hand. Susan gasped and called for a medic from the backup security vehicle outside. "I'm okay," I assured her, "but the wineglass didn't survive."

She bent down to assess the injury. Her dark suit faded into the shadows, accentuating her pale skin and blond hair. Twenty-eight and happily married, she was one of my favorite bodyguards. She met my eyes, expression worried. "What happened?"

I gave her, and the growing crowd behind her, a bright, vapid smile. "I think I must've had too much of House Durand's excellent wine."

Twitters rose from the bystanders. No one was quite brave enough to insult me to my face—I was the daughter of a High House after all—but they weren't laughing *with* me, either.

Susan, who was used to my antics, didn't bat an eye, and that was somehow worse than the pitying looks from the crowd. I wanted to tell her that I wasn't this person, that I'd built this facade when I didn't know any better and now I was trapped.

But of course I couldn't.

So I smiled while the medic extracted the glass from my hand and slathered it in regeneration gel. And I smiled as I moved through the crowd of vicious gossips who barely veiled their clever slights behind concerned looks and condescending advice.

At twenty-one, I was the youngest von Hasenberg heir. People thought that made me gullible, so I played into the narrative. I flitted from group to group, bubbly and shallow, more concerned with fashion and shopping than war and treachery. It was an exaggeration of my normal personality, but some days the mask was harder to wear than others.

Lately it had been harder still, especially when I could clearly hear the whispers that trailed in my wake.

None of them were kind.

It didn't help that I remained stuck here on Earth while all of my siblings went gallivanting off across the universe. They insisted on treating me like a child, never mind that I was an adult in my own right. I loved them to death, but they were smothering me.

Every day the thought of getting in my ship and pointing it at a distant planet grew more and more appealing. Only honor, duty, and love kept me earthbound. We'd all worried after Ada had left, and while her story had turned out for the best, I didn't want to put my brothers and sisters through another round of anxiety.

Not yet, not when everything was so unstable.

So I stayed at the party, because socializing was the one thing I was good at. I mingled, and laughed, and ignored the barbs. And if it all felt empty and hollow, I ignored that, too. House Durand was an ally, and we needed all the allies we could get while at war. I was here to strengthen that relationship.

It was all I could do.

For now.

TWO DAYS LATER, I FELT LIKE A SPRING THAT WAS WOUND too tight. My hand had healed, thanks to the regeneration gel, and I hadn't had any more accidents, but I couldn't settle. Enclosed in my private office, I paced and worried. I'd designed the space to be soothing, with pale green walls and antique wooden furniture, but right now it felt oppressive.

After months of careful planning, everything was finally coming together, with one tiny exception—I still had to tell my sister Bianca what I'd done. I'd scheduled breakfast with her, so at least I wouldn't have to carry this anxiety all day. Not that the rest of my schedule was any better. After Bianca, I had to face one of Mother's official House brunches.

One thing at a time.

I tucked away my restlessness and painted on the face I showed the outside world, then smoothed a hand down my pink-and-blue polka-dot dress. It flared around my knees and made me look young and carefree. My wardrobe tended toward bright colors as a distracting visual camouflage.

I checked my smile in the hallway mirror on my way out. There was too much tension around my eyes. I blinked and tried again. *Better.*

I didn't really look like a von Hasenberg. My four oldest siblings had all taken after our father, with strong features, ruddy skin, and light brown hair. Ada and I had taken after our mother, with more delicate features, golden skin, and dark brown hair. Ada had also inherited Mother's blue-gray eyes, but mine were a more common golden brown.

I joked that my five older siblings had used up all of the good genes, a joke that hit a little too close to home considering how sick I'd been as a child, but I liked the anonymity of not being immediately recognized as a member of my House.

My reflected smile turned wry. I was never anonymous, not really, but sometimes it was nice to pretend.

I continued down the short hallway to the living room. If my office was an oasis of calm, my living room was a riot of color. The walls were white, but large, colorful abstract prints adorned them. My furniture was all brightly hued. A lime green sofa, orange chair, and purple tables somehow formed a beautiful, cohesive design. The interior decorator I'd hired had earned every credit I'd paid her.

This was my public face, shown even to the few friends who were close enough to get to see the inside of my suite. We were all liars, to one degree or another.

Susan waited for me in the hallway outside, wearing her trademark dark suit, today paired with a pale pink shirt. "Going out, Lady Catarina?"

"I am heading to breakfast with Bianca, but I want to stop by a coffee shop on the way."

She inclined her head in agreement and silently fell in behind me. I liked her because she always instinctively seemed to know if I wanted to be left alone with my thoughts or if I wanted idle chatter to fill the silence.

We stepped outside and I let my gaze drift over the city. Serenity, the headquarters of the Royal Consortium and the only inhabited city on Earth, was just beginning to wake, bathed in the brilliant gold of early morning sunlight.

The city was laid out in a circle and each High House owned a quarter. The quarters were divided into sectors starting from the middle. The Royal Consortium government buildings were in the very center, colloquially called Sector Zero. The family residence for each quarter took up the entirety of Sector One. The other nine sectors contained shops, offices, residences, and all of the amenities found in a large city.

The closer the sector was to the center of the circle, the more expensive it was to live and work there. Also, the buildings closer to the middle tended to be shorter, driving up prices even more due to the lack of supply. It made for an interesting view as the city grew taller and taller in the distance. Sector Ten was almost entirely skyscrapers over a hundred stories tall.

I took a deep breath, closed my eyes, and let the warmth of the sun shrink my worries back into manageable sizes. There were *some* benefits to being stuck on a planet.

And being able to go outside was a major one. I spent a lot of time outdoors because my earliest memories were of the white walls and locked windows of a medical center. As a child, I'd spent hours staring wistfully out of the small window in my room. I'd been sickly, despite the nanobots in my blood that were supposed to keep me well, and I still carried side effects from my numerous treatments.

I masked the side effects, like I masked my true personality, but these secrets were much more important to keep.

I opened my eyes with a sigh. Secrets and lies seemed to be all I dealt in these days. It was exhausting.

Susan and I entered the House transport, and I set the destination for Bianca's favorite coffee shop. The transport lifted into the air with the familiar, soothing thrum of the engine.

My mind drifted and landed on the exact thing it shouldn't: the unknown man at the club last night. My best friend, Ying Yamado, had persuaded me to go out with her, and I'd caught sight of him as soon as we walked in the door.

A stranger was hardly unusual, but this man had been captivating. Powerfully built and radiating quiet confidence, he was likely a soldier on leave. He wasn't my usual type, but I'd been drawn to him like a moth to flame. I'd caught sight of him a few times, but before I'd worked up the courage to go say hello, he'd vanished.

And now my mind was stuck on him.

I acknowledged the attraction and then let the thought go.

He wasn't for me, not even for a night. It took a while, but I let him drift from my thoughts and focused on centering myself for the day to come.

By the time we landed, I felt calmer. It wouldn't last, but I'd take what I could get.

THE SMALL COFFEE SHOP IN SECTOR EIGHT OF THE VON Hasenberg quarter bustled with customers, but the line moved quickly. I was meeting Bianca for breakfast at her apartment, but I wanted to bring her something she loved, and this shop served her favorite coffee. And if it helped to soften her up for the news to come, that wouldn't be a bad thing, either.

After securing our coffees, Susan and I returned to the transport and lifted off, trailed by an additional House von Hasenberg security transport—an unfortunately common sight now.

Ian Bishop was the director of House security, and between the attack on Ferdinand and his relationship with Bianca, he'd become even more overprotective, especially once Father kicked Bianca out of her suite in the main house. She and Ian shared a penthouse a block away from the main House von Hasenberg complex, but you'd think she lived deep in a war zone from the way Ian worried.

It was kind of adorable, unless you wanted to walk to see your older sister—then it was just annoying. In the past few weeks, Director Bishop had made a security team shadow me even for the short walk between the main house and their apartment, so I wasn't surprised that one followed us now.

Bianca's penthouse spanned the entire top floor and would have cost a fortune if our House didn't own the property.

Ten stories tall and situated on the corner of the block, the building was made of smooth gray stone. It had a view of the House von Hasenberg gardens as well as the ornate stone main house itself. Personally, I thought Father let her have the location because he wanted her to be able to see what she was missing.

I didn't think it had worked because in the last two months she'd been as happy as I'd ever seen her, even after the forced move.

The penthouse had its own private entrance from the street. I swiped the identity chip in my right arm over the reader and the entry door popped open. Bianca had always given her siblings free access to her suite, and that practice carried over here, too.

The entryway opened into a tiny lobby with a single elevator and a set of stairs behind a locked door. On the far side of the elevator, another door opened to an office and lounge for visiting bodyguards. While Bianca might not mind her siblings running roughshod over her privacy, that same attitude did not extend to our guards. Both the elevator and stairs opened only here and in the penthouse, so having the guard wait at ground level had been deemed acceptable.

It didn't hurt that the person making the rules was deeply in love with my sister and would do anything to make her happy.

The elevator required another identity check. I took the few seconds alone to check my smile in the reflective elevator doors. I didn't usually hide my true feelings from my siblings, but I didn't want Bianca to worry about me, not when there were so many other, more important, things to worry about.

Bianca's living room was a study in retro-industrial looks. Silver chain link curtains spanned the large windows and glittered in the sun. The furniture was sleek and black. Exposed ductwork in the high ceilings added additional visual interest, and a single vivid painting saved the room from being utterly colorless.

The air was rich with the smell of cinnamon and sugar, but my sister was conspicuously absent. "Bee?" I called.

"We're in the kitchen!" she yelled back.

My smile slipped at the *we*. I didn't know anyone else was joining us for breakfast, but if Bianca was yelling like that, then it couldn't be anyone too important. Maybe our oldest sister Hannah was back on Earth. She had taken some much-needed time away, but I hadn't expected her back for another month or two.

The living room and dining room were one large, open space, but the kitchen was tucked away out of sight. Bianca liked to cook and her vast kitchen reflected that. It had the full range of high-end appliances as well as two oversize synthesizers.

I took in the scene at a glance. An unknown man and woman sat at the bar while Bianca bustled around. My sister had on a casual outfit and *flats*. The only time Bianca went without towering heels was around close friends and family. So who were these two and why had I never met them before? They turned my way, and I froze.

It was the man from the club.

I blinked and switched into public mode, mind racing. *What was he doing here?* I had a feeling that the pause hadn't gone unnoticed by either of them as they tracked my progress into the room.

The woman had pale ivory skin, strawberry blond hair, and a lean build. Her eyes were sharp and neutral. Not unfriendly, more like undecided. The man had light brown skin, dark hair, and heavy musculature. His square jaw had a few days of dark stubble adorning it. His features were too strong for traditional beauty, but he was damn attractive all the same. His expression was even more guarded than the woman's.

He did not seem to recognize me. That should have brought relief, but I felt a vague sense of disappointment instead.

Both of them wore close-fitting black shirts. I'd bet utility pants and boots hid behind the bar. Not Consortium types, then. Were they Ada's friends from Sedition?

I realized I'd been staring for a beat too long and turned to my sister with a wide smile. "Bianca, you didn't tell me you had visitors," I admonished. "I would've rescheduled! And I apologize, but since I didn't know you had guests, I only brought coffee for you."

She accepted the coffee with a hug and a grateful smile. "These aren't guests, these are my friends Alexander Sterling and Aoife Delaney." She pronounced the woman's name *EE-fa*. "They helped me rescue Ferdinand. I wanted you to meet them."

I turned back to them. "Thank you so much for your help," I said sincerely. I'd gotten only the barest of details out of Bianca about how she'd found Ferdinand and gotten him out, but based on the introduction, I bet these two were a big part of it. We owed them a great deal.

The woman waved off my words. "Your sister more than paid us," she said. Her voice was pleasant, with just a hint of a lilt. She was likely lower to middle class from one of the more isolated planets where Universal Standard wasn't taught as rigidly.

Bianca put a tray of warm sticky buns on the small table in the kitchen's breakfast nook. "Shall we talk over food?" she asked a little too brightly.

I narrowed my eyes at her. What was she plotting?

While Bianca could have easily ordered food from the synthesizer, she preferred cooking. And, truth be told, synthesized food had nothing on Bianca's cooking, so I was always delighted to eat at her table. Today she didn't disappoint. The informal kitchen table was laden with four different kinds of pastries, all homemade, as well as bacon, eggs, and roasted potatoes.

The round table seated four. I sat next to Bianca. Alexander took the seat across from me and Aoife sat on my left. If anyone else noticed the tension in the air, they didn't show it. I was generally very good at reading people, but Alexander gave me nothing other than that he had good manners. I had to force myself not to stare at him.

"How goes the investigation?" Bianca asked.

My gaze cut to hers, but I couldn't tell what she was doing. "I don't want to bore your guests," I demurred. Why would she bring up House business in front of strangers? I was looking into Ferdinand's kidnapping. Both Hannah's husband, Pierre, and House James were involved, and that wasn't information we wanted shared.

"Not guests," she reminded me, "*friends*. And they are here to help."

I kept the shock and suspicion off my face. "Help how?"

"From what I've seen, you've wrapped up everything you can do here. What is your next step?"

While Bianca had been chasing after Ferdinand, I'd muscled my way into the investigation here on Earth, and I'd refused to give it up once she returned. Bianca had reluctantly agreed to let me help, but only if we worked together.

No one trusted me to be able to do anything on my own.

We had found the ties between Pierre and House James, but hadn't been able to tie House James to any of the other Houses or the Syndicate, despite Bianca's uncanny ability to gather intelligence. Either House James was acting alone or they were being very, very careful.

But so was I.

Over the last two months, I'd slowly expanded my circle of friends to include Lynn Segura and Chloe Patel, the two young women who had been caught talking shit about Bianca. Lynn was a genuine delight. Chloe was *not*. But both of them were friends with Stephanie James, youngest daughter of House James.

And every year, Stephanie James hosted a summer retreat at House James's estate outside Honorius. It was part vacation and part informal networking event, but mostly it was a chance to get out of Serenity and have some fun away from censorious eyes. It also coincided with the stunning annual Bouman meteor shower.

When guests weren't busy trying to steal kisses while watching space rocks burn up in the atmosphere, Honorius had some of the best haute couture shopping in the 'verse. House James also offered an assortment of entertainments on their sprawling estate, including an excellent hover bike rally-cross racecourse.

Invitations were highly coveted in Stephanie's circle of friends and acquaintances, and this year Chloe was finally old enough to help her best friend host—a task she had taken up with gusto.

Based solely on our brief friendship, Chloe had been cheeky enough to invite me, and through me, Ying Yamado, the daughter of High House Yamado. She was aiming high, which is exactly what I had expected. If even one of us accepted, it would be a major coup for her.

I had let her stew for two days before accepting, and then

I'd talked Ying into accepting, too. But now I had to break the news to my overprotective older sister. In front of *friends*.

"I'm attending Stephanie James's house party in two days. I will be gone for at least two weeks."

Bianca smiled, which immediately put me on guard. That was not the reaction I'd expected. "That's perfect," she said.

Concern whispered through me—something odd was going on. "I thought you'd be against it," I said, fishing.

Bianca's smile softened just a tiny bit. "I don't love sending you into danger, Cat, you know that, but we need information, and right now, you're the one best positioned to get it."

I glanced at our silent dining companions. They were both pretending to focus on their food, but I caught Alexander's gaze. His eyes were a rich, warm brown. Despite his guarded expression, he had kind eyes, not what I would expect from a man with his build. Once again, I was struck by the fact that he looked like a soldier—or a bodyguard.

And then, like a light blinking on, suspicion hardened into certainty. I turned back to my sister. "Bianca," I said slowly, "why are Ms. Delaney and Mr. Sterling here?"

Bianca's smile never faltered. If anything, it got brighter. I was not going to like whatever came out of her mouth next.

She proved me right when she said, "Aoife is going to be your bodyguard while you're in Honorius."

"I already have a guard," I reminded her. "Several, actually."

"None like me," Aoife said without an ounce of humility *or* arrogance. It was less a boast and more a statement of fact, one I was inclined to believe based on nothing more than her attitude and confidence.

I might be the most sheltered of my siblings, but I was still a von Hasenberg. I'd grown up around—and trained with—all types of people until the side effects of my childhood became too difficult to hide. Aoife had the calm self-assurance of someone who knew that she could take anyone in the room and come out ahead.

I briefly wondered how she would fare against *me*.

It was a silly thought because I'd given up real fighting long ago—it was too dangerous for me. But that didn't mean I was going to roll over. "That may be true, but I've worked with my current guards for years. I know and trust them." I also understood how they thought and how they might be influenced.

Aoife's flawless composure was impossible to read, but I smiled apologetically at her. She inclined her head slightly, seemingly not offended.

My eyes snagged on Alexander. For such a big man, he had a way of fading into the background that was almost uncanny. If not for my humming awareness of him, I might've overlooked him completely.

"And you?" I asked him directly. "Why are you here? Are you Ms. Delaney's partner?" I glanced between them. "Or husband?"

A slow smile broke over his face and he chuckled quietly. My breath caught. He was utterly captivating when he smiled and for the first time I envied the beautiful woman next to me.

I felt his gaze like a physical weight and fought the prickling awareness trickling through my system. He focused on me intently, but I'd bet half my fortune that he also remained aware of everything else happening in the room and could react in a heartbeat.

What would it take to capture *all* of his attention?

I shoved the question away. He wasn't for me. Someday, I would marry for the good of the House, and until then, I preferred my men more manageable.

"We are partners," he said. His voice was low and delicious, a velvet rumble I felt in my chest. He had no discernible accent.

Partners could mean anything from business partners to romantic partners. Without knowing which, I had to stop mentally ogling him. I didn't pursue taken men.

I turned my attention back to Bianca. Mischief flittered through her expression before she smoothed it away. "Alex is here for you."

I forced myself not to react to the tiny thrill of pleasure I felt at the words. I frowned at her, not liking where this was going. "What do you mean?"

"He's going with you to Honorius as your plus one."

CHAPTER TWO

No." The denial was as flat and hard as I could make it. I knew from the set of Bianca's mouth that she expected me to argue and that she expected to win, but I wouldn't be moved. Taking someone was allowed by the invitation, but everyone would assume we were lovers. We would be rooming together, would have to spend all of our time together.

We would have to pretend to be a believable couple.

Alexander was exactly the opposite of the men I'd dated in the past. The others might not know me well enough to question it, but Ying would. She'd want to know why I'd brought a man she'd never met before. Our story would collapse.

"No," I repeated, just in case there was still any doubt. "If you must, send him with me as a guard."

"Guards won't have the same access as guests," Bianca said. "You could take him places where it would seem odd to take a guard."

"I'm the daughter of a High House," I said drily. "If I wanted my guard to jump into the pool with me, fully dressed, someone would run to fetch a towel."

"You don't want to give House James any reason to think

you are there for more than shopping and relaxation. A secret, illicit affair is juicy enough that it might blind them to your true purpose. And Alex can slip away and search for information while you socialize."

The pieces came together. "You knew I was going." No wonder she had capitulated so easily. Alexander hadn't been checking me out at the club, he'd been *following* me, on Bianca's orders. Sharp disappointment mixed with acute embarrassment. Thank heavens he'd vanished before I'd tried to chat him up or this meeting would've been a whole lot more awkward.

Sending Alexander and Aoife with me had been Bianca's plan all along. She didn't think I could handle it. Something like sorrow tried to rise at her lack of faith in me, but I masked it with a practiced smile.

Bianca grimaced. "Technically, *Ian* knew you were going. He asked for my advice."

"Director Bishop needs to stay out of my personal communication." Bitterness gave my voice bite.

Bianca's laugh echoed off of the walls. After years of being too subdued, it was a shock when Bianca laughed. The sound of her joy hit me so hard, I almost didn't mind that she was laughing at me. *Almost.*

"I told him something very similar about my own communication and it got me exactly nowhere, but you're welcome to try," she said. "Good luck."

I sighed and got back to my main point. "It won't work. No one will believe it. Where would I have met him? He doesn't exactly scream Consortium. No offense," I said belatedly.

Alexander grinned. "None taken."

"He and Aoife can be my guards," I said, trying to compromise. "No one will blink if I bring an extra, not with the war."

Bianca's expression turned shrewd. "Are you meeting someone there?"

I laughed. "If you think I need to go all the way to Andromeda Prime to get laid, you really have been gone for too long." Although the thought had definitely crossed my mind. Perhaps a little harmless fun would ease the restlessness I'd been feeling lately.

"It's settled, then. You and Alex will go as a couple. Aoife will go as your guard."

"It is *not* settled," I countered.

Bianca continued as if I hadn't spoken. "You and Alex can spend the day together today, get to know each other."

"Bianca Isabella, do not make me bust out your full name," I said. "I am not going to meet anyone, but I am not above flirting my way into information, either. That will be impossible if I show up with a companion. I have already thought this through, and I have a plan, let me run with it."

Granted, it was a loose plan—go to the party, get information—but it was *mine*. I'd been working on getting an invite to this party for months, and now that the hard part was over, Bianca wanted to swoop in and take charge, because she didn't trust me to do it. It stung.

My sister deflated, barely visible, but I caught the minute slump in her shoulders and the haunted look on her face. She wouldn't meet my eyes when she said, "I'm not trying to step on your toes, Cat. I just want to keep you safe. All of my information and I couldn't stop what happened to Ferdinand. And now my network is sending me mixed signals, but I feel like something big is coming. I don't want you to be unprotected when it hits."

If it had been pure manipulation, I would have ignored it, but there was a painful honesty to Bianca's voice. Restless frustration rose. I pushed it back. It wasn't Bianca's fault that I was stuck on Earth. That was my choice.

Still, I bit my tongue against the urge to give in, to smooth the way. I *hated* causing Bianca pain, but if I didn't stop this now, I'd find myself in Honorius with Alexander as my fake lover, my own plans in ruins.

Perhaps I needed to leave sooner than anticipated.

"Let me think about it," I said. "I know you are only trying to help, but you sprung it on me without warning, and my schedule is already jam-packed today." I gave Alexander and Aoife another apologetic smile. "I really do appreciate your offer to help, more than you know, but it's an unexpected boon. I'll need to adjust my own plans."

"Of course," Aoife agreed easily. "We have time."

FOR ONCE, I WAS GLAD THAT I WAS EXPECTED AT Mother's brunch because it gave me the perfect excuse to leave Bianca's early. Despite remaining mostly quiet, Alexander was impossible to ignore, and I still couldn't tell what kind of partners he and Aoife were. Distance was my friend.

An invitation to Maria von Hasenberg's semimonthly brunch was one of the most coveted in the Consortium social scene. Any event held by a High House always drew intense interest, but Mother knew how to generate the most buzz without any apparent effort on her part.

The draw was so strong that two weeks ago, Anne Rockhurst, matriarch of High House Rockhurst, had shown up to make nice and drink mimosas while our two militaries plotted the quickest way to destroy each other.

The brunches were always intimate, with between ten and fifteen guests. Both men and women were invited, but invitations were per individual—no extra guests allowed—and the guest list was always eclectic. Today's guests included House members, of course, but also the ambassador to a planet no one had ever heard of, a fashion designer, and an astrophysicist.

Bianca remained cut from the list, much to her delight and my dismay. Mother was upset that Bianca had chosen her own happiness over the House's best interest. She conveyed that disapproval in the most public way she could without officially banishing Bianca. All of my other siblings were out of town, so that left me to fend for myself.

I hoped I'd be seated near the astrophysicist, so I would have someone interesting to talk to.

With the nice weather, brunch would be outside, one tiny positive. I slipped into the building, Susan on my heels, and made my way to the formal breakfast room. The doors had been thrown open and a small crowd clustered on the terrace outside. A long table had been set up, covered in white linen, glittering crystal stemware, and shining silver cutlery. The gardens made a colorful backdrop, perfectly manicured to look wild and natural.

Never let it be said that House von Hasenberg did anything by half measures.

I smoothed my face into a pleasant smile and stepped outside. The first person to notice me was Tae Yamado, the second son of High House Yamado. He was a handsome man, with light golden skin, short black hair, and dark eyes. When he moved toward me, my smile turned genuine.

Tae was Ying's older brother and she loved him as fiercely as I loved my siblings. He was the most soft-spoken of the Yamado children. If he hadn't been a decade older than me and happily married, I would've tried to snag him, though as the spare, he was out of my league.

He'd married for the good of House Yamado, but by all accounts, he and his wife were making it work. I kept praying for a rogue meteorite to take out his older brother Hitoshi, so that Tae would become heir, but so far, my prayers went unanswered. Tae seemingly had no interest in House politics anyway. It was too bad Ying was the youngest, because she was the most qualified to lead the next generation of House Yamado.

"Cat, you look lovely, as always," Tae said. He kissed the air next to my cheek.

"Flatterer. What did you do to deserve getting dragged to this special hell?" I asked, my voice pitched for his ears only.

"Mother is under the weather, so I'm attending in her stead. I tried to con Ying into it, but she already had plans with Elizabeth Rockhurst that she couldn't break."

I chuckled at his wary expression, but it was smart for House Yamado to schedule events with both rival Houses on the same day. That way, it wouldn't seem like they were playing favorites in the war, and they would be able to gather intel from both sides.

"Well, now you get to escort me around and learn all the latest society gossip. Aren't you lucky?"

He held out his elbow. "I am indeed, Lady Catarina. Lead on, and please don't leave me alone with the vipers."

I patted his arm. "I'll do my best. How's your wife?"

His face softened. "She's very well, thank you for asking."

We both pasted on our social smiles and waded into the fray. Most of the gossip was worthless, but I kept my ears open for anything about the war. I doubt anyone had better information than we did, but it didn't hurt to pay attention.

Mother stood conversing with a short, spare, older man. Lord Henderson was the head of House Henderson. Rumor had it that he was angling for my hand in marriage regardless of the fact that he was old enough to be my father. I'd been raised to think of the House first, but I didn't know if I could force myself to marry Henderson. He made my skin crawl.

And I couldn't help comparing him to Alexander Sterling's warm brown eyes and muscular build. To say Henderson did not fare well in the comparison was a vast understatement.

When Mother saw me with Tae, her mouth compressed into a tiny frown. I bit back a smile and tucked my hand more securely into the crook of Tae's elbow. No doubt I would be seated near Lord Henderson for the meal, but for now, I could enjoy my moment of freedom.

Tae and I floated from group to group, charming and bubbly. Well, *I* was charming and bubbly, Tae mostly just nodded along or offered noncommittal grunts. Still, I was glad of his company because his presence shielded me from having to fend off other suitors, namely Henderson, who watched me with a predatory gaze.

While we were between groups, I noticed a woman in her late thirties standing alone. She fidgeted with her dress and looked like she wished she were somewhere else. I towed Tae in her direction. "Hello," I said, extending a hand as we approached, "I don't believe we've been introduced. I'm Catarina and this is Tae."

Sharp, wary brown eyes took our measure from behind the clear lenses of her glasses. Odds were her vision was perfect, thanks to the range of corrective options, but she'd decided to use glasses as a fashion statement—or possibly as camouflage. She had curly dark hair, deep brown skin, and high cheekbones. She was on the striking side of beautiful, but the other guests had taken one look at her glasses and cheap dress and written her off.

After a few seconds, she shook my hand. "I'm Esteri Kryer. I'm an astrophysicist for the Royal Consortium Defense Force."

It sounded like she'd repeated the same phrase more than once and expected it to send us running.

The RCDF, as it was more commonly known, was tasked with keeping the peace in the 'verse. Most people thought of soldiers when they thought of the RCDF, but the RCDF also employed a huge number of scientists and researchers.

Before I could ask her what she did, a tinkling chime indicated it was time to take our seats. Tae held out his other elbow to Esteri and she accepted with a nod and a grateful smile. He led us to the table. Mother always seated herself at the head. The rest of us were scattered along its length, not by order of importance but by Mother's whim.

My name card put me at the final seat on the side of the table closest to the house. Being at the end meant I could only converse with three people: the person next to me, the person across from me, and the person diagonally across from me. It would've been a rare gift, but I doubted Mother meant it that way.

It did not surprise me when Tae was seated as far away from me as possible and Lord Henderson settled across from me. Esteri was seated next to Henderson, and an older lady from one of the lower houses was seated next to me. Mother had neatly boxed me in with who she'd thought were the most boring guests so I'd be forced to talk to Lord Henderson.

Too bad for her, I actually *liked* talking to scientists.

"Cat, you look ravishing today," Henderson said with a smile that was half leer.

I hadn't given him permission to use my nickname or drop my title, but that didn't seem to matter. I smothered my distaste under a cool smile. "Why thank you, Lord Henderson. How is your grandson? Let's see, he must be five or six by now, right?" I waited for him to nod before I continued. "How time flies. Your daughter must be so proud and you must be *delighted* to be a grandfather."

My tone was carefully polite, but in point of fact, his daughter was a few years older than me. His line was secure for two generations. He had no reason to pursue me other than as a tie to House von Hasenberg and because he was a dirty old man.

His smile went tight. "My family is very well, thank you for asking. And please, call me Rupert."

I made a noncommittal noise and turned to Esteri. "We were interrupted before. Please, tell me about your job at RCDF. What do you do as an astrophysicist?"

"I work on optimizing the equations that the gates use to track celestial bodies," she said. "My doctoral thesis was on a novel new way to predict orbits, and I've taken that research further with the RCDF. Now we're attempting to translate it into computational improvements."

Gates were the giant supercomputers that could calculate safe jump points millions of light-years away for spaceships using faster-than-light travel. Even small optimizations in the calculations would mean big gains for the people who relied on the gates every day to safely navigate the cosmos.

"Fascinating," I said, and I meant it. "So do—"

"Yes, fascinating," Henderson interrupted, "but we don't want to bore Lady Catarina with all this talk of work. She's much more comfortable discussing fashion." He paused and flicked a meaningful glance at Esteri's dress. "Oh, but I suppose you wouldn't know anything about *that*, would you? Too bad." He laughed and went so far as to give Esteri a patronizing little pat on her arm.

Esteri's face tightened into a mask of anger, but she bit her tongue and bowed her head. "Of course, forgive me, Lady Catarina."

I gave Henderson a bright smile filled with teeth. "Actually, I would like nothing more than to hear what Dr. Kryer has to say. I find her work very interesting, and it is important for us all." *Even you, you misogynistic asshole.* I kept the barb to myself. It wouldn't do to insult one of our potential allies outright while we were in the middle of a war.

Esteri looked between us, but something in my expression must've convinced her that I was serious. Her smile turned sly as she launched into a technical discussion of her job. Honestly, I followed less than half of what she said, even though I'd grown up in a High House with the best tutors money could buy. The lady next to me was practically asleep.

I understood gates and the technology behind them at a high level, but Esteri knew them down to the minutia. Listening to her explain her research and how it affected the inner workings of the gates was truly fascinating. She kept talking, I kept asking what I hoped were intelligent-sounding questions, and Henderson kept being thwarted every time he tried to change the subject.

It was a delightful brunch.

Unfortunately, when it was over, Lord Henderson made a beeline straight for my mother, presumably to complain about my behavior, so when Esteri made for the exit, I followed. Susan, my bodyguard, fell in behind us.

"Susan, call us a transport," I murmured. I could practically *feel* Mother's eyes burning a hole into my back. I linked my arm through Esteri's. "Where are you headed? I'll give you a lift."

"You don't need—" she started.

"You'd be doing me a favor."

She inclined her head in agreement, and we cut through the house to the family entrance where a House transport waited for us.

We climbed in and Esteri set the transport's destination to the fiftieth floor of a building in Sector Nine. The transport lifted smoothly into the air, shadowed by another transport in the black and gold of House von Hasenberg colors—our security detail.

I pulled a card from the pocket of my dress and handed it to Esteri. "Lord Henderson is known to be vindictive. If anything happens—anything at all—contact me and I'll fix it. Even if it doesn't seem related, like your project loses funding or you get reprimanded at work seemingly out of the blue, contact me."

"I was happy to help," she demurred.

"Yes, but I don't want that help to cost you something you clearly love. That card contains my private contact information. If Lord Henderson acts against you, contact me and don't let your pride get in your way. Handing him a victory isn't winning. I can't do much about him elsewhere, but I can do this."

"But you're a von Hasenberg. Surely there's something you can do to get rid of him?"

My smile was grim. "Not when his attention is in the best interest of the House."

Esteri's eyes widened in surprise. I smoothed my expression into a pleasant social smile. I didn't need to burden a near stranger with my personal feelings. I was extremely privileged. If that privilege sometimes felt like handcuffs, well, that was my problem, not anyone else's.

I pivoted the conversation back to her research and asked a few more questions about how the gates worked. Now that I didn't have to worry about sounding smart, I could ask the questions I really wanted answered.

Esteri never once made me feel stupid, even when I asked questions that didn't make sense. And she was *phenomenally* smart. This year alone, she'd helped to increase the gate algorithm's efficiency by 5 percent. I made a mental note to put her on the roster of potential House employees. That way, if the RCDF was ever stupid enough to fire her, we'd be ready to snap her up.

The transport landed and Esteri exited with a wave, still clutching the card I'd given her. When the door closed behind her, I let out a sigh. "Think she'll contact me?" I asked Susan.

"No, not unless something terrible happens."

"That's what I think, too. I'll have to keep an eye on her."

CHAPTER THREE

After I dropped off Esteri, I had several stops scheduled. Avoiding Mother was just a bonus. She'd already sent me a terse message, demanding my presence, but if I was constantly busy with House tasks then she couldn't get angry when I didn't show up.

Or, rather, she couldn't get *angrier.*

I pressed my fingers against my eyes; I was being pulled in too many directions. With the war, marrying Lord Henderson *would* bring in desperately needed ships, supplies, and troops from House Henderson, which might save Benedict's life, along with the lives of many of our soldiers.

Benedict would vehemently oppose the union, even with his life on the line, but perhaps it was time to grow up and do my duty. If only that duty weren't so distasteful.

I swiped my identity chip over the reader in the transport and set the destination to a bakery in Sector Five of the Rockhurst quarter. When we arrived, I bought myself a coffee and Susan a spiced tea. She turned down my offer of a pastry, so I ordered a dozen pastries to go.

We continued to the Khadela quarter, aiming for a tall

apartment building in Sector Seven. It wasn't usually a good idea to drop in on a pregnant woman unannounced, but I happened to know that Lady Pippa August worked constantly, no matter what her condition. As the matriarch of the burgeoning House August, she had her hands full.

She also loved pastries, specifically the ones I'd just bought.

House August had yet to decide who to back in the war. They weren't solid allies with any of the High Houses and tended to deal with each of us equally. It was my job to charm her to our side, but over the last couple of months, I'd found I also enjoyed her company.

She received me in the informal sitting room, an upgrade in friendliness since my last visit. She started to rise when I entered, but I waved her off. She was young for a matriarch, not yet forty, and had a delicate, petite build. She had golden-brown skin and big, dark eyes set in a face that was more cute than stunning, but her fragile appearance belied an iron will and a mind sharp enough to cut. This close to her due date, her stomach was as big as she was.

Her eyes widened in delight when she caught sight of the box in my hands.

"Lady Catarina, those had better be what I think they are or I'm going to have to ask you to leave. Junior here," she motioned to her rounded stomach, "has been kicking my kidneys for the last hour. If those aren't pastries, I'm going to cry."

I handed her the box with a flourish. "See for yourself."

"You are a saint," she vowed, tearing the lid in her haste to open the box. She grabbed a pastry, took a large bite, and groaned in delight. "Delicious. Help yourself to the tea. Susan, you, too," she said over my shoulder. "I need a minute with this eclair. How did you know this was my favorite bakery?"

That was Bianca's doing. I didn't know where my sister got her information, but it was spookily good, as evidenced by this morning's ambush. It was all fun and games until she turned her skill on me.

"Lucky guess," I answered with a grin.

Pippa wasn't buying it, but she was too busy with her sugary snack to press harder.

We chatted for half an hour, catching up on gossip and news. We both knew I was here to try to win her to our side, but we didn't talk politics or war. She told me how her husband had started hovering as she entered her final month of pregnancy and how it was driving her crazy, but her tone was fond. They were a rare love match, and it was obvious he worshipped the ground she walked on.

I reluctantly took my leave, aware that the rest of the day was not going to be as much fun as my time with Pippa. I crisscrossed the city, running errands for special delights and delivering them along with my bubbly personality. The next three Houses all had older, crankier members, but I kept my smile fastened to my face and didn't let them rile me, no matter how sly their comments.

Bianca had dubbed this my charm offensive, and she was right. As the youngest, there wasn't a lot I could do for House von Hasenberg right now—other than marrying—but I could socialize. I could ensure that other Houses thought of us fondly.

And so I did, but it was draining as all hell.

WHEN I FINALLY RETURNED HOME, MY FACE HURT FROM smiling and a tension headache clamped my temples. I wanted to crawl into bed and stay there, but tonight's gala required a House von Hasenberg representative and I was it.

I entered my suite and headed straight for the bedroom.

I'd already procured the two trunks I would take, but I wasn't yet sure how to get them to my ship without tipping off Director Bishop that I planned to leave early. That was a problem for future me—too bad the future was mere hours away. For now, I had to pack before getting ready.

One might expect a summer house party to be a casual affair, but apparently Stephanie James and Chloe Patel did not agree. Guests had been advised that the James household dressed for dinner. *Every night.* Who did that? Psychopaths, that's who.

I quickly selected two weeks of fashionable outfits with the ease of long practice. Dresses, skirts, slacks, blouses, and all of the various undergarments and accessories were carefully packed and placed in the first trunk. More utilitarian clothing went into the second trunk, along with a selection of weapons and other handy gadgets. On top, I packed a few specialty outfits: swimsuits, riding habits, hiking gear, and a cold weather coat. Most of it probably wouldn't be needed, but I liked to be prepared.

And the extra clothes also nicely concealed the weapons and gear.

I locked both trunks and hoisted them onto the narrow cargo sled I'd used to retrieve them from storage. When I picked up the paired beacon, the sled lifted from the floor and floated after me. I parked it in the living room, just out of sight of the door.

Now I just had to spend a few more hours socializing, come home, grab the sled, and make it to my ship before Ian or Bianca realized I was on the move. I huffed out a laugh. No problem.

TONIGHT, I REPRESENTED HOUSE VON HASENBERG AT A charity gala for the families of fallen soldiers. With the war, it was a little too on the nose, but no one seemed to care. Elizabeth Rockhurst had also attended, representing House Rockhurst. She'd raised an eyebrow at me during the opening speech. At least I wasn't the only one who saw the irony.

My gown was a deep, bright pink that complemented my golden skin and dark hair. The skirt flared around my knees and the modest cut made me appear younger and more innocent than I was. It was effective camouflage in a crowd of jaded socialites.

I glided from group to group, renewing acquaintances and making new connections. One of the benefits of being the daughter of a High House was being welcome nearly everywhere. And I had superb recall where names and faces were concerned.

Ada was excellent with numbers and Bianca unearthed impossible-to-find information, but I could remember the name of a person I'd met once two years ago. My skill was a lot less practical, but it was fantastic for building a large social network and keeping up my charm offensive.

My circuit of the room brought to me to an elderly woman clad in the deep black of mourning. She acknowledged me with a short nod. Wilma Sollorz had lost her beloved wife less than a month ago. Their adult daughter had taken over the House—with Wilma's blessing—but I knew Wilma must feel unmoored after so many changes.

"Lady Sollorz, how are you this evening?" I asked gently. "Can I get you anything?"

"No, thank you, child." She patted my arm. "You always were the kind one. Don't lose that."

"I will do my best," I murmured as a sliver of guilt stole through my system. In my opinion, kindness was selfless. My actions were decidedly *not*. I enjoyed socializing and brightening people's days, but I did it with the full knowledge that they were likely to think better of House von Hasenberg because of it.

I was the worst kind of hypocrite.

"I heard Lord Henderson is aiming for you," she said with the complete lack of tact that only advanced years and a secure place could bring. "Are you going to accept him?"

"He hasn't asked me," I hedged.

She leaned close, her dark eyes shrewd. "If you ever need help, you only have to ask. I may not be as powerful as a Rockhurst or a Yamado, but I will help you. No one should have to endure that cad unwillingly."

Warmth softened my expression into a genuine smile of gratitude. "Thank you, Lady Sollorz. I appreciate it. But if it comes down to it, my sisters will have my back."

She nodded knowingly. "It's good that you have someone to look out for you, but my offer stands." She peered over my shoulder. "Speak of the devil." She looped her arm around mine. "Actually, I do feel a need for some fresh air. Escort me?"

"Gladly." I'd been dodging Lord Henderson all evening, and I was perfectly happy to continue the trend.

When he caught my eye, Henderson smirked. Anxiety tightened my stomach. His smug expression boded ill for me, but there wasn't anything I could do about it right this second.

I escorted Wilma out onto the balcony while Susan quietly shadowed us. We were in one of the taller buildings in Sector Six of the Yamado quarter. A gentle breeze drifted around the tall glass panels that had been installed as both railing and wind block. The gorgeous view glittered with lights below us and stars above us. I could stand out here all night.

"Such a beautiful city," Wilma murmured, "with such a dark heart." She shook herself. "Don't listen to this old woman's raving. Enjoy the night air and remember what I said."

"I will, thank you. Have a good night."

She headed back inside. I let her go, content to remain for another minute. A few other people were enjoying the outside air.

"Incoming," Susan warned quietly.

I turned around and found Lord Henderson making his way toward me, smug look still firmly in place. I couldn't quite summon a smile, but at least I didn't actively grimace at his approach. That was as much as I could do.

"Lord Henderson," I said flatly.

"I told you to call me Rupert, darling," he said.

"And I told you to call me Lady Catarina. It seems neither of us will get what we want."

"Au contraire, *darling*. I had a very fruitful talk with Lady von Hasenberg this morning after our brunch. She gave me permission to court you openly. You will attend the symphony with me tomorrow night."

Long practice kept the distaste out of my expression. "I already have plans, and then I will be traveling for two weeks. Perhaps we can schedule something when I return." I got the whole sentence out without a single inflection that expressed my true feelings. I should get a gold star. And a stiff drink.

Henderson's face clouded with anger. "Lady von Hasenberg said you would clear your schedule for me."

I smiled sweetly. "She was wrong."

He stepped threateningly into my space. "Listen here, you little c—"

In a heartbeat, Susan had switched places with me.

"Threaten Lady Catarina again, and I will be forced to defend her," she said calmly. "Return inside. Now."

Henderson's hands clenched, his face livid with rage. "This discussion is not over," he snarled at me over Susan's shoulder.

"Yes, it is," I said. "Run back inside before I forget that you're an ally." I bit back all of the other insults I wanted to lob at him. The less I said, the less likely he'd be to run back to Mother and tattle on me.

He turned and stalked away.

"He's going to be trouble," Susan predicted. "We should return to House von Hasenberg before he rallies."

I sighed. I hated ceding ground, but I was done here anyway. "Very well. Let me say my good-byes. Please call us a transport."

She nodded, and then stayed closer than usual while I found the hosts and made my excuses. She didn't relax until we had settled in the transport and it lifted off.

"Thank you for defending me," I said. I could've handled him myself, if it came down to it, but she didn't know that.

She waved me off. "I was just doing my job."

"You were doing more than that. You could've let it slide until he physically harmed me. You didn't. I appreciate it. And if he tries to come after you, let me know. I will hire you myself if I need to."

"Thank you." She paused, seemingly debating something. Finally, she said, "Will you accept his suit?"

I stared out of the window. Even the sparkling lights of Serenity offered no comfort. "I don't know. I find him revolting, but every day the war drags on, my brother is in mortal danger. And if I spurn Henderson, he could align with Rockhurst just to spite me."

We made the rest of the trip in silence. Susan saw me to the door of my suite and then retired for the evening when I told her I'd be staying in. I didn't want her to get in trouble when I disappeared.

My best chance of success would be in the early hours between midnight and dawn. I really should sleep for a few hours, but the chances of that happening were nil. Instead, I changed into dark pants made of sturdy material, a stretchy black top, and heavy boots. Then I double-checked my packing, paced, and thought about what I was going to tell Bianca once I was in the air.

Hours later, I still wasn't sure what to do about that last one, but it was time to leave anyway.

There was no point in subterfuge—I would either make it or I wouldn't—so I headed straight for the secondary hangar where my ship waited. Confidence was key in cases like this, so I sailed by the barely awake hangar guard without a backward glance.

Chaos sat right where I'd left her, a tiny little spaceship covered in mottled black-and-gray camouflage paint. The name was an inside joke. My older siblings had lovingly dubbed me a chaos monster when I was young, thanks to my ability to slip away and get into mischief whenever I was feeling well enough. While the nickname had finally died, I'd thought it was perfect for my ship.

It didn't hurt that the ship was smaller, faster, and stealthier than most of the ships in our fleet—the perfect agent of chaos.

I swiped my identity chip over the control panel and unlocked the cargo door. The ship only had two levels. The cargo bay in the aft spanned both, but didn't have much horizontal area. The sled with my two trunks stacked vertically took up a third of the floor. I wouldn't be running any resupply missions in this ship unless I turned off the gravity and stuck supplies to the walls.

I closed the cargo door and retracted the ramp, then headed upstairs to the flight deck. The top level also contained my quarters and the mess hall. The bottom level contained the medbay, guest quarters, exercise room, and maintenance access.

Because *Chaos* was so small, I'd forgone the traditional three-station layout on the flight deck. I'd kept the captain's station, but I'd merged navigation and tactical into one station. I rarely had guests on my ship, and I could control the whole ship from the captain's console. I would've omitted the second station, too, but some small part of me still hoped to find someone who wanted to go on adventures with me.

I slid into the captain's chair. The window shutters were closed, but the displays showed an empty hangar. Time to see if my ship had been grounded or not.

"*Chaos*, take us into orbit."

The ship chimed an acceptance and I felt the subtle vibration as the engines engaged. The engine noise ramped up and the ground dropped away in a dizzying rush. I laughed with joy. I was *flying*.

Chaos rocketed upward and the vast expanse of space opened before me. Something loosened in my chest and I felt like I could breathe again for the first time in months. I'd missed this.

I plotted a course for Honorius and the ship requested a jump point from the gate. Because it was stupid early, we were fifteenth in the queue. Earth's gate was blazing fast, so in less than a minute, the engine noise changed as the FTL drive ramped up. My stomach dropped, then a heartbeat later, the noise peaked and fell silent.

The emptiness of space had been replaced by the distant view of Andromeda Prime. The planet hung suspended in the inky depths of space, sparkling red and blue in the sunlight. Andromeda Prime was one of the oldest occupied planets outside of the Milky Way and every House had a large holding here.

My com chimed with a message. I checked it and cringed when I saw Bianca's name. The only reason my sister would be awake now was if she'd been told that I'd left. Damn Ian for not letting her sleep until a decent hour.

And damn me for not sending my explanation sooner.

I opened the message and frowned. Rather than demands, anger, or disappointment, it was just three short sentences: *Be careful. I love you. Forgive me.*

I was still trying to puzzle out exactly what she meant when the door to the flight deck slid open.

CHAPTER FOUR

t took a second for my brain to process exactly how wrong it was that a door on my *presumably empty* ship had just opened without me opening it. Adrenaline dumped into my veins. I jerked violently, grabbed for a nonexistent blaster, and then whipped around to face the threat with my hands up in a defensive position.

Aoife yawned widely as she entered, stretching her arms over head. Behind her, Alexander's eyes quickly flickered around the room before landing back on me. His expression remained impossible to read.

"You couldn't have waited until morning?" Aoife complained.

Shock stole my voice. When I finally found it again, I could only growl, "Bianca . . ."

"Your sister cares about you," Aoife agreed. "She figured you'd run. It's what she did, after all. So she let us crash on your ship in case you moved up your plans. Surprise." Her tone was dry as dust.

"I'll kill her."

"I'm sure she would welcome you back on Earth, if you'd

like, but you better hurry. She has her own trip scheduled. Otherwise, we need to make plans. You and Alex have less than two days to get your stories straight."

I dropped my hands and took a deep breath. I tried to shake off the adrenaline and anger flowing through my system. I'd spent my whole life charming people, subtly manipulating them into doing what I wanted while they thought it was their own idea.

I smoothed my expression into my friendliest smile and relaxed the tension around my eyes. "I appreciate that you're willing to go so far to help us, but I am more than capable of taking care of myself. When we get to Honorius, I'll pay you whatever you are owed and we can part ways."

"Bianca has you dead to rights," Aoife said, "but I'll tell you what. If you can make it through the door, I'll believe that you can take care of yourself and let you go your own way in Honorius. If you can't, you're stuck with us—and Bianca's orders."

I eyed her and Alexander. Neither was *directly* between me and the door, but both were close enough that I wouldn't stand a chance in a fair fight, even with my advantages.

I borrowed a bit of Mother's haughty stare. "That is a fool's bargain," I sniffed. "I don't have time for this."

I made it past Aoife and was mere steps from the door when warm fingers closed gently around my wrist and pulled me to a stop. Goosebumps rose along my skin and I suppressed a shiver. I glanced up at Alexander and raised an imperious eyebrow. His eyes crinkled at the corners, as if he was trying not to smile.

"Clever," he murmured, his voice deep and velvety smooth, "but you won't get out that easily, not unless you are willing to admit defeat."

"Unhand me."

"Agree to take us with you."

I lunged for the door, far faster and stronger than I appeared. I'd spent so long learning to moderate myself that even this tiny break felt like freedom. Yet, somehow, impossibly, Alexander anticipated the move. He looped an arm around my waist and used my own momentum to spin me farther into the room. He let me go and stepped back slightly, but he kept the light grip on my wrist.

We stared at each other in shock for an eternal second before I remembered my mask. "What does it matter to you?" I demanded. I had to distract him.

His expression was impossible to read. If he had questions, he hid them well. "Bianca wants you safe and we owe her a debt."

My eyes narrowed. "What debt?"

A grin touched his mouth. "One between her and us."

"You are the most infuriating man I've ever had the displeasure of meeting," I growled. It wasn't exactly true, but warm tingles ran up my arm where he touched me and his voice kept sending delicious shivers skating along my nerves.

"He gets that a lot," Aoife chimed in from behind me.

I stiffened. I'd forgotten she was here, and worse, I'd forgotten they were partners. I ordered my wayward body under control.

"Giving up?" she asked.

"Never," I vowed.

I STOPPED TRYING TO ESCAPE LONG ENOUGH TO LAND *Chaos* in the House von Hasenberg hangar on top of our main building in Honorius. I wasn't due at House James until tomorrow night, so I might as well spend tonight in the penthouse, in my own bed, as I'd planned. Unfortunately, I hadn't planned on having guests.

Aoife swore that she would let me go on my own if I could escape the flight deck, so after landing, I spent the next four hours attempting to do just that. I tried talking my way out, sneaking out, and occasionally just running for it when they moved away from the door, but I limited myself to normal speed and strength. I couldn't risk arousing suspicion, not after the first attempt had failed.

I'd been sickly as a child. By all accounts, my siblings had sailed through their training, but I'd struggled with the physical tasks, often too tired and too weak to complete them. It was one of the reasons my brothers and sisters still babied me so much—I'd worried them for years.

The doctors had tried a variety of treatments, but nothing had worked until I was nearly a teen. At twelve I'd gotten dramatically worse and then dramatically better in the span of six months. By the time my thirteenth birthday rolled around in the fall of that year, I was healthy. Father had been especially interested in my recovery. I'd had to undergo so many tests. And each time I excelled, he pushed me harder.

I was so happy to be able to use my body without pain or fatigue that I'd strived and trained and practiced until the day I'd broken my adult sparring partner's arm—a week before my thirteenth birthday.

Father had been *so proud.* For the first time, he'd looked at me with something other than cool disinterest. He'd looked at me like I was *special.*

And then he'd sat me down and shattered my dreams, one by one.

I hadn't just been sick, I'd been a test subject. I was an experiment—the first one who had lived. The doctors treating me had tweaked my DNA, altering who I was. I would be the House's greatest hidden weapon. Stronger. Faster. *Better.* A killer hidden behind a pretty face and a High House name. I would be welcome everywhere; I could kill anyone.

My elation had morphed into horror.

Father must have noticed. Albrecht von Hasenberg was nothing if not observant. He explained precisely what would happen if I told anyone. First, they would kill me, because I was an abomination in the eyes of Consortium law. Then they would kill my doctors. Then they would strip House von Hasenberg of our status and kill anyone who knew about what had happened. My siblings would die if I told them, so I had vowed to take the secret to the grave.

I had to give it to him—Father knew *exactly* how to manipulate me.

With no other options, I'd kept training, but I'd refused to hurt my sparring partners. Father, being the problem solver than he was, had put me in the ring with a convicted killer and told me to fight or die.

I'd very nearly died. I still woke up sweating and wondering if I should have.

Alone and trapped, I'd done the only thing I could: I started to hide my abilities. After all, if I wasn't special, then Father couldn't use me as a weapon. And if I was the first successful experiment, then no one would know that the effects weren't temporary.

Over the next three months, I'd begun to slow my responses and pull my punches. I'd gotten my ass kicked so hard and so often that Father began to believe that my abilities really were fading. I'd caught him shouting at my medical team more than once.

Thanks to a careful, sustained campaign on my part, everyone thought the side effects had faded. That I was just a normal woman.

But the DNA changes remained, so I had to be very, very careful. Any bloodwork had to be done through specific House doctors, and I'd been advised that having a child would be risky—as if I wanted to burden an innocent with a secret like this. The other High Houses would love nothing more than to crucify House von Hasenberg for illegal gene manipulation.

I was still tested every six months, but moderating my abilities during testing was second nature now.

I could fake normal almost as well as if I *were* normal.

And I'd risked that hard-won stability just to escape having an extra guard for a couple of weeks. I shook my head at myself and blamed it on the fatigue dogging my steps. I hadn't slept well this week, and now I'd been up for over twenty-four hours straight.

I endured another half an hour before nature's call made the game far less fun. I was either going to have to concede or epically humiliate myself.

"Very well, you can come with me as my guards," I agreed mutinously. It took most of my willpower not to wiggle in place.

Aoife wasn't having it though. "I will be your guard, and Alex will be your guest. That was Bianca's requirement." Her slightly evil grin said she hadn't missed my nervous pacing and longing glances at the door.

Fifteen minutes later, I'd had all I could take. "Fine, you win this round. Let me out."

"Promise you won't try to ditch us once we're out of the ship."

"I promise," I grated out.

She nodded and moved away from the door. I made a beeline straight for the en suite bathroom in my quarters. Once I'd taken care of business, I splashed some cool water on my face.

My eyes had circles under them and I looked as exhausted as I felt. Sleeping was the first order of business.

Alexander and Aoife were waiting for me in the cargo bay. "Feel better?" Aoife asked with a grin.

It was impossible to stay mad at her. It wasn't her fault Bianca had sent her to babysit me. I was a job for them, and it wasn't fair of me to make their job harder just because I didn't appreciate Bianca's meddling. "I do, thank you."

"What is your plan for the day?"

"We should have the penthouse to ourselves. First, I need to sleep for a few hours. After that, I don't know."

"We should spend the day together. You and Alex need to get comfortable with each other and I need to see how you move through the world."

I glanced at the big, silent man in question before asking her, "Are you sure you don't mind me getting comfortable with your partner? We'll have to act like lovers in public."

Aoife's grin turned sly. "I don't mind sharing."

"That's fine, but I do. It won't look natural. We should stick to you both being my guards."

She burst out laughing. "Bianca said you'd be persistent. Let me put you out of your misery: he's my adopted brother. Get as comfortable as you like, but for the love of all that's sacred, don't tell me about it."

Heat bloomed in my cheeks. I'd been trying to talk her out of continuing with the plan, but now all I could think about was getting *comfortable* with Alexander. I shook my head. I needed sleep so my brain would start functioning again.

But before that, I needed to ensure Alexander was on board as well. I turned to him. At a meter seventy-eight, I was a fairly tall woman, but he had at least twelve centimeters on me. He had broad shoulders, a flat stomach, and thick legs. His height combined with his muscular build made me feel almost petite next to him. "Did you agree to this plan or did Bianca railroad you into it?"

"Your sister is plenty fierce," he said, "but I agreed because I think she's right. You'll be safer if I am your guest rather than merely your guard."

"And pretending to be lovers isn't going to bother you?"

His smile stole my breath. "You're clever and determined. Any man would be lucky to stand by your side." He met my eyes. "But if having me around like that is going to make you uncomfortable, we'll come up with another plan."

Aoife made a sound of protest, but Alexander held up a silencing hand. "Personally, I think it would be the wrong call, but I don't want you to be uneasy because of me. The decision is yours."

He'd just handed me the exact outcome I'd wanted, and yet I hesitated. Focused on me like this, he was overwhelmingly attractive. Dark hair fell across his forehead and his brown eyes were flecked with black and gold. I would definitely be uneasy with him around, but not for the reasons he thought, and I was oddly reluctant to use his kindness against him.

"Let's see how today goes," I hedged. "I had my own plans, but Bianca wouldn't have insisted without a good reason. However, if we can't pull off being a convincing couple, then we'll have to consider some other options."

He inclined his head in agreement. Aoife huffed out a disgruntled breath, but she didn't argue.

I left my trunks stacked in the cargo bay and stepped out into the hangar. I had spare clothes in my room, so there was no reason to unpack and repack just for one night. Aoife and Alexander each carried a small bag. The house was unoccupied, so I'd been able to land in the small hangar on the roof, which meant just a short elevator ride down into the penthouse proper.

The penthouse was split into three floors. The top floor held all of the public spaces because it had the best view. The middle floor was for guests, and the lowest floor was for family. Access between the floors was restricted. Guests could go up to the public spaces, but not down into the family level.

I swiped my identity chip over the control panel next to the elevator. "Did Bianca or Ian add you to the House security list?" I asked.

"Yes," Aoife said.

"Then you'll be able to access all three floors, but you won't be able to enter any of the family suites on the bottom floor. Guest suites are on the middle floor and they are all unoccupied, so you can pick whichever you like."

"We're staying with you," Aoife said. "I don't trust you not to sneak out, and you and Alex need to get used to being together."

I was too tired to argue, so I called the elevator. "Fine, let's go. But you'll have to sleep on the couch and floor because I don't have guest rooms."

Aoife narrowed her eyes at me. "Are you okay?"

That drew a reluctant grin. "I'm dead on my feet, but don't worry, I'll be back to bedeviling you after I get a few hours of sleep."

I led my silent entourage to my suite on the family floor. It was a much smaller version of my suite at home, with very similar decorations. From here, you'd never know we were at the top of a building, because the only room with an outside view was my bedroom.

"Did a color palette throw up in here?" Aoife asked, looking around with wide eyes.

"I see you've volunteered to sleep on the floor. That's kind of you. I'm sure Alexander will appreciate your sacrifice." I waved an arm at the kitchenette. "There's a synthesizer in the kitchen if you're hungry. Since I didn't let the staff know I was coming, there won't be any real food in the fridge, but you can order something from the main kitchen if you want."

I pointed to the left. "The guest bath is there. My bedroom, office, and bath are down that hall." I waved to the right. "If you leave, you won't be able to get back in unless someone opens the door for you. The suite computer answers to Jarvis, or you can use the panel on the wall. Let me find you some bedding."

I started toward the linen closet, then paused and turned around. "I guess we could move up to a guest suite. They have multiple bedrooms. I don't know why I didn't think of that before. You'll be more comfortable up there."

"This is fine," Alexander said. "Aoife can have the couch and I'll sleep on the floor in your room."

He was pushing, to see what I would do, but I was too tired to play these games right now. "Okay. Fair warning, though, my floors are as hard as rock."

He shrugged. "I've slept on worse."

So had I, but that didn't mean I was eager to repeat the experience. I opened the closet and handed them both extra bedding. "I'm going to try to sleep for at least four hours, so you're on your own until after lunch."

Aoife nodded and made her way back to the living room. I led Alexander to my bedroom. The walls were a pale peach and the furniture was white. A wall of windows with a tall glass door overlooked the balcony. Beyond, Honorius was just waking up under the early morning sun.

If Alexander was surprised by the decor change from the living room, he didn't show it. His gaze quickly swept the room, then he began to lay out his bedding along the wall between the door to the rest of the suite and the door leading outside.

"I'm going to darken the windows, if that's okay with you," I said. When he nodded, I turned on the bedside lamp, then had the suite computer dim the windows until they were an opaque black. Without the outside light, the room faded into twilight, lit only by the lamp.

Now that we were alone, the strangeness of this situation struck me. I tried to remember if anyone other than family or staff had ever seen this room and I came up blank. I knew Bianca wouldn't risk my life with someone she didn't trust completely, but *I* barely knew him and now he had invaded my sanctuary.

He glanced up and caught me staring. He froze for a second, then quietly asked, "Would you prefer that I sleep in the living room?"

His voice was rich and deep and smooth. Here, unguarded, he had the tiniest hint of an accent, but it was too slight to place it accurately. "Tell me something about yourself. How old are you? Where did you grow up?"

"I'm twenty-six. I grew up in the outer rim."

The outer rim consisted of the settled planets the farthest from Earth—and farthest from the moderating influence of the RCDF. They weren't completely lawless, but it took a certain kind of hardiness to thrive on an outer rim planet.

It did not escape me that he'd answered my questions, but only in the vaguest possible terms. He stood still, waiting to see if I would ask him to leave.

"Are you familiar enough with Consortium etiquette to pass as my guest?"

He shrugged. "I know enough."

"Show me?" I asked quietly. "Pretend I am Chloe Patel.

She's rich, spoiled, and a bitch—just like me—so you won't have to stretch your imagination too far." I painted on my social smile, cooled it until it had a chilly bite, and tipped my chin up to an arrogant angle. I raised one imperious eyebrow. "And *you* are?" I demanded with a dismissive little sniff.

Alexander transformed before my eyes. Before, he'd sort of faded into the background, despite his size. Now he loomed, even from across the room. When he approached, it was with a predatory stalk, his expression sharp, haughty, and fierce. Awareness shivered down my spine.

He stopped too close and took the hand I'd instinctively offered. He bowed over it and pressed a searing kiss to my skin. When he rose, his expression was knowing, like he'd looked into my head, pulled out every dirty thought, and approved of them all. "I am Alexander Sterling, my lady," he said, his upper-class accent sharp enough to cut glass. "The pleasure is mine."

I had long ago become inured to empty flattery and pretty faces—or so I had thought. Alexander smashed straight through that disinterest until it was a struggle to keep my mask in place. "Charmed, I'm sure," I said coolly.

By his grin, he knew that I wasn't nearly as unaffected as I pretended. "Would you honor me with this dance?"

Before I could decline, he'd swept me into his arms. He hummed a tune under his breath, and after an initial stumble on my part, we swept into an easy waltz. He was light on his feet and a natural lead. His gaze was hot on my face and I could feel the play of muscles under my hands.

I pulled us to a stop. "You are dangerous, Alexander Sterling."

"Not to you," he disagreed. He'd reverted to his normal accent. "And call me Alex."

CHAPTER FIVE

I stared at my reflection in the bathroom mirror and willed myself to calm down. Alexander—now Alex—had flustered me, and I felt like I needed a cold shower. I shivered as I remembered his knowing grin. Maybe two cold showers.

After I'd dawdled as long as I could without looking like I was hiding, I returned to the bedroom. Alex was sitting on his pallet, looking at his com. He glanced up, and I tilted my head toward the bathroom. "All yours."

He nodded his thanks and gathered his bag. Once he was gone, I slid into my enormous, fluffy bed. I looked at his sad little pile of blankets and hardened my heart. *No.* This was his decision. I'd offered an alternative and he'd chosen this. He could live with his choices.

"Jarvis, lights twenty percent." The overhead lights flared to life, slightly brighter than a night-light setting. Alex would be able to see, even after coming out of the fully lit bathroom.

I set the windows to gradually lighten in four hours. The sunlight would wake me without the need for a harsh alarm. I checked my com one final time, but I hadn't gotten anything else from Bianca. I wondered if she was getting updates from Alex or Aoife, or if she assumed no news was good news.

With nothing left to do, I turned off my bedside lamp and closed my eyes. Restless energy pulsed under my skin, but I feigned sleep.

Alex returned with a whisper of sound. He settled on his pallet and turned the overhead lights off. He was perfectly still and quiet, without so much as a discontented sigh. It would've been so much easier to ignore him if he'd acted disgruntled, but his quiet acceptance sent sympathy and guilt swirling through my veins. He had to be uncomfortable, but you'd never know it.

I lasted for maybe ten minutes before I sighed and whispered, "Are you awake?"

"Yes." His voice rumbled from the dark. "Do you need something?"

"Jarvis, lights five percent." The room was still deeply shadowed, but I had excellent night vision and could see clearly even in deep darkness. However, this would be easier if I could pretend the shadows hid us from each other. "Bring your pallet. You can sleep on the other side of the bed. On *top* of the covers."

There was a long, silent pause. Finally, he asked, "Are you sure? I don't mind sleeping here."

"But I do," I grumbled. "This bed is giant and it's petty to make you sleep on the floor because you agreed to help me. Hurry up before I change my mind."

He stood and gathered his bedding. He wore a T-shirt and pajama pants. I acknowledged the flare of disappointment, then ignored it and glued my gaze to the ceiling. I wasn't sure if this was the best idea ever or the worst, but I was never going to get to sleep if I kept worrying about whether or not he was comfortable.

He rounded the bed and laid out his bedding. I tracked him

via sound and kept my eyes firmly pointing upward. The mattress shifted as he climbed into bed—the bed I currently occupied. I banished all improper thoughts before they could form. I needed sleep and nothing else.

Alex turned the lights off. Once the blissful darkness hid my face, I peeked in his direction. I could just make out his form, cloaked in shadow. He was on his back, staring at the ceiling, much like I had been before. He did not look relaxed. I grimaced in sympathy, then closed my eyes. Just because I *could* see him, didn't mean I *should*. Darkness made for a reasonable expectation of privacy, and I wouldn't violate his. I rolled away from him, away from temptation. I was being ridiculous.

"Thank you," Alex murmured quietly.

"You're welcome. Good night."

"Good night."

Exhaustion pulled at me, but I couldn't settle. I wasn't used to having someone in my bed, and especially not a virtual stranger. My hookups were with people I knew and trusted, but even then, they were more of the *that was fun, don't let the door hit you on the way out* variety. Now, every little noise kept me awake. Alex apparently didn't have the same trouble. He fell asleep with enviable ease. It took a long time, but eventually his deep, even breaths lulled me into dreamland.

I AWOKE TO MIDDAY SUNLIGHT STREAMING THROUGH the window. I felt good, like I'd slept hard. It took me a second to remember where I was, but when I did, I jerked my head around to check the bed. It was blissfully empty, which was nice because sometime in the past four hours I had migrated over until I was pressed up against the edge of where Alex's bedding started.

My cheeks heated in mortification. I could only pray that

I'd moved after he'd already left the bed and that I hadn't driven him out. Or worse, snuggled up against him. I groaned and covered my face. That's what I got for being nice. Unless Alex brought it up, I would pretend it had never happened.

I slid out of bed and got ready for the day. I wasn't sure exactly what my plan was, so I decided on a pair of slacks and a fashionable blouse. If Alex didn't already have appropriate clothes, then we would have to go shopping.

But, before that, I needed to talk to Bianca. The time in Honorius closely matched Universal Standard Time, the time in Serenity, so Bianca should just be finishing with lunch. I wanted to talk to her face-to-face, or as close as possible, and the only way to do that with the distance separating us was in HIVE. The acronym stood for High Impact Virtual Environment, and it was one of the tiny handful of technologies allowed to use the FTL communication channels.

I moved to my office and closed the door, glad I hadn't run into anyone on the brief trip down the hall. I used the terminal built into the desk to log in to HIVE with my official account. The room dimmed and the projectors came to life, surrounding me in the virtual environment.

My desk disappeared and the living room of my suite in the towering stone von Hasenberg building snapped into place. The room was bright and colorful, like all of my public spaces. I sat on a bright blue sofa and the wall of windows in front of me looked out over snowy mountain peaks, despite the fact that I was in the middle of a city.

Virtual reality could be bent to the user's will, given enough money, but sometimes it made for a rough transition. I closed my eyes for a second and waited for the feeling of vertigo to settle, then sent Bianca an invite to join me.

A few minutes later, her avatar appeared in the middle of

the room. She was also using her official account, so her avatar matched her usual appearance. Based on the avatar's stiff movements, she was connecting using smart glasses and not from her office.

I stared at her, silent. Now that she was in front of me, hurt warred with love.

"I'm sorry, Cat," she said quietly. "I couldn't let you go alone. Please don't hate me."

I sighed. "I don't hate you, Bee, but I wish you'd recognize that I'm an adult and able to take care of myself. I had my own plans, but I was still going to ask you to send Alex and Aoife as my guards once I'd arrived."

She moved and sat next to me. She looked out the window. "You changed the view."

"I got tired of the beach." I wasn't going to let her change the subject that easily. "How much do you trust Alex and Aoife? How much do they know?"

"I trust them both and Ian vouches for them, too. I gave them the basics: House James coerced Pierre into putting the hit on Ferdinand, but we still don't know if they were acting alone or at the behest of someone else. You're going to the party to find additional information. House James may know you're digging for info and would very much like for you to not find anything, by whatever means necessary."

"No one sees me as anything other than the spoiled, shallow daughter of a High House. I am tolerated because I'm fun and bubbly and because friendship with me brings a certain level of social power. No one would expect me to be running an investigation into Ferdinand's kidnapping."

"You don't give yourself enough credit," Bianca said, "but don't underestimate House James, either. They pulled off a complicated attack without leaking any information. And we still don't know who in House Yamado is responsible for the looped video from the night Ferdinand was taken."

Both Ian and Father had made inquiries of House Yamado about the looped video but they'd gotten nowhere. I'd asked Ying about it, but she didn't have any information, either. I trusted Ying to tell me the truth, which meant Lord Yamado was keeping it very hush-hush. I suspected they'd found a high-level traitor and had quietly taken care of it without ever admitting fault.

"House James gains nothing by attacking me, and Agatha James is smart enough to know that." The matriarch of House James was rumored to be a cunning woman. I had met her twice, briefly. Most recently, I'd met her during a tea hosted by Chloe Patel a few weeks ago. Lady James had been pleasant, with no indication that she was plotting treachery against my House.

"They stand to lose everything if you start poking around and uncover their plot. Lady James is also smart enough to make your death look like an accident, so be careful. I know you resent me forcing Alex and Aoife on you, but I also know you understand why I did. I would do anything to keep you safe, Cat."

"I know you would." And that was the truth. Bianca was a fixer; she expressed her love by fixing problems. In her mind, my going alone to the house party was a problem, and she'd come up with a solution because she loved me and wanted me to be safe and happy.

I was a soother. It was in my nature to smooth things over, to quietly apologize even if it wasn't my fault. I'd spent a lot of time as the peacekeeper for my five siblings. As the youngest of six, I'd learned negotiation and manipulation early, but I was trying to do better at setting boundaries and standing my ground.

"I just wish you'd worked with me rather than dictating,"

I said quietly. "You didn't even wait to see if I had plans of my own before you rode roughshod over them."

Her face fell and she took a deep breath. "I'm sorry. You're right, of course," she agreed. "And I yelled at Ian for doing the exact same thing to me." Her laugh was bitter with an edge of self-deprecation. "I've become Father."

"No. You do things out of love. I know that. Father does things because he's an asshole. But you can't protect me forever."

"Oh, I absolutely can and will. But I will endeavor to ask rather than dictate from now on, okay?"

"That's all I ask. Thank you."

She inclined her head. "Is there anything else you need from me?"

"Alex and Aoife are quite enough, thanks."

She grinned at my less-than-enthusiastic tone. "I have to go," she said, "but keep me updated and send me a message if you need anything. I'm going on a short trip and will be in and out of communication range, but I'll respond as soon as I can."

"Where are you going?"

"Just a little business trip," she said, which meant she didn't want to talk about it on potentially insecure channels.

"Keep *me* updated," I demanded. "Are you taking Ian?"

Her avatar mirrored her enamored smile. "Yes. I tried to talk him into staying behind, but he wouldn't hear of it. We should be back in a few weeks."

"You're leaving Father to hold down the fort on his own?" Ferdinand and Hannah were both off-planet, too. Ada lived in Sedition, and Benedict was at war. With me gone and Bianca leaving, Father and Mother would have to attend any events that expected House von Hasenberg participation, or cancel and risk alienating our allies.

"It will be good for him to realize what it's like when we're not always at his beck and call." Bitterness had crept into her tone. She had not forgiven him for opposing her relationship with Ian.

"Just as long as he doesn't decide we're expendable," I muttered.

"He'll be delighted to have you home. He doesn't appreciate how much work you do. See you in a few weeks. Stay in touch."

"Bye, Bee. Stay safe."

She waved and her avatar blinked out. I logged out and the lights in my office came back up. I sighed. Bianca trusted Alex and Aoife, Ian trusted them, and she'd sent them with me as her way of showing love. I was stuck with them.

I guessed I might as well get them up to speed and come up with a plan that wouldn't destroy the months of hard work I'd already done just to get an invite to the house party.

I FOUND AOIFE AT THE KITCHEN TABLE, SIPPING A STEAMing mug of coffee. "Good afternoon," I said.

"Good afternoon. You look better. Did you sleep well?"

"Yes. You?" I asked as I headed for the synthesizer. I needed caffeine and food.

She nodded. "Your couch is more comfortable than it looks. Alex went to find the gym. He should be back soon. What's on your agenda for the day?"

"Do you know if Alex brought the appropriate clothes to pose as my guest?"

"Yes, Bianca helped him pick out his wardrobe. He has enough clothes for two weeks."

I killed the little flare of jealousy before it could start. Of course Bianca knew him better. And she'd also known he needed clothes, so she'd taken care of it—see: *fixer*. My public persona was an exaggeration, but I really did love shopping, and I would've loved to shop with him. I rarely got to shop for men, and clothing all of that muscle in high fashion would've been a treat.

I shook my head in disappointment and focused on food. The synthesizer had a list of my favorite meals already programmed in. It was afternoon, so even though this was my first meal of the day, I chose a soup and sandwich combo, then added a vanilla latte and hit the start button. The machine hummed, then a bright *ding* announced the order was ready.

I pulled the tray out and joined Aoife at the table. "If he already has clothes, then we need to see if we can play a convincing couple. If so, we'll go out and be seen together later today so it won't seem odd when I show up at House James with him tomorrow night."

"You've decided to work with us?"

"I talked to Bianca. She trusts you, and she's trying to look out for me, in her own way. If Alex and I can play a convincing couple, then I will take him as my guest. If not, then you'll both come with me as my guards." And if I needed to, I'd slip away from them both and do a little snooping on my own, as I'd originally intended. I did not think Aoife would appreciate that plan, so I kept it to myself. "Do you have anything you need to do before we head over tomorrow?"

"Ideally, I'd like to spend some time sparring, to see how you react to threats. My job will be easier if I can predict what you'll do."

I hated sparring. I blew on a scalding spoonful of soup to cool it. The synthesizer could make food at any temperature, but I liked my soup just a little too hot to eat right away. Now it gave me a reason to delay while I figured out how to get out of sparring.

Finally, I said, "What I do depends on the threat. If I can safely escape, that's always my first choice."

"Always? What if by leaving, you're putting someone else in danger?"

"Depends on the person," I said with a grin, then sobered. "I've had the same sort of risk assessment training that body-guards and soldiers receive. I excel at reading people and sit-uations. I won't risk myself stupidly, but if I think I can help someone I care about, I'm going to do it. I do not expect my guards to follow me into those situations."

"But you know they'll follow you anyway."

My smile was sly. "If they wouldn't, then they wouldn't be my guards for long."

"You're both the best and worst kind of person to guard."

"I'll try to keep my heroics to a minimum for the next two weeks. There aren't many people attending I would want to rescue, anyway. And despite Bianca's worries, I don't think House James is stupid enough to kill me at their own house party."

"I hope that doesn't become your epitaph."

The doorbell interrupted my response. "Alexander is at the door," Jarvis, the suite computer, said.

I raised an eyebrow at the lack of a last name. Someone didn't want his full name in the system. "Let him in."

The door opened and Alex entered, wearing dark slacks and a crisp, white, button-down shirt. He'd rolled the long sleeves up until his forearms were exposed. He looked cool and sexy and untouchable. He'd adjusted his attitude to match the clothes—he radiated confidence and was impossible to ignore.

He was arresting, but I couldn't help but wonder which version was a mask. Was his true face this hard-edged man who took up more than his fair share of the space in the room or the quiet, unassuming man who faded into the background? Or was his truth somewhere in the middle, like my own true personality?

I put down the spoon that I'd forgotten halfway to my mouth. "Welcome back," I greeted him.

"Thank you."

Well, this wasn't incredibly awkward at all. I turned back to my food. I usually had no trouble reading people but both Aoife and Alex were damnably opaque. It left me feeling unsettled and off balance.

FOR THE PAST TWENTY MINUTES, ALEX AND I HAD BEEN trying to act like lovers, to see if we could pull it off. I stared at him, trapped between conflicting desires. All I had to do was fail and he would accompany me to House James as a guard. But I *hated* failing. It was one of the reasons I hated sparring so much. I didn't know if Bianca had tipped him off or if he'd just gotten lucky with the guess, but now I was determined to prove that I could be his fake lover.

I mentally rolled my eyes at myself. I could spot manipulation at fifty paces, but that didn't mean I wasn't susceptible to it.

I sank deeper into my public persona. I needed the reminder that this was all *pretend*, an illusion as fake as my smile. "Alex, darling, there you are!" I crossed the room to him and slid an arm around his waist.

It felt right, especially when his arm came around my shoulders and he brushed a kiss against my temple. I had to work to keep my smile in place and my body relaxed. I wasn't successful.

"Relax. You look like you want to run away," Aoife said from her place on the sofa. It wasn't her first comment.

"Can I kill her?" I asked under my breath, my smile still firmly attached.

Alex's chuckle rumbled through me. "I'd rather you didn't."

"Just a little?"

His chuckle turned into a full laugh. "Aoife, why don't you go check out the rest of the house for a while? There's a deck with a nice view on the top level."

Some sort of silent communication passed between them, but she grumbled and got up. "You have an hour, then we have to come up with another plan."

Once she was gone, I was somehow both more relaxed and more nervous. I fell back on my training. "Ready to try again?" I asked brightly.

His expression softened. "Drop the mask, and let's talk. What is bothering you?"

I rubbed at my face. "I don't know. This should be easy. Charming people is what I *do*."

His gaze seemed to see too much. I broke eye contact.

"What if you pretend I'm one of your siblings?" he asked.

"I don't know what your family is like, but—"

"We just need to be affectionate; we don't need to fuck in the halls." Uncertainty flashed across his face. "Right?"

I squashed that mental image, but I couldn't suppress the shiver. "Well, I won't promise we won't come across some of that, especially during the meteor viewing nights, but guests are not expected to perform publicly, no. This is not that kind of party."

"You had no problem hugging your sister in front of strangers. Just pretend I'm your brother."

"That's not going to work."

"Why?"

"Because I'm not attracted to my brothers."

I'd meant to shock him, and it worked. His expression went carefully blank. "Oh."

Well, that answered that question—whatever I was feeling was definitely one-sided. I forced myself to laugh lightly. "Don't look so worried. I know this is fiction." I waved between the two of us. "So let's figure out how to make it work before Aoife comes back and yells at us."

"Have you ever taken a guest to a house party before?"

"No."

"So there's no precedent. We can make our own rules. How would your friends expect you to treat your lover in public?"

I grimaced. There wasn't really precedent for that, either. My hookups had been discreet. There had never been a public staking of claim. Still, Alex brought up a good point. "Most of the people at the party see me as a bubbly socialite, not too bright but always fun. Since I'm bringing someone for the first time, I need to be smitten, and that means flirtatious and affectionate, perhaps a little blind to the fact that I'm being manipulated."

"Can you do that?"

Here it was, my final out. I could say no and Bianca's interference would cease to plague me. I could do exactly as I'd planned from the beginning, but with Alex and Aoife backing me up in case things got hairy.

The word hovered on the tip of my tongue, but the pleading, worried look that Bianca had worn popped into my head.

Fuck.

"Yes, I can do it," I said with a sigh. The trick would be remembering that no matter how real it seemed, it was only an act on his part. "Let's try again."

Alex nodded and prowled toward me. I gave him a flirtatious smile. "Did you miss me?"

He pulled me into a loose embrace. "Yes," he murmured
with just the right hint of heat and longing. After a beat, his
expression turned serious. "If I ever make you uncomfortable,
and you don't feel like you can say anything without breaking
cover, you only have to tap me twice and I'll back off. Try it."

I patted him twice on the chest and he slowly drew away
with a teasing grin. It looked completely natural. He was once
again putting control back into my hands. Quietly. Effortlessly.

Alexander Sterling was far more dangerous than I'd given
him credit for.

CHAPTER SIX

E ventually I'd gotten over my initial jitters and no longer froze when Alex pulled me into an impromptu embrace. We looked natural enough to fool everyone at the party except maybe for Ying Yamado, the only person who knew me well enough to be suspicious. I could always pull her aside and ask her to keep it quiet if she got too curious.

"We need to get our basic story straight," I said. "Things like where we met, how long we've known each other, and who you are." We were standing close together, getting used to each other's presence.

"Simple lies are the easiest to remember. When was the last time you were away from Earth?"

"Three months ago."

"Then we met three months ago. Bianca introduced us. We hit it off and now we're enjoying each other's company outside of the watchful eye of your family. I'm friends with one of Bianca's business associates, but we're keeping it very hush-hush. You'll introduce me just as Alexander, which will add to the whole illicit affair vibe."

"If I do that, the other guests will be insufferable to you."

His smile stopped my heart. "Catarina, I could not care less what a bunch of pompous Consortium types think about me. Present company excluded, of course."

"Of course," I agreed drily. "And call me Cat or everyone will know we're faking."

"Cat," he agreed, smiling down at me.

I very firmly reminded my stomach that this was *fake* and therefore it had no business flipping over. I distracted myself with more questions. "What should I tell people that you do for a living?"

"I'm a partner at a private security firm."

"Is that true?"

He shrugged. "True enough. What are you hoping to find at House James?"

"A detailed journal of their treachery, openly laid out on a convenient side table." I said it with a completely straight face.

Alex's eyes gleamed in amusement, but he gamely nodded in agreement. "That would be ideal, but assuming they're not quite that accommodating, do you have a plan?"

"I do." First, I planned to attempt to crack into one of their terminals. That would be my best chance of success, but I also planned to poke around in an office or study if I got a chance. Some people clung to hard copies of blackmail material because even a skilled hacker couldn't delete paper and data chips. And being in the house would give me a chance to eavesdrop, snoop, and skulk about.

I doubted Alex would approve of any of those plans, so I kept them to myself.

He grinned knowingly, but rather than pressing, he changed the subject. "How old are you?"

"I'm twenty-one."

"How old are the rest of the guests?"

"Anywhere from eighteen to midthirties," I said. "Why?"

"Just gathering information."

My attention swung to the door as Aoife let herself in. She'd either disabled the lock on her way out or hadn't closed the door all the way. She took us in at a glance. "Better," she said. "Now that you're comfortable with each other, let's see what kind of self-defense training you've had."

"That's not going to happen," I said.

"Why not?"

"I don't spar. I've been trained. I can get myself out of most situations. If it comes to it, I'll fight like hell, but I don't spar."

"I won't hurt you," Alex murmured.

That drew a reluctant smile. He would never guess that *I* was worried about hurting *him*. "I believe you, but that doesn't change my mind. I won't spar. If you force the issue, I'll let you hit me." And then I wouldn't ever trust him again.

Alex looked at me for a long time. "Last night you asked me to show you that I could handle myself at a Consortium event. Return the favor. Show me that you can keep yourself safe. We don't have to full-on spar, but show me that you can dodge a simple attack and escape. Please."

The please did me in. I sighed. This was such a bad idea. "Fine. I will dodge one attack and then run away."

He squared up to me. I dropped into a ready stance and mentally started my sparring refrain: slow, gentle, careful, *slow*. I needn't have bothered, though, because he came at me like a tortoise.

I straightened, and he immediately pulled back. "While I appreciate your care," I said, "I'm not that fragile. Come at me like you mean it or it won't prove anything when I dodge. You've got one chance."

He nodded and we both took our ready stances again. I wasn't sure if he was going to try to grab me or hit me, so I stayed light on my feet. I couldn't win a grappling match against him without giving myself away.

He attacked without a single twitch of warning. His fist flashed toward my middle, fast, but I could already tell he was pulling the punch. If this were a real fight, I would dodge the fist and slide in closer, under his guard, then hammer a blow to his throat. When it came down to it, I fought to win and that often meant fighting dirty. But for this demonstration I only needed to escape. I dodged the fist, feinted at him to put him on the defensive, and then, while he was off balance for a split second, I turned and vaulted over the sofa before he could make a grab for me.

When I turned back, Alex and Aoife watched me with identical calculating expressions. I hadn't used any excessive speed or strength. I'd barely done anything. "What? I escaped, as requested."

"You've been trained," Alex said at last.

I rolled my eyes. "I told you that."

"You were holding back."

"So were you. This was a friendly demonstration, not a real fight. You wanted proof that I could take care of myself. I provided that proof. Are you unhappy with the result? I tried to tell you that I didn't need guards constantly. If you've changed your mind about accompanying me, I'll still pay you what you're owed."

His jaw firmed. "We're going with you; that hasn't changed. I'm glad to know that you can hold your own." He met my eyes, his gaze oddly intense. "But don't hold back in a real fight, not for any reason. If it's you or them, you can't afford to underestimate your opponent."

It sounded like a warning. My answering smile was grim. "If it's me or them, it's going to be me."

He nodded. "Good."

HONORIUS HAD A POPULATION OF TEN MILLION, MORE than ten times larger than Serenity, and the sheer scale tended to boggle the mind for the first few days of a visit. It was the largest city on Andromeda Prime, but dozens of other vast cities dotted the planet, with thousands of smaller towns and settlements nestled in between. Millennia ago, when Earth became uninhabitable, the majority of the population had resettled on Andromeda Prime before spreading to ever more distant and untamed planets.

The von Hasenberg building was in the central business district. While it was a good area for making deals and networking, it wasn't the most fun or fashionable area. For that, we needed to head east, to the entertainment district.

It wasn't far and the weather was beautiful, so we decided to walk. Andromeda Prime had extended seasons, but Honorius was situated near the equator, so it had mild weather all year long. Today was sunny with a warm breeze.

Alex and I walked arm in arm while Aoife trailed along behind us, a shadow in her dark clothes. No one recognized me as we entered the main entertainment district. In fact, Alex drew far more interested looks than I did, which was a nice change. I reveled in the anonymity even as I plotted the fastest way to break it.

I stopped at a cafe in the middle of the trendiest block. If anyone would recognize me, it would be here. And indeed, the hostess took one look at me and a table magically became available. We sat outside in a prime location while we enjoyed an afternoon cocktail.

Aoife went to scout the area, leaving Alex and me alone. We were in public, so we both slid into our roles as a couple. We smiled and shared little touches and chatted about nothing in particular. Mostly I chatted and Alex listened, but he was a surprisingly good conversationalist for someone who stayed quiet much of the time. It was so easy that at some point I stopped pretending and actually enjoyed myself.

As long as I didn't let myself get emotionally entangled, I could enjoy our time together. And if shivers danced up my arm every time he brushed his fingers across my knuckles, I would just keep it to myself.

We were on our second drink when I heard my name being called. I looked up to find Chloe Patel bearing down on me with Stephanie James trailing along in her wake. Chloe had tan skin and dark brown hair. She was attractive, but she had enough money and skill to edge toward beautiful with clever makeup and gorgeous clothes.

Stephanie James had blond hair and peaches-and-cream skin. She had a wholesome beauty and a perfect, curvy figure that she showcased with excellent tailoring. She tended toward timidness in conversation, but little peeks of stubbornness had made me think that a steely backbone and sharp mind hid under her placid attitude. Chloe liked everyone to think that she was in charge of their friendship, despite being two years younger than Stephanie, but I wasn't certain it was true. When Stephanie wanted to do something, Chloe did it.

"Catarina, I thought that was you," Chloe called as they drifted closer to our table. She'd started dropping my honorific more and more and I hadn't corrected her. I'd been cultivating this relationship for months. If she felt more important because she didn't have to call me Lady Catarina, then that was fine by me.

Chloe looked at Alex, and then, pointedly, at our hands on the table, barely touching. She didn't go quite so far as to raise an eyebrow, but she was angling for an introduction or explanation.

I painted on my social smile. "Chloe, how surprising. I didn't expect anyone to be in Honorius early. Hello, Stephanie." Because I outranked them, I didn't need to use their honorifics, but I usually did, out of politeness. Dropping them could imply closeness, but it could also imply disdain. It was all about the tone, and I left mine purposefully vague.

Chloe's eyes narrowed as she tried to figure out if I was being friendly or not. I hadn't immediately introduced Alex, another social faux pas, but I might as well get the gossip mill well and truly started, and there was no bigger gossip than Chloe Patel.

"And who is your companion?" she dared to ask.

"Oh, this is Alexander," I said and then paused. I knew this was the path I had to take, but it still rankled, just a little. And now there would be no turning back. "He will be joining me at the house party as my guest." I looked to Stephanie. "I apologize for the late notice, but he didn't think he would be able to get free. He surprised me this morning. You don't mind, do you?"

"Of course not," she agreed stiffly.

"Delightful!" I cast a smitten glance at Alex, only to nearly break cover at the amusement dancing in his eyes. I waved a hand toward the women. "Alexander, meet Chloe Patel and Stephanie James. They organized the party, and Stephanie's family is being kind enough to host."

Bianca said she'd briefed him on the basics, and she must have included House James's involvement because his gaze sharpened before he turned his focus to Stephanie. He gave her a charming grin.

She blushed prettily and returned his smile. "It's nice to meet you, Alexander. I'm so glad you were able to join Lady Catarina."

"The pleasure is mine," he said. "I apologize for any inconvenience my presence causes." Neither woman was immune to his voice and Stephanie practically tripped over herself to assure him that it was no trouble at all.

While they chatted, Chloe turned to me with a catty smile. "So where did you and Alexander meet? Wait, it's not *Lord* Alexander is it?" she asked, all false innocence.

I reminded myself that I needed to remain friends with Chloe for at least the next few days. Still, I let ice creep into my tone. "It is not, but as my guest I'm sure he will be treated with all due respect."

"I'm sure," she murmured.

Somehow I was not reassured.

She was doing exactly what I'd expected her to do, but I felt bad that Alex would bear the brunt of her cattiness for the next two weeks. She wasn't quite brave enough to insult me to my face, not after Bianca had cut her socially at an event a few months ago, but she would absolutely feel justified in slyly insulting Alex.

And if she could knock me down a few pegs in the process, I'm sure she wouldn't lose any sleep over it.

Chloe touched Stephanie's arm, pulling her from her conversation with Alex. "We should go so Catarina can return to her date," she said. "We'll see them again tomorrow." She practically vibrated with the need to share the juicy gossip that had just landed in her lap. She didn't want anyone else to wander by and scoop her.

They said their good-byes, bobbed shallow curtsies, and

then slipped away. Chloe pulled out her com before she was out of sight.

"Did you know that you'd run into them here?" Alex asked.

"No, but I knew if any guests were already on-planet then they would likely be in this area. It was just luck that it was Stephanie and Chloe who found us first. We should go before we get mobbed with curious onlookers. Let me pay for the drinks and then we'll go find Aoife."

He tilted his head, indicating the area behind me. "She's at the corner of the building. And I already took care of the drinks."

I blinked at him, stunned into silence. When I went out with friends or on dates, it was implicitly assumed that, as the daughter of a High House, I would pay for everything. I didn't mind, not really, because I could easily afford it, but it stood out when someone at least *offered* to pay, even though I always turned them down.

I couldn't remember the last time that someone had quietly taken care of the bill for me.

"Thank you, but I'll repay you," I said at last. This cafe was very chic, which meant very expensive.

"No."

He'd surprised me again, but I refused to back down. "Of course I will. You're helping me. You aren't responsible for expenses on this trip."

The stubborn set of his mouth told me that I wasn't getting anywhere. I couldn't believe that I was actually arguing with someone about who was going to pay. It was so far outside normal that it helped me to remember that this was all fake. I'd butted heads with stubborn men before, so I just smiled and thanked him again.

And then I planned how to slip him a credit chip when he wasn't looking.

I TOOK US ON A MEANDERING PATH HOME, THROUGH A rougher neighborhood. After a few minutes, Alex leaned over and whispered, "We're being followed by a group of kids."

"I know. If you see them, point at them. It helps them learn how to stay hidden." I'd seen a few younger kids, just learning the ropes. I was gratified to see that they looked well taken care of.

Two more turns and I slipped into a dim alley. Neither Alex nor Aoife protested, but both stuck close to me. Maybe this guard situation would work after all.

Halfway down, a slender figure melted out of the gloom. They were young, still in their late teens, with deep brown skin and bright blue hair, shaved into a short Mohawk. I'd made the mistake of addressing them as "she" when we'd first met, due to their delicate build, but I'd quickly learned they preferred gender-neutral pronouns.

"Took you long enough," they said.

"I didn't want to surprise you, so I wanted to give your kids time to get word back to you."

"I've known you were on-planet for ages. I figured you'd swing by at some point."

I turned to my temporary bodyguards. "Aoife and Alex, meet Skout. They keep an eye on the street kids and refuse all offers of respectable employment," I teased. It was a discussion we'd had many times. They were happy where they were, and they kept an eye on the most vulnerable kids, as well as ensuring everyone's safety, so I let them be.

They rolled their eyes. "You couldn't afford me."

I laughed. "True. Do you need anything? Are the shipments coming through on schedule?"

Skout's eyes softened. "Yes, thank you. The addition of medical supplies was really helpful. We had a bad round of croup last month."

"You have my address. If you need anything else, you only have to ask. If I don't spend my money on you, I'll just buy some ridiculous party dress, so you might as well take advantage."

"I will."

We both knew it was a lie, but I smiled and nodded. I made a mental note to add a few more items to the next shipment. "I will be on-planet for the next two weeks, but I'll be out of town, so if you need anything you can either send word to House James or to me directly."

They grimaced in distaste. "What are you doing with them?"

"Spying."

That got me a sly smile. "Need help?"

"Have you heard anything I should know?"

Skout shook their head. "Nothing concrete, but most of House James are assholes. If one of my kids was lying in the street dying, they'd step on them on their way across, then bitch about the blood on their shoes."

"If you hear anything, let me know. I'll pay twice the standard rate."

"You are such an easy mark," Skout said with a laugh. They looked at Alex and Aoife. "You have your work cut out for you, if you're trying to protect this one."

Aoife smiled faintly. "We're good at our jobs."

"You let her walk into a dark alley."

"There are twelve children in this alley, but only two are

armed with ranged weapons. I could take them both out before they pulled the trigger. And that was not an invitation to try, because I will shoot to kill." ·

Skout's eyebrows rose. "Lady C might survive in House James after all."

I waved a hand. "No one is shooting anyone. We have to go, but let me know if you find anything interesting or if you need anything else. And tell your urchins to stop trying to pick-pocket Consortium peers. I know they are juicy targets, but I can bail out only so many kids before local law enforcement stops talking to me."

"I'll spread the word."

We said our good-byes, then we left the alley. We were nearly back to the von Hasenberg building before Alex asked, "You sponsor a gang of street kids?"

"*Sponsor* is a strong word. Skout is too proud for that. I send them shipments every two weeks of food and clothes and other supplies. Skout won't accept credits directly, but they never turn down food and supplies, especially with hungry mouths to feed."

"How did you meet them?"

"Skout tried to pickpocket me a couple of years ago. They didn't expect me to be aware enough—or fast enough—to catch them. Seeing that I was interested in their story, Skout bargained answers for their freedom and I agreed. They were already climbing the gang hierarchy and trying to look out for the other kids, so I helped them along."

An unnamed emotion glowed in Alex's eyes. "I bet it blew their mind when you didn't immediately call the RCDF."

I smiled. "I hope so. It's not much, but it's something I can do. If everyone did something—especially those like me with the most to give—the 'verse would be a better place."

"Too bad the rest of the Consortium doesn't feel the same way," Alex said bitterly.

"Some do. I know it doesn't seem like it, but we're working on it. Someday it'll be better."

"That doesn't help today."

"I know," I said quietly.

It was something I struggled with daily, but if I told him, he wouldn't believe me. I just had to keep on keeping on and work for the change I wanted to see. One woman wasn't going to change the 'verse, but I was going to do my damnedest to ensure I was doing my part.

WE RETURNED TO THE HOUSE AND AOIFE WENT TO CHECK on the supplies she'd left in *Chaos*. Left alone with Alex, restless energy burned under my skin. This afternoon had been surprisingly great and I was dangerously close to forgetting that it was all a ploy. I needed to burn off some energy.

"I'm going to swim," I said. "I'll be back in an hour or so. I gave you and Aoife suite access, so you can come as go as you please. If you need anything, you can ask Jarvis."

"Would it bother you if I joined you?"

I hesitated for a split second as my brain short-circuited at the thought of Alex in nothing but swim trunks.

He glanced away. "Never mind," he murmured.

"No, sorry." I shook my head. "You're welcome to enjoy the pool. I'm planning to swim laps, so I'll be poor company, but I don't mind."

He met my eyes as if judging my truthfulness before finally nodding. "My clothes are in the ship, so I'll go change and meet you there."

I said a silent prayer of thanks. If I hurried, I could be in the water and swimming before he arrived. "Sounds good. See you in a bit. If you get lost, you can ask the house computer to direct you."

He left, and I dashed to my bedroom to change. My lap swimming suit was a modest one-piece that was designed to reduce drag in the water. It flattened my chest and did not enhance any part of my figure. For one crazy second, I thought about changing into one of my bikinis, but I was going to swim to reduce restlessness, not encourage it.

I threw on a dresslike cover-up and made my way to the fitness center. There was a lounge pool on the top floor, open to the outside, but the fitness pool was buried in the middle of the building. It was twenty-five meters long and nearly eight meters wide with three marked lanes. It was also blissfully empty when I entered.

I grabbed my swim cap and goggles from my locker. Once on, the display in the goggles came to life, overlaying distance, time, and heart rate on a transparent screen. I removed my cover-up and slid into the cool water.

With a wave, the goggles began tracking and I kicked off from the wall. I swam a few laps of warm-up, then pushed myself in hundred-meter sprints. I lost myself in the smooth rhythm of each stroke and the flip turn at the ends of the pool. Finally, finally, I began to settle.

After an hour, I felt centered again. I'd swum nearly four kilometers, but if I wanted to, I could easily swim four more. In the water my abilities were less obvious, except for my endurance, so it was one of the few places where I could use my full strength and push myself without seeming suspicious.

I swam a lazy two-hundred-meter backstroke to cool down. I delighted in the feel of my body operating at peak efficiency. My muscles were warm and pliable and I felt like I could take on the world thanks to the endorphins rushing through my blood.

Cooldown complete, I reluctantly hoisted myself out of the pool. It was only after I'd removed my swim cap and goggles that I realized I was not alone. Two lanes over, Alex glided through the water nearly silently, his stroke clean and fluid. I watched, mesmerized, as he flipped and turned back toward this end.

Had he been here this whole time? I didn't know anyone who liked to swim as much as I did—or who could keep up with me.

For such a big man, he sliced smoothly down the lane. He was shirtless, and I caught teasing glimpses of tawny skin with every stroke. I felt like a voyeur, but I couldn't seem to tear my eyes away. Athletic prowess had always been a weakness of mine.

When he neared the wall, I expected him to turn and continue, so it took me a second to realize that he hadn't. Now he was staring at me staring at him.

Heat rushed into my cheeks, but I managed to calmly ask, "Are you done or resting?"

"I'm done." Rather than moving toward the ladder, he effortlessly lifted himself out of the water using only the edge of the pool and his strength. The solid muscles in his arms and chest flexed and I was once again transfixed. His swim trunks were designed for lap swimming. They clung from his waist to his knees, leaving very little to the imagination.

Oh. My. God.

I turned away after I'd gotten an eyeful, my face flaming. It wasn't fair that he managed to look like the statue of an ancient hero come to life in his lap swimming suit while I looked like I hadn't hit puberty yet.

I stepped in the drying booth and waited for the two-minute cycle to be completed. At the end, my skin was dry and my suit and hair were barely damp. If I had wanted to wait longer I could have gotten completely dry, but I planned to shower after I returned to my room, so I just needed to be dry enough not to drip all the way there.

Alex had also dried. I watched him out of the corner of my eye while I pulled on my cover-up. He donned a shirt and wrapped a towel around his waist.

I tried not to think about the fact that, in just a few short hours, he would be back in my bed.

I failed.

CHAPTER SEVEN

Raventhorpe, House James's main property, was located outside Honorius on a pastoral piece of land lush with fields, forests, and gently rolling hills that stretched for kilometers in every direction. They had a smaller residence in the city proper, but the house party was always held in the country, the better to see the meteors. The shopping district was a twenty-minute transport ride away.

The property had a spaceport and guests were invited to bring their ships. Because I thought I might have to make a quick escape, I took them up on the offer. *Chaos* gently touched down on the landing pad. I cut the engines and took a deep breath. Time to sell the lie I had to live for the next two weeks.

Alex and Aoife met me in the cargo bay. Alex wore an expertly tailored dark blue three-piece suit that matched the blue accents in my orange sundress. He exuded the perfect cool arrogance common to Consortium nobles. Aoife wore dark slacks and a white blouse. If she had a blaster, I couldn't detect it. She looked relaxed and confident.

If we were lucky, they would show us to our rooms and allow us to change and rest before dinner. If not, we'd have to socialize over tea before being allowed to escape.

A new trunk had been added to the cargo sled. I picked up the beacon and the sled lifted. "Ready?"

They nodded, so I lowered the cargo ramp and opened the door. I tucked my worries and fears away behind a mask of aristocratic boredom. A pair of strapping young men in House James uniforms waited at the bottom of the ramp.

"Welcome to Raventhorpe," the blond said with a bow. "I am Aaron. May I take your luggage? It will be delivered directly to your room."

I handed over the sled's beacon. "Thank you."

"You're welcome, Lady Catarina. David will show you to the house." He waved to the dark-haired man next to him. David bowed.

I locked *Chaos*. Alex offered me an arm, then we followed David toward the main house, Aoife trailing behind us. The spaceport was off the corner of the building, but the path curved around so we approached directly from the front.

Raventhorpe was an impressive building, all red stone and imposing lines. It was five or six stories tall and rectangular in shape. Large, evenly spaced windows spread across the building's face. It looked far older than it was, a design decision that added to its gravitas.

A uniformed, gray-haired butler swung the door open as we approached. The foyer was lined with dark wood paneling and an enormous chandelier hung overhead. It felt claustrophobic and I had the sudden urge to turn around and leave. I didn't believe in omens, but if I did, this would be a bad one.

The butler dismissed David with a subtle gesture. "Welcome to Raventhorpe, Lady Catarina. Lady Stephanie and a few of the other guests are enjoying tea in the green salon if you would like to join them."

I hid my grimace behind a polite smile. "That would be lovely, thank you."

Alex tucked my hand farther into the crook of his elbow. When I glanced up, his gaze was concerned. I minutely shook my head. I was going to have to face everyone sooner or later, so it might as well be sooner. I couldn't say that though, so I gave him a weak smile.

The butler stopped outside the closed doors to what was likely the green salon. "If your guard would care to refresh herself, I can have someone show her to her room."

My eyebrows rose. I addressed the largest concern first. "*Her* room? Is she not staying in my suite?"

The butler sniffed lightly. "I apologize, my lady, but the guest accommodations at Raventhorpe are not suites. Staff and guards are roomed on the upper floors."

"And the room next to mine?"

"All of the guest rooms are currently spoken for, my lady. Once again, I do apologize."

Usually, I would be elated to get away from my guard, but I was in a hostile House and my own House was at war. A universe of possibilities flashed through my mind. If I protested, it could tip them off that I knew about their involvement with Ferdinand. Or they could be expecting me to protest so they could move me away from the other guests, possibly to the family wing, which would give me better access to their rooms, but also give them better access to *mine*.

My eyes narrowed. Had Bianca known about this? As far as I knew, she'd never been to Raventhorpe, but I'd learned not to underestimate the extent of Bianca's intelligence network. This could very well be the reason she'd insisted I bring Alex.

I did not want to make an enemy of the butler. He would

be a powerful ally if I could win him to my side, so I smiled brightly. "Thank you for letting me know. I'm sure Aoife will enjoy having time to herself. But for now, I'd rather she stayed with me, so she will be here for the introductions, if you don't mind. Then she can find her room before dinner."

The butler unbent slightly at my friendly tone and lack of screaming complaints. "Very good, my lady. I will ensure someone is available to show her up to her room whenever she is ready. Shall I announce you and . . ." He trailed off delicately with a glance at Alex.

I firmly affixed my public mask and gave Alex an adoring look before returning my gaze to the butler. "This is Alexander. Please introduce us as Lady Catarina and guest, if you don't mind." I giggled softly and leaned in, as if I was imparting a secret. "I want to handle the personal introductions myself."

"As you wish." He crossed the hall and slid open the doors to the green salon. Heads swiveled our way when the butler cleared his throat. "May I present Lady Catarina and her guest." He stepped aside. Alex and I swept into the room on a murmur of intrigue. My hand curled possessively around his arm, something the sharp-eyed guests in the room did not miss.

I could not have asked for a better entrance. I could hear speculation and curiosity in the low murmurs. Stephanie James and Chloe Patel stood near the far windows, deep in conversation with another lady from a lower house. I cataloged the room as I crossed to greet the hostesses.

We must have been nearly the last to arrive because over a dozen people sat and stood in little conversational cliques around the room. Most of them were distant acquaintances, easily ignored, but two stood out: Ying Yamado, the youngest daughter of High House Yamado, and Joseph James, Stephanie's middle brother. Ying was the only true ally I had in this crowd, and Joseph had not been included on any of the guest lists I'd seen. I hadn't expected anyone else from House James to be in residence.

I nodded at Ying. She grinned back, tipped her head minutely toward Alex, and raised one eyebrow. My answering grin was full of secrets. Her eyes narrowed and I knew I'd be in for an interrogation as soon as she got her hands on me.

Cira, Ying's favorite guard, stood with her back to the wall and watched the crowd with an impassive expression. She was the only guard I saw in evidence. She acknowledged Aoife with a tiny nod.

I let go of Alex to exchange air kisses with Stephanie and Chloe. Chloe took the opportunity to link her arm through mine and drag me around the room, introducing me as "my dear friend Catarina von Hasenberg" to people I already knew.

I murmured the correct responses while surreptitiously casing the room. The green salon was a fairly standard reception room, though one decorated tastefully—and expensively. The name came from the seafoam-green walls, augmented with real wood wainscoting. There were, sadly, no evil plans neatly labeled and sitting out on a side table.

When Chloe finally pulled me to Joseph James for an introduction, I brought my attention back to the conversation. He bowed over my hand and pressed a light kiss to my skin. When I raised an eyebrow at him, his mouth curved into a devilish grin.

Joseph was a handsome man, but unlike his fair sister, his skin was tan and his hair was dark brown. He had hazel eyes and striking cheekbones. He was a couple of years older than me and an outrageous flirt. I didn't know him well, but I'd always liked him.

Until his family had decided to kill my brother.

"Joseph, it's nice to see you again," I said. "Have you met Alexander?" Joseph was tall and lean, with an athletic build. I was surprised to find that he looked almost gaunt next to Alex's muscled bulk.

"I don't believe I've had the pleasure," Joseph said. The two men sized each other up. Alex's expression was as chilly as I'd seen it. Joseph apparently took it as a challenge and turned back to me with a mischievous light in his eye. "My sister tells me you're into gardening. You must let me give you a private tour of Raventhorpe's gardens before you leave."

Before I could answer, Alex slid an arm around my waist and tucked me into his side, dislodging Chloe's hold on me. "We would be delighted to tour the gardens," he said smoothly.

There was no way for Joseph to retract or narrow the invite without seeming rude, so he just grinned and tipped his head, acknowledging his defeat. "I am at your service," he said. "If you'll excuse me." He bowed to me, ignored Chloe, and moved to talk to someone across the room.

Well, that was one way to make a statement—one Chloe did not miss. Her face was a mask of anger as she watched him leave. When she noticed my gaze, she smoothed a smile into place. "I didn't realize you and Lord Joseph were acquainted."

"We've met a few times. He's entertaining."

"And what of Alexander?" she asked snidely. "Have you forgotten him so soon, even though he's plastered against your side?"

I didn't have to fake the cold smile I gave her. "Tread lightly, my dear, or Joseph won't be the only one who ignores you this trip."

The dig landed true and she flushed in outrage.

I nodded politely to her and turned to find Ying, pulling Alex with me. I might as well dive headfirst into the inquisition, otherwise she'd be even more curious about why I was avoiding her.

"Brace yourself," I whispered under my breath. He squeezed me, a silent acknowledgment.

Ying broke off from her group when I approached. She was gorgeous, with pale skin, straight black hair, and dark eyes. Her delicate beauty and lithe frame masked a cunning, razor-sharp mind. She was two years older than me, and despite being a few centimeters shorter, she had a commanding presence.

She pulled me into a hug. "You're dead to me for keeping a man that hot a secret," she whispered.

I pulled back with a grin. "Ying, this is Alexander. Alex, this is Lady Ying Yamado, youngest daughter of High House Yamado."

Alex bowed over her hand. "It is a pleasure to meet you, my lady," he said in his perfect aristocratic accent.

"Likewise," Ying said. She glanced at my empty hands. "Chloe didn't even let you get a drink before dragging you around the room." She *ts*ked under her breath. "Let's fix that. Alexander, be a darling and fetch Cat a drink, would you?"

It was not a subtle bid to get rid of him. Alex glanced at me. I nodded. "A coffee would be lovely."

Once he was out of earshot, Ying leaned in close. "No *wonder* you were desperate to attend this party. Wherever did you find him and does he have a brother? Or a sister?"

I thought about Aoife, guarding my back, and shrugged. "Not that I know of," I said.

As if drawn by my thoughts, Ying peeked around me. "And did you get a new guard? You're full of surprises today."

Most people would never have realized that Aoife was new. They treated guards as interchangeable parts and didn't notice when they were swapped out. But Ying wasn't the daughter of a High House for nothing.

"Bianca insisted," I grumbled. It took no effort at all to infuse that statement with annoyance. "And since I couldn't tear Susan away from her husband for two weeks, I agreed. This is Aoife. Aoife, meet Lady Ying and her guard, Cira."

Cira Zapata had olive skin and dark blond hair, pulled back into a braid. She wore dark slacks and a light blouse, with a jacket covering a shoulder holster. She was in her early thirties and had been Ying's guard for years. Her wife also worked for House Yamado in an administrative role.

Aoife bowed shortly to Ying and nodded to Cira.

"So, tell me about Alexander," Ying demanded.

"We met a few months ago. I didn't think he'd be able to make it, which is why I didn't mention anything. That and I didn't want Mother to hear about it until it was too late."

"Is it serious?"

"No," I said. "We barely know each other." I smiled at the truth in that statement. "But it's fun."

"What am I supposed to do now that you're going to be sneaking off every five minutes?"

I waved an arm at the variety of beautiful people in the room. "Pick someone and enjoy yourself?" I grinned. "Isn't that why you decided to come?"

She pouted at me. "Of course! But I thought we'd be on the hunt together. At least now my competition has gone down." Her gaze drifted around the room before settling on Joseph. "I'm not going to step on your toes if I choose him, am I?" she asked on a low murmur.

"No, but I hope you like a challenge. He'll flirt with anyone, but rumor has it that he's extremely selective when taking it further than that."

Ying thrived on challenge. Her eyes lit up. "In that case, I should get started." She pointed a finger at me. "I'm not done with you, but we'll adjourn until after dinner. I want to speak to your mystery man."

I inclined my head in agreement, but I was already trying to figure out the best way to get out of it. "Good luck."

She tossed her head, sending her long hair swinging. "Darling," she drawled, nose in the air, "I don't need *luck* when I have *skill*."

I burst into laughter and she joined me. Heads turned as the other guests tried to figure out what we found so amusing. I was glad that Ying had come. It was nice to have a friend in this sea of lies.

After Ying wandered off, Alex returned, and I wondered if he'd been surreptitiously waiting for her to depart. He handed me a delicate china cup and saucer. His hands were big and calloused, but he handled the cup with the utmost care.

"Thank you," I said.

"I wasn't sure how you liked it," he said softly, "so I guessed."

His voice was a delicious caress. If he could bottle that effect, he would be a rich, rich man.

I took a sip of coffee. It was creamy and slightly sweet. I hummed in appreciation. "It's perfect, thank you."

"You're welcome."

I took another fortifying sip. "Ready to mingle?"

He grinned. "If we have to."

I agreed completely.

———

I HAD FIELDED SLY QUESTIONS FOR NEARLY HALF AN hour before we were allowed to escape to prepare for dinner. Aoife retreated up to her room after tossing a significant glance at Alex.

A uniformed maid led us up to the end of the third-floor wing. As the highest-ranking guests, Ying and I were each given corner rooms. Ying waved and disappeared into the room across the hall.

Alex and I entered our own room. He closed the door, enclosing us in silence. I relaxed for the first time since landing. The room was much like the rest of the house, too ornate for my taste, but obviously expensive. Dark, heavy furniture anchored pale pink walls. Windows on two walls looked out over pristine lawns and the forest beyond. A large bed dominated the room, but a small sitting area was tucked near the glass door to the balcony.

A tall door led into the lavish bathroom. An enormous shower and a tub big enough for two took up most of the space. The tub sang a siren song, and I promised myself that I would make use of it before I left. The vanity and mirror included a built-in cosmetics kit that meant I wouldn't need the portable one in my trunk.

When I returned to the bedroom, Alex was sweeping the room for bugs and cameras. He moved into the bathroom, then came back and stepped close. He brushed his lips against my temple and whispered, "There's a bug in the corner. What do you want me to do?"

"Video?" I asked, just as quietly.

He shook his head.

"We'll let Aoife find it. Until then, play along." When he nodded, I moaned. "We can't. We don't have time before dinner," I protested at my normal speaking volume.

His eyes laughed at me even as he growled, "We'll make time. Now get naked."

"You naughty man."

A tap on the door interrupted us. Alex cursed vividly and I had to smother a giggle. I crossed the room and swung the door open to reveal Aoife. "Aoife, you have terrible timing, but I guess you might as well come in. How was your room?"

Her eyes narrowed, but she seemed to catch on. "My room was nice." Once I closed the door, Alex signaled that we had a listener. "Have you swept for bugs?" she asked.

I laughed nervously. "Bugs? Like an infestation? If there are bugs in here, I'm sleeping on my ship. I don't care how rude it makes me seem."

"I meant listening devices, Lady Catarina," Aoife said with the perfect touch of exasperation.

"Oh, I knew that. No, I didn't check. I was distracted." I giggled. "You can do it for me, though, right?"

"Of course, my lady." Aoife swept the whole room. While she did that, I pulled out my com and did a sweep of my own. It's possible my com was more sensitive than whatever they were using, especially if Director Bishop hadn't equipped them with von Hasenberg standard-issue devices.

Aoife and I both found the same bug Alex had warned me about. Aoife loudly admonished me to be more careful and then destroyed it.

Another sweep revealed the room was clean.

"Is bugging personal rooms common?" Aoife asked.

"Common enough. Could be House James, could be someone on staff, or one of the guests could've snuck it in. It's hard to say, but there's a reason I usually sweep new places before I say anything incriminating. We'll have to recheck every time we return. How is your room really?"

"It's fine. Smaller than this, obviously, but it has its own bathroom. It's on the fifth floor and the path down here isn't direct. It will take me at least a minute at a run."

A lot could change in sixty seconds if I needed Aoife badly enough for her to run. "Let's hope it doesn't come to that."

But I didn't rely on hope when preparation could be used instead. I crossed to my trunks and swiped my identity chip across the lock on the box of supplies. I lifted the clothes out and unlocked the secondary container.

Alex and Aoife watched without comment until I started pulling out blasters. "What are you doing?" Aoife asked.

"Planning ahead." The three blast pistols I removed were in holsters that were backed with a special adhesive. With the press of a button, they'd stick to nearly anything. Then, when it was time for removal, press the button again and a small electric current rendered the adhesive nonsticky.

The holsters were excellent for concealing weapons around a room in places where the cleaning staff was unlikely to look. I moved to the sitting area and attached a pistol under the coffee table. I practiced drawing the blaster to ensure it was positioned well—I'd learned that lesson the hard way when I'd been unable to draw my gun on a training mission thanks to the edge of the table I'd hidden it under.

My self-defense tutor had been less than impressed.

"Are those bio-locked to you?" Aoife asked.

"No. If you need to use you them, you can."

"So can anyone else."

I shrugged. My bigger, more dangerous weapons were locked to my identity chip, but these little blast pistols were weapons of last resort. If I needed to use one, then things were already terrible. I stuck the second one behind the nightstand by the bed and the last one under a cabinet in the bathroom. The room was covered enough that I was never more than three meters from a weapon.

It would have to do. I repacked the trunk and locked it, then set about finding a dress to wear to dinner.

"Am I supposed to attend dinner with you?" Aoife asked.

"It depends on what kind of message I'm trying to send. If guards attend dinner, they usually sit or stand behind their principal for the duration of the meal, eating on their own either before or after the formal dinner. I think that's stupid, so I usually dismiss my guards until the meal is over. If I bring you, it'll be out of the ordinary for me. And it'll imply that I don't trust the host."

"Which you don't," Aoife said.

"True, but I don't necessarily want them to know that."

Alex snorted, but it was Aoife who said, "No wonder Bianca wanted us to come with you. I bet your other guards wouldn't have any problem letting you run off on your own, especially when it makes their lives easier."

It was true, but I'd be damned if I admitted it.

"You are too clever for your own good," she said.

"You're here, aren't you? Clearly, I'm not that clever."

Aoife smiled, a true smile that tipped her from beautiful to stunning. "I have no doubt that it's a problem you're still working on."

Also true, but I also wasn't going to admit that, either.

"This is why Bianca wanted me to attend as your guest," Alex said. "I'm expected at dinner, while Aoife would cause questions. I can protect you when she can't."

"I can protect myself." And now I sounded like a petulant child. I took a slow, deep breath. "I appreciate your concern. I know you're trying to help. Everyone is always trying to help." I shook my head. "Sometimes I wonder if my public ruse isn't a little *too* good. Even my siblings underestimate me."

"Bianca doesn't underestimate you," Alex said quietly. "She warned us about you, about how quick and perceptive and cunning you were. She told us we'd have to stay on our toes or you'd leave us behind."

"Your sister had nothing but praise for you," Aoife agreed. "But she also knew that with our help, you'd be more protected. We're not your enemy. We're not here to stop you. We're here to help you find what you need and get out safely."

I wished I could trust her, but perhaps she could be useful even if I didn't. "How are you at reconnaissance?"

Her wicked smile was answer enough.

CHAPTER EIGHT

Formal dinners were always an interminable affair, but tonight's was made worse by the unanticipated attendance of Lord and Lady James. I had expected Stephanie's parents to vacate the estate for the duration of the party, as was their custom, but they sat at the head of the wide table as imperious as royalty.

Because we were the highest-ranking guests, Ying and I were seated next to them. We shared a pained grimace before settling more firmly into our public personas. Alexander sat on my right and Joseph James sat across from him, next to Ying. Ying's guard Cira was nowhere to be seen.

Everyone was dressed in formal elegance. The men wore tuxedos and the women wore formal gowns. No one looked especially pleased to have to dress for dinner. The boned bodice of my gown dug into my waist. This was my first time wearing it to a seated event. It would also be my last.

Lady Agatha James smiled a shark's smile at me. "How did you and Alexander meet?"

"My sister introduced us," I said. I hid a grin when shock briefly crossed her face. Even if my father wouldn't approve, my siblings were not without power of their own and having them on my side meant she couldn't use the relationship against me.

"And how is your brother? I heard about the terrible attack. You have my condolences." Her tone was perfectly polite and her expression held nothing but earnest well wishes but something rang false. I'd always excelled at reading people, and even Stewart, Lord James, was paying close attention to me now.

I gave her my most guileless smile. Bianca would immediately know that I was up to something, but Lady James didn't have my sister's insight. "He is well, thank you for asking. The attack was a tragedy, but I'm so glad we got him back. I believe our security forces know who is responsible, so we should all sleep a little easier."

"Oh? Who was it?" she asked with just a touch too much interest.

"Father didn't discuss the details with me," I said with a dismissive flick of my fingers. Then I leaned in and lowered my voice. "But I heard it was the Syndicate."

It was the rampant rumor around Serenity, so I wasn't telling them anything new. Agatha relaxed and smiled at Stewart with a slightly raised eyebrow, as if to say, *I told you so.*

My hand flexed under the table as I imagined lunging at her and wrapping it around her throat until she told me why they'd wanted my brother dead.

Alex slid his hand over mine and squeezed gently. "I, for one, am glad your brother is safe now," he said, his voice warm. I glanced at him and he must not have liked whatever he saw in my face, because he raised my hand and brushed a kiss over the back of my knuckles.

Ying sighed at the romantic gesture.

The shock of his mouth on my skin coupled with the warning look in his eye was enough to remind me of why I was here.

"Me, too," I replied lightly. "Otherwise I would've had to stay home and miss the legendary meteor shower."

"You've never seen them?" Ying asked.

"No, there was always something else going on. I'm delighted that this year I will be able to fix that. Thank you for your hospitality, Lady James."

She inclined her head, accepting the praise as her due.

"Stephanie did not mention that you and Lord James would be in residence." Nor did the youngest James look particularly pleased by the addition. That end of the table was distinctly sullen. "How long do you plan to stay?"

"Stewart has business in Honorius, but with the meteor shower, we decided a stay in the country was preferable to our city residence."

I had to assume they planned to stay for the duration, which meant my own plans needed to be adjusted. It would be more difficult to sneak around if they were constantly underfoot, but it also meant I would have more opportunity to study them.

"Will you be expecting more guests?" Ying asked.

"None that are planning to stay, but a few may drop in for dinner or meetings. You know how it is."

We all nodded politely and the conversation drifted on to more mundane topics. Alex was the perfect dinner guest—funny, attentive, and well-mannered. He'd won Ying over before the second course. By the time dessert finally arrived, Lord and Lady James were laughing at his jokes.

He might be even better at this game than I was.

And excellent liars should not be trusted. I should know—I was one.

If Alex noticed my cooling regard, he didn't show it. After dinner, the younger guests retired to the green salon for a nightcap while Lord and Lady James disappeared into the library. Another hour of socializing and I was *done*. Even a seasoned socialite could reach the end of her patience when every other comment was a subtle dig at her fake date.

Ying pulled me aside when my smile started looking more like the baring of teeth. "Your dragon look is scaring the peasants," she said drily. "Let's commandeer a bottle of wine and move to my room."

"That sounds lovely, but if you don't mind, I think I will retire for the evening. This dress is killing me. Tomorrow night?" She nodded easily, her eyes already searching for Joseph. "Happy hunting," I murmured.

She blushed and winked at me. "You, too." Then, with a laugh, she moved away.

AOIFE HAD BEEN BUSY WHILE ALEX AND I HAD BEEN stuck making nice with the people who'd betrayed my House. She had scouted the first and second floors as part of her security patrols. My own research had given me the basic layout of the building, but Aoife confirmed the rooms I knew about and added several more that had been guesses.

After reporting, she returned to her room, leaving me with Alex. The black tuxedo added a civilized veneer to the untamed look he usually sported. It was incredibly effective. I knew it was camouflage and still I was drawn to him.

"Did I do something wrong at dinner?" he asked.

I frowned. Perhaps he wasn't as oblivious as I'd thought, but it was easy to give him the truth. He'd played his part perfectly. Just because I was unsettled by his level of skill at lying didn't mean he'd done anything wrong. "No. Why?"

His gaze traced over my face, but he shook his head. "What's your plan now?"

"First, I'm going to get out of this gown. Then I'm going to set up a device to probe their network for vulnerabilities. After that, I'm going to sleep. Agatha and Stewart are an unexpected complication, but it might be a boon. I'll have to think about it. What about you?"

"I'm going to ensure that any assassins who attempt to nab you during the night have a bad time." He said it with a perfectly straight face, but he broke into a grin when I laughed.

"I appreciate it. Shout if any bust in while I'm changing and I'll come help you kick their asses." I grabbed a change of clothes and retreated to the bathroom.

Safely locked behind a solid door, I let my gown slide to the floor and sighed in relief. I took a deep breath without the boning pressing against my skin. I changed into pajama pants and a tank top with a built-in bra. I wanted to lull Alex into thinking that I really was going to sleep, while still being decent enough to slip out into the house. I hadn't lied, exactly, I'd just left out a few steps in my plan.

I washed my face and let my hair down. My scalp tingled from where the heavy weight had been pinned up. I usually didn't bother, but formal wear meant formal hair. *Bleh.*

Although, it also meant that I'd get to see Alex in a tux again, and that was worth something. I might not trust him, but he certainly wasn't hard on the eyes.

I gathered up my dress and let myself out of the bathroom. I dumped the dress over the back of a chair. It was slightly better than the floor, which is where I'd really like to drop it.

Alex disappeared into the bathroom while I dug through my trunks, looking for the gear I'd need tonight. I put a silencer and a vanisher as well as a few other items in a small bag and tucked it next to the trunk. I didn't want to have to risk the hinges squeaking when I snuck out later.

I also pulled out a security tablet. I wasn't nearly as good as Bianca at cracking into foreign networks, but I'd had training—all von Hasenberg children had. I would have to be careful or House James would know I was poking around. I pulled up a general-purpose script and set it to run one query every two to six minutes. The timer was random to make it look less like a script, and it would refresh the news feed at the same time to provide some connection noise for cover.

By the time I was done, Alex was out of the bathroom, dressed in loose pants and a dark T-shirt that stretched across his chest. "Where should I sleep?"

The bed was smaller than the one we'd shared in my suite but large enough for two people. The floor was hard even with the rugs that softened parts of it. The sitting area had a tiny sofa that would be laughably too small for him. He waited patiently.

"Can you keep your hands to yourself?"

"Yes." His eyes crinkled at the corners, but he didn't mention that both times that I'd awoken, it had been on his side of the bed. He'd been gone before I awoke, but apparently I was a restless sleeper. Or a stealthy cuddler.

"We'll share the bed. I want the side by the door."

Alex nodded and headed for the other side. It was late, but not late enough to be up roaming in the halls undetected, so I climbed into bed with him. I pretended that I was getting into my own bed, alone.

It did not help.

I could feel the heat of him, just centimeters away. The bed had seemed much larger from across the room, but now that we were here, Alex's broad shoulders took up more than his fair share.

I turned off the light before my face gave away the level of my embarrassment—and interest.

"Good night," he murmured.

"Good night."

I DOZED, OFF AND ON, FOR THREE HOURS. ALEX'S BREATH-ing was deep and even. I slipped from the bed one careful centimeter at a time, but he didn't stir. The mattress did an excellent job of isolating movement.

The room was dark, but I could see well enough to make my way to the bag I'd left near the trunk. I pulled out the silencer and clicked it on. Now I was surrounded by a two-meter radius of silence. No noise inside that radius would be transmitted outside, nor would any wireless signals. This silencer was one-way, so I could still hear the sounds around me. I tucked the silencer in my pocket.

Next, I pulled out the vanisher. This was a new piece of tech that House von Hasenberg had been working on for a while. It was currently undergoing field testing, but I hoped that it would work tonight or I'd have a lot of explaining to do. Working correctly, it would keep me from appearing on any form of electronic surveillance—camera, thermal, and everything else.

Our engineers were trying to combine the two pieces of technology, but for now, I had to carry both. I clicked the vanisher on and put it in my other pocket. I made sure both items were secure. I also had a handful of tiny wireless bugs. If House James was diligent about security, they would quickly find them, but if not, I might get lucky. A few other odds and ends went into my pockets, and then I tucked my com into my bra.

Finally, I performed the complicated finger motions that disabled the main identity chip in my right arm. I didn't bother activating my secondary chip. None of my backup identities had access to Raventhorpe. With no active chip, I at least had plausible deniability because no chip readers could grab my identity wirelessly.

I crept toward the door. With the silencer I didn't have to be as careful, as long as I didn't get close to the bed. Alex remained still and quiet, his breathing even. It was deep in the early hours of the morning. I would not get a better chance than now.

Despite the silencer, I winced when the door hinges creaked. It was a slight sound, but it would've been enough to wake me. I edged from the room, checking the hallway for any other stray guests.

If questioned, I was either heading to the library, on the second floor, to borrow a book, or the kitchens, on the first floor, for a cup of tea. It wouldn't do me much good if I was caught in a room I shouldn't have been in, but then I'd play it off as drunken sleepwalking.

My bare feet didn't make any sound on the thick rugs running the length of the hallway. I walked slowly but purposefully. If I was caught, creeping around would be immediately suspicious, while wandering around deliberately implied I had nothing to hide.

Raventhorpe was still and silent around me, cloaked in deep shadows. I probably should have worn a pair of smart glasses to explain why I could see in the dark so well, but it was too late now. I could always pretend I was testing new tech.

I bypassed the wide main staircase for the narrower back stairs. The first-floor study was tucked away at the back of the house. It was also closer to the kitchen if I got caught. The stairs dumped me out into a small butler's pantry near the kitchen, dark enough that I had trouble making out more than large features like doorways.

I crossed the room and slid the hallway door open. My mental map served me well; I was just two doors down from the study. The hallway was dark and quiet, and no light glowed from under any of the doors.

The study's door handle refused to turn. Locked, but with an old-fashioned key rather than a keypad or biometric scan. The James's insistence on making this house appear antique was a boon. It was a mere moment's work to pick the lock.

I eased the door open and slipped inside. A wall of windows overlooked the side yard and Andromeda Prime's twin moons produced enough light for me to be able to see well. I clicked off the silencer for a few seconds while I ran a scan for cameras and bugs. My com showed one camera in the far corner that had a clear view of the entire room.

The study was a long rectangle. From where I stood, the space opened up to the left. In front of me, a sitting area had a sofa and two wingback chairs. At the far end, a massive, ornate desk sat behind two uncomfortable-looking chairs. Bookcases lined the wall beside me, filled with leather-bound books that I'd bet good credits had never been opened.

Books were the perfect place to conceal bugs. I carefully hid an audio bug near the sitting area, taking care not to leave any fingerprints, then I hid a video bug pointing at the desk.

Now came the tricky part.

The vanisher made me invisible to the camera, but it was less good at hiding the objects around me. Things held in my hands or very near my body would be hidden, but changes to the room would not. So if I opened a desk drawer or moved some papers, those actions would be perceptible. If someone watched the video, they would see things moving around but not who was moving them. It would be a very short logical leap to guess that the hidden person was me.

I moved toward Stewart's desk; it was frustratingly clean. Not a single paper marred its smooth surface and accessing the built-in terminal would definitely show up on the video. I carefully tried the drawers, barely pulling to see if any of them were locked. Only one drawer resisted, and it was not locked with an easy-to-pick metal key.

The codebreaker in my pocket could crack it. It was so, so tempting, but common sense won in the end. I had more places to check, and if Stewart James was smart, he'd be monitoring access to the drawer. The codebreaker would find the right combination, but a middle-of-the-night unlocking might trigger some warnings.

I methodically checked the rest of the room, looking for a hidden safe or secret cache. I didn't find anything. None of the paintings covered safes, and short of pulling all of the books off the shelves, I couldn't find anything there, either.

If there was any evidence in this room, it was either in the desk or the terminal. I circled back to the desk and ran my fingers over the ornate carvings, feeling for a hidden button. *Nothing.*

The locked drawer sang a siren song. The proof I needed could be sitting just centimeters away. Or it could be a very clever honeypot, just waiting to trap the unwary, so I tamped down my impatience. I had two weeks to find what I was looking for. There was no reason to rush foolishly, no matter how tempted I was.

I pressed my ear against the door to the hallway. When only silence greeted me, I slipped out and locked the door behind me. The rest of the ground floor consisted of public rooms that held little chance of being useful, so I moved toward the back stairs. Both the library and Stewart's private office were on the second floor.

I slid open the door to the butler's pantry. After the moon-light in the study, the interior now appeared pitch black. Before my eyes had time to adjust, strong arms snaked out and yanked me into the murk.

CHAPTER NINE

F ear gave me strength and overrode my usual moderation. I jerked free, spun, and threw a blind punch. It connected with a solid wall of muscle, hard enough to send a small flash of pain jolting up my right arm. My attacker hissed out a breath but otherwise didn't make a sound.

My eyes adjusted and I could make out a large, shadowy figure, probably male. I threw another punch, one he swiftly dodged. I aimed a quick flurry of blows at him. After I got him down, I could call for backup and question him. Half of the hits landed, but the stubborn bastard stayed up. I wished I could use my feet, but barefoot I was as likely to break a toe as to do any damage with a kick.

I should have brought a weapon.

"Stop," Alex whispered, "it's me."

I froze as a new fear took root. I had been fighting at *full strength*, thinking I was under attack. Fear gave way to fury, blazing bright. "What the fuck were you thinking?" I whispered fiercely.

"Aoife is tracking the night guard. He was coming down the main stairs."

"So you just fucking grabbed me? Is your voice broken?"

"I'm sorry. You surprised me, and I reacted without thinking."

I rubbed my hands over my face and tried to get the anger to settle. Honor made me ask, "Are you hurt?"

"No." There was a strange inflection in his voice.

"Are you sure?"

"I'm sure. We need to move. Were you headed upstairs?"

"Yes. I have a silencer."

"I know."

I let him guide me into the stairwell. We climbed cautiously. When I stopped at the second floor, he sighed but only said, "The guard is on the main floor. If he sticks to his pattern, he'll be there for another half an hour."

In the brighter light of the hallway, I could make out his features. He wasn't wearing smart glasses, but seemingly had no trouble seeing. I watched as he scanned the hallway. Yes, definitely seeing.

"Did Ian give you a vanisher?" I asked. At his blank look, I elaborated, "For the cameras."

"No, but Aoife put the system on a loop before you slipped out of the bedroom."

I closed my eyes in frustration. "That was stupidly risky. I had it under control."

"We didn't know that," he murmured quietly.

It shouldn't hurt, to be underestimated by strangers, but it did. It hurt every time and the pain only seemed to be growing worse. How much longer would I be able to play this game before I shattered completely?

I pushed the hurt away and plastered a smile on my face. "Well, since it's been done, let's make the most of it."

Alex looked like he wanted to say something, but I turned

and led the way to Stewart's private office. Once again, the door was locked with a simple metal key, which meant that anything truly valuable was probably hidden away behind electronic locks. I picked the door lock while Alex played lookout, then we were in.

The office was smaller than the study, and the room stretched away from the door rather than off to the side. Close to the door, two comfy chairs were arranged near a fireplace on the right wall. A cigar box and a crystal decanter of dark amber liquid sat on the table between the chairs. Farther in, a large desk, facing into the room, hunkered down in front of a pair of tall, elegant windows. I guess Stewart didn't like looking at the scenery.

The left wall was lined with glass cases displaying all manner of collectibles—antique vases, bits of carved sculpture, ancient weapons. This was a fortune on display, which must mean the security was better than it appeared.

"Stay away from the cases." Alex nodded. He'd stood beside me while I'd surveyed the room and hadn't moved. "I'm turning off the silencer for a second to check for transmitters. Be quiet."

Another nod. I ran the scan, then clicked the silencer back on. There were a *lot* of transmitters in here. The scan had created a rudimentary model of the room, and the sensors were overlaid on the map. The display case was rife with them.

I turned the com so Alex could see the screen. "Stay *far* away from the cases. I'm going to search the desk. Look around and see if you can find a safe."

With the cameras on a loop, I could search more thoroughly than I had in the study. I opened each desk drawer, checking for hidden compartments and false bottoms. There weren't any, and none of the drawers were locked. I rifled through the few papers I found. There were a few interesting tidbits—their House was not as well off financially as they would like it to appear—but nothing at all concerning gambling debts, Pierre, the Syndicate, or Ferdinand.

I had hoped I wouldn't have to search Lord and Lady James's personal rooms, but that hope was slowly dying.

I tucked an audio bug under the desk. Perhaps it would be missed in the mass of other transmitters. I straightened and movement caught my eye. Alex waved me over from near the fireplace. He was outside the influence of the silencer and wasn't risking one of the many sensors in here picking up his voice. Smart.

I crossed the room to him, and he slid a piece of trim aside to reveal an electronic keypad about chest high. It took me nearly a minute to find the hidden seams in the wainscoting at the bottom of the wall that would open when the correct code was entered.

"How did you find it?"

"I pushed on everything. This moved."

If the drawer had been a temptation, this was nearly irresistible. It would take the codebreaker less than two minutes to crack the code. Before I'd spent a full day at Raventhorpe I could figure out why House James had thought their plan for Ferdinand was wise, and what they might be planning next.

My fingers twitched.

Alex had wandered away, and now he cocked his head, as if he was listening to something. He came back into the silence field. "Aoife said the guard just broke from his normal pattern and is heading for the stairs."

"You think he's on to us?"

"Hard to say."

He was very carefully leaving the decision in my hands,

but I could read the tension on his face. I sighed and silently promised the safe I'd be back for it soon. "Let's go."

Alex slid the trim back into place and then we left, locking the door behind us. I could just hear the guard's shoes on the marble main stairs as we dashed for the back stairs. We moved quickly, counting on the silencer to muffle our steps.

The third floor was still and quiet. We were halfway down the hallway when I heard the distinct sound of a door opening ahead of us. Between one breath and the next, Alex swept me into a shallow alcove and pressed his muscled body up against mine, pushing me back against the wall and both of us deeper into shadow.

I froze, electrically aware of every centimeter of him. Wide chest, tapered waist, thick legs. And muscles *everywhere*. The simmering desire I'd felt since I first laid eyes on him flared to life, and I wanted to rub against him like a cat. His warm breath ghosted over my cheek. I could turn my head and kiss his jaw, taste his skin.

A feminine giggle brought me back to myself. A deeper voice whispered a low response, and then the sounds of an enthusiastic kiss made me shift uncomfortably, my desire still burning too hot.

Alex's breath hitched and he pressed into me a little tighter. The growing bulge pressed into my low belly told me he wasn't unaffected by our inadvertent eavesdropping, especially when the woman moaned low in her throat, a sound of pure pleasure.

I rocked my hips against his, a tiny, barely-there movement. Alex surged against me, pinning me firmly to the wall. I went molten and slid my hands down his back a centimeter at a time, feeling the muscles flex and twitch under my exploring fingers. I couldn't quite reach his spectacular ass, so I settled for pulling his waist in, fusing us even closer. I bit back a moan.

Alex hissed under his breath, a sound so low that the couple couldn't possibly have heard him, but they finally broke apart with a few more whispered words. Steps crossed the hall, then two doors clicked closed.

Alex waited a moment before backing off so quickly that I stumbled. Acute embarrassment smothered my desire like an avalanche of icy water. Of course he was trying to get away—his body was having a natural reaction to external stimulus, and I was trying to hump him like a dog.

My face flamed, but I ducked my head and practically ran for the safety of our room.

Our room.

I needed a dozen cold showers and about a thousand years before I'd be able to face him again. Unfortunately, I had neither.

When the door closed behind us, Alex opened his mouth, but I held up a single finger. I turned off the silencer and scanned the room for new bugs. None showed up. I clicked the silencer back on so we could talk in peace.

I slowly unpacked my pockets while I tried to figure out what I wanted to say. Alex waited quietly, close enough to be in the silencer's field, but not crowding me.

It was cowardly, but I couldn't talk about my behavior in the hallway, not yet. I needed to apologize, and I would—in the morning. So I gathered my tattered dignity and asked about my original concern. "Were you ever asleep?"

"Yes. You woke me when you left the bed."

"Why didn't you stop me?"

"I'm not here to stop you. I'm here to help you." Aoife had

said something very similar and I hadn't believed her. With Alex's declaration, maybe I was starting to. Tentative trust bloomed. He continued, "I hadn't planned to interfere at all, but I was worried that you didn't know about the guard."

"I didn't," I admitted quietly. "Did I bruise you? Let me check."

Alex's grin was quick and rueful. "For such a small thing, you hit like a freighter."

It would take someone with his muscled build to consider me "small." There was a question there, in his expression, one I refused to answer. Instead, I gave him a different truth, at least part of it. "It's one of the reasons I don't spar. Please let me make sure that you're okay. Where did I hit you?"

He lifted his shirt, revealing tawny skin stretched tight over flat, rippling abs. And there, in the middle of his stomach, a fist-shaped bruise, already purpling. I felt sick. While I'd been busy groping him, he could've had internal organ damage. Shame glued my eyes to the damage I'd caused. I really was a monster, just like Father wanted.

I must've made some sound because his fingers feathered over my jaw, bringing my gaze up to his. "I'm fine, Cat. I surprised you and got what I deserved."

"No one deserves that. Do you have nanos? I know I hit you more than once. Where else?" I tugged on his shirt, trying to see what other damage I'd done.

He covered my hand with his own. I froze. "I have nanos. I'll be fine. None of your other hits landed so hard. You shouldn't worry. It takes a lot to put me out of commission, and this doesn't qualify."

"You could have internal injuries." Worry made my voice wobble, and useless tears pressed against my eyes. I was emotionally exhausted. I sniffled.

He pulled me into a gentle hug that didn't feel fake at all and stroked a hand over my shoulder blades. "*Shhh*, I am fine."

I blinked. I was *not* going to cry over this. I gingerly wrapped my arms around his waist and accepted the comfort he offered. "When I was younger, I accidentally broke my sparring partner's arm." The confession popped out of me without warning. I tensed. Father could not find out that I'd been moderating my strength this whole time. "Please forget I said that."

"You'll find me a much tougher opponent," he said carefully, "if you want to spar."

I buried my face against his shoulder and shook my head. "I can't risk it." For any number of reasons.

He did not ask me any more questions, just held me in a loose embrace. My mind knew that this wasn't real, that he was just playing his part, but my heart . . . my heart wasn't so savvy. I drew away with a sigh. "If there is any change for the worse, any sort of twinge that feels out of place, I want you to promise me that you'll go use the diagnostic table in *Chaos*. Please."

He nodded. "I will, but don't worry. I'll be good as new in a few hours."

I doubted bruising that deep would heal in a few hours, even with nanobots helping him along. He wasn't moving like he hurt, but I would keep an eye on him. I was lucky that he wasn't asking me more questions. I didn't know what it was about him that snuck under my armor, but I had to be more careful.

"Did you find anything in the study?" he asked.

"Not really. There was one locked drawer, but I didn't search as thoroughly as we did in the office. I didn't know the cameras were on a loop, and the vanisher has limitations. I left a couple of bugs, so we'll see if anything comes of them. How did Aoife get into the security system so fast?"

"Bianca gave her a script."

I rubbed my temples and tried not to be furious with my sister. I failed. Bianca could've given *me* that script and helped me along. Instead, she'd given it to the person she'd assigned to babysit me, because my own sister didn't trust me. Bianca had bought the lie I'd sold. She thought I was incompetent.

Or maybe I *was* incompetent and just too blind to see it. Bianca was the smartest person I knew. If she didn't believe in me, then maybe the universe was trying to send me a sign.

It wouldn't be the first. Father certainly thought I was a failure.

Doubt crept in around the fury. Hurt stabbed deep and I couldn't quite tell if it was directed at Bianca, Alex, or *myself*.

"Why didn't you tell me?" I demanded. "I thought you were here to *help*." The bitter, sarcastic bite in my tone was impossible to suppress. My mask felt paper thin.

"I didn't know Aoife had gotten it working until after you'd left."

"But you knew it existed."

He inclined his head. "I did."

"Is there anything else that exists that I should know about?"

"No."

"No, there's nothing else, or no, I shouldn't know about it?"

He did not respond. I supposed I should be glad that he chose to misdirect rather than lie to my face, but I was too angry to see much difference. Part of that anger stemmed from the fact that I wanted him to be on *my* team, not Bianca's.

My hands curled into fists as the emotional turmoil tempted me to do something unwise. I locked myself in place, a roiling tower of fury, doubt, embarrassment, and shame.

Alex glanced at my fists. The corner of his mouth tipped up. "You want to spar so you can hit me again?"

I did, badly, which proved just how out of control I was. "I don't spar," I ground out.

"Good. You shouldn't fight when you're angry."

"I'm not angry—I'm furious. And you shouldn't presume to know what's best for me." But even as I spoke, doubt edged out the fury. I should be happy that Bianca was taking care of me, since I was doing a hell of a job of mangling it on my own.

Exhaustion, sorrow, and disappointment merged into a toxic soup of bitterness. "Go to sleep, Alexander. I'll see you in the morning."

"Are you going to search anything else tonight?"

"No."

His steady gaze held mine, questioning my sincerity.

I huffed out an unamused breath. "It's too late—or too early, I suppose. People are more likely to be moving around. Further searches will have to wait until tomorrow night."

"Are you okay?" The bitter twist of my mouth seemed to be answer enough because he asked, "Is there anything I can do?"

I rebuilt my mask, piece by piece. In the span of two breaths, I was once again Catarina von Hasenberg, youngest daughter of a High House—fun, bubbly, *not too bright*. I would not forget myself so easily again, even if the mask pinched more than usual.

I summoned my public smile. "Go to bed. Tomorrow is going to be a long day. I think hover bike racing was on the schedule and I'd rather you didn't take yourself out on a tree because you blinked for too long."

"There's a schedule?" Alex asked with a raised eyebrow. He'd also retreated behind a pleasant mask. We were all fake here.

I laughed lightly. "Oh, yes. Our time in Raventhorpe has been broken down into fifteen-minute increments with military precision. It's less house party and more minute-by-minute mandatory fun."

"And are you going to sleep? I would hate to lose *you* to a tree." A strange edge had crept into his tone.

"Of course, after I shower and check on the security com."

He caught my fingers as I was turning away. "Cat, please go to bed. I will move to the floor. I don't want to chase you from your own bed."

"Silly man, as if I could be chased away so easily." I laughed and gave him a flirtatious smile.

He frowned and met my eyes. "I'm serious."

I let my mask slip, just a little, so he could see the hard truth behind my words. "So am I."

He stared at me for a moment longer, then let me go. I locked myself in the bathroom and climbed into a scalding shower. I let the water run over my head, blocking out everything. Eventually, my thoughts turned to Alex.

Why did I let him rile me so easily?

I was honest enough to admit that attraction and resentment were driving factors. I needed to get my head back in the game. Alex worked for Bianca, not me, no matter how much I wished it was different. I could try to sway his loyalty, but I had a feeling it would not be easy. So I needed to keep him at a distance, an impossible task when we were supposed to be a couple.

I really should've thought this through more before agreeing, not that I had much—or *any*—choice in the matter. Bitterness tried to rise again, but I pushed it down. I would just have to make do. I was excellent at it and I wouldn't let a pretty face distract me from that.

Armed with new determination, I left the shower, put my pajamas back on, and checked on the security com. It was linked to the bugs I'd planted. It would record and transcribe the audio the bugs picked up. I set up some keywords that would trigger an alert on my com, but so far, nothing had been recorded and none of the bugs had been discovered.

With no remaining excuses to procrastinate, I headed to bed. Alex lay on his side, facing away from the middle. He didn't move when I slipped under the covers.

Weariness weighed me down, but it took a long time for sleep to come. It wasn't until I was finally drifting off, right on the edge of consciousness, that I realized I'd been attacking Alex at both full strength *and* full speed.

And he had dodged half of my attacks.

CHAPTER TEN

Morning came far too early, but at least we'd get to spend a good part of the day outside. It might not help me figure out House James's plan, but it would give me time to get my head on straight. And often, socializing was just as useful as snooping, so today might not be a loss anyway.

I dragged myself from bed and got ready while Alex was in the shower. Today I would wear my riding habit: tight breeches, tall boots, a high-collared shirt, and a jacket with tails that had flexible armor reinforcements on the back and arms.

As a play on the subdued traditional colors, I'd chosen bright gold breeches, a vibrant purple shirt, and an emerald green jacket. My tailor had done her job and the colors had enough undertones in common that it worked. I looked perfectly put together. I'd argued for dyed boots, too, but she'd talked me down to black. When I checked myself in the mirror, I conceded that she might have had a point.

Alex emerged from the bathroom in an all-black riding habit. His was more functional and less showy than mine, but it fit him perfectly. With his size, it had to have been tailored.

Bianca must've known my plans for weeks because even with a rush order, a complete custom outfit would take a day or two to make—not to mention all the rest of his clothes.

His gaze flickered over me and seemed to snag on my breeches. I had nice legs—strong and muscled—and he seemed fascinated by the taut gold cloth covering them. I was so, so tempted to turn around and pretend to pick something up off the floor because I knew that these particular breeches did incredible things for my ass, but I restrained myself with a silent admonishment to behave.

In fact, I still needed to apologize for my behavior the night before. That doused my desire to play.

"Now I see why we must wear these ridiculous clothes," Alex murmured.

"Just be glad you get to wear all black and still be considered dashing. Clothes are both weapons and armor, and Consortium women have elevated them to an art form." I waved a hand at my own outfit as an example. "What do you see?"

He paused to consider, his eyes sweeping me from head to toes and back. "Color. It fits you well. It would be hard to fight in."

"Yes, yes, no. This fabric is made for movement. It's no harder to fight in than anything else I own, and far easier than many things. Would you like to know what my fellow Consortium ladies would see?"

"Yes."

"They would see the color, but they would see how skillfully the seemingly disparate colors are woven together to create a cohesive whole. That takes a good eye or a talented tailor or both. They would know how expensive this fabric is—and it is, hideously so. They would know that it was hand stitched and custom made, just for me. The colors imply that I'm immature and spoiled, but rich enough that it doesn't matter. And finally, the design does not follow any of the current trends, which means I'm powerful enough to forge my own path."

"All of that from a bit of cloth?"

I laughed. "All of that and more. It's why Bianca made you get a new wardrobe, and presumably oversaw all of the details. She doesn't like playing the game, but she's very, very good at it."

"What do my clothes say, then?"

It was my turn to assess him. The material was very fine. Perhaps not as dear as mine, but in the same neighborhood. The unrelenting black was a good foil for his light brown skin. It also emphasized his size, and the excellent tailoring showcased his physique. The jacket had a split hem, made for movement, and almost military styling. His tall, black boots had thick soles. The outfit was simple enough that it would work in both formal and informal events and no one would bat an eye if he wore it on the street.

"You're rich, with good taste, but a little boring and you generally play it safe. You have a military background. You either didn't want to draw attention to yourself or you purposefully chose this outfit because the simplicity would be its own attraction, but I'd have to see you in action to figure out which."

His eyebrows swept upward.

"On a more personal note, the jacket design was your idea, not Bianca's. You talked Bianca down from whatever she had designed to this simpler version because you would've felt awkward in a more stylish option. You fought to wear 'normal pants' instead of breeches. She wouldn't budge, but she did allow the cut of the breeches to be a little looser than usual. You like to blend into the background, which you thought you were doing, but you didn't realize aloofness makes you more desirable to a good chunk of the Consortium population."

Surprise and suspicion chased each other across his face. "You guessed all of that from my clothes?"

"Yes. Was I right?" He didn't answer, which was answer enough. "What did Bianca want you to wear?"

"Some kind of fussy jacket. In salmon."

I hummed in thought. Bianca had a good eye. Salmon would be a superb color for him, but perhaps not for hover bike racing. "Let's head downstairs. Breakfast should be informal this morning, then we'll get to have some fun."

He gestured for me to go ahead. "Lead the way."

I gathered my courage. "Before we go, I need to apologize for last night. My behavior was unacceptable, and I'm sorry. It won't happen again."

"What do you mean?" Alex asked with a frown.

He was going to make me spell it out. My face heated, but it was no less than I deserved. "In the hallway. I should not have touched you without permission." I cleared my throat nervously. "You've made your feelings clear, and I overstepped. I'm sorry."

"If you'll recall, I touched you first."

"Yes, but you did it to protect me. I did *not*."

Alex prowled closer. "What feelings did I make clear?"

I tried to retreat behind my public mask, but Alex shook his head. "No, no masks. Tell me."

My prayers for the floor to open up and swallow me whole went unanswered. My face had to be bright red, but Alex was relentless, waiting patiently for me to answer. I could *feel* his gaze.

Was it possible to die of embarrassment? Apparently not, because I was still alive.

I sighed and quickly confessed, "I am aware that you are not attracted to me. I should've respected that last night and kept my hands to myself."

He chuckled softly. "Oh, Cat, you could not be more wrong." With that bombshell, he turned and exited the room.

CHAPTER ELEVEN

Breakfast was quiet, and I couldn't even glance at Alex without blushing. Ying caught me and gave me an inquiring look. At my minute head shake, she smirked. I was adding fuel to the inquisition that was coming, but I couldn't discuss it across an open table. Plus, I needed time to process everything that had happened.

After breakfast, we broke into teams of four for the hover bike race. Hover bikes were small, nimble craft that were ridden astride and open to the elements. They floated above the ground on anti-grav boosters and could reach speeds over two hundred kilometers per hour when running flat out. Racing one required a blend of skill, art, and science.

I loved the thrill of it.

This was one area where I got to be close to my true self because I'd made a point of throwing myself into various dangerous hobbies over the years. Every time I picked a new one, I flamboyantly hired a host of the best instructors money could buy. Thanks to them, as well as my standard House upbringing, I could race on land, water, air, or space with equal skill.

Having an outlet made the rest of my public persona easier

to bear—most of the time. This morning I was still struggling with the toll yesterday had taken. A good ride was exactly what I needed.

Alex and I had formed a team with Ying and Joseph. Ying was lovely in a burnt orange jacket, cream breeches, and deep brown boots. Joseph kept sneaking glances at her when he thought no one was looking. He wore the traditional black jacket, tan breeches, and black boots.

House James had two dozen matched racing bikes in a garage built specifically to hold them. The garage opened onto the starting line, and stands lined the far side because the House hosted qualifying races for the intergalactic hover bike rallycross championship. They usually fielded at least one team of their own, and Joseph had been their driver of choice for a few years. He was quite successful, but I had a feeling that Ying hadn't pulled him into our group because of his racing prowess.

Each group was "discussing strategy," which seemed to mean flirting and laughing for most of the groups around us, but Joseph's competitive nature had seemingly overridden his penchant for flirtation. "Have you ridden before?" he asked us. When we all nodded, he continued, "Are any of you any good?"

I laughed. "Not as good as you, maybe, but I can hold my own with most amateurs. Damien Quint taught me how to ride."

He looked stunned. "How in the hell did you get Damien to give you lessons? And how did you know I race?"

Damien Quint was one of the all-time greats of hover bike rallycross. These days he was a near hermit, so Joseph's stunned surprise wasn't misplaced.

"Even Damien isn't immune to the right offer," I said with a wink. "And I follow rallycross. Your circuit was one of the reasons I accepted Lady Stephanie's invitation. I had hoped to try it."

Joseph shook his head in wonder, then turned to Ying and Alex. "What about you two? Any more surprises?"

"I've ridden, but I'm not very good," Ying admitted with a grimace. "I thought it was going to be a tour, not a race."

"A race is just a fast tour," Joseph said with a grin, "but I'd be happy to escort you on a more *leisurely* circuit whenever you like."

Ying rolled her eyes, but a faint blush stained her cheeks.

Alex said, "I'm familiar with hover bikes but not rally-cross."

Joseph heaved a dramatic sigh. "It's up to you and me, Lady Catarina."

I wrinkled my nose at the title. "Well, since I'm going to be saving you from the ignominy of defeat, you might as well call me Cat."

His smile was warm and genuine. Perhaps he was merely trying to gain my friendship, as I was his, but if so, he was the best actor I'd ever seen. I wanted to believe that he had no idea what his House had done to mine, but that was a dangerous assumption.

Joseph laid his com on the table and it painted a map of the course in the air above it. "The circuit is five kilometers long and includes two creek crossings, a tunnel cut into the rock, blind corners, and numerous jumps." He pointed to the various places on the map. "The bikes are limited to a meter from the ground except in the jump zones. There are three straights for passing, one short and two longer. Any questions so far?"

Aoife straightened from her position against the wall. "Has the circuit been swept by security?"

"Yes. The entire length is monitored."

"Is it possible for me to ride double with Lady Catarina?"

Joseph looked between us, obviously trying to judge why

she wasn't asking me. "It's possible," he allowed, "if she's skilled enough. The weight of another rider makes the bike trickier to control. And if you move in a way she doesn't expect, it could be catastrophic."

While technically true, he'd overplayed the danger a bit, and I appreciated it. I'd already had this argument with Aoife. Going out alone was certainly a risk, but this was one of the few parts of this trip I was actually looking forward to—I wasn't going to skip it. As a precaution, I'd worn my shielding cuff. It looked like a wide bracelet, but it could deflect blaster bolts long enough for me to escape or for Aoife to intervene.

Aoife studied the projected map with a frown. From a security standpoint, it was a nightmare. There were too many access points and too much distance for her to cover on her own. "I want a bike that is not hobbled with height restrictions," she said. "I will observe from the air."

"Of course," Joseph agreed easily.

She turned to me. "Do not leave this building until I return."

"Where are you going?"

"I'm getting a different weapon. I'll be back in five minutes." She handed me her blast pistol. I accepted it by grasping the grip with two fingers and holding it away from my body, like she'd handed me a live snake. Her eyes narrowed slightly as she tried to determine whether I was acting or not. "In the unlikely event that someone attacks before I return, shoot them."

I shuddered dramatically. "*Hurry.*" I gingerly set the pistol on the table. It was a standard-issue von Hasenberg security weapon, biometrically locked to House members and security personnel. It would be useless if anyone else tried to pick it up and use it, but it would be quite enlightening.

"Cira will keep an eye on us both," Ying offered.

Aoife inclined her head in gratitude, then strode off toward *Chaos*. I wondered what sort of weapon she expected to find. There were rifles in the armory, but she wouldn't have access to them. Maybe she'd brought her own supplies and had left them out of sight.

Aoife was barely out of the door before Stephanie and Chloe approached the table. I tried not to view it as an ill omen, but it was difficult.

"Hello, brother," Stephanie greeted. Chloe stopped far too close to Joseph and smiled up at him. He returned the expression with a tight smile of his own. I mentally rubbed my hands together at the potential for drama.

"Hello, sister. Lady Chloe." He edged closer to Ying on the pretense of turning to include her in the group.

"We're planning to do a slow group circuit before the warm-up laps, to give everyone a chance to see the whole route," Stephanie said. "I wasn't sure if you wanted to join us or not. If so, would you mind escorting some of the newer riders?"

"I would appreciate your expert guidance," Chloe said, simpering. She was a few years younger than me and this was her first season, so I tried to cut her some slack, but her technique needed work. She wouldn't catch Joseph like that. He was the type of person who craved a challenge, not fawning affection.

Still, as a gentleman, he was stuck, until Ying decided to throw him a rope. "I'm sorry, ladies, but Joseph has already agreed to escort me around the circuit and I plan to hold him to it." She laughed lightly. "I need all the help I can get."

Chloe's smile was filled with ineptly concealed jealousy. "Of course, Lady Ying, I understand," she gritted out. "Joseph, another time, perhaps." She was conceding the battle, not the war. She turned to me. "And what about you, Lady Catarina?

Wasn't hover bike racing last season? Haven't you moved on to some new frivolity this year? Do you even remember how to ride?"

Her face was a pleasant mask, but her eyes gleamed with malice. Oh, someone was big mad that I'd threatened her yesterday. Now she was feeling brave in company and with Stephanie James at her side. As if I wouldn't be rude to both hostesses if it suited my purposes.

I didn't rise to her baiting, and instead laughed lightly. "I suppose we'll find out soon enough."

She shook her head with a poorly concealed sneer. "Come, Stephanie, let's check in with the others." The women drifted away.

"You have my gratitude, Lady Ying," Joseph murmured.

"You can repay me by making sure I don't make a fool of myself on the circuit today."

"Of course, it will be my pleasure. Would you like to ride with me for the first lap so I can point out the dangers?"

Ying paused long enough that I figured she was going to turn him down just to be ornery, but then she dipped her head in reluctant agreement, a tiny smile hovering on her lips. "If I ride with you, I expect you to teach me how to cheat without getting caught." Unlike Chloe, Ying knew exactly how the game was played.

Joseph's eyes widened and he clutched at his chest dramatically. "And give away my best secrets? You demand a high price, my lady."

She leaned in. "I'm worth it."

If Joseph had been the swooning type, he would've been laid out at her feet. Instead, he bowed low. "I have no doubt, Lady Ying. Shall we?" He offered her his elbow and she slid her arm through his.

Alex's eyes twinkled when he offered me his own elbow. "Shall we?" he murmured in perfect imitation.

Butterflies fluttered in my stomach, but I was going to have to talk to him sometime, and this was a nice, neutral opener. I slid my hand into the crook of his arm. "Do you know what Aoife was going to get?" I asked in a low voice.

"Her rifle, most likely. She's a crack shot with almost anything, but her long-range rifle is her baby. She could hover on a bike in the middle of the circuit and hit a person-sized target at speed on the ground anywhere on the course."

"So I shouldn't challenge her to a shooting competition?"

"Not unless you want to lose. Or stroke her ego. But it's big enough already."

I laughed. "I'm going to tell her you said that."

"Go ahead. I say the same thing to her face, I'm just usually wearing combat armor when I do it," he said with a grin.

"Are you excited about the race?"

He shrugged. "I like riding, but I'm more interested to see what you can do. I bet you give Lord Flirtatious over there a run for his money."

"I appreciate the vote of confidence, but while I'm decent, he's semipro and this is his home course. He's going to trounce me. I would be happy to beat Chloe, though."

"Vindictive?"

My grin was sharp and full of teeth. "Of course. Aren't you?"

"When I need to be."

Aoife rejoined us, a long blast rifle strapped across her back. She hadn't bothered trying to conceal it and she had a point—nothing would disguise a gun that big. It was a specialty weapon, designed for long-range, high-powered shots. Even at a distance the blaster bolt could punch through combat armor and keep going.

"Alex told me to challenge you to a shooting competition because you're terrible and I would definitely win." I said it with a straight face and an earnest expression.

"He's right," she agreed easily, but her smile had turned predatory.

"Oh, you're good," I murmured.

"I am," she said without an ounce of humility.

THE HOVER BIKE PURRED UNDER ME, ATTUNED TO MY EV-ery shift. The course was narrow and curvy here, winding through dense trees, but the heads-up display in my helmet gave me a few seconds' warning of what was ahead. This was my third lap on my own and I was starting to get a feel for the course.

The jump button illuminated as I came into the jump zone. Ahead, a stack of fallen trees blocked the track. Timing jumps was where races were won and lost. Jump too early and the bike would arc higher than necessary, costing precious seconds, but wait too long and the safety system would kick in, jumping for you, but at a much slower pace.

I mashed the button a heartbeat before the end of the zone. The bike skimmed over the top of the logs, low and fast. I whooped in delight and my teammates, tied into the com in my helmet, laughed with me.

"That was cutting it close, Cat," Joseph warned, "but nicely done. I see Damien taught you well, the lucky bastard." Since Joseph didn't need more than one practice lap, he was monitoring the rest of us from the garage.

As soon as I slid around the corner onto the longest passing straight, I jammed the throttle wide open. The bike surged forward and the ground and trees flashed by in a blur of brown and green. I could see the rider in front of me, even though we'd started a minute apart for the warm-up laps.

I wanted to catch him.

I hunkered low over the bike, pressing my chest to the angled, padded frame, legs back and arms forward on the separate steering controls. A clear windscreen showed my speed and other information in addition to the heads-up display, but nothing else blocked the forward view.

It felt like flying and I reveled in every second of it.

I leaned to the right as the straight became a sweeping curve that led into the tunnel. If the bike's sensor system didn't think it was going to make a clean tunnel entry, the bike would automatically slow or stop. It didn't eliminate crashes, but it made them far less fatal than they once had been, especially on a tricky circuit like this.

Our bikes were also locked into amateur mode, which upped the safety and decreased the overall speed. Still, even limited, I slowly closed the distance between me and the rider in front of me. At the next jump point he jumped early and I streaked under him. The safety system wouldn't let him come down on my head, even if he tried.

I left him behind and flew through the tight corners and gentle hills of the final third of the track. When I returned to the start line, I reluctantly slowed down and pulled into our team's pit area and parked the bike. I could do this all day, but that was supposed to be my final warm-up lap. Maybe I would get to ride some more after the race. I couldn't remember what else was on the schedule, but perhaps no one would notice if I skipped it.

And maybe I could persuade Joseph into disabling the amateur lock on my bike.

Alex settled his bike beside me. It gently sank to the ground and rested on the landing pads. He'd started two people behind me, but he must've passed the person in front of him, too. I took off my helmet so our conversation wouldn't be broadcast to the team. "I thought you weren't a racer."

He swung off the bike and pulled his helmet off. "I said I wasn't familiar with rallycross, but I've had my share of fun on a hover bike before."

That was proven true when Joseph showed us our lap times. Alex was a mere second slower than me. Joseph had beat us both by more than five seconds, an eternity in a race, and Ying trailed by a half dozen seconds. But, overall, our team was the fastest during the warm-up.

I leaned into Alex. "Your time was pretty good. Think you can beat me during the race?"

"Maybe."

"Want to make a friendly wager?"

His answering grin was slow and delicious. It sent heat spiraling through my veins. "What do I get when I win?"

"Fighting words already. You should be more concerned about what you forfeit when you lose."

"Name your terms, my lady."

I paused. I hadn't really thought that far ahead. I was naturally competitive, but an additional wager might give me the edge I needed to pull off a truly spectacular time. "What do you want?"

He backed me into the wall behind me and caged me in with his arms. He wasn't touching me at all, but I was hyperaware of the heat of his body. The overhead lights cast shadows on the sharp planes of his face. To everyone else, it probably looked like he was stealing a kiss. I had the intense urge to make that fantasy a reality.

"That's a dangerous question," he growled quietly. "Are you sure you want to know the answer?"

Wordlessly, I nodded, nearly hypnotized.

He leaned in until his cheek nearly brushed mine and his lips were next to my ear. "I want you," he breathed, "to spend a week with me. No pretense, no obligation, no plots, just you and me."

I shivered and desire burned bright, but it was tempered by a heavy dose of caution. People rarely wanted me for *me*, so I tried to decide what he really wanted. Nothing I came up with made any sense. He already had a connection to my family through Bianca and he couldn't possibly be stupid enough to assume that I would be manipulated into marriage. If he was, I'd be happy to disappoint him.

It's not as if I was going to lose, anyway. "Deal."

He pulled back enough that I could see his face. "What do you want?"

He'd asked for a week of my time, something worth a small fortune to many people. What did I want in return? What could I ask for that held the same value?

I stared at him for a few more seconds. "If I win, I want you to stop working for my sister for the next two weeks. I will pay whatever fee she's promised you."

He sighed and dropped his arms. "I can't agree. I'm sorry, but I gave her my word. I won't break it."

Disappointment warred with respect. Disappointment won. "Never mind. It was a silly idea anyway."

I started to step around him, but he stopped me with a hand on my arm. "Ask for something else," he urged, his gaze intense. "Please."

"Fine, if I win, I want you to tell me about the debt you owe to Bianca. And how you were able to dodge my punches last night." I hadn't meant to add the second requirement, but the question had been bothering me all day. I'd never had a sparring partner who could keep up with me, and I'd trained with our elite soldiers.

Alex stared at me for long enough that I thought he was going to decline, but finally he said, "Deal."

And now I was desperate to win.

THE RACE CONSISTED OF FIVE LAPS OF THE CIRCUIT. IT was far shorter than a standard fifty-two-lap race, but likely longer than some participants would enjoy. I, however, would love every moment.

All eyes were on the starting lights. As soon as they went out, Joseph and I launched off the line, everyone else behind us. Joseph easily edged me out going into the first turn, but I stayed in front of Alex. The bottom corner of my helmet's display showed me everyone's position on the course. Right now, we were all clumped together, but as the race progressed, we'd spread out.

With how good Joseph was, five laps were not enough time to do much more than cling to second. I could still see him in the distance, which was something, but I was slowly losing ground, and Alex's bike remained glued to my ass. If we went into the first straight this close, he'd likely overtake me.

And I really wanted those answers, dammit.

I pressed myself against the bike frame, trying to be as aerodynamic as possible. Adrenaline thrummed through me, and I couldn't stop smiling. I was truly enjoying myself for the first time in months.

I timed the first jump perfectly and gained a few meters of breathing room. Alex made up some of the distance in the first straight, but he couldn't get around me. I gained ground on the jumps, while he gained ground on the straights, but I held him off at the second straight, too. We plunged into the brief darkness of the tunnel, then swept through the rest of the course.

Joseph had crept farther ahead, mostly out of sight. Alex and I were neck and neck, and Stephanie was just a few seconds behind us. The rest of the field was scattered around the track and the last stragglers were about to be lapped.

On the second lap, Alex lost less ground on the jumps. By the third lap, he was reeling me in. I pushed my bike wide open on the longest straight and kept a lot of the speed going into the sweeping curve to the tunnel. The bike had proved that it could handle it, and I'd done this enough to know I could handle it, too.

Then, fifty meters from the tunnel, the bike died without warning.

I careened toward the ground and a sheer rock wall with no hover, no brakes, and no steering. I hit the emergency restart, but it did nothing. I didn't have time to try anything else; I was going to crash and there wasn't a damn thing I could do about it.

I had two heartbeats to decide if I should try to ride it down—yes, because it was sturdier than my body—then the bike hit the dirt.

yanked on the steering controls and leaned back and left, trying to lay the bike over sideways so it wouldn't roll. I had the strength to do it, and I might've been successful if the front landing pad hadn't caught on a protruding root.

The front dug in and the back bucked up.

Everything seemed to slow down. If I couldn't get clear, the bike would land on top of me and crush me beyond what any medbay in existence could fix. I reacted on instinct, throwing myself to the right, into the middle of the track. If I survived the next five seconds, then I would have to worry about getting hit by the bikes behind me, but that was a very big *if*.

I threw my left arm out in order to twist around and land on my back, where the armor in my coat was the strongest, but an iron grip clamped around my left wrist. My legs hit the ground and I jerked as the additional drag felt like it was going to dislocate my arm. I might have screamed, I don't know, but time snapped back to normal.

Alex had caught me with his left hand. I had a second to glance up at his helmeted form before we plunged into darkness, barely clearing the tunnel opening. My eyes adjusted, and I could see the wall whipping past, centimeters off my right side. Looking backward, I watched my bike tumble end over end before slamming into the rock wall in a fiery explosion.

I was not dead.

The realization broke me from my shock. I had to get off the ground. Alex was lifting me as high as he could, but he wouldn't be able to hold me for long. My boots were getting shredded, and in another few seconds, it would be my flesh that would be tearing away. The bike was slowing, but it wouldn't be soon enough.

I swung my right arm up and caught his wrist. "Lift me up behind you on three," I shouted, not sure if my com still worked. "One, two, three!" I kicked off with my feet. He swung me up and around. I let go of his wrist to grab his right shoulder and clung to him as I tried to get my legs to work well enough to straddle the bike.

Once I was seated, I wrapped my right arm around his waist and held on for dear life. He let go of me and I awkwardly wrapped my other arm around him, too. Everything hurt. My left arm and shoulder throbbed enough that it was probably dislocated. My legs stung and ached. My heart raced.

But I was alive. Somehow, miraculously, I was alive.

With nothing left to fight, the full impact of the last minute hit me, and I trembled from head to toe. If I hadn't jumped or if I had jumped the other way, I would be dead. If Alex hadn't caught me, I would be dead. If my additional weight had pulled us off course by even ten centimeters, I would be dead. I squeezed my eyes shut and focused on breathing.

It took me several long minutes to realize that we had stopped. We were off the course, in a little clearing surrounded by trees. Alex was trying to gently remove my arms from where they were welded to his waist. I let go with a hissed curse. Moving my left arm caused blinding bolts of pain up and down the limb.

Alex swung his right leg over the front of the bike, then he stood and turned to me. "Where are you hurt?" he demanded, his voice muffled by our helmets. My com must've been out, which made sense because it was tied to my bike. I felt trapped by the clear plastic face shield. I wanted the helmet *off*. I used my right hand to unhook the chin strap, but I lacked the leverage to pull it off one-handed.

"Let me help," Alex said. When I nodded, he carefully removed my helmet, then removed his own. His expression was completely flat. "Where are you hurt?"

"My left shoulder is dislocated."

"I can pop it back in for you, or you can wait for a doctor."

"Do it."

He skillfully manipulated the joint back into place. He was as gentle as he could be, but it still hurt like a son of a bitch. Tears leaked past my tightly closed eyelids.

"Try moving your arm."

I swallowed my sarcastic reply and lifted my arm a few centimeters. The pain was tolerable. I met his gaze. "Thank you."

"Are you hurt anywhere else?"

"Nothing major. My feet and legs are a bit torn up, but my boots mostly protected me. It looks like you won our bet, although I guess we're both going to be marked DNF—did not finish. Joseph is going to be so sad we lost." I was rambling. I clamped my mouth shut.

"What happened?" Alex asked.

"Bike died in midair. I tried to ride it down, and when that didn't work, I bailed. You saved my life."

Something stark and dangerous flashed across his face before he smoothed his expression. "Someone tried to kill you."

"Looks like it, yes."

Now he frowned. "You're in shock."

"Yep. I can't stop shaking."

"Would a hug help?"

I held out trembling arms. He stepped closer and tenderly wrapped me in a comforting embrace. I laid my head on his shoulder and my breath hitched. He rubbed a soothing circle on my back.

Someone had tried to kill me and nearly succeeded. Tears pressed against my eyes. I bit my lip to prevent them from falling. "Thank you," I whispered. "If you hadn't been there . . ."

"You scared the shit out of me," he admitted quietly.

My laugh had a watery edge. "Yeah, I scared the shit out of me, too. And of course it had to be when I was actually having fun for once. What are the odds that I can persuade you not to tell Bianca about this?"

"Nil," he said. "Your sister deserves to know that someone is actively threatening you."

He was right, of course, but that didn't mean I had to like it. The overhead whine of a hover bike engine brought my head up. Aoife descended into the clearing. She wasn't wearing a helmet, so it was easy for her to yell at us. "You took your com off!"

"My bike blew up," I muttered. "Cut me some slack."

She heard me and rolled her eyes. "Not you."

"This was more important," Alex said. He pulled away and I had the irrational urge to drag him back, like a human safety blanket. "Did you find anything in the garage?"

"No, it was empty by the time I got there. No one unexpected on the course, either."

"One of the other riders could've had an override," I said. "Whoever it was had to have had deep access, though, because none of the bike's fail-safes were triggered. It just died in the air between one second and the next."

"There's no chance it was a random failure?" Aoife asked.

"No."

She nodded. That was the answer she'd expected, but she was covering all of the bases. "Did you pick that bike or was it given to you?"

I thought back. Joseph had led our group to the bikes. Had he nudged me to a certain bike? I didn't think so. If he had, then it was the subtlest direction I'd ever seen.

"I'm fairly sure I picked my own bike, but if they already had the override code ready, it would take only a few minutes to modify it for a specific bike."

"Is there any way to track what happened?" Alex asked.

"Maybe, if the diagnostic box from the bike is recovered. The others must know something happened because they were behind me. How did they react? Do they know I survived?"

"They do not know. Alex got you off the course before the others arrived. I'm listening in on the main com channel. Ying is currently demanding an immediate investigation by the RCDF, into both the crash and Alex, since he's missing, too. Chloe and Stephanie are trying to talk her down in an attempt to salvage the party. Joseph sounds legitimately distraught. The other guests are in shock. They're all heading back to the garage."

"Let's see what they do when I rise from the dead."

"Cat—" Alex started.

"No. I'm here for a reason. That remains true. And they just tipped their hand—House James wants me dead."

"Or someone is framing them," Aoife said.

"Or someone with deep access to their proprietary racing

bike system is framing them," I allowed. "Let's go before Ying gets the RCDF involved."

AOIFE, ALEX, AND I RETURNED TO THE GARAGE. YING was facing the door and shouting at Stephanie and Chloe, so she was the first to notice that I'd returned. Her eyes widened and she looked so relieved that I felt bad I'd let her believe I was dead even for a few minutes. She rushed toward me. "Cat!"

Stephanie and Chloe spun around, identical dismayed expressions on their faces. Chloe rallied fastest, painting on a relieved smile. "Catarina, I'm so glad you're okay. You had us all worried! What happened? I was so far behind you that I only saw the aftermath of the explosion."

The rest of the group drifted over, curious about the crash and how I'd survived. I caught a few disappointed looks, but I also found some genuine relief among the faces in the crowd. A few people were happy I wasn't dead. Or maybe they were just happy Ying wasn't going to get the RCDF involved.

I'd thought about how I was going to play this on the way over. Accusations would let House James know that I had reason to suspect they wanted me dead, so playing dumb—as usual—might get me more answers. I gingerly slid off the hover bike. My legs looked worse than they were, thanks to the mangled boots, but they were still tender.

Ying cast a suspicious glance at Alex, then stepped close and pulled me into a hug. "*Are* you okay?" she demanded quietly.

"Yes. I'll explain later," I breathed.

She nodded and let me go. I turned back to Stephanie and Chloe. "I lost control of my bike on the curve before the tunnel. If Alex hadn't grabbed me, I would've died." I barely had to fake the tremble in my voice.

Neither Joseph nor Ying looked like they believed me, but Stephanie wore a sympathetic smile. "How awful!" she murmured. "And how lucky for you that Alex was there to save you."

"Has a crew retrieved the diagnostic box?" Alex asked, his voice cool. "I want to know what happened."

"From what I saw of the wreckage, it's going to be a total loss. I doubt the safety crew will be able to retrieve anything," Stephanie said.

How convenient. I decided to press a little. "Damien Quint told me those boxes are indestructible. Surely your safety crew will be able to salvage it."

Her expression tightened with annoyance. "Perhaps I am wrong. I hope so. I am quite curious as to what caused such a catastrophic accident on one of our safest bikes."

Oh, she was good. She had deftly shifted the blame for the accident on to me while sounding appropriately sympathetic.

Chloe threaded her arm through Stephanie's. "Since the race had to be canceled early, the kitchen staff laid out snacks and punch in the gardens for us to enjoy before lunch. I think we all could use something to settle our nerves. If you'll follow us."

They trotted off and the group followed them. Ying and Joseph remained behind with me and Alex.

"What happened?" Joseph demanded. "And don't try that same bullshit line with me. I watched you practice. You didn't lose control."

He was the enemy, but he seemed compellingly sincere. Perhaps shock would break his mask—if it was a mask at all. "My bike died. Lost all power while in the air. I had to bail and it was only luck that Alex caught me. I thought I was going to hit the ground at speed."

Ying blanched, her eyes wide in horror. Joseph's response was more nuanced. Shock, surprise, fury, and suspicion all chased one another across his face. "It was either a one-in-a-million fluke or someone tried to kill you," he said at last.

Alex loomed closer, his voice soft and deadly. "Yes, on a bike you provided for her. Care to explain yourself?" Strip away the veneer of civility and Alex was huge and intimidating. He always held himself so still, so carefully, that it was easy to overlook just how many muscles hid under his clothes.

Joseph did not shrink away. He met Alex's gaze without flinching, as serious as I'd ever seen him. "I've never seen a bike fail like that on its own. There are perhaps six people here who could override this bike's safety features and disable it in midair. I am one of them, as I'm sure you're aware, but it wasn't me. I would not harm Lady Catarina."

"Who else could've done it?" Alex demanded.

"Anyone in my family, given enough time. They have access but perhaps not the know-how. The head mechanic. Maybe the safety chief."

"And can *you* figure out who did it?"

Joseph looked away for the first time. "You're asking me to potentially betray the people closest to me."

"Because those people tried to kill one of your guests. Wouldn't you like to know who did it and why?" Alex asked. He was all hard edges and ruthless logic.

"I'll see what I can find out," Joseph agreed slowly.

"Thank you," I said. "I'm going to go get changed."

"I will go with you," Ying said. "Joseph, you and Alexander can go start looking into the incident."

Alex started to protest, but I shook my head. Ying and I needed to talk. She still had doubts about what had happened, and she was purposefully trying to separate us. She wouldn't believe anything I said while he was there. "We'll have our guards," I told him. "Go with Joseph."

He looked at Aoife over my shoulder, then inclined his head in agreement. "Let me know if you need anything."

Ying let me set the pace. I was stiff and sore, but I'd been very, very lucky. I tried to ignore the fact that I had nearly died, but it lurked in the back of my mind.

Aoife scanned the room for bugs. The scan came back clean. Either House James had better technology than I'd given them credit for, or more likely, they assumed I would be dead.

Ying turned to Cira and Aoife. "Why don't you two check out the balcony?" She cut off Aoife's protest before it could start. "Leave the door open."

After getting a nod from me, Aoife retreated outside with Cira.

"What is going on?" Ying asked.

Ying was my closest friend. She was also the daughter of a rival High House. That usually didn't matter, but it might now. To give myself time to think, I sat and tried to pull my boots off. Considering they were shredded, it was far harder than it should've been.

"Can I trust you to keep anything I tell you to yourself, even if it might help House Yamado?" I finally asked her. It had been our unspoken agreement for years, but I needed the confirmation of her word.

She settled on the chair across from me. "Will it *hurt* House Yamado if I don't tell Father?"

"No, the threat is to me, not you—as you might have noticed." My voice was dry, but I still felt shaky as I wrestled the first boot off.

"Then you can trust me to keep your secrets."

I hobbled to my trunk and dug out the silencer. I clicked it on, then resettled in my chair. I wished I could trust her with my biggest secret, but that was too much to ask, even of my best friend. Instead, I entrusted her with something I'd only shared with a handful of people, most of them family.

"This does not leave the room," I said. When Ying nodded, I continued, "We have reason to believe that House James was behind the attack on Ferdinand."

Her eyes widened and she leaned in and hissed, "Then why are you *here*?"

I tugged off my other boot. My lower legs were scratched, but the red marks were already fading as my nanos worked. "We need proof."

Understanding dawned and she sat back. "Did you volunteer or were you the most expendable?" she asked quietly.

I laughed. "I volunteered *because* I'm the most expendable. And because I was desperate to escape Lord Henderson."

"You know if you say the word, he will no longer be a problem." Ying might look delicate on the outside, but she had a core of icy, ruthless pragmatism. The few people she cared for were held protectively close and everyone else was considered a pawn. It had taken me years to figure out which I was.

She continued, "Speaking of problems, who is Alexander really?"

I searched her face. I'd been planning to lie to her, to spin a story of a secret affair, but the attack had shifted things. Perhaps it wouldn't be so bad to have another ally. "Bianca sent him and Aoife with me as protection."

Something relaxed in her face. "Ah, that makes sense. I couldn't figure out why you hadn't told me about him." The hurt was buried, but I'd known Ying for a long time.

"I'm sorry I lied to you. I met him a few days ago and

promptly tried to leave him behind. Bianca, as usual, was ten steps ahead."

"So he wasn't responsible for the accident?"

I bit back the instinctive denial and really thought about it. Double-crosses were common enough that I should consider it. "No," I said slowly, "I don't think so. He could've easily let me hit the ground, but instead he made an impossible catch that put him at risk of losing control of his own bike. There are easier, safer ways to build trust."

"Are you fucking him?"

"No."

Ying didn't pull her punch. "Do you want to be?"

"If it wouldn't complicate everything, yes. As it stands, no."

"At least you're honest with yourself. So who do you think tried to kill you?"

"I don't know. There are too many pieces in play. But I think Stephanie and Chloe both knew about it, even if they didn't actually carry out the attack. So the question becomes whether Chloe is working alone or on behalf of House Patel."

"To what end?"

House James had wanted Pierre, Hannah's husband, to sign over mineral rights in Antlia once Ferdinand was dead and Hannah named heir. The Antlia sector was the only known place in the universe where alcubium had been found, and it was essential to House Rockhurst's new, secret, faster FTL drives.

Whoever controlled the supply would control the 'verse. It was why we were currently at war with Rockhurst. That motive made sense: eliminate the heir, get priceless mineral rights with a contract binding enough that the Consortium would have to enforce it over House von Hasenberg's protests.

We thought House James might be working with Rockhurst, but adding a second lower house changed the equation. One House plotting against us was a nuisance; two Houses started to look like a rebellion. And House Patel generally aligned with House Yamado, not Rockhurst. So what did they get for switching loyalties?

I blew out a frustrated breath. "I don't know. I know what House James wanted, and it didn't involve House Patel. It also didn't involve killing me."

Killing me made no sense, even if they knew I was here on false pretenses. My death would accomplish nothing except to anger Father, which should be the exact opposite of what they were trying to achieve.

Unless they could pin the blame on someone else. Someone like Lady Ying Yamado, daughter of the only High House currently staying out of the war.

The pieces snapped into place, showing one possible scenario. It was plausible enough that I had to warn her.

"If they had succeeded, the attackers might have tried to frame you, Ying. You need to be very careful because you might be their next target."

"Why would they do that? What do they gain?"

"War."

She nodded thoughtfully. "I will be careful."

The situation had changed, and as much as I hated to admit it, Bianca had been right to insist on Alex and Aoife. I needed to find proof and get out. And take Ying with me. If I gave them a chance, House James would try again.

And, next time, I might not be so lucky.

CHAPTER THIRTEEN

The rest of the day passed in a blur. I must have faked normal well enough because people stopped asking if I was okay. Or perhaps they were all upset that I was still alive. Either way, I found myself stretched out on a blanket with Alex in the middle of Raventhorpe's massive back lawn. Full night had fallen, but the twin moons hadn't risen yet, so the sky was inky black and sprinkled with stars.

I could hear low murmurs from the other people around us, but the words were lost to the open air. We were out to enjoy the first night of the meteor shower, but it seemed that most people had paired up, more interested in what was happening on the ground than in the sky. Ying had lured Joseph onto her blanket. They were somewhere to our left, far enough away that I could barely hear them.

Alex lay next to me. He'd been attentive but strangely distant since the accident. A bright green streak burned across the sky. My breath caught as more and more meteors appeared, painting the sky with flashes of color.

It was *spectacular.*

An hour later, couples started moving back inside as the

air turned chilly. Ying stopped by, the light in her com on the lowest setting. "Are you coming?"

I was cold, but I wasn't ready to head in. I didn't know when I'd get to see something like this again. "No, not yet. I'll see you tomorrow."

I was so caught up in the meteors that it took me a long time to realize Alex had shifted onto his side. He was staring at me instead of the sky. I flicked a glance at him, and he met my eyes.

Last night's suspicion came back to me. "You can see," I whispered.

He leaned in, his voice as soft as mine. "So can you."

That was the problem with observant people—they noticed things you'd rather they didn't. I went back to watching the sky while I tried to figure out if there was a way I could ask him about it without getting asked in return. And if there was a way I could ask him to keep the information to himself without making a big deal of it.

He seemingly read my mind. "Your secret is safe with me."

I breathed through the panic. He was fishing. I could do the same. I turned to him. "Oh? Is your ability a secret then?"

He chuckled and the husky sound sent shivers racing over my skin. "My secret is safe with you, too, whether you admit it or not. Mutually assured destruction."

"You trust me to keep your secret?"

He was quiet for a long time. Finally, he said, "I trust you to look out for your own self-interest. If you reveal my secret, then you risk me revealing yours. I don't think you'll take that risk."

He wasn't wrong, but it stung to be laid bare so casually and brutally.

My panic faded, replaced by intense curiosity. I stared, unseeing, at the sky. *How* could he see in the dark? Did he know?

Had he gone through the same thing I had? I knew my genetics had been altered, but no one had explained exactly how—or why. I assumed it was to cure my sickness, and the ability to become a weapon for the House had just been a lucky side effect, but I didn't *know*. And now I couldn't very well ask without a whole lot of uncomfortable questions.

"Does Bianca know?" Alex asked.

I surreptitiously looked around. There was no one in view and Alex's voice was low. We were in our own little bubble, so I shook my head. "No one knows. You?"

"I don't think so. But she has surprised me before."

I glanced at him out of the corner of my eye. "Do you know why you're the way you are?"

Shock and surprise flashed across his face. "You don't?"

We were getting dangerously close to secrets that I didn't want to reveal, even to someone with secrets of his own. "Did you and Joseph find anything this afternoon?"

He clearly didn't want to let the subject change stand, but he ran a hand through his hair and blew out a breath. "Nothing definitive. Unsurprisingly, the diagnostic box was unsalvageable, but the main maintenance computer did record a lockdown override just prior to your crash. But there's no way to know where it came from."

"We need to find proof quickly and get out. I told Ying to be careful. It's possible they are trying to send our Houses into war by pinning the blame for my death on her or vice versa. Otherwise, why would they try to kill me? It serves no purpose."

"It prevents you from digging around further and provides a powerful distraction."

"You think they're hiding something else?"

Alex shrugged. "Could be. Attempting to kill you on their

own property is a dangerous tactic. If they suspected you knew about their involvement in Ferdinand's abduction, they could just remove all proof from the house. You either have them extremely rattled, or they were planning to use your death to their own advantage. We just need to figure out which it is."

"If I died, Father would send the RCDF to investigate. House James would have to be certain that they could withstand the investigation—or that the results wouldn't matter."

I mulled it over while watching meteors blaze colorful trails overhead, but the motivation didn't become any clearer. House James had upped the stakes far more than I had expected and I didn't know why.

And not knowing drove me crazy.

Alex had moved close enough that I could feel the heat radiating from his body. I wished I could turn to him and lose myself in mindless pleasure for a few hours. I needed the release—both literal and figurative. Nearly dying had put me on edge. Frustration made it worse.

I kept my hands to myself and sat up. "Ready to go inside?"

He stood with fluid ease, then offered me a hand up. I healed fast, but my left shoulder was still a little tender, so I gave him my right hand and let him haul me to my feet. I turned on the light on my com while he gathered and folded the blanket.

"Are the others still up? Do you want to join them?" Alex asked.

It was just after midnight. Most people had probably sought their beds, with or without company. "No and no."

A shadow moved in the dark. I spun and lifted my light. Aoife squinted as I blinded her. "Do you mind?"

I dropped the light back to the ground and ordered my pulse to slow. "I thought you went to bed."

"I was patrolling. And watching the meteors. And eaves-dropping."

"Learn anything interesting?"

"You might have been the only couple who was actually here for stargazing."

I laughed. "Don't tell me you've never hooked up in the dark. It's practically a requirement at a party like this."

Alex growled something too low for me to catch and Aoife laughed.

My com vibrated. When I checked the screen, my breath caught.

"What is it?" Alex demanded.

"It's an alert from the security com monitoring the bugs. Sentiment analysis on the recording from the study found raised, angry voices."

Alex stepped closer. "What are they saying?"

"I don't know. I can't tap into the stream remotely. Why don't we go find out? We can stumble in on them."

"Absolutely not," Alex and Aoife both said at the same time. They hadn't realized that I had been joking—*mostly.*

I turned and headed toward the house. "It's creepy when you do that. You know that, right?"

Alex fell into step beside me. "You have no idea who or what is in there. It could be a trap. It could be Lord and Lady James arguing about the roast they served for dinner. Barging in blind would be a mistake. You have the recording. Listen to it, then decide what to do."

"I'm going to."

"You shouldn't—wait, what?"

"Barging in blind *would* be a mistake. I'm agreeing with you." I smiled at him. "Is that so hard to believe?"

His expression told me that he didn't quite trust me. And

he was right to be suspicious. While I might not be planning to *enter* the study, I certainly planned to walk past it. *Slowly.*

Alex protested quietly when I turned from the main door and headed for the kitchen. I ignored him, and he and Aoife followed me.

I slipped through the kitchen door and snagged an apple from the basket on the counter. I didn't think I would be caught, but if I was, then I had an excuse to be in this part of the house because the main entrance led into a hallway that bypassed the kitchen and study entirely.

I settled firmly into my public persona, looped my arm through Alex's, and swept us out into the hallway that led past the study. The study door was firmly closed, but light glowed from under the edge. I walked as slowly as I could manage, leaning on Alex like I was still injured and a little drunk.

A trio of raised voices could be heard through the door—two masculine, one feminine. I couldn't make out their words, and the voices cut in and out, as if they were in a malfunctioning silence field, but one of the men had the lilting accent common to the Silva family. The Silvas ran the Syndicate, the largest crime organization in the universe. The Consortium had spent years trying to wipe them out, to no avail.

I could only hope that my bug was still recording because if a Silva had risked coming here in person, then House James was either deeply in debt to them or planning something big.

We were almost back to the main hall when I heard the study door start to open. I backed into a shadowed art niche set into the wall and pulled Alex with me. Aoife eased through the doorway into the main hall before silently melting into the shadows.

I tugged Alex's head down to mine as an unknown person stepped out of the study. "Kiss me," I murmured.

He hesitated for a heartbeat, his eyes questioning, then his lips covered mine, softly, slowly, barely touching. I'd meant for it to be a platonic kiss between friends, a way to deflect suspicion about why we were in the hallway.

I'd thought I had it under control. Instead, I *ignited.*

I pressed up toward him, desperate for more. His mouth opened, or mine did, and then his tongue slid against my own. His kiss reflected his personality: slow, deliberate, *thorough.* I moaned and lost myself in the delicious sensations. Distantly, I heard footsteps but they didn't register for several long seconds. When Alex pulled back, I realized the footsteps were heading *away* from our hiding place and this might be my only opportunity to see who had been in the study.

I leaned past Alex and peeked down the hall but only caught a glimpse of a dark-haired man in a suit disappearing into the kitchen. It could have been anyone.

Following would be a bad idea, but I entertained it for a few seconds before sighing and turning away. Alex looked completely unruffled while heat still swirled through me, muddling my thoughts. I'd asked him to kiss me and he'd complied. Insecurity tried to rise, but I discarded it. His tongue had been in my mouth. No matter what mask he wore now, he'd wanted to kiss me.

And I'd wanted to kiss him.

This attraction was a complication I didn't need. And now that I knew how good it would be, the temptation would be even worse.

I retreated behind my public persona and let out a nervous, slightly tipsy giggle. "Do you think they saw us?" I asked in a too-loud whisper. I wasn't positive this hallway was under surveillance, but better to be safe.

"No."

I pouted. "Too bad."

Alex's eyes crinkled at the corners as he fought not to laugh. "Let's get you to bed."

Aoife reappeared. She moved entirely too quietly for comfort. "Do you need help?" she asked.

"I've got her," Alex said. He bent and easily lifted me into his arms. Thanks to my muscle mass, I was much heavier than I looked, but Alex didn't even seem to notice. Aoife led us up the main stairs. The rest of the house was still, dark, and quiet.

When Alex showed no signs that he was tiring or uncomfortable, I snuggled into his arms and leaned my head against his shoulder. Not too many people could carry me so effortlessly, so I decided to enjoy it while I could. Plus, I hadn't been *entirely* faking my limping walk earlier—I was sore and tired. Today had been a thousand hours long.

Aoife swept the room for bugs and trackers while Alex set me back on my feet. "Thanks for the lift," I said.

"You're welcome."

We were both ignoring our scorching kiss. I tried to convince myself that it was for the best. I failed.

"The room is clean," Aoife said.

"Did either of you see who left the study?" They both shook their heads. "Then let's hope the video caught something."

I sat down with the security com. Aoife paced. She'd been in constant motion since the attack and I didn't know what to say to her to get her to settle. I had as much trouble reading her as I did Alex. I was so used to understanding people's motivations that not knowing was super frustrating.

I turned my attention to the device in my lap. The security com automatically surfaced data the software had tagged as potentially important. Even with the filters, it was still a large amount of data. I jumped to the place where the sentiment analysis had first identified anger.

Both bugs in the study were set to stream data in real time rather than buffering it for later transmission. There were pros and cons for each option, but real-time streaming meant I might get *some* data before the bug was discovered. Buffering meant I might get everything, but if the bug was discovered before the designated transmission time, then I would get nothing.

Whoever was in the study was definitely using a silencer, but not a quality one because it kept cutting in and out, leaving me with choppy audio and still images. Silencers were rigidly regulated and getting caught with one without authorization meant an automatic ten-year sentence. As the daughter of a High House, I had permission. House James did *not*.

But the black market thrived for a reason.

It was difficult to piece the recorded conversation together from two-second clips interspersed with five seconds of silence. The tone was definitely angry, and they seemed to be talking about the hover bike failure.

Then a sentence caught my attention. I played it again.

"You—tarina von—dead b—o excuses—take car—myself."

Trying to fill in the blanks was a guessing game, but based on the rest of the conversation, the man with the Silva accent was upset that I wasn't dead already and he was planning to fix it. The other two were trying to placate him, but it wasn't going well.

"That sounds like a threat," Alex said from behind me.

I locked my muscles against the urge to jerk in surprise. I'd forgotten Alex and Aoife were hovering nearby. I had the com set to a low volume, but apparently it was loud enough for them to listen in.

"This audio is awful, but I agree. It seems pretty clear that they knew about the 'accident' and are upset that I'm not dead. The man sounds like a Silva, but it's hard to say for sure. I'm hoping to find a picture."

I turned my attention to the video clips, and Alex leaned over my shoulder to see the screen. I was excruciatingly aware of him, but I kept swiping through the video clips. Lord and Lady James were easy to spot. The dark-haired man was far more difficult because he spent most of his time facing away from the camera.

"Stop," Alex said at the same time my hand froze above the screen. Finally, one frame showed the man's face—and it was a face I recognized.

Alex cursed. "Pack your stuff. We need to leave, now."

I closed my eyes against a wave of bright, burning anger. There was no mistaking Riccardo Silva's face. He was one of the younger sons of the main branch of the Silva family. He was smart and cruel and power hungry.

And he was the man responsible for cutting out my oldest brother's tongue.

CHAPTER FOURTEEN

I couldn't believe that Riccardo Silva had been less than five meters away, and I'd let him escape. I clenched my fists against the helpless fury and disappointment. Once again, I'd failed.

Alex was right, too. If Riccardo was here, then things were far worse than I had expected. Silvas rarely left their ships because they were hunted by the RCDF throughout the 'verse. I needed to leave, pronto.

But not before I cracked open the safe in the study.

"What do you know about Riccardo Silva?" I asked.

"He has a grudge against Bianca," Aoife said. "And he maimed your brother."

Bianca had told me that Alex and Aoife had helped her rescue Ferdinand, but this proved it. No one outside of family knew what had really happened to my brother. Most people didn't even know that he'd been hurt because Father had sent him off-planet just days after his return.

I nodded slowly, thinking it through. "If Silva and House James are working together, then I have to warn Father and the rest of the House. We thought Silva had been hired for a single job, not a collaboration. I need to know what they're planning even more than I did before."

Because right now the pieces pointed toward open rebellion, if not against the whole Consortium, then at least against House von Hasenberg. I had to find out how extensive it was—my siblings' lives depended on it.

"Pack your stuff," I said, "but be quiet about it. Anything you can't afford to leave behind should be on your person, if possible. I have to get one of my trunks to *Chaos*. It has too many useful supplies to be left behind."

I stared at it, trying to figure out how to sneak it out. If I took it through the house, even with the vanisher, I risked getting caught leaving. Maybe the balcony? I switched my gaze to the door, considering it.

"How full is it?" Alex asked.

"Three-quarters." I grimaced at him over my shoulder. "I brought a lot of stuff. I can carry it easily enough, but I don't want to drag it through the house. Taking it over the balcony will be tricky—many of the weapons and electronics inside shouldn't be dropped from the third story." I headed off the obvious question. "And sadly, I didn't pack a rope."

"I can climb down with it," Alex said. At my skeptical side eye, he smiled. "Have a little faith."

"Okay. First we'll get the supplies to the ground, so we can grab them on our way out, then we'll hit the study after everyone is asleep. I don't suppose one of you brought a codebreaker?"

"I have one," Aoife said reluctantly, "but I still agree with Alex that we should leave now before they have a chance to try something else."

I'd already decided the potential reward outweighed the risk, so I ignored the second part of her sentence. "You and Alex can hit the office while I'm in the study. If we're going to be set-ting off alarms anyway, then we might as well hit both."

"You're not going alone," she said, "but nice try. I can han-dle the office while you and Alex are in the study. Or, better yet, Alex and I can handle both while you wait outside."

I laughed. "I don't know what about our interaction so far makes you think that was even an option, but you get points for persistence." I tapped my fingers against my lips. I felt like I was forgetting something. It took me far longer than it should've to remember Ying—I was a bad friend.

"I have to let Ying know what's happening. I already told her to be careful, but I need to let her know I'm leaving." And persuade her to leave with me.

As the plan ballooned in complexity, so, too, did the chance of failure. I had to get the three of us, my trunk, Ying, *and* her guard out of the house without getting caught, after stealing from two locked, potentially alarmed safes. No problem.

"Aoife, go pack what you need and pretend to go to sleep. When it's time, can you loop the security video again?"

She nodded.

It was half past midnight. Late, but not late enough for sneaking around. "After you leave, we'll turn out the lights so anyone watching will assume we've gone to sleep. Alex can take the trunk down and hide it on the ground. Then, after we've given everyone a couple of hours to find their own beds, we'll crack the safes and head to *Chaos*."

Aoife didn't look entirely convinced, but she left for her room after a long look at Alex. He closed the door behind her, then turned off the lights and perfectly navigated through the dark room. He smiled when he caught me watching him and sprawled in the chair across from me.

It still made me very nervous that he knew part of my

secret. I had to suppress the desire to tell him exactly how important it was that he keep quiet. He could destroy my life. He could destroy *me.* But if I made a big deal of it, I would draw even more attention to the very thing I wanted him to forget. I bit my lip and let it go.

I needed to warn my family that something was happening. I put on a pair of smart glasses because they produced less light than a com. They were already paired to my personal com, so I used them to set up a secure connection. I didn't want House James to be able to easily intercept my messages. If they wanted to, they'd have to work for it.

Our sibling chat channel was filled with the usual gossip, but nothing like the bomb I was about to drop on everyone. I assumed either Alex or Aoife had already snitched about the attack to Bianca, so I decided to give my siblings all of the information I had. I summed up the hover bike failure, the weirdness from Chloe and Stephanie, and Riccardo Silva's presence in one dense paragraph.

None of my brothers or sisters had posted messages recently, so I also included a paragraph about my plan to raid the safes and then get the hell out. No one was around to tell me not to do it, but in the unlikely event that I didn't make it, at least they would have enough information to destroy House James on my behalf.

I knew what it was like to be the one sitting at home waiting for news and only getting partial updates—it sucked.

That done, I sent a formal note to Father, warning him about the new treachery taking place in House James. I had considered waiting until I left, but an early warning with little information was better than no warning at all. I told him I'd send an update once I learned more and to *not* send the RCDF while I was still here.

It was late in Universal Standard Time, so hopefully he wouldn't see the message until in the morning when it wouldn't matter anyway. Because when Albrecht von Hasenberg made up his mind, no amount of pleading or logic would change it. And I could absolutely see him sending in the RCDF and mucking up all of my plans.

Family taken care of, now I debated how I was going to alert Ying without alerting the household. I could send her a message, but it ran the risk of interception. I suppose I'd have to grab her on my way down to the study and her guard could meet us there. It wasn't ideal, but it was the best I could do.

Now I had to wait.

I looked through the display on my glasses to Alex lounging across from me. "You should get some sleep. I'll wake you when it's time."

"I could say the same to you."

I chuckled quietly. "I'm wound too tight for sleep."

"Want to spar?"

"No." Alexander Sterling already knew far too much about me. Sparring would be a very bad idea, no matter how much I wanted to see what he could do. I'd never fought with someone who could match my speed. It was nearly as tempting as kissing him again.

Clearly, I needed to keep my butt in this chair and my mind on the mission.

"Afraid you'll lose?" His voice was soft, a low rumble of velvet and gravel.

"You won't taunt me into it. But if it makes your ego feel better, then sure."

His mouth twitched, like he was fighting a grin, before flattening into a pensive line. "Why can you see in the dark?"

If he'd been trying to blindside me, it worked. The casual reference to an ability I'd kept secret for nearly half my life still shocked me, and I struggled to keep my expression even, to not show the panic that caused my pulse to race.

I must not have been very successful because he frowned at me. "What's wrong?"

Now it was my turn to shake my head. "Nothing." I paused, then continued despite my earlier misgivings. "If you tell anyone, I'm as good as dead. You know that, right?"

He leaned forward, as serious as I'd ever seen him. "I did tell you that it would be *mutually* assured destruction. I know the consequences, perhaps better than you. I will not risk either of us."

I still didn't know if I could trust him, but at least he understood the gravity of the situation. I had to hope that he wouldn't accidentally let anything damaging slip. "Thank you."

He looked like he wanted to add something else, but he just inclined his head and went back to a relaxed slouch. I wished I could relax so easily. Anxious energy thrummed under my skin as I thought about all of the ways tonight could go wrong, all of the ways I could fail. The clock ticking through the seconds in the corner of the glasses' display didn't help.

I stood, too anxious to sit still, and crossed to the trunk that held all of my gear, the trunk Alex assured me he could climb down three stories of balconies to the ground. I swiped my right arm over the lock and the trunk opened. I removed the clothes and dropped them on the floor—the time for subterfuge was over. Alex needed this trunk to be as light as possible.

I unlocked the bottom compartment and pulled out the codebreaker, silencer, and vanisher. I also removed a blast pistol and a belt holster. Once the compartment and the trunk were closed and locked again, I dug through the clothes on the floor until I found a pair of utility pants, a long-sleeved shirt, and a pair of thick-soled boots, all in black.

Alex watched me without saying anything. Technically, he could carry the trunk down while I changed clothes, but I wanted to see how he did it, so I ducked into the bathroom without a word. I'd changed into a casual summer dress after dinner. It was one of my favorites and I hated to leave it behind, but if I took everything I liked, then I'd have two trunks full of stuff.

I stepped out of the dress and pulled on the far more practical clothes and boots. Clothes were a first line of defense for me. People drew many conclusions based on nothing but an outfit, a bias I ruthlessly exploited. Most of my outfits were carefree, frivolous, and very, very expensive.

Utility pants and boots were not. One of my masks stripped away.

I returned to the bedroom and dropped the dress on the pile of other clothes. I put the codebreaker, silencer, and vanisher into the cargo pockets of my pants, then slung the belt holster around my waist. The blaster went into the holster and I was ready to go.

The trunk was a meter and a half long, and nearly a meter deep and high. Packed as it was, it weighed almost twenty kilograms. Climbing it down would be tricky.

"Are you ready for me to take that?" Alex asked, seeing the direction of my gaze.

I glanced at him. He was still sprawled in the chair, but he'd changed into dark clothes and heavy boots. The short sleeves of his shirt stretched around his biceps, drawing attention to his exquisitely muscled arms. The man was a damn work of art.

One I didn't want to see broken on the ground below my balcony.

"Can you climb it down, truly? You're no good to me if you fall and crack your head. The supplies in the trunk aren't worth your life."

A slow grin broke across his face. "While I'm glad you value me more than your gear, your lack of faith wounds me."

"What do you need me to do?"

He rolled to his feet, grin still in place. "Just watch."

The thought of sending him over the balcony with a large, heavy box made the anxiety under my skin worse. "There's still room inside if you want to store anything."

"I'm good. I'll carry my bag. Now stop stalling."

He stopped in front of me, close enough to touch. We were shrouded in darkness, but it didn't offer privacy. I could see him clearly, and I was struck again by his height and the breadth of his shoulders. My gaze fell to his lips. I could offer him a kiss for luck, to see if earlier was real or just a fluke.

I held back the words by the thinnest of threads. Instead, I said, "Please don't die."

He nodded, and I moved out of the way. He picked up the trunk, testing the balance, then crossed to the ornate glass door that led outside. I followed him out. The generous balcony was surrounded by a stone balustrade. I peered over the side.

Below was the second-floor balcony, an identical match to ours. The ground floor had landscaping flowers and shrubs near the building and grass leading out into the yard. Without a trunk, I could easily shimmy down to the next balcony and then to the ground, but I wouldn't try it with an unsecured burden.

I heard the slightest brush of fabric on stone and then out

of the corner of my eye, I saw Alex disappear over the rail. I stifled my cry and dashed to the side where he'd vanished. He hung from the bottom of our balcony by one hand, his toes on the railing below. His other hand held the trunk by one of the handles on the end.

Alex let go of the balcony and landed quietly on the balustrade below, perfectly balanced. He crouched down and went over the railing, hanging from the top by one hand. He tucked the trunk between his calves, then used his now free arm to climb down until he hung from the bottom of the first-floor balcony. He grabbed the trunk, held it out of the way, and dropped lightly to the ground.

He'd made it look so easy that I didn't even have time to worry.

He disappeared around the corner of the house toward the ship. That hadn't been the plan, but not having to return to this side of the house might be a good idea. He was gone for long enough that I began to wonder if he'd taken it all the way to *Chaos*, but then he returned just as quietly as he'd left.

I hadn't thought too much about how he was going to climb up again. I should've sent him with the vanisher and he could've just come through the house, but before I could suggest dropping it down to him, he ran at the wall, vaulted off it, then turned and caught the bottom of the first balcony.

He pulled himself up without any apparent effort in a show of strength that did terrible, wicked things to my pulse.

He stood on the railing below and jumped up to catch the bottom of our balcony. My breath caught when his feet left the relative safety of the balustrade, but his grip was strong and sure. He heaved himself up, caught the top of the railing, and then he was standing in front of me, not even breathing hard.

Physical prowess was my catnip and all of the anxious energy pulsing through me had morphed directly into lust. When his grin turned knowing, I straightened my spine, pulled on my public mask, and gave him a dazzling smile. "Well done, thank you. Where did you hide the trunk?"

"On the way to the ship. I'll grab it after we hit the study."

"Sounds good. Now we wait." Had he edged closer, or had I? Either way, Alex stood within reach, a temptation that was difficult to resist. The memory of our kiss lingered, no matter how I tried not to dwell on it.

I needed to clear my mind.

"I'm going to wait inside," I said. "Close the door when you're done out here. And thank you again." I beat a hasty retreat before my libido made a fun—but unwise—decision.

I didn't escape far, just to the sitting area inside the door. I slid down to the floor, then sat up straight, crossed my legs, and closed my eyes.

I heard Alex return inside and close the door. "What are you doing?" he asked.

"Meditating," I said without opening my eyes. "Would you like to join me?"

"Does it help?"

I didn't know precisely what he was asking about, but the answer was the same anyway. "Yes."

I heard him settle on the floor, then grunt. "My legs don't bend like that."

"Just sit any way that will be comfortable for an extended period of time." Once he stopped moving I continued, "Have you meditated before?"

"No."

"The goal is to quiet the mind, to be still and peaceful in the moment." A bitter smile twisted my lips. "It's never been hard for me, probably because my mind is mostly empty anyway, but others find it more difficult. Everyone has their own way of getting to stillness. A common beginner practice is to count your breaths. Breathe in for a certain count, out for the same count, slow and deep. Anywhere from three to eight is typical, so do whatever feels right. Try to focus solely on the numbers and if your mind drifts, gently pull it back to the count."

We sat in silence for a few minutes. My awareness of Alex made my own meditation far more difficult than usual, so I followed my own advice and lost myself in counting.

"Now what?"

"Now you're meditating. Do it for as long as you like and stop when you're done."

"That's it?"

I laughed quietly, eyes still closed. "That's it."

He made a noncommittal noise, but then settled back into silence. It took me a long, long time to find stillness.

Then it took no time at all for that stillness to shatter.

CHAPTER FIFTEEN

At first, I thought the sound of breaking glass, cut off abruptly, was a figment of my imagination, then some-one slammed into me and flattened me to the floor. The unmis-takable sound of a blast pistol being fired next to my head was enough to jerk me back into the present, filled with adrenaline.

I opened my eyes to find Alex poised over me, shooting at an unknown assailant. He shot again and I revised my assess-ment to unknown *assailants*, plural. Alex's body blocked my access to the blaster on my hip, so I reached for the pistol I'd hidden under the coffee table, moving quickly but carefully to avoid ruining his aim.

The sounds in the room were wrong, short bursts that were cut off rather than fading out. The people who had entered were using silencers, albeit poor ones, but it meant that I couldn't get a clear count of how many we were up against.

I disabled the adhesive and the holster fell into my hands. I drew the pistol. Alex fired again. It was so weird not being able to hear the shots hit. A body sprawled on the floor near the balcony door, unmoving.

A head and gun peeked around the doorway and I shot on instinct. The attacker silently fell to the floor.

The furniture blocked my view of the rest of the room. "How many left?"

Alex shot, then ducked down, his face centimeters from mine. "Five, at least. Aoife is on her way."

I still wore my shielding cuff. It had been inactive during the race—and wouldn't have protected me from a fall, anyway—but after the crash, I'd thought it prudent to wear it through dinner. The silver cuff was designed to look like a bracelet that, while a little plain, was fashionable enough to wear with any outfit.

The cuff encircled my right wrist. I swiped my left hand across it, from the inside to the outside and back again, then held my hand in place for two seconds until the cuff buzzed once. Active, the cuff could deflect up to eight shots, but from this close, the protection would likely be halved. I would have to make it count.

When I tried to sit up, Alex pressed a hand to my shoulder, while returning fire with someone near the bed. They must've come in the windows in addition to the balcony doors.

"I have a shielding cuff," I hissed quietly. "Let me up. I can distract them and give you a chance to attack."

"No," he bit out without looking at me. Gone was the quiet, soft-spoken man I was used to. In his place was a hardened soldier, focused and deadly.

My cuff pulsed and a blaster bolt was deflected toward the ceiling. *One.*

I pushed myself up just as the bedroom door was kicked open. "About time," Alex growled.

Aoife flashed a grin and launched herself into the chaos. She created a wave of death as every shot found a head. She'd taken out three in the space of three seconds. I'd never seen anyone shoot like her, and neither had our attackers. While we froze in shock for a heartbeat, she and Alex took out the remaining two.

Holy shit.

A faint sound broke me from the shock, and I lunged up. "Ying!"

Aoife nodded, already in motion, and I followed her, drawing my other pistol. We darted across the hall. There were definitely sounds of blaster fire coming from Ying's bedroom, which hopefully meant she wasn't dead in her sleep. "I have a shielding cuff," I told Aoife. "It will deflect three more shots."

She nodded and kicked the door in. She took in the situation at a glance and threw herself into the room, shooting as she went. I followed with Alex behind me. Ying was apparently holding her ground in the bathroom. The five surviving assailants did not expect us to appear behind them.

Aoife picked them off with uncanny precision, while I mostly tried to shoot the enemies without hitting her or Ying. I could shoot with either hand, but I was less accurate with my right. The soldiers in the room turned and my cuff vibrated twice in rapid succession. The next bolt grazed the top of my shoulder, far too close to my head. Alex shot the attacker before she could try again.

"Ying, are you okay?" I asked. My voice felt loud after the weirdly half-silent battle we'd just fought.

She emerged from the bathroom with a blast pistol in each hand. She had on smart glasses and moved gingerly, favoring her right side. Her right arm dripped blood. "I'm hit in the arm, but my nanos are dealing with it. With the silencers, how did you know I was under attack?"

"They hit my room, too. Get ready, we have to leave, now.

Is your ship here?" I asked as I bent to examine the nearest attacker. Dressed in black combat fatigues and light body armor, the man could be a soldier or mercenary anywhere in the 'verse.

"No, I took a transport from Honorius," Ying said.

"You'll ride with us, then. Call Cira if you haven't. Tell her to meet us at *Chaos*." I quickly searched the body. I pulled out what looked to be the prototype silencer they were using, but he didn't have anything else of interest. I ran my com down both of his arms, but his identity chip was either disabled, removed, or suppressed—definitely a soldier or merc.

"Cira received my emergency alert and confirmed she is on her way down from her room," Ying said. "She should be here any second."

I stood and tucked the prototype silencer in my pocket. "Okay, grab anything you can't leave behind. Alex, you're with me. Aoife, hit the office. I want everything in the safe. Ying, are you okay on your own until Cira arrives?"

"I'm here," Cira said from the doorway. She was slightly out of breath, but otherwise seemed fine.

"Take Ying to *Chaos*. It's in the spaceport. We'll meet you there in ten minutes." Cira had been a shock trooper in the RCDF for a decade. She would keep Ying safe until they made it to the ship.

Everyone assembled looked ready to argue, so I cut them off. "Now is not the time. We have a very narrow window until we are attacked again or the whole house wakes up. You all know what to do. Go!"

I headed for the back stairs, Alex on my heels, and the rest of the group followed. Aoife broke off on the second floor to hit the office. On the ground floor, Cira and Ying continued toward the back door while Alex and I headed for the study. I clicked on the silencer and vanisher before we left the butler's pantry.

"How do you want to do this?" Alex asked.

"Speed over stealth."

The hallway was empty and no light appeared under the door of the study. I'd holstered my second blaster, but kept the first in a low ready position. Alex took me at my word and kicked in the door. We rushed the room but it was as empty as it had been last night when I was here.

I moved directly to the desk and pulled out the codebreaker. I placed the small, rectangular device against the drawer's control panel and activated it. The codebreaker was designed to open electronic locks, but it took time. The more complex the lock, the longer it took.

And we were sitting ducks until it finished.

While I worked on the desk, Alex had closed and barricaded the door. I suppose that meant we'd be taking a window exit, which wasn't a bad plan, all things considered. He paced in the dark, watching both the door and windows.

Codebreakers were rare enough that most locks only had the most basic defense against them and would open in a few seconds. The lock on this drawer was proving better than most. As time slid past, I began to wonder if it was going to open at all.

Three minutes later, the codebreaker finally chirped and the drawer opened. It was filled with paper, but I didn't bother reading any of it. I had been serious about speed over stealth, so I pulled the entire drawer from the desk and dumped it on the pristine desktop.

I searched the empty drawer for a hidden compartment, and found a small one at the very back that included some hard credit chips and a data chip. I shoved them in my pocket, replaced the drawer, and bundled all of the papers into a stack nearly four centimeters tall—there was a *lot* of paper here.

Someone in the hallway rattled the doorknob, then pounded

on the door when it wouldn't open. Alex had his bag strapped over his back. It would be more secure than my cargo pockets, so I waved him over until he was inside the silence field. "Does your bag have room for this?" I gestured at the stack of paper.

Rather than answering, he silently opened the bag and shoved the papers inside. "We need to go. I haven't seen anyone outside yet, but stay alert. Aoife is climbing down from the office. She's going to meet us on the way to the ship."

Alex and Aoife were obviously wearing mics and earpieces, and once again they'd left me out of the loop. "We're going to have a long talk about the meaning of teamwork once this is over," I groused.

He moved to the window, shoved it open, and knocked out the screen. "I'm sorry. I was planning to get you connected before we left, but then everything went to shit and there was no time." He waved me forward. "Let's go. And turn off your silencer."

I gave him a jaunty salute and clicked it off, then hopped through the window, blaster first. The lawn was empty, but we were on the other side of the house from the rooms where Ying and I had been attacked. I moved aside, but stayed in the coverage provided by the landscaping along the building.

Alex silently landed beside me. "Aoife is drawing fire on the other side of the building. At least two attackers. She's going to distract them while we break for the ship. Move fast."

"Did she see Ying?"

"She didn't say."

Worry pressed on my chest as we dashed across the yard. A glance back showed lights in a few of the upper-level windows. Our fight had finally awakened some of the guests.

A blaster bolt sailed by, close enough that I could feel the heat. With nothing to hide behind, I dove to the side. I spun and came up shooting. Two attackers had rounded the back of the house from the direction of the study.

Alex and I shot the same one, giving the other time to get off another shot. Based on the grunt, it must've hit Alex, but he shot milliseconds after me and both bolts found their target. The assailant collapsed.

I pushed myself to my feet and checked on Alex. "Are you okay?"

"I'll live," he grumbled. "Grazed my shoulder."

"Can you walk?"

"Yes. Let's go before anyone else tries to kill you."

We veered off the path to grab my trunk—which Alex wouldn't let me carry—and then we were at the spaceport. I didn't see Cira or Ying, but *Chaos* sat where I'd left her with the cargo ramp down and door closed. All of the surrounding ships had been here when I'd landed, so either the soldiers had been lying in wait the whole time, or they had come from somewhere else.

There was a lot of empty ground between me and the ship, but it couldn't be helped. Delaying would only give our attackers more time to get in position. Alex must've agreed because he didn't try to stop me when I sprinted for the ship.

I swiped my identity chip over the control panel and the cargo bay door slid upward. I ducked inside before the door was all the way open, and Alex came in behind me. The lights came on automatically and I blinked against the brightness. "*Chaos*, how many people are onboard?"

"Two passengers in the cargo bay, Captain."

I figured Ying hadn't hacked her way into my ship, though she probably could have, but that left the question: where was she? She knew what *Chaos* looked like and this was the only spaceport on the grounds.

Alex set the trunk on the floor. "Aoife is on her way. Her attackers are down."

I got my first good look at him. His shirt had a ragged hole at the top of his left shoulder and the fabric around it was plastered to his skin with blood. "Holy shit, that's not a graze. Get to the medbay before you bleed out."

He glanced down at his shirt with a grimace. "It looks worse than it is. My nanos have already stopped the bleeding. I'll be healed by tomorrow." He said it with an oddly expectant look in his eye.

I knew exactly what he was aiming for, but there was no way in hell I was giving him any more of my secrets—even if those secrets were shared. My own blaster graze, which actually was a *graze* and not a chunk of missing flesh, would be healed in an hour or two. Fast, even for someone with top-of-the-line nanobots.

And impossible to hide.

Thanks to the tests, Father knew I retained my healing abilities, but as far as he knew, that was all I'd kept. Even if this particular secret wasn't entirely secret, I didn't need Alex having any more power over me.

"I'm glad you're not too hurt. Please have Aoife keep an eye out for Ying and Cira."

If he was disappointed that I didn't pick up the gauntlet he'd dropped, he didn't show it. He nodded and relayed the request. I moved to the door and scanned the area around the spaceport. A flicker of movement on the path leading to the house turned into Cira and Ying. Ying had Cira's arm over her shoulder and both women looked the worse for wear.

"Alex, with me!" I dashed toward the two injured women without waiting to see if he would follow. Up close, it was easy to see that Cira had been shot through the leg. "What happened?"

Ying answered, "We hit a team staging in the backyard, then had to work our way around in cover because of Cira's leg. You took them out in the yard. Thanks for not leaving us."

"Of course I wouldn't leave you. But I only have one diagnostic table. Which of you needs it more?"

Ying and Cira each answered with the other's name. Ying's arm was bloody, but it didn't appear to be dripping anymore, where Cira's leg was. "Alex, please help Cira to the medbay, then–"

Aoife sprinted into view. "Time to go!"

Alex swept Cira into his arms and ran for the ship. I urged Ying into a run and we all scrambled aboard. Once Aoife cleared the door, I retracted the ramp and closed the cargo bay door. "Alex, medbay is on the bottom floor. Get Cira in the diagnostic scanner. *Chaos*, take us into orbit."

Cira complained, but Alex just carried her down the hall to the medbay. The ship's engines rumbled to life and ramped up as we lifted off. I headed for the flight deck. Ying and Aoife followed. I wasn't sure if our attackers had a ship, but if they thought to tangle with *Chaos*, then they would get a surprise. My little ship was well equipped for both defense *and* offense.

"Where are we headed?" Ying asked as I dropped into the captain's chair. I waved her into the second console and she sank down with a grateful sigh. Aoife sat in one of the chairs along the wall and pulled out her com.

"For now, we're headed to space so we have room to maneuver if we need to. After that, it's up to you. I can drop you back in Honorius for your ship, or you can ride back to Serenity with me. I have to report to Father about everything that happened."

"You think they're trying to push us into war."

The soldiers who had attacked weren't using stun pistols. They'd been aiming to kill both of us. The only thing that would do was push both of our Houses into war with House James, not each other. "I don't know what they're doing."

"Have either of you checked the news?" Aoife asked. Her tone was oddly flat.

I hadn't, and I hadn't gotten any replies from my siblings, either, which was a little weird. I'd expected them to jump down my throat, especially Ada, who was on a planet where it was late afternoon. "What's going on?" I asked, as I pulled up the news feed on my console.

"Widespread attacks," Ying whispered, staring at her com in horror, "including Serenity."

"Who was targeted?"

She looked up, her eyes huge in her pale face. "Everyone."

CHAPTER SIXTEEN

Ying had been exaggerating, but only a tiny bit. An event at House Yamado where all three High Houses were scheduled to attend had been targeted. There were a few pictures of smoking buildings, some pleas for help, a picture of what seemed like at least a battalion of soldiers, and then nothing.

Messages to Serenity went unanswered and the RCDF ships dispatched to check it out had not returned or sent any word. At least not any *public* word. The military reports from the RCDF to the House's private network told a different story.

Four ships had been sent. Two were destroyed almost immediately by Earth's ground-based defenses. The third became a shield for the fourth to get a message out, but the gate was unavailable—either powered down or destroyed, the message didn't say. The fourth ship had just enough time to launch a com drone with a manually plotted jump point near Andromeda Prime before it was presumably lost as well.

Four large military vessels, destroyed in a blink.

RCDF was in an uproar, as they didn't know who the attackers were or how many forces they had on the ground. They also didn't know who was in charge, if any of the High Houses had lost their leaders, or if this was a coup attempt by one or more Houses.

It was chaos.

On top of that, reports were coming in of attacks in other areas, including one in Sedition. The holo image showed a smoking ruin where Rhys Sebastian's home used to sit. I'd visited it once because it was also the home were my sister Ada lived.

Terror stabbed deep, and I prayed to any god who would listen that she'd made it out alive. Or better, that she hadn't been there at all.

Despair and helplessness threatened to drown me, but I didn't have time to break down. I needed a plan and I needed it now. I sent an emergency message to our sibling channel asking for status updates. Anyone with a signal would get an audible alert, no matter the time.

"This was a coordinated attack on the High Houses and all of their heirs. Ying, do you know the status of any of your family members?"

Her face was still too pale, but her voice was steady. "No. My parents and both of my brothers were on Earth. You?"

"My parents were on Earth, but my siblings were not. They also hit Ada's house in Sedition, but I don't know her status. Benedict is at war. Hannah, Ferdinand, and Bianca didn't publicly disclose their locations, but they haven't responded to my messages, either. Do we know anything about Rockhurst? As far as I know, Richard is in Antlia with Benedict. Anyone else?"

"I think Elizabeth was off-planet, but I don't know for sure. Is it the lower houses?"

"Some of them, certainly. Riccardo Silva met with Lord

and Lady James in their study tonight, so I would not be surprised if the Syndicate was also involved."

"They have to know they can't hold Earth. What is their plan?"

I wasn't so sure about the first part. Earth was designed specifically to be a stronghold for the Consortium elite. It had the best orbital and ground-based space defense complex in existence, but a relatively small deployment of ground troops because no one expected a ground war. With a few carefully placed traitors, a battalion could take the command center, and if their info was good, then they knew about the backup location as well.

But if their information wasn't good, then there might be a chance to turn the tide. Only a few people knew about the backup command center, and, aside from Ying and myself, they were all unaccounted for. Unfortunately, that meant I was my family's best hope. I wished I had Ada's confidence or Bianca's intelligence. I would even take Benedict's boisterous arrogance.

But all I had was me.

It wasn't enough, but I was still a von Hasenberg—I wouldn't go down without a fight. I had to get to Earth in order to help. And one tiny ship, fast and undetectable thanks to heavy stealth, might be able to slip through the defenses.

It was potentially suicide, but it was *possible.*

And then Benedict and the RCDF and anyone else who wanted in on the fun could come in to sweep up the ground forces.

I took a deep breath. "Presumably, they intended to wipe out the existing High Houses, and then use the power vacuum to divvy up the spoils and name some new High Houses. By surviving, we've thrown a bit of a wrench in that plan, but I have to get on-planet and get the defenses down before the lower houses decide that maybe the Syndicate isn't so bad after all. We can't afford a war with everyone."

"Absolutely not," Aoife said. At the same time, Ying asked, "Are you serious?"

"I am. But I'm happy to let you out wherever you'd like to go."

Ying's jaw firmed. "They have my parents and Tae. I will go with you." Her oldest brother Hitoshi did not merit a mention.

"Neither one of you is going anywhere," Aoife said. She stood and paced, glaring at us.

"I'm not asking you to go. I will drop you back in Honorius and pay for your starliner fare to wherever you like, Aoife, you and Alex both."

"I've *studied* Earth's defenses." She slashed her hand through the air. "It's suicide."

"For a big ship, maybe. *Chaos* is small and nimble, with the best stealth technology money can buy. If any ship can break through, we can." If I didn't fuck it up. And that was a pretty big *if*.

"Or you can die like everyone else. Let's say you get to the ground. Then what? Are you going to single-handedly take out that battalion I saw in the pictures?"

"If I have to."

She laughed, a harsh, grating sound. "You sound just like your sister, but at least she had the good sense to have a plan and take backup."

I flinched as the barb hit. Even if it wasn't true—I did intend to have a plan and as much backup as I could manage—it drove home how everyone saw me. Stupid, worthless Catarina. Good for socializing and nothing else.

It was a mask I'd voluntarily donned, but sometimes it was *unbearable*. And sometimes, I wondered if it was a mask at all.

"What is going on?" Alex asked from the doorway.

"Catarina is planning a suicide mission. Maybe you can talk her out of it." Aoife stormed from the flight deck.

Ying stood. "I'm going to go check on Cira. We will talk later, yes?" When I nodded, she, too, left the room.

To keep myself busy, I plotted a course for Sedition on APD Zero. I could get in the queue, drop Alex and Aoife off in Honorius with sufficient fare for a starliner anywhere, and then go check on Ada. But rather than giving me a place in the gate queue, I got back an error. Alex said something I didn't catch. I waved him off while I frowned at my console and tried again.

Nothing.

The gate wasn't responding. I looked at the time stamps on the news I'd been reading. The newest articles were from almost two hours ago. When I refreshed the feed, nothing new came up. I switched to a local news source and found I wasn't alone.

No one could get jump coordinates or communications through the gate. Even HIVE was down. We were effectively cut off.

The attackers had instigated an emergency lockdown of every gate in the 'verse. Designed to be used in cases where quarantine or containment were necessary, individual gates could be remotely disabled from Serenity, but it hadn't been used in my lifetime—at least, not that I knew of. And I'd never heard of a case where all of the gates were disabled at once.

It would've taken at least three high-ranking RCDF officers to authorize the lockdown and they shouldn't have acted without a signed order from the Royal Consortium. We had traitors upon traitors.

A message popped up from Skout, who ran the gang of street kids in Honorius. They'd kept it infuriatingly brief: *The Syndicate is in Honorius. Rumor has it, they're looking for you. Watch your back. You can send my payment to the usual account.*

The last line made me smile. Skout might not accept credits as charity, but they definitely wanted them as payment for a job well done. I sent the agreed upon payment. With the gates down it would take it a while to go through, but they'd see I paid.

Alex moved closer and caught my eye. "What's wrong?"

"Serenity was attacked, my sister's house in Sedition was attacked, and now the gates are down. *All* of the gates. And I heard from Skout. They caught wind that the Syndicate was looking for me in Honorius."

"Your sister Ada?"

I glanced sharply at him. "You know Ada?"

"No, but I know Rhys Sebastian, and I believe she was living in his house. Is there any word from them?"

"The news didn't mention any deaths, but I haven't heard from Ada, so I don't know. The pictures looked bad."

"Damn." Alex blew out a breath and gripped the back of his neck with one hand. "What did Aoife mean by a suicide mission?"

"I'm going to Earth."

He chuckled, but it didn't sound happy. "That would do it. How are you going to get there without a gate?"

"*Chaos* has an emergency jump point near Earth." Normally, civilian ships didn't get emergency jump points, but I was the daughter of a High House. Once I'd started investigating House James, I'd thought it prudent to have a backup.

Emergency jump points were only used when a ship was

too far from a gate and needed to jump immediately because of imminent danger. They weren't as reliable as the gates, so they were strictly used as a method of last resort.

I'd say this qualified.

But if I jumped to Earth, I'd be stuck. I could try jumping out blind, but that was a good way to end up in an unexpected asteroid. Many cocky captains who had decided to risk the small but significant odds had fallen victim to their own hubris.

So I had to gather all of the supplies I needed before I jumped. And see if I could hire a merc unit or two to serve as backup. I changed course for Honorius.

Alex broke me from my thoughts. "Why do you want to go to Earth?"

"My friends and family are there, and I think I can make a difference." My parents had raised me from a distance, through a series of tutors and increasingly difficult training missions. I was a House asset and treated as such. Albrecht and Maria might be bastards the vast majority of the time, but they were still my parents. Filial loyalty demanded I at least find out what happened.

"How will your presence make a difference?"

I sighed. I didn't begrudge him for doubting me. Hell, *I* doubted me. "I don't know if my parents survived. If they didn't, our House has no direction. With the gates down, none of my siblings will be able to step in, and even if they could, I'm uniquely suited to landing in hostile territory." It was as close as I wanted to get to mentioning my abilities, but Alex seemed to understand what I meant.

"You can't take out a battalion."

"No, I can't. I'm better suited to stealth. But I can gather up our forces and hit the backup location. It's possible the attackers don't know about it, or if they do, that it's only lightly defended."

"You've made up your mind."

I smiled grimly. "I have. I don't expect you or Aoife to accompany me. You're welcome to stay here in the von Hasenberg building until the gates come back up." I paused and considered it. "Actually, with all of the other attacks, that might not be safe. I'll book you into whichever hotel you prefer."

"Why not let the rebels take over? Bow out gracefully while you can?"

"Because I don't think they are rebels, not really. I think it's a few lower houses and the Syndicate. And while I know the current government has problems that Father and the others are reluctant to solve, the Syndicate will be far, far worse. If they get a foothold, they'll rule the universe even more ruthlessly than the Royal Consortium. And the lower houses working with them are idiots not to see that."

We were interrupted when my console lit up with warnings. An unknown ship was targeting us. The automatic defense prevented them from getting a lock, but they were closing the distance. I pulled up the information *Chaos* had gathered.

We were being hunted by an unflagged destroyer.

"Fuck!" My hands flew over the console. I dropped us into deep stealth to cut all signals from the ship and then ramped the engines to full power to give us maneuverability. I pressed the ship's internal intercom button. "Secure yourselves. It's about to get bumpy." I followed my own advice and clipped in to the restraints in my chair.

Alex dropped into the navigation and tactical console and clipped in. He tapped on the console then scowled. "Give me access to the weapons' systems."

I unlocked his console but warned, "There's a destroyer on

our ass. Don't get us in a firefight unless there is no other option. I'm running stealth."

I pulled up the list of nearby destinations. *Chaos* could jump up to three thousand light years without the help of a gate, but all of the big occupied planets and stations were farther away than that. *Dammit.* I needed supplies before I jumped to Earth.

More warnings flashed on my console and the ship shuddered as the shield deflected a blast. A blast from *in front of us*. A second destroyer had joined the fight. And while their systems couldn't lock on to us, their manual targeting seemed to be working just fine.

Chaos trembled as Alex fired on the destroyer behind us, but their shields deflected the shot. I could not take on two destroyers and win.

"We're jumping local," I said. "Keep them off of us until I find a destination."

I frantically searched the jump list again for the most promising option and found a small station at the very edge of *Chaos*'s capability. This ship had the best internals in the 'verse. If the destroyers wanted to follow us, they would have to jump twice. By the time they waited out their FTL cooldown for the second jump, we'd be long gone.

I locked in the course and slapped the jump confirmation button just as the shield took another glancing hit.

The engine noise ramped up, then fell silent as my stomach dropped and we jumped. The view changed. There was no longer a pretty planet below us, just a vast expanse of empty space. In the far distance, lights from the space station flickered like a distant star.

"Where are we?"

"S2BAP8. A small station outside the destroyer's jump radius. I'm going to take us in. We'll wait out the FTL cooldown on the station."

Alex nodded in acknowledgment.

Still in stealth, *Chaos* wasn't transmitting any registration data. I hastily swapped the registration to backup data that showed the ship was registered to one of the many shell companies I owned. It would not be traceable back to me, or to House von Hasenberg.

Now to see if my gamble had paid off, I brought the ship out of stealth and requested a berth. I received provisional clearance to land in bay twelve, assuming I paid a truly staggering amount of credits.

I paid.

I approved the automated flight path and *Chaos* headed for our home for the next six hours while the FTL cooled down. The mandatory wait gave me a convenient deadline for getting supplies and backup—if this tiny station even had any to offer.

I wasn't holding my breath.

CHAPTER SEVENTEEN

Station Two of Beta Andromedae Primus Eight—or S2BAP8—was not much to look at. The planet it was named after, BAP Eight, had originally been terraformed for use as a farming planet. Then as synthesizers took over most food production, the planet had fallen out of favor. A few hundred thousand hearty souls still lived on-planet, eking out a living by trading with the station and travelers headed deeper into Andromedae space.

Needless to say, the traffic wasn't exactly thick.

The station had a dozen levels and a listed resident population of a little over three thousand. Built in a starfish configuration around a central core, landing bay twelve was at the end of one of the arms. The bay was secured by both an atmospheric shield and a heavy blast door, so leaving would not be a quick process.

Alex had been strangely silent since the jump, but as *Chaos* settled in the landing bay, I snuck a glance at him. I'd been too caught up before, but now I realized that he'd changed his shirt. "Did you get bandaged while you were in the medbay?"

He nodded. "Cira patched me up with some regeneration

gel after I took care of her leg. The injury is going to put her out of commission for a day or two, even with the regen gel."

I didn't have time to wait for her to heal. I needed to strike while everything was still in flux, but at the rate I was losing allies, I'd be storming Earth alone. Hopefully S2BAP8 had a whole bunch of hungry mercs willing to risk life and limb for a shot at an astronomical reward—and who wouldn't stab me in the back at the first opportunity.

Alex glanced at me. "You're planning to enter the station?"

"Yes, but not until a decent hour. I'm going to grab a few hours of sleep, then go in search of supplies and people. I'll pay the fare for you and Aoife to get back to Andromeda Prime. I don't have the hard credits on me for what Bianca owes you, but if my bank account isn't frozen, I can initiate the transfer. This far from a gate and with communication down, it'll take a couple of weeks to go through, but I can give you enough hard credits to cover the gap."

Alex didn't contradict me and I felt a tiny stab of disappointment. Of course he wouldn't want to go to Earth. I was on a fool's errand and I'd be lucky if I could persuade anyone to accompany me. Ying might also change her mind, now that the gates were down and turning back wasn't an option.

"I'm going to talk to Aoife, then hit the rack. Don't leave the ship without me." At my raised eyebrow, he softened his tone. "Please."

"Before you do that, would you mind bringing me the papers from your bag? And whatever Aoife managed to grab from the office?"

He nodded and left the flight deck.

I fished out the credit and data chips I'd stolen from House James. There were three hard credit chips and one data chip. I used my com to check the amount on the credit chips. I blinked and checked again, but the total came back the same. There was a shocking amount of money on these three chips.

Like instantly become a lower house kind of money.

Hard credit chips were not tied to bank accounts. Like the paper currency of old, if a credit chip was lost, the money was gone. If this money had come from House James, I'd just bankrupted them. I could pay off Alex and Aoife no matter how much Bianca had promised them.

I could hire an army of mercenaries.

Why would any House keep such a ridiculous amount of money on hard credit chips? The only answer I could think of was for untraceable bribes. But a payment this big would buy a small, sparsely inhabited planet in an out-of-the-way part of the 'verse.

Or pay off the Syndicate after they took out three High Houses.

Nothing I'd learned about House James led me to believe that they had this kind of ready capital. No, this was blood money paid for by multiple Houses. But how many were involved?

The data chip might shed some light, but it was more dangerous than credit chips. I needed a secondary com that I could put in quarantine mode. I unclipped from my seat and headed down the short hall to my quarters.

My suite took up the entire starboard side of the ship from the flight deck to the cargo bay. The door opened to a tiny sitting room that connected to a small study on the right and a bedroom on the left. The bedroom had an en suite bathroom. The sitting room was a bright orange and the furniture was as colorful as in the rest of my public spaces.

My bedroom was a more subdued pale yellow that reminded me of sunshine even in the depths of space. I swiped my identity chip over a plain piece of wall paneling and the panel slid aside to reveal my personal armory.

Filled with weapons and supplies, the secret closet was shielded from all but the most sensitive scanners. I grabbed the com I needed, then locked the credit chips in the hidden, built-in safe. I couldn't carry that much money on me into the station or I'd be begging for trouble. I closed the panel and it automatically locked.

The com I'd grabbed, like all of my coms, was a von Hasenberg specialty, which meant it had features not found in standard off-the-shelf devices. A quarantine mode was one of those features. It shut down all external communication and turned on processing protection. Inserted data chips would be read and the data placed in safe storage where no executables were allowed to run.

I didn't know if the data chip was protected by a virus, but if I was hiding a secret Syndicate contract for toppling the three High Houses, I'd include one. Plus, it was better to be safe than sorry.

I inserted the chip and waited for the data to be copied. Once it was done, I crossed my fingers and opened the files, but after delivering a fortune in credits, the universe was not feeling particularly generous any longer—the data was encrypted.

The com had chips designed to crack encryption, but it would take a while. If I was very lucky, the time would be measured in hours. If not, it could be days or months. For now, I would have to move forward with the information I already had.

A KNOCK ON THE SUITE DOOR PULLED ME AWAY FROM the com. I dropped it on the desk in my study to let it continue working, then opened the door. Alex stood on the other side, holding a stack of paper with a gold necklace on top. I stepped back so he could enter, and he blinked as the sitting room wall color assaulted his eyes.

"Ao—"

I shushed him before he could finish the name, then picked up the necklace. It was as beautiful as it was fake. It didn't seem to be old enough to have sentimental value, so the only reason to lock it in a safe was to ensure anyone who broke in would steal it.

I used my com to scan the necklace and paperwork for bugs and trackers. Both scans came back positive on the necklace. I couldn't remotely disable them with my com, which meant they were high-level tech, so I smashed the necklace under my heel until the scan came back negative, then put the pieces in a signal-proof pouch.

Once I was done, Alex broke his silence. "How did you know?"

"I can spot fake jewelry at thirty paces. I should've scanned it before we left, but things were a little dicey."

"Will they follow us here?"

"Eventually, but they would've done that before. If a ship jumps back to Andromeda Prime and relays the signal, then they might get here faster than if they were choosing destinations at random, but we'll be long gone either way."

Direct FTL communication was expensive and finicky, so stations far from the gates like S2BAP8 relied on passing ships and com drones to relay messages. Even now their news cache would be updating with information from *Chaos*. I'd considered locking down the ship's communications, but I wanted the mercs I hired to know what they were signing up for. It would cost me more, but hopefully it meant I would get a crew who meant business.

Alex handed me the stack of papers. "Are you going to go through those before you sleep?"

I stepped into the office and dumped the paper on my desk with the com. "No. I probably should, but if I do, I'll be asleep and I still need to talk to Ying."

Alex had followed me silently, moving with a quiet grace that belied his size. He was tall and broad and muscled, but he moved like an athlete or dancer—or a very deadly soldier. He leaned against the office doorway, seemingly harmless.

"How do you do that?" I asked with a frown.

"Do what?"

I waved a hand at him, trying to encompass everything. "Blend into the background. Be inconspicuous. Look harmless."

A lazy grin tugged at the corner of his mouth. "What makes you think I'm not?"

"Please. I've seen you shoot." And I'd fought him, very briefly, hand to hand. He was far from harmless.

He straightened, and once again his presence felt heavy in the room. "You do it, too," he said. He stalked toward me until he was less than an arm's length away. "When you're playing nice with others, you go all soft and helpless. It's a mask and a form of manipulation, but it's all about body language."

I liked the language his body was speaking right now. It took all of my willpower stop myself from licking my lips and staring at his mouth.

He lifted an arm and barely touched my shirt where I'd been shot. "Did you bandage your shoulder?"

In truth, with all the drama, I'd forgotten about it. A glance showed a small nick in my shirt where the bolt had grazed me, but my shoulder wasn't bothering me. My nanos had already taken care of it. "It was barely a scratch. It's already healed."

"May I check it? Please?" His voice was whisper-soft temptation.

"It's fine," I grumbled, but I pulled my shirt over my head. Alex's eyes dropped to my chest before he blinked and focused on my shoulder. I had on a plain sports bra that held everything firmly in place and was not the least bit enticing. Too bad.

Alex's hands were gentle on my skin as he cupped my shoulder and brushed away flecks of dried blood. The blaster bolt had sliced a path through the top of my left shoulder about the width of one of his fingers and a millimeter deep. The wound was pink and shiny as my natural healing and nanos raced to repair the skin.

While he inspected the wound, his thumb traced back and forth over my clavicle, so lightly that I wasn't sure he knew he was doing it. It was a motion meant to soothe, but all it did was make me more aware of him. I held perfectly still, afraid that movement would snap him back to reality and I wasn't ready for this moment to end.

I closed my eyes against the urge to sway into him. It had been so long since someone had gathered me close and offered me comfort for no other reason than that I needed it. I had so many superficial acquaintances, but so few true friends.

He touched my jaw, tilting my face up to his. "Are you okay?"

A look proved that he was closer than he had been. I could see the flecks of black and gold in his brown eyes and the dark stubble shadowing his jaw.

And still his thumb caressed my collarbone.

He was going to leave for Andromeda Prime in the morning. This might be my last chance to see if our kiss was a fluke. I needed to know. *For science.*

Decision made, I lifted my hand to his chest. His muscles were firm under my fingers. I glanced up at him from under my lashes. "May I kiss you?"

"Please." The demand sounded like it was ripped from him, his voice deep and delicious.

I ran my hand up his chest and around the back of his neck, into the soft strands of his dark hair. I took my time. There was no rush and I wanted to savor this moment. If things went poorly on Earth, this could be my last kiss *ever*.

I pushed the thought aside and focused on Alex.

I closed the distance between us, until my chest brushed against his. Once again I bemoaned my bra selection, but based on the heat in his eyes, he wasn't complaining. I stretched up and brushed my mouth against his, once, twice. Tingles shivered down my spine, tightening my nipples and causing heat to pool low. And I'd barely started.

The first kiss was *not* a fluke.

I licked into his mouth and he met me with a low groan. The hot slide of his tongue against mine threatened to send me up in flames. His hands clamped around my hips and he pulled me close, until I could feel the heat of him through my remaining clothes. I wrapped my other hand over his shoulder and tried to pull him even closer. In different circumstances, I would've climbed him like a tree. Instead, I settled for devouring his mouth.

He backed me into the desk, then wedged a thick thigh between my own. My moan ended in a gasp as he pressed exactly where I wanted him. His hands flexed and he rocked me against him in delicious little movements.

I broke the kiss to suck in a deep breath. Alex's eyes were dark with desire. I wasn't the only one feeling the heat between us. One-night stands were not usually my jam, for a host of reasons I had trouble remembering right now.

His lips brushed against the corner of my mouth, my jaw, and the spot on my neck that made me arch and moan. I snuck a hand under the hem of his shirt and ran my fingers across the rippling muscles of his abs. He made a low sound of pleasure and tugged me closer, so that I was practically riding his thigh.

I lifted the hem of his shirt and he pulled it off, exposing hard-packed abs and a solid chest. I ran both hands up over his nipples, causing him to hiss out a breath.

He hooked a finger under the edge of my bra. "Take this off."

I grinned at him. "I will, as long as you understand that there's no sexy way to get out of a sports bra."

"Can I help?" His voice was velvety soft, but his eyes were on fire.

"*Please.*" I lifted my arms. "Straight over my head."

His fingers slipped under the band, then he slowly drew it up over my breasts. When my nipples sprang free, he groaned low, a sound I felt more than heard. Still, he didn't rush. By the time he was done, I was squirming in place.

He tossed the bra on my desk, then lowered his hands to my bust, hesitating just before he made contact. His scorching gaze met mine. "May I?"

"Gods, yes. Please. I'm dying here."

He smiled and cupped each breast in a warm hand, then flicked his thumbs over my pebbled nipples. I arched into him with a moan. "Do that again."

He lowered me back onto the desk and then his hot mouth closed over my nipple and pleasure exploded. I threaded my fingers into his hair to hold him there and he obliged, licking and sucking until I was mindless and writhing.

I gasped out a demand and he switched sides, trailing little nibbling kisses as he went. Somehow, this side was even better than the other. I'd never had chemistry like this before. If it was this good *now*, how was I going to survive sex without losing my mind?

I suppose I'd just have to find out.

I was calculating just how fast I could get our pants off when a noise broke through the bliss. It wasn't until it repeated that I realized someone was knocking on the door to my quarters. I pushed myself up onto my elbows, trying to snap out of the pleasurable haze.

Alex moved with me and pressed a kiss against the side of my neck. "Ignore it."

"It might be important."

He groaned, but it was tinged with resignation. He knew about duty, too. He put on his shirt while I struggled into my bra, then he helped me with my shirt and smoothed my mussed hair. I didn't think it was going to fool whoever was knocking, but it was better than answering naked.

I opened the door to reveal Aoife. She looked over my shoulder and her grin turned knowing. "How are we going to bunk?"

I bit back my first instinct, which was to ask Alex if he wanted to stay here. I needed to sleep, and I needed to plan, and if he was here, I would do neither.

"You and Alex can share the crew bunk," I said, striving to keep my voice steady. "I'll put Ying on the sofa in here and Cira can stay in the medbay. Does that work for you?"

"Yes. Don't leave the ship without one of us."

"I'm going to talk to Ying, then sleep for a bit. I'll be leaving in about four hours if you want to join me." I needed at least that much sleep or I'd be dead on my feet.

"We'll be there." She tilted her head toward Alex, her expression unreadable. He edged around me and out into the corridor. I couldn't see what passed between them, but Aoife left with a murmured parting.

Alex turned back to me. "Please don't leave the ship without us."

"I wasn't planning to. One of you needs to be there to book your seats to Andromeda. And if you have time, maybe you can help me screen mercenaries."

He nodded. "I will." He lingered for a moment, then leaned in and pressed a gentle kiss to my lips. Desire flared again, but he pulled back before it could blaze out of control. "Sleep well."

"You, too."

We both headed down to the lower level. I was not going to let this be awkward between us. We'd kissed. He'd tasted my nipples. It was earth shattering. No big deal.

I shoved the thoughts aside and mentally prepped for how I was going to tell Ying about the gates. I tried to anticipate her questions. I wouldn't blame her if she bailed, and I had to make sure my expression didn't guilt her into continuing when she wanted to leave. I pulled on my public mask and tucked away my emotions.

Alex stopped in the crew quarters while I continued to the medbay. The tiny room had only a single diagnostic table and enough space for a few people to move around. The pristine white walls contrasted with my usual public style, but medbays were supposed to look plain and sterile.

Cira sat on the table, a slightly loopy grin on her face. Her pants were missing and her leg was bandaged. Regeneration gel sped up healing, but it burned like the devil while it worked—or so I'd been told. It was likely that she had been dosed with a painkiller.

Ying sat in the guest chair that folded down from the wall. She turned and her smile fell at the look on my face. "What's wrong?"

"The gates are down."

Ying stood with a frown. "All of them?"

"I believe so, yes. Both Earth and Andromeda Prime are

down. We jumped to a nearby station after Andromeda's orbit got a little crowded with two destroyers that would've liked to shoot us down. I'm still going to Earth. I have an emergency jump point that will get me there, but it's going to be a one-way trip until the gates come back up. You need to decide if that's a risk you're willing to take."

"It's too dangerous, my lady," Cira said. She scowled as she tried to focus through the painkiller. "We need more backup. Like a battle cruiser. Or ten."

"I'm going to hire a mercenary crew to back us." Maybe if I said it with enough confidence, it would actually become true.

"What about Alex and Aoife?" Ying asked.

I sighed, reluctant to reveal the truth, but Ying deserved to know. "They also believe it is too dangerous. They will be returning to Andromeda."

"What will you do if you can't hire any mercs?"

What could one person do, really? Maybe nothing, but I couldn't live with myself if I didn't try. "I will go alone."

Ying nodded, as if that was the answer she'd expected. "I will go with you. What are best friends for, after all? Dying a completely avoidable, horrible death together seems like it qualifies."

"Ying . . ."

She shook her head. "I'm kidding. I understand why you're going. It's the same reason I am—my friends and family are trapped there. Maybe the two of us won't make a difference, but maybe we will. If you say you can get us on Earth, I believe you."

"Think about it for a while longer," I said. "I'm going to sleep for a few hours, then go check out the station and see who I can find for backup. Alex and Aoife are in the crew bunk. I can fold out the couch in my quarters or I can make you a pallet here, whichever you prefer."

Ying looked at Cira. "Will you be okay here alone?"

"I'll be fine. Wake me up before you leave the ship."

"I will. Message me if you need anything." She picked up the small bag at her feet and turned to me. "I'm ready when you are."

"I've added you both to the passenger list," I said, "so you can come and go as you please. You can also ask *Chaos* to relay messages and locate crew. If you need food, the mess hall is on the upper level. Cira, if you get hungry, you can use the ship's intercom to alert one of us and we'll bring you something. Don't walk on that leg."

She waved me off. "I'll be fine."

"Message me," Ying said, her tone firm. Cira grimaced but nodded.

I led Ying up to my quarters. We folded out the sofa and made the bed in silence. Finally, when we were done, Ying broached the subject we were both reluctant to think about. "Do you think our families survived?"

The pictures I'd seen had not left a lot of room for hope. If they were at the gala, then the odds were good that they hadn't survived. Although, I'd underestimated Father before—to my detriment. "I don't know. Was Tae scheduled to be at the event?"

She bit her lip. "I don't know. Mother would not have attended, as is her usual habit, but Father would've included one of my brothers. It's usually Hitoshi because he's the heir, but Tae sometimes goes in his place."

Ying respected her parents but she had no love for her elder brother, and I didn't blame her. Hitoshi Yamado was an asshole of the first order. He was the one case where I thought the current High Councillor—the official title for the head of a High House—was better than the next generation.

Her jaw firmed and the hint of vulnerability was hidden behind a ruthless smile. "Either way, we'll make them pay. They may think we're weak and wounded, but all they've done is piss us off."

I matched her smile with my own. We would definitely make them pay.

CHAPTER EIGHTEEN

Morning came too soon and too early. I groped for my com and groaned when the alarm didn't stop. I fumbled it and had to hunt for it in the bedding while it continued to wail. Well, at least now I was good and awake.

I dressed and got ready as quietly as I could. I slipped the silencer and vanisher in my pockets. I hopefully wouldn't need them, but better safe than sorry. For the same reason, I wrapped a utility belt with a blaster around my waist.

I planned to sneak out and let Ying sleep, but she was sitting up, waiting for me. "Sorry," I murmured. "I didn't mean to wake you. I'm going out to find us some backup. Would you like to come along or stay here?"

"I will stay here and keep an eye on the ship and Cira."

"Okay. I should be back in an hour or so. We have about an hour and a half until we can jump again. I'd like to be ready to go by then."

"We'll be ready."

"I have my com if you need me."

She waved me off. "Go find us some backup. We'll be fine here. Do you mind if I use your bathroom?"

"Help yourself. There are spare clothes in my closet." Ying was a little shorter than me and she had a more delicate build. "If you cinch them up, there should be something that will work for you."

She nodded. "Thank you."

I raised my hand in farewell, then stepped across the passageway to the mess hall. Alex and Aoife sat at one end of the table, speaking in low tones. I nodded to them, then ordered a pastry and a steaming cup of coffee from the synthesizer. The machine beeped and I pulled out my meal. There was only a single table, but I hesitated to sit next to them. I didn't want to interrupt their conversation.

Alex solved the problem by nudging out the chair next to him. "Join us."

"Thank you."

"Are you still set on your suicide mission?" Aoife asked.

"Unless new updates came in overnight. Are the gates back up?"

"No."

Damn. I'd hoped that given a few hours, someone on Earth would take back control. Were any of the Houses even fighting back? The High Houses would be on lockdown, but based on the firepower I'd seen in the photos, that might not last long.

I sighed. "Then I'm still going."

She muttered something under her breath that sounded a lot like "whole family is stubborn as fuck."

I ate my breakfast in silence and started mentally listing all of the things I needed to pick up. S2BAP8 was probably too small to have most of my wish list, but I'd have to make do. I dumped my dishes in the recycler and waved at Alex. "Ready?"

He and Aoife both rose, but neither of them looked too

happy. I took a deep breath and slipped on my public mask. "Are you going out with us?" I asked Aoife.

She slanted a glance at Alex. "Against my better judgment."

"After you look at the departure schedule for transport back to Andromeda, let me know what you decide on and charge the fare to my account."

She didn't reply, so I shrugged and the three of us left *Chaos*. The ship's cargo bay door locked behind us. The landing bay was a dingy white covered in gray and black smudges. It hadn't been painted in a decade at least. It was also oddly quiet.

The hatch into the main corridor squealed on rusty hinges as Alex forced it open. The corridor itself wasn't much better. The paint was peeling and the overhead light panels flickered, in dire need of replacement. It seemed like the whole station needed work.

I could reach up and touch the ceiling. I tried not to think about it. Stations were built to minimize materials, not maximize comfort. Spacers—those who grew up on stations and ships—found the low ceilings and close walls comforting. Surfacers like me, who grew up on planets with wide-open skies, often found them claustrophobic. The flickering lights didn't help.

"I paid a small fortune to dock here. They need to put some of that money to use."

"I'm sure the station master's quarters are just fine," Aoife grumbled. Sadly, she was probably right.

We didn't meet anyone in the long corridor. The airlock into the station proper seemed to be in moderately better shape than the rest of what I'd seen. It quickly cycled us through into the station's outer ring.

I'd downloaded a station map to my com. Much like Serenity, the station was divided into ring quadrants and sectors, but it also had floor levels. We were on the main level. Most businesses were on this level because it led to the landing bays and had the most foot traffic.

Though foot traffic seemed to be almost nonexistent. The few people I saw all appeared to be station employees on their way to their shifts. They did not make eye contact.

"I'm going to wander through the market section on my way to the bar," I murmured.

"A bar for breakfast?" Alex asked.

"You ever seen an empty bar on a station, no matter what the hour? I'll get a drink and scope out the mercenaries. And see what kind of gossip I can pick up." Stations usually operated on Universal Standard Time, but they rarely had a true night. Days were split into two or three shifts, depending on the task, and people were always at the bar as body clocks often didn't match Standard.

Alex agreed with a reluctant grin.

The directions to the largest bar were displayed along the bottom of my smart glasses. Not only were bartenders excellent resources, most mercs looking for work kept at least one person stationed in the main bar because it was a natural gathering place.

I expected Aoife to break off now that we were in the station, but she trailed along behind us. Alex stalked at my side, his body a tense line. "What's wrong?" I asked.

He paused in scanning our surroundings long enough to flick a glance at me. "You ever been to a small station where there's not a crowd of vendors, children, and pickpockets waiting to meet an arriving ship?"

I didn't spend a lot of time on small stations, but nothing about the current situation seemed too unusual. "Maybe they didn't know we were up and about."

"Someone knew. I don't like it. What supplies do you need?"

"Weapons, explosives, and people, though not necessarily in that order." I'd also kill for some combat armor but that would be a stretch. The more of the station I saw, the more I pared my list. I might be pleasantly surprised, but I doubted it. Anything of value was long gone.

The market section was nearly empty. A few businesses were still struggling to stay open, but they were the ones that catered to the station occupants more than visitors. None sold weapons.

Unless there were specialty merchants on the upper levels that were still in business, I would have to hire mercenaries who had decent supplies. Most mercenaries should—at least the good ones—but it limited the pool of possibilities.

The bar was a hole-in-the-wall and that was saying something considering the rest of the station. The interior was dim and grimy. Rickety, mismatched chairs surrounded small, chipped tables. The patrons didn't look much better. Many of them were deep into their cups, and for the ones who weren't, it seemed like it was only a matter of time.

The bartender was a massive man who looked like he broke people in half for fun. He was in his forties and missing an eye. Rather than a prosthetic, he wore an eyepatch. His mouth turned down when I approached the bar. "The cocktail lounge is on level three."

Public mask firmly in place, I gave him my sunniest smile and slid onto a barstool that threatened to wobble over onto the floor. Only a quick grab for the bar saved me from embarrassing myself. Alex and Aoife sat on the two stools flanking me. "I appreciate the tip, but I find cocktails too sweet. I'll take a good beer or whisky any day. Got any you'd recommend?"

"No."

I laughed. "In that case, we'll have three beers. Whatever you have on tap."

He pulled three beers into questionably clean glasses. He set them on the bar, but I made no move to reach for them. When I continued to watch him without moving, a grudging smile tipped up the corner of his mouth. "Weren't born yesterday after all, were you?"

"Not last I checked. How much?"

"Twenty credits." When I kept waiting, he added, "Total."

It was a little high for what was going to be shitty beer, but I handed him a hard credit chip with a hundred credits on it. "Keep my tab open."

He nodded silently. Now that the price had been settled, I picked up my glass and took a tentative sip. My nanobots would protect me from most poisons and waterborne diseases, but they couldn't protect my taste buds. The synth beer was even worse than I'd expected. I kept my pleasant expression only through force of habit. Alex and Aoife didn't touch their glasses.

The bartender smiled slyly. "Good, yes?"

"No," I said, "but you knew that already."

He didn't bother to hide his amusement. "It was on tap, as requested."

"Straight from the bilge system of some derelict freighter, I'm sure."

He shrugged carelessly. "What brings you to S2BAP8?" He pronounced it *stew-bap-eight*. Officially, station and planet names were initialisms—each letter was supposed to be pronounced individually. But the public rarely followed that rule if there was any way to pronounce it as a word. Thus BAP Eight became *bap eight*.

"I need weapons, supplies, and mercenaries, if there are any around who aren't drunk."

"Any mercenaries who aren't drunk aren't on S2BAP8 anymore."

I glanced around. I'd always been good at reading people, at figuring out what motivated them. Money was a good start, but some people craved power, status, or danger as much as monetary reward. Figuring out what drove people was the first step in figuring out how to manipulate them.

None of the patrons in the bar were the least bit interested in motivation. They hadn't looked up when we entered and they didn't care now that we'd decided to stay. If this was the best S2BAP8 had to offer, then I'd be going to Earth alone.

If only the destroyers hadn't been in orbit around Andromeda. If only the gates weren't down. *If only, if only . . .* A jump back to Andromeda would give me better supplies and people, but it meant dodging the destroyers for the FTL drive's twelve-hour cooldown.

I eyed the bartender. "You're not drunk. Interested in earning a pile of credits?"

His laugh sounded rusty and ended in a cough that rattled in his chest. "I've had enough of other people's wars. I'll stay here with the drunks, thanks."

"What about supplies?"

"They left with the mercenaries."

"Well, aren't you just a barrel of sunshine." I took another sip of my beer. It remained revolting.

"I've never seen anyone go back for seconds," the bartender said, a touch of respect in his expression.

"Perhaps bilge water is growing on me." It wasn't, but I'd drain the glass if it got me information. I took another sip.

He wiped a surprisingly clean cloth over the bar's surface. "What kind of supplies do you need?"

"Weapons, explosives, armor. Pretend that I'm single-handedly waging a war. I need everything for that."

"What about these two?" He waved to Alex and Aoife.

"They're too pretty to go to war," I said with a straight face.

The bartender broke into loud guffaws. "You're all right, lady. I'm Harvey. You got a name?"

I bowed slightly from my seated position. "Catarina von Hasenberg, at your service."

CHAPTER NINETEEN

Alex and Aoife groaned simultaneously. Harvey's good eye widened and he looked me up and down, like he could see the truth in my skin. "You're a von Hasenberg?"

People generally reacted one of two ways when they learned who I was: greed or anger. I was interested to see which camp Harvey fell into, so I answered him simply. "Yes."

He glanced around, but the drunks hadn't moved. "You shouldn't be here," he hissed.

"I didn't have much choice, so you'll have to clarify what you mean. Do you mean here in the bar or here in general? Is there some specific threat to me?"

He leaned across the bar. "This is a Syndicate station."

I casually took another sip of my beer when I wanted nothing more than to freeze. "What do you mean?"

"The station master is running weapons, drugs, and worse for the Syndicate. It's why all the mercs who can have cleared out. And word on the street is that Riccardo Silva wants any von Hasenberg detained for pickup."

That was far too specific for him to be making it up. "Why are you telling me this?"

"Because you're going to make it worth my while."

I toasted him with the terrible beer. "So there's nowhere to get supplies?"

"No. You need to leave as soon as possible. The station master was drunk as hell last night, but sooner or later someone is going to wake her up with the news that your ship is in the landing bay. Then you'll be stuck."

I didn't tell him that my ship wasn't registered to me. Someone would have to recognize me first, and I didn't look anything like my father. Plus, Harvey's idea of stuck and mine were probably different, but I let it go. "Are passenger ships running to Andromeda?"

"Twice a week. The next one leaves in a few hours."

"You sure you don't want to escape the drunks?"

He shook his head. "I've got family on BAP Eight. I have to stay and keep an eye on them."

"Close out my tab." He did, and handed the credit chip back to me. I swapped it for a chip with two thousand credits on it, then slid the new chip across the bar and tapped it twice. "If I make it out alive, I'll send you five times this much. And if anyone asks, I told you my name was Luisa."

The credit chip disappeared into his pocket. "Good luck."

My silent shadows stood with me and we left the bar. Once we were out of sight, I turned to them. "Think there is any chance I'll find supplies?"

"Unlikely," Alex admitted. "This station is dead. You saw the market."

I had, but I wasn't ready to give up just yet. "I'm going to do a quick search of the upper levels while you get your seats booked for the flight to Andromeda. I'll meet you back at the ship in thirty minutes."

"It's a bad idea," Alex said.

"Understood. I'm doing it anyway. See you soon."

"Wait, I'll come with you." He turned to Aoife. "We'll meet you in half an hour. If we don't, come find us."

She nodded and disappeared down the corridor leading to the passenger ships. Alex and I took the elevator to the third floor. The hallways were deserted. I entered what appeared to be the only shop on the floor.

The shopkeeper looked up in surprise. She was around my own age, and she flinched when she caught sight of Alex. "I already paid this month."

"We're here to buy, not collect," I said. "I'm going to war and I need supplies. Do you have anything?"

She frantically waved her hands. "No, of course not."

I pulled out the silencer and set it on the counter. I clicked the middle button, turning it on. The shopkeeper stared at it with wide eyes. "Do you know what this is?" Her head dipped in a barely perceptible nod. "I am Catarina von Hasenberg and I need weapons. So I'll ask again: do you have anything?"

"I don't, my lady, but I know someone who might." She looked around like people were going to jump out of the walls at any moment. "Go down to negative five. Someone will meet you at the elevator. Hurry."

"Thank you. Do you need help? I'll pay your way to Andromeda on the next ship."

"No, I'm okay. I have family on BAP Eight. This isn't such a bad gig, most of the time, but the Syndicate has been leaning on us harder than usual lately."

"I need sturdy, dark clothes for someone who is slightly shorter and thinner than me. Do you have anything?"

She pulled out a few items and I bought everything in

Ying's size. We often shopped together, so I knew all of her sizes, just as she knew mine. The total was under a hundred credits but I tripled it before I paid. "Thank you," I said. "Negative five?"

The shopkeeper agreed quietly, but she wouldn't quite meet my eyes. Alex grabbed the bag of clothes before I could reach for it, so I swept the silencer back into my pocket, though I didn't bother turning it off.

Once we were out of the shop and down the hall, I asked, "Think it's a trap?"

"I'd give it even odds."

"Not ideal. What do you think?"

"If they're running weapons for the Syndicate, then they might have something useful. But they could also be leading you into a little-used part of the station to rob you or worse. Aoife will find us if we don't return in fifteen minutes, but a lot can happen in fifteen minutes."

I could control many less-than-ideal situations because people routinely underestimated me. But I also had to worry about Alex and Aoife. I had no doubt that they both could take care of themselves, but I was no longer just risking myself.

And based on what I'd seen so far, the weapons I would find would not be worth the delay in getting off-station. "Let's return to the ship."

Alex didn't bother hiding his relief. "I think that's smart."

I nodded and clicked off the silencer. The elevator took us back to the main level. It remained as empty as it had been before. "Well, that was a waste of time. Hopefully Aoife was more successful and got you booked on a flight back to Andromeda. Let's go get your stuff."

Alex walked beside me, alert and light on his feet. "Will you go to Earth without supplies? Or will you attempt to go back to Andromeda?"

I sighed and ran a hand over my face. "I don't know." Both options had downsides. I wished Ada were here. She'd always been better than me at tactics. And if she were here, then she wouldn't be anywhere near the smoking ruin that was her house.

I couldn't remember the last time I'd been cut off from all of my siblings. Even on missions where stealth was a priority, I'd always had the *option* of sending a distress call or asking for advice. I didn't realize how much I'd depended on that support network until it was gone.

Now I had to make my own decisions and live with the consequences.

"Unless Ying objects, we will head directly to Earth. Both of our Houses have hidden caches of supplies. I *should* have enough firepower onboard to keep us safe until we can claim one of them. And once I'm in the solar system, I can communicate with our security staff and the RCDF."

Alex shook his head, but he didn't say anything. I pulled him to a stop and handed him a credit chip. "This chip has ten thousand credits on it. I know it's probably not what Bianca promised you, but it should be enough to last until my transfer goes through. Tell me how much she owes you and I'll initiate the payment before I jump."

"You don't owe us anything. Our agreement was with Bianca." Alex tried to return the chip, but I held up my hands and backed away.

"Bianca is my sister and she's unavailable right now. I don't mind settling her debts." I smiled. "Don't worry—I'll be sure to charge her interest on the loan."

Alex stared hard at me. "Aoife and I are going with you."

My heart leapt before I realized what must've changed his mind. "No matter what your debt, Bianca would not expect you to risk your lives on a suicide mission," I said, my tone gentle. "Whatever you agreed to do, your promise has been fulfilled. Go back to Andromeda and wait this one out. Aoife already bought you tickets."

"She didn't. She went searching for supplies. Whoever is behind the attacks on Earth also attacked Rhys," he said. "That makes it personal. And we can't get to him until the gates come back up. So Earth is it. And you're going to need the help."

He wasn't wrong.

WE WERE NEARLY BACK TO *CHAOS* WHEN A DISTANT alarm began to wail. I glanced at Alex. "What are the odds that doesn't have anything to do with us?"

He grimaced. "Let's hurry."

The hatch to the landing bay squeaked open, revealing *Chaos* just where I'd left her. The rest of the bay was, thankfully, empty. We entered the ship and found Aoife already onboard. I settled into the captain's chair on the flight deck and requested launch permission. It took over a minute, but eventually the request was denied without a given reason. The heavy blast door protecting the landing bay remained closed.

I keyed the ship's com to the flight controller's channel. I was the daughter of a High House, and I sank all of the command and icy hauteur of my status into my tone. "If you do not open the bay door, I'm going to blow it open with my blast cannon."

They didn't respond. A few seconds later, they tried to override my ship's controls, but *Chaos* was immune to such control unless it came from a High House or the RCDF directly. And still they didn't open the blast door. If the station master wasn't awake yet, she would be soon. I needed to move.

"Will you really blow the door?" Ying asked.

"Not unless I have to." Several thousand people lived on the station. And while the loss of pressure in a single, sealed landing bay should be a nonissue, the maintenance level of the station didn't give me great confidence about their ability to weather an emergency. "I'm going to try to override it from the console in the landing bay first."

"Let me do it," Alex said.

"I would, but I have only two nonemergency space suits on board and they are both sized for me. I didn't expect to be hosting a party." Ships were required to carry enough emergency space suits for the max passenger capacity. They were big and shapeless, designed to fit nearly everyone, but poorly. Moving around in one was a nightmare.

Quality space suits were thin, light, and sized for a snug fit. They had a little give, but not nearly enough for Alex's broad shoulders to fit into my suit. And it would be faster for me to do it in a proper space suit than wait for him in an emergency suit.

"*Chaos*, promote Ying Yamado to first officer." A chime acknowledged the command. "If things get dicey, get us out of the landing bay and I'll come through the airlock. And don't wreck my ship."

Ying inclined her head in agreement.

"I'll go with you," Aoife said.

"Are you trained for zero-g?"

She nodded.

We were similar enough in size that she could wear my second suit, so I waved for her to follow me. It was faster than arguing.

We suited up in record time. My helmet's heads-up display

showed my oxygen level and the status of the suit, including the maneuvering kit. Everything was green. The built-in com would allow me to communicate with Aoife and the ship.

I strapped on a belt with a pair of holstered blasters as well as a combat knife and a can of foam sealant. I hoped none of it would be needed, but the universe was currently kicking my ass, so I wasn't taking any chances.

Aoife looked alien in the white suit and sleek white helmet with its darkly tinted visor. I knew I looked very similar. It would be hard to tell us apart from a distance.

We exited the ship and headed straight for the manual override console. We were halfway across the landing bay when the hatch to the corridor opened and a quartet of soldiers entered. We had exactly zero cover, but *they* didn't have Aoife. She took down two of them before they got shots off. A blaster bolt winged by far too close for comfort, but then I hit one and Aoife hit the last one.

"I'm going to secure the hatch, you deal with the override," Aoife said. She didn't wait for confirmation before loping off toward the hatch. She didn't make it before the power was cut and the landing bay went pitch dark.

The override console was no longer an option. The outer door should be wired with emergency charges and a detonator that would work even without power. But without power, the atmospheric shield wouldn't work. Blasting the emergency charges would also decompress the landing bay and potentially send *Chaos*, Aoife, and myself jettisoning into space.

There should also be an emergency vent to slowly decompress the landing bay, but it would take at least ten minutes. Once the pressure dropped low enough, the hatch to the corridor would seal shut, but until then, we'd be vulnerable to attack. "Aoife, how long can you hold the door?"

"There's a manual turn lock, and I'm holding it closed. The soldiers on the other side haven't figured out how to open it. Unless they want to risk an explosion or cut through the wall, I can hold this all day."

"I'm going to vent the landing bay. Ying, retract the ramp and close the cargo door. We'll come through the airlock."

She acknowledged the request while I looked for the emergency controls. Usually they would be on an exterior wall away from the blast door, so that if something went wrong there was a good chance of remaining inside the landing bay instead of hurtling through open space.

I found the controls behind a stack of heavy crates. The detonator and air vent controls were locked behind a sturdy metal cage. I broke the cover protecting the lock. If the power had been on, an alarm would've sounded. Without power, the rest of the station wouldn't know what I was doing until they saw the air being vented.

The detonator consisted of two flip switches protected by metal covers that individually locked in place with twist locks. It was designed so the chance of accidentally blowing a hole in the side of the station was as minimal as possible. Next to the detonator, the large, circular air valve handle did not budge when I tried to turn it. I checked the labels just to make sure that someone hadn't installed it backward, but no, it was still lefty loosey to open it. The valve had seized up and routine maintenance hadn't caught the issue.

Surprise, surprise.

I gripped the handle and heaved, using every ounce of strength I possessed. For a long second, nothing happened, then, finally, the valve broke free with a metallic squeal. The vents along the top of the landing bay opened and the air began to flow.

A peek out the window revealed the escaping air, so I spun the valve wide open. I hoped the vents themselves had gotten more safety checks than the rest of the station or our gradual decompression might be more energetic than desired.

I gave the others a status update. "The vent valves are open. Don't leave the ship without a suit. When the bay pressure drops below seventy-five percent, the inner hatch will seal closed. Assuming they've maintained that safety feature."

"It may not matter because we don't have that long," Aoife warned. "The soldiers look like they're getting ready to plant charges and blow the hatch."

"Are they in space suits? Does it seem like they're bluffing?"

"No and no."

By now, they had to know I was venting the bay. Maybe they thought they would get through the hatch before the pressure dropped low enough to kill them, but even if they did, I could just blow the outside blast door and they would all die. *Horribly.*

"Ying, is the flight controller talking?" I should be able to hear it over my com, but I asked just in case I'd somehow missed it.

"No, nothing."

I had two options: blow the outer door now and risk *Chaos*, Aoife, and myself, or wait until after they blew the hatch and risk killing everyone in the hallway. The second option would also cause all of the air from the corridor outside to vent directly past Aoife and *Chaos*. And if the main airlock between this arm and the station failed, the whole station could collapse.

"I'm blowing the landing bay door now. Aoife, hold on. Ying, be prepared for the pressure change."

Both murmured their agreement. I twisted open the detonator covers and flipped the switches before I could second-guess myself, then grabbed on to the metal cage. A series of small *pops* seemed to last forever, then the door creaked and banged open on rusty hinges.

Normally the door slid open and closed, but with no power, trying to manually slide open a door was a sure way to end up in space. But station designers had built in an emergency hinge so the door could be explosively separated from the track and swing open in an emergency without becoming a several-thousand-kilogram projectile that could hit the rest of the station.

Unfortunately, the lockout that was supposed to lock the door in the open position failed and after swinging all the way open and then rebounding back, the door ended up half-closed.

At least the rest of us fared better. *Chaos* had shivered as the air rushed out of the landing bay, but Aoife and I were far enough away from the door that we were okay. However, that wouldn't remain true for Aoife if the soldiers outside blew the hatch. The flow of air from the corridor would sweep her out the landing bay door. "Aoife, get to the ship. I'll get the door because I'm closer."

I sprinted for the landing bay door without waiting to see if she would argue. Standing on the edge of a station, staring into empty space was always a trip. I knew as soon as I left the landing bay, I'd leave the artificial gravity, so it was impossible to fall—if I stepped out the door, I would gently drift until I used the maneuvering thrusters to return. But mere knowing didn't reassure my lizard brain. It insisted I was *IN DANGER*.

And sadly for my lizard brain, I was going to have to go out there because in here there wasn't a good angle from which to push the door. I'd have to rely on my maneuvering thrusters to provide the force to open the door. I did not have time to panic, no matter how much I wanted to.

I clipped an emergency autotether onto my belt, pulled out a few meters of line, and stepped into space. The transition from gravity to weightlessness always fucked with my head as my inner ear tried to figure out what the hell I was doing.

The partially opened blast door slowly drifted into reach. It had plenty of handholds, so I pulled myself out until I was at the very edge. The farther away from the hinge, the easier the massive door would be to move. I tightened my grip. "Artemis," I said, addressing the suit by nickname so it wouldn't transmit the command over the com, "move forward at five percent." The suit chimed its acceptance of the command and I felt the thrusters come on, barely moving me.

I wanted to slam the door open, hop into my ship, and get the hell out of here, but this was one instance where patience truly was rewarded. If I moved too quickly, the door would just bounce closed again—and smash me in the process.

"Cat, you need to get inside, now," Alex said, his voice somehow both calm and urgent.

"I'm almost there."

"You've got incoming. The door is open enough. *Chaos*'s hull shielding can take the hit to nudge it out of the way."

I looked out over my right shoulder and saw a space troop transport approaching. It was basically an open shuttle that carried the soldiers in space suits to their destination. Because it wasn't pressurized, or even enclosed, the soldiers didn't have to wait on an airlock. They also wore specially designed, armored combat suits made to fight in a vacuum.

My space suit was nice, but it wasn't space-combat nice.

I activated my reverse thrusters for a split second and let go of the door. Once I was clear, I jerked the tether twice.

It should've activated the return reel. Instead, the first pull caused me to drift toward the landing bay, but the second pull caused the tether to go slack in my hand.

A moment later, the end of the tether drifted past.

The goddamned *emergency tether* had broken and left me drifting in open space.

CHAPTER TWENTY

Panic pushed my heart rate sky high. My stomach soured, and even with the temperature regulation in the suit, sweat broke out across my forehead. Drifting in open space was one of my fears. I'd moderated my strength just so this exact thing wouldn't happen, though the tether should've been unbreakable even at full strength.

"Cat, what's going on?" Alex asked. "Your vitals are all over the board."

The smooth baritone of his voice broke me from the panic. I wasn't in open space, not really, I was a handful of meters from a landing bay and my ship, in a suit with full maneuvering capability. I detached the worthless tether from my belt and tossed it toward the approaching transport. The thrusters in my suit automatically corrected for the slight spin I'd caused with the throw.

"The tether broke, but I'm okay," I said. "Artemis, return to *Chaos*." The suit automatically located the ship and activated the thrusters to guide me back into the landing bay. The heads-up display calculated my travel time as thirty seconds.

I asked the suit to show what was behind me, and a small

video from the camera on the back of my helmet came up in the bottom of the display. The transport was closing in fast because it didn't have to be as careful about movement as I did with my tiny thrusters. I should clear the landing bay before they reached me, but it would be close.

I increased the power to the thrusters. The landing bay opening was a huge, impossible-to-miss target and I was already heading in the right direction. I didn't need to be quite so cautious.

The transition from gravity to zero-g was trippy, but the transition back was a good way to end up face-first on the deck. My suit had recognized the presence of the field and had positioned me upright, but even knowing it was coming, the loss of weightlessness caused me to stumble a few steps and nearly fall.

I shook my head, as if I could shake off the dizziness, and staggered toward *Chaos*. Aoife, who should already have been in the ship, appeared at my side and helped me along. And by helped, I mean dragged.

"Do you want me to attack the transport?" Ying asked.

"Not unless you have to. Open the airlock door and lower the ramp, then take off as soon as we're inside. If they don't get out of the way, that's their problem."

Aoife and I climbed the short, steep airlock ramp and sealed the door behind us. I used the control panel to retract the ramp and felt the engines engage as Ying piloted *Chaos* out of the landing bay. I trusted Ying—or I never would've given her control of my ship—but I was desperate to be back in the captain's chair.

Finally, the airlock cycled us through into the pressurized interior of the ship. I stripped off my helmet and ran for the flight deck. The rest of my suit would have to wait.

We were nearly out of the landing bay and the troop carrier had fallen back to just outside the door. Alex sat at the second station, watching the console. Ying ceded her place at the captain's console and I slid into the seat. There were no other ships in sensor range that could pose a threat.

I looked at the three other people on deck with me. "This is your last chance to bail. I did not get any help, but I will be jumping to Earth as soon as we're clear of the station."

Cira was still in the medbay, but Alex, Aoife, and Ying all nodded their agreement. We were really going to do this. It was either my best idea ever, or my worst, and only time would tell.

We cleared the station and the space around us remained empty. If the station had any ships capable of stopping us, they weren't using them. Maybe the Syndicate wasn't paying them enough to take on a fully armed and armored House ship.

Chaos needed another half an hour before our next jump, so I plotted a course toward vacant space and brought the ship into full stealth. Luck hadn't been on my side lately, but it owed me a quiet thirty minutes without any new surprises.

I took a deep breath and tried to let go of some of the adrenaline that had been riding me hard all morning. I acknowledged just how much I hated being outside in space with nothing but a space suit to protect me. I liked taking risks, but *calculated* ones, and open space had too many variables that I couldn't control.

But I'd done it, and I was safe.

Ying had a pair of my pants cinched around her waist and rolled at the hem. That reminded me. "Ying, I bought you some clothes, but I don't remember what happened to them. Alex did they make it onboard?"

"I dropped the bag in the mess hall."

I dipped my head in gratitude. "We have thirty minutes until our next jump. Everyone should use it to get ready because we'll all need to be clipped in for the jump and subsequent sprint to Earth. The compensators can only do so much and I expect I'll have to surpass their capability before all is said and done."

Ying left the flight deck to change and ensure that Cira was clipped in to either the diagnostic table or a seat, depending on her injury. Aoife left to change out of her space suit. I needed to do the same, but I enjoyed a moment of peace and quiet. They would be few and far between for the next couple of days.

"Are you truly okay?" Alex asked quietly.

"Yeah, but I'm nervous and second-guessing myself. Just because I'm convinced that this is the right plan doesn't mean that it *is*. I wish I could talk to my siblings. Ada is the tactician. Bianca is the information specialist. Hannah is the diplomat, and Benedict is the soldier. Ferdinand is the best of all of us. I'm none of those things, but I'm the only one who can get to Earth right now, so it falls to me."

"You're giving yourself too little credit. I've seen you do all of those things in the past few days."

I snorted. "Just because I *can* do them doesn't mean I can do them *well*."

"You found the information you were looking for, evaded an attack, escaped, came up with a plan, and persuaded your allies to go along with you, all despite fierce resistance."

"Doesn't mean it will work," I grumbled. I wasn't sure why I was so hung up on this, but after a lifetime of trying—and failing—to measure up to my siblings, it was a sensitive topic.

"Of course it doesn't mean it will work. That's why plans evolve. And you know it. You're just arguing for the sake of arguing. But you won't change my mind. You can hide all you want, but I've seen you, and you're amazing."

Trust Alex to drop perhaps the single nicest thing anyone had ever said about me into our conversation like it was no big deal. I blinked at him in astonishment.

His slow smile did all sorts of interesting things to me. "I wouldn't recklessly invade a planet with nothing but five people and a tiny ship for just anyone, you know. You can do it. And you know it."

He was right. I might not be a tactician or a diplomat or a soldier, but I had determination and a knack for succeeding against all odds. I gave him a sharp nod. "I'll make it work."

"And we'll help you."

I grinned. "They won't know what hit them."

AFTER CHANGING OUT OF MY SPACE SUIT, I RETURNED to the flight deck. I'd kept my blasters belted around my waist. We should have time to prep once we were on Earth, but being a little prepared now didn't cost me anything.

Alex had gotten up to pace, but neither Aoife nor Ying had returned yet. We had fifteen minutes until we could jump again and nerves kept me on my feet. I leaned against the wall and watched Alex stalk back and forth across the small flight deck.

He paused and focused on me. "Walk me through the plan."

"Earth is protected by an orbital array as well as ground-based laser and blast cannons. Serenity has additional protections, but we're not aiming for the city, at least not at first. We'll be most vulnerable while entering the atmosphere, so we'll come in fast over whichever pole is closer." At his inquiring look, I added, "Fewer cannons cover the poles."

"If we're not heading for the city, where are we heading?"

"House von Hasenberg has several supply caches hidden around the planet. Supplies will be our first objective. If we're caught entering the atmosphere, then we'll lose some of the element of surprise, but surprise won't help if we don't have enough weapons."

"What will you do if you find that the attackers are rebels and people are celebrating the fall of your House?"

I shrugged. "Join the celebration."

Alex arched a skeptical eyebrow. "You'd give up your power so easily?"

"I'm the youngest of six children. My 'power' is to marry for the good of the House, whether I want to or not. Right now, Father wants to marry me off to a man old enough to be my grandfather. Hannah's husband is a traitor, Bianca's marriage nearly killed her, and Ada ran away to avoid the same fate."

"Why stay at all?"

It was a question I'd asked myself for years. My fortune was secure; I could disappear and leave the mess for someone else to fix. And I'd been tempted—so tempted—but the easiest way to implement changes was from the inside. "Optimism and loyalty, not to my House, but to my siblings. I don't want to worry them. And we are changing things for the better, but it's a slow process. A powerful name helps."

"Everyone in power thinks they're doing what's best and nothing ever changes," Alex said bitterly.

He wasn't wrong. I'd had many long conversations with Ferdinand about exactly that point. Ferdinand was the most like Father of any of us because he'd borne the brunt of Father's lessons. But, even as a child, Ferdinand had decided to follow a different path. He'd protected Hannah, and together they'd protected the twins, until it all snowballed down to everyone protecting me. It might be suffocating at times, but I'd never once doubted that I was loved.

And I'd never doubted Ferdinand's drive to make changes that benefited everyone, not just House von Hasenberg.

"Father is an asshole, but I believe in my brother. I'm going to Earth for him, and for the billions of people who will suffer even more if the Syndicate takes over. The Consortium might be full of arrogant, self-indulgent assholes right now, but at least there are *some* checks and balances. A Silva dictatorship will be worse. But if we get there and things are not what I expected, I'll reevaluate. And you are free to bail whenever you like."

Alex stalked toward me, so mesmerizing that I almost missed his words. "You're always trying to get rid of me. How has that worked out for you so far?"

He stopped close enough that I could reach out and touch him. He loomed, even without trying, and his broad shoulders blocked out the room.

I rolled my eyes at him, but couldn't quite meet his gaze. "I'm giving you options. You know I desperately need your help."

"Then why do you keep trying to get me to leave?"

"Because I don't want you to risk your life out of obligation to Bianca!" I closed my eyes and collected myself before I revealed something I'd rather not.

I'd already skated dangerously close to a truth that was as stupid as it was selfish: I wanted him to do it for *me*. Not because I was Bianca's sister or the daughter of a High House or someone who could help him in the future, but just because I was a person he found worthy of his help.

Alex touched my jaw, a feather-light caress that I thought I imagined until I opened my eyes and saw how close he was.

"I'm not here for Bianca," he murmured. "So stop trying to get rid of me. You're going to give me a complex."

That pulled a reluctant grin from me. "Well, I wouldn't want that." I met his eyes, so he could see both the sincerity and everything I was unwilling to say aloud. "Thank you."

He dipped his head and my breath caught. He moved slowly, giving me time to retreat, but I was perfectly happy where I was. When his lips finally covered mine, I felt like I'd been waiting an eternity.

Then it took no time at all for desire to blaze.

His lips were warm and firm and I wanted to taste them forever. I wrapped a hand around the back of his neck and tugged him closer. When that wasn't enough, I wrapped a leg around his hip.

Clever man that he was, he knew exactly what I was doing. I felt him smile against my mouth, then he cupped my ass and lifted me so I could wrap my other leg around him. I clamped my lower body to his, and he groaned deeply. It vibrated through me, sending pleasurable tingles racing along my nerves.

I was determined to make that happen again.

Thanks to my strength, I didn't need him to hold me up, which meant his hands were free to roam—and roam they did. After another squeeze of my ass, they slipped under the hem of my shirt and caressed the skin of my low back, before slowly moving north.

I tentatively tested our balance by rocking against him once, twice. He was rock solid—in more ways than one.

Assured that I wouldn't hurt him, I set a quick rhythm. Squeeze my legs to lift a few centimeters, release to slide back down.

"*Fuck*," Alex hissed out. He'd spread his legs and thrown his head back. The thick bulge I could feel through both sets of clothes told me just how much he was enjoying this. He pressed exactly where I needed him, and my whole focus became driving us to release.

I was close, *so close*, when *Chaos* chimed a five-minute warning. I snarled at the universe, and Alex cursed. I was trying to decide if I had time to finish anyway when the flight deck door slid open. "Ha!" Ying exclaimed. "I knew it! Don't let me distract you; I'll be in the mess!" The door slid closed.

I banged my head against Alex's muscled shoulder. Unfulfilled desire pulsed through me, hot and insistent, but already the adrenaline from earlier was rising, spiking my anxiety levels.

"Sorry," I murmured, unlatching my legs.

"Next time, I'm locking the fucking door," he growled. He slowly withdrew his arms, his reluctance clear. I knew exactly how he felt.

I grinned ruefully. "Deal."

We both took a moment to rearrange our clothes and let our bodies settle. By the time we were done, Alex's expression was grim, and I knew my own matched it as I started mentally running through possible scenarios. I would have one shot at getting us on the ground safely.

I could not screw it up.

The console showed a countdown as well as our current flight plan when I slid into the captain's chair. Alex took the secondary console where he could control the navigation and tactical systems—if I gave him access. "Can you handle the ship's offense?" I asked.

"Yes. Aoife and I are both fully qualified pilots."

"Okay, you're in charge of the guns. I'm going to attempt to slip through unseen because we don't have enough firepower to take out the orbital array or the ground cannons. However, if another ship starts firing on us, the guns are yours. Don't get us in a fight with the RCDF."

His eyes crinkled at the corners as he smiled. "No promises."

I sent Ying a message and she returned just before the one-minute warning. She had changed into the clothes I'd bought for her. Her wide grin was completely unrepentant. She slid into a seat along the wall and clipped in. "Cira is secured but unhappy about being stuck in the medbay."

"As long as she's secure." I hit the button for the ship's intercom. "Aoife, you have ninety seconds to either get to the flight deck or secure yourself in your quarters."

"I'm on my way," she responded.

I checked our flight plan again. We were set to jump to *Chaos*'s emergency jump point, which at cruising speed was about an hour from Earth. I planned to jump fully stealthed and stay that way for the entire trip. Earth's defenses were designed to concentrate fire on targets within twenty minutes of the planet, so we should be well outside their range, but there was no reason to risk it.

Once we got close, I would take over manually and fly us on a somewhat meandering path to the closest pole. The goal was to look like an organic piece of space debris rather than a ship. *Chaos* was designed to be invisible to both radar and lidar. And full stealth shut down all transmissions, including the automatic positioning messages that ships used to avoid collisions. We would be completely dark and silent.

Aoife arrived on deck thirty seconds before the jump. She clipped into the seat next to Ying.

The time ticked down in agonizing increments. It reached zero and the engine noise changed as the FTL drive ramped up. It was time to do or die.

I just hoped it wasn't die.

CHAPTER TWENTY-ONE

The jump went smoothly. The emergency jump point proved good and we didn't end up inside the moon or another ship, so we were off to a stellar start. Now I just had to get us to Earth.

I plotted a sweeping course to the North Pole, which was marginally closer to our current position. It also had the benefit of being dark, which wouldn't protect us from the sensors, but would at least shield us from normal human vision.

"If everything goes well, we'll be on the ground in sixty-three minutes," I said. "I'm not picking up any other ships or signals, but I've got us in deep stealth, so that's not unexpected."

"Can you tell if the gate is up?" Ying asked.

I brought up a list of the raw messages *Chaos* had received passively. There was a lot of noise coming from Earth, but I didn't see any of the usual gate transmissions. "I don't see anything, but I can't tell for sure, not without potentially giving us away. I'll ping it once we're on the ground. I am seeing a lot of other message traffic, mostly encrypted."

The next forty minutes passed with tense silence and

sparse conversation. With just another twenty minutes to go, we were now within prime range of the orbital array. I'd already shut down the engines and we coasted silently toward Earth. I'd have to fire them up again to slow us down before we slammed into the atmosphere, but I'd wait until the last second because the heat signature would give us away.

In full stealth, *Chaos* wasn't using any active sensors, so we could only find other ships visually or if they were transmitting positioning data. So far we hadn't found anything, but that also wasn't too unexpected.

I'd already closed the window shutters in preparation for landing, but the transparent video screens that covered the windows were transmitting the video from outside the ship. Earth loomed large in front of us. The pole was dark but bright sunlight limned the horizon, turning it blue and gold.

And just beyond the horizon, sunlight glinted off metal. I brought the forward video feed up on my console and zoomed in to maximum magnification.

I blew out a slow, quiet breath. The question of Silva's involvement was now definitively answered because at least one of their giant battle cruisers was in orbit around Earth. I put the image up on the main screen.

"Is that a Syndicate ship? Can they see us?" Aoife asked.

"That is definitely a Silva ship, but we're in the planet's shadow and not emitting any light. We should be hidden for now. Once I fire the engines they may be able to sense us."

"How long until then?"

"Five minutes. Then it's fifteen minutes to the ground."

"Are we landing at the Pole?" Ying asked.

"No, we're just getting close enough to lose the ground cannons, then we're headed for a supply cache."

"There's a second ship," Ying said. "You can just see the

bow peeking out on the left. The Syndicate ship isn't one of our designs, but the second ship is."

I squinted at the image. The second ship was even farther away. Ship identification had been part of my training, but a part that I'd hated and avoided whenever possible. I could recognize whole ships with decent accuracy, but I was hopeless at piecemeal identification. I supposed the bow did look like it could be vaguely Yamado, but I had no idea what kind of ship it was attached to.

"It's a House Yamado battle cruiser. Is that a red stripe?" Ying leaned forward as if that would help her see.

With the angle, distance, and sunlight, I couldn't see well enough to know if the ship was painted red or not. Ying apparently agreed with me, because she shook her head. "I can't tell."

Top-tier House Yamado ships were painted to show their allegiance to both the House and their captain. The overall House colors were yellow and red, but each family member had a personal color, as well. Ying's was azure, which I knew because many of her clothes also incorporated the color.

And, as the heir, I was pretty sure Hitoshi's color was red.

"Was Hitoshi's battle cruiser scheduled to be here?"

"No. *Vermillion* should be on a routine patrol of the outer rim. And Hitoshi would rather destroy the ship than surrender it." Her voice was flat and cautious.

I tried to keep my own tone level and not accusatory. "You know I have to ask: is there any chance that he's working with Silva?"

"I don't know. My gut says no. Hitoshi is cunning and ambitious, but he's too smart to get tied up with the Syndicate." Then she quietly added, "I hope."

"Are any of House Yamado's battle cruisers unaccounted for? Do you sell that type of ship to third parties?"

"None of our ships are missing, but we do sell battle cruisers to the RCDF. Other than that, no."

"Damn."

We all watched the two ships until they disappeared behind the planet. I checked the other views, but nothing else was visible.

I waited as long as I could before I brought *Chaos*'s engine up to full reverse thrust. Almost immediately alarms started going off. After a brief debate, I brought up the shields. It was another possible target point, but if we were hit without a shield, we'd be toast.

"The orbital targeting system is taking an interest in us," Alex warned.

We didn't have a lot of room to maneuver, and too many adjustments right now would just alert the system that we were definitely a ship and not space debris. I kept us on the same course. In another five minutes we'd be low enough to be past most of the orbiting cannons, but we'd still have to avoid the ground defenses.

Usually, the orbital defense system didn't act without human intervention. Once the system was confident an object was a potential threat, it would alert the operators and they would approve or deny an attack. But if they'd changed it to emergency lockdown, then automation took over and the system operated without supervision. That would be worse for us, because rather than waiting for human approval, which took some time, the automated system would try to eliminate us on its own.

A couple of minutes later, *Chaos* blared a short, sharp warning. I flexed my hands on the manual controls but didn't alter our course.

"Cat—" Alex started.

"I see it. The defense system is locked on our heat signature, not the ship. We're still going too fast to shut down the engines, but if we deviate from our course, we'll be fired on immediately."

"You're playing chicken with a computer."

"The autopilot would've taken evasive action as soon as a lock was detected. The defense system doesn't have enough confidence to determine if we're a ship or not, so it's testing us."

"What happens when it decides?"

"It'll start shooting."

If we were very lucky, the system would assume we'd burned up in the atmosphere and not send the battle cruisers after us. Although they could land, they were unwieldy in the air and usually only landed for emergencies, but their real threat was the air wing they usually had onboard. *Chaos* was good, but she couldn't outgun a flock of fighters.

We were out of range of the orbital cannons and low enough to be in the atmosphere. I'd just begun to cautiously hope that we would make it to the ground undetected when *Chaos* repeated the target lock warning and followed it with a solid tone.

I jerked the controls hard to port and felt the pull on my restraints as the compensators failed to counteract the force of the turn. The first cannon blast skimmed by our starboard side. "They know we're here. Get the decoy and jammer drones in the air," I barked at Alex.

The console showed me the approximate location of the cannon that had fired on us. It was far off to starboard. At our current rate of descent, we would be under its firing zone in approximately twenty seconds. I dodged starboard as another blast just grazed the outside of our shields.

It was going to be a long twenty seconds.

"Where are my decoys?" I demanded.

"They're out, but the system is ignoring them."

"Jam their tracking. I need another fifteen seconds."

The heat of reentry now exceeded the heat produced by the engines. There was no hiding from the thermal imagining, but the jammers would at least make it more difficult to target the ship itself.

I flew us on a jerky path that put the restraints to the test. I heard something crash from the direction of the mess hall, and the ship complained with a litany of new warnings about exceeding force tolerances. That would be a problem for future me, assuming we made it to the ground in one piece.

The next blast glanced off the shield, setting off a new round of warnings. The defense system was getting better as we slowed down. I pushed us as fast as I dared and we plummeted toward the surface.

In the dark, I had only the ship's systems to guide me. We dropped out of the firing zone and I ramped up the engines to slow our descent. My console glowed with a dozen warnings ranging from informational to major.

But we were in one piece.

I brought *Chaos* far enough out of stealth to scan our surroundings and check for communications. The sky was clear of other ships but the surface was being buffeted by strong winds and ice. I kept our heading the same. I would dip into the top of the storm to lose any drones sent to track us, then head south toward the nearest supply cache.

"How much damage did we take?" Ying asked.

I looked over the various warnings. "Not too much, considering. The ship is still spaceworthy, but the hull shielding took quite a bit of heat from our entry and needs to be replaced. As long as we don't plan to land hot on another planet with atmosphere, we're good."

My com pinged as I received a batch of new messages. Hopefully that meant that someone in House von Hasenberg was still alive and fighting, but I would have to wait until we were on the ground to check.

Ying's com pinged and a second later her breath caught, but I didn't have time to ask her about it. "Two drones inbound," Alex warned at the same time the ship chirped an alert.

"Don't engage unless I can't lose them in the storm."

The ship bucked as we dropped into the heart of the blizzard. Between the darkness and the whiteout, I was flying completely blind with only the instrument readings to guide me. I edged closer to the ground.

"First drone pulled off," Alex reported.

I banked away from our plotted course to keep us in the storm. I needed that other drone gone, but it proved damned persistent. "Shoot it down," I said.

Alex acknowledged me with a grunt, his hands already flying over his console. I heard the lock tone, then a second later the blip chasing us disappeared.

One final sweeping circle didn't draw out the second drone, so I dropped *Chaos* back into full stealth and headed for the supply cache.

CHAOS SLID UNDER THE NATURAL ROCKY OVERHANG AND disappeared from the sight of anyone looking for us from above. And based on the number of drones I'd had to dodge, someone was actively searching for us. Sadly, my trip through the storm hadn't fooled them into thinking we'd crashed.

The ship settled to the ground with a gentle bump and I breathed out a sigh of relief. We'd made it. For better or worse, we were on Earth.

"That was exciting," Ying said with false cheer, "but let's not do it again anytime soon, okay?"

"Works for me," I agreed. It would take me a month to use up all the adrenaline I'd produced in the last twelve hours. I turned to look at her. Deep lines bracketed her mouth, but when I met her eyes, she barely shook her head. Whatever it was, she didn't want to talk about it in front of the others.

I pulled out my com. "I'm going to check my messages before we head out. If you need to do anything to get ready, now is the time. I'll meet you in the cargo bay in ten."

The others nodded and pulled out their own devices. I skimmed the messages I'd received. The destruction was even worse than what had been reported in the initial messages. House Yamado's ballroom was obliterated. House Rockhurst and House von Hasenberg had also suffered attacks on their buildings. All three appeared to have weathered the attacks well enough to remain mostly standing, but Bianca's apartment was a smoldering ruin.

Someone knew exactly where to find all of the High House heirs, but didn't have insider information about whether or not the heirs were home at the time of the attacks, so they were taking a scorched-earth approach.

Both of my parents had been at the gala. There were no status updates on either of them, but the House network had blown up with messages. With Albrecht and Maria both out of the picture and everyone else, including Ian, off-planet, Marta Stevens, the deputy director of House security had taken over. I'd worked with her on the initial investigation into Ferdinand's disappearance and I liked her quite well. She'd ordered everyone into the stronghold and was sending small teams out to search for survivors.

I couldn't risk sending her a message yet, but I would once we were closer to Serenity. If anything had happened to Father and Mother, I would be the default person in charge of the House until communication to Ferdinand was restored.

I really, really did not want to be in charge of our House, even for a short time.

From Marta's messages, both Anne Rockhurst and Ren Yamado had attended the gala. There were no mentions of any of the heirs, but all three High Councillors were currently unaccounted for. They were all presumed injured, possibly dead.

The news caused a riot of emotions. My feelings for my parents were complicated—at best—but they were still my parents. I felt a certain amount of filial loyalty that could be classified as love, I supposed, though it paled in comparison to the love I felt for my siblings.

On one hand, I would be sad if Mother and Father were dead, but on the other, I would be profoundly relieved, which made me feel guilty. But Ferdinand would never force me to marry someone I couldn't stand, no matter how badly the House needed the alliance. Perhaps I was just being selfish. Mother would certainly think so.

I put away my com. Alex, Aoife, and Ying were all staring at their devices with grim expressions. Apparently they weren't getting good news, either.

"Mother and Father are missing," I said. "Our deputy director of security is in charge of the House right now. I didn't see anything about the RCDF forces on the ground, but we can assume that at best they are scattered, at worst lost."

"How many troops does the RCDF keep on Earth?" Aoife asked.

"Generally, a battalion is stationed on the surface to police Serenity and defend the command center, but the majority of

Earth's defensive forces are in ships. At least four battle cruisers patrol the solar system at all times, each with two battalions of ground troops and a similarly sized air wing. As far as I know, all four battle cruisers were lost in the initial attacks."

Those ships each had over four thousand troops onboard. Losing one was a tragedy; losing four was unfathomable.

I continued, "In addition, each House employs a number of private security personnel. I know we have over a hundred people on our security staff. Probably two-thirds of them are ex-military or field-trained."

"Will they fight for you?"

I shook my head. "I don't know."

"They will," Ying said. "Your bodyguards adore you because you care about them. You can ask Cira if you don't believe me." She caught my skeptical look and asked, "When is Susan's birthday?"

"February fifth."

"And what did you get her this year?"

"A necklace that I saw her admiring while we were out shopping, plus dinner and theater tickets for her and her husband."

"A *sapphire* necklace and box seats to her favorite sold-out show," Ying corrected. "She was the envy of the Serenity security forces for a month. Everyone wants to work with you because you remember their birthdays, ask about their kids, and treat them like family. They'll fight for you."

Aoife nodded in agreement, but I still wasn't convinced. A necklace wasn't the same as risking one's life. Susan and I spent a lot of time together. Taking care of her was less about my charm offensive and more about being a decent human. And I knew for a fact that Ying knew Cira's birthday, too, so I was hardly unique.

I slid out of the captain's console and rose to my feet. "Ying, would you mind helping me for a second?" When she stood, I waved to Alex and Aoife. "I'll meet you in the cargo bay in five minutes." It wasn't subtle, but I didn't have time to be subtle.

Ying followed me to my quarters. Once the door closed, her shoulders slumped and her face crumpled. "Father is dead," she whispered.

I pulled her into a hug. Her breath hitched and she buried her head against my shoulder. I squeezed her tight. "I'm so sorry."

She slowly pulled herself together and stepped back, wiping away her tears. "Mother is alive, but Tae's status is still unknown. Hitoshi wasn't at the event. He survived, and he wasted no time taking over the House. Father's body isn't even in the ground yet." Her voice had a bitter bite.

"Was Tae at the gala?"

"It's unclear." She sighed. "What about your family?"

"Mother and Father both attended, and they are both still unaccounted for."

Ying squeezed my arm. "I'm sorry." When I nodded, she asked, "Have you heard anything about House Rockhurst?"

"I heard Anne attended, but that's it."

"Me, too."

We stood for a moment, just letting the enormity of what had happened sink in. No matter what happened now, the universe was forever changed. It could be an improvement, or it could be the start of something far worse. Only time would tell.

"Let's load up on guns and get moving. The faster we get the defenses down, the faster we can get some backup."

Ying went to update Cira, and I headed for the cargo bay. Both Alex and Aoife had donned lightweight ballistic armor and sported high-powered rifles.

"Where's your armor?" Alex asked, concern in his voice.

"I'm getting there." Much like in my quarters, the cargo bay had a hidden armory panel in the wall. I swiped my identity chip over a seemingly random spot and the door popped open. I pulled out a pair of rifles and two sets of the same type of lightweight armor that Alex and Aoife wore. Because it was sized for me, it would be a little big on Ying, but the fit shouldn't be too bad.

Alex helped me put my armor on, and when Ying arrived, Aoife helped her into the second set. I didn't think we'd need it, but with drones in the air it was a smart precaution. I slung my rifle over my shoulder and put on a pair of smart glasses. They connected to my com and gave me heads-up directions to the bunker.

We left *Chaos* and ventured into the prickly winter forest, dappled with morning sunlight. The air had a frosty bite and I wished I'd grabbed a cloak with a temperature regulator to keep me warm.

Trees towered over our heads, bare limbs providing some cover from the sky. Leaves crunched underfoot and the underbrush was thick and healthy. Looking at it now, it was hard to imagine that Earth had ever been in such bad shape that humans had abandoned it completely, but it had taken the Consortium decades to terraform it back into a habitable state.

Old photos from before the terraforming showed dry, bare dirt and small, sickly plants. Now, centuries later, it was as rich and alive as the ancient paintings had made it seem. The Consortium had made the entire planet a natural park and being out here with nothing around, it was easy to see why.

Animals had been reintroduced as well, but black bears were the largest predator common to this area and they mostly left humans alone. They should also be hibernating now. None of the other small animals posed a threat. As long as whoever had taken over Serenity hadn't been able to track our flight path, we should be safe.

And even if they had tracked us, drones would be useless here. They would have to send ground troops and that took time. If we were lucky, we'd be gone before the first ship arrived.

With a cautious glance at the sky, I led us deeper into the forest.

CHAPTER TWENTY-TWO

T hick underbrush full of thorny plants scraped across my armor. Supply cache locations were secret and the bunkers themselves were hidden, so there was not a clean path to follow. The bunker was only five hundred meters from the ship in a straight line, but we ended up walking nearly double that because of the steep ravines and underbrush.

This particular bunker was set into the side of a hill. The door was under a small overhang and obscured by camouflage netting and natural plants. Even knowing it was there, my eyes would've skipped over it without the helpful icon from my smart glasses.

I swiped my chip over the reader and also input a six-digit code. The door unlocked and I pulled it open with cold fingers. Our entrance would not be reported to House von Hasenberg. If I had used the alternate code, it would appear to work exactly the same, but it would send a silent emergency request back to the House—useful in case someone was forced to open the door against their will.

The lights came on, revealing the first of five rooms. All

of our bunkers were laid out similarly, and all von Hasenberg family members regularly trained on simulations to ensure we'd know exactly what to do in an emergency. When time mattered, you didn't want to get lost in your own damn bunker.

We were standing in the main supply room. It spanned the entire width of the bunker and was filled with cabinets and shelves. A short hallway in the middle of the back wall led to a mess hall, bathroom, and war room on the left, and a large bunk room on the right. Each bunker could comfortably support up to fifty people and could be pushed to support twice that if necessary.

Ying looked around with interest. This was likely the first time she'd personally seen the inside of a von Hasenberg supply cache. She caught me watching her and grinned. "I'll keep it to myself, cross my heart—even the parts our spies got wrong." Her exaggerated wink made me chuckle. She continued, "Our caches are similar, except you enter in a hallway that runs the whole length of the bunker. It means fewer people can hold it against attack."

"It also makes it easier for someone to prop the door open and shoot anyone trying to escape. Like fish in a barrel."

Ying waved me off. "That's why we have the *secret exit*, of course."

I pretended to write in an imaginary notebook. "Note to self . . ." We both grinned at the ridiculousness and then broke into laughter. It was good to remember how to laugh even when things were terrible.

Looking around, I realized I probably should've made a list of high-priority items. "We'll have to limit what we take to what we can carry because I don't think the sleds will make it through the brush. We can each wear a suit of powered combat armor, but we'll have to carry a spare for Cira. I'd rather not make two trips if we can avoid it, so let's get moving. Feel free to dig through anything in here."

Ying and Aoife headed off to look for supplies, but Alex stuck close to me. Once we were alone, he murmured, "Have you been trained to fight at full strength? Do you know what you are capable of?" When I slanted a sharp glance at him, he held up his hands. "Whatever you tell me goes no further. I swear it."

Alex was incredibly observant. He'd noticed I could see in the dark, and when I'd attacked him, he had to have noticed how hard I hit. By answering his questions I wasn't really giving him anything he hadn't already guessed—or so I told myself. "Briefly. And I mostly know my limits thanks to my own experiments."

He ran a hand down his face. "They really didn't tell you what they did to you?"

I dodged the question by asking one of my own. "Were you sick as a child, too?"

He cursed under his breath. "Were you sick before or after the treatment?"

"Before." I'd been sick for as long as I could remember. The treatment had cured me.

A furious look crossed his face before he smoothed it away. "Were you weak, tired all the time, and in constant pain?"

I couldn't stop the shock from showing on my face, which was answer enough. I didn't like where this was going. The list hit close to home, but there were many illnesses that had those symptoms; it didn't mean anything. I brought the conversation back to the relevant point. "It's been a while, but I know how to fight if I have to."

Alex looked like he wanted to argue, but instead he nodded curtly. "Aoife is going to keep an eye on Ying until Cira is healed, so you're stuck with me."

"I think you mean that you're stuck with me. Try to keep up." I smiled to take any unintentional sting out of the words.

He leaned in, expression intent. "I like being stuck with you."

I flushed and wished once again that we'd met in different circumstances. If only Bianca had introduced us sooner, we could've gone on a date like a normal couple instead of racing across the universe, hunted by a crime syndicate.

I could've peeled him out of that tight shirt and mapped his abs. With my lips.

I jerked my gaze away from his chest and back to the supplies surrounding us. Now was not the time, no matter how much I wished it was. I cleared my throat. "We should find the armor first, then decide how much we can carry and what we might need."

"What kind of supplies do you have in here?"

"A bit of everything. Weapons, armor, and packaged food and water in case the synthesizers go down. It's a space designed to hole up or resupply a platoon well enough to take back whatever was taken. We have heavy weapons and explosives in addition to the standard blasters and blast rifles. Armorwise, there should be a dozen or more suits of powered combat armor."

"Artillery?"

"Only portable mortars and lightweight rocketry. Maybe a drone or two. Everything had to break down small enough to fit through the door. We have a few larger caches, but they're closer to Serenity, and we're more likely to get caught if we try to get to one."

"We'll make do. Let's see the combat armor."

Powered combat armor protected better than the ballistic armor I currently had on, but not as well as a fully mechanized combat suit. It was a lightweight compromise, powered enough to assist with moving the armor's extra weight, but not nearly as much as mechanized suits, which made soldiers superhumanly strong.

Alex and I each picked armor in the closest generic size, but generic armor didn't fit nearly as well as the custom armor I'd left in House von Hasenberg's armory. In the future, assuming I survived this little expedition, I would get another suit made and store it on *Chaos*.

After trying it on to ensure I'd chosen the size correctly, I stripped off the pieces and carefully arranged them together off to the side. Beside me, Alex did the same.

"Do you heal faster than normal?" he asked quietly.

I blinked at the unexpected question and automatically deflected. "Of course. I have the best nanos money can buy, and they are renewed every year."

He turned to me with a frown. "You know what I mean."

Desire was easy, but trust was so, so difficult. If I kept handing him pieces of me, he would have enough to destroy me completely. I met his eyes. "I have exceptional natural healing," I said. "Must be my excellent von Hasenberg genes."

He didn't need a map to read between the lines. "Good."

When he didn't press further, I nodded and led him deeper into the shelves. "Is there anything in particular you would like, besides artillery?"

"Explosives," he said immediately.

The shelves were not labeled, and while the organization followed a pattern, it wasn't one easy to discern if you didn't already know it. So when I found Ying and Aoife digging through crates of explosives, I raised an eyebrow. "How lucky that you found the explosives so quickly," I commented drily.

Ying grinned and mimed locking her lips closed. Having a

best friend who was also a member of a rival High House was an interesting experience sometimes. Never mind that I could do exactly the same thing in any House Yamado supply cache.

We sorted through the supplies and filled two crates with grenades, rockets, and malleable blocks of explosives. By the time we were done, we had enough explosive power to level a small civilian complex—or put a sizable dent in a military building.

Ying and Aoife went to get their armor situated while Alex and I continued hunting for supplies. Sadly, we didn't find any prototype shields, one of the things I'd been hoping to obtain. My cuff would have to be it, but it only protected me and one extra person if they were standing very close.

Alex and I filled two more crates with weapons and electronics, then picked up a small drone. With Cira's armor, we'd each be hauling back two full crates. It wouldn't exactly be pleasant, but we should be able to make it in one trip.

I was tempted to grab more, but *Chaos*'s cargo hold was tiny. Six crates—plus the one I'd taken to Andromeda—would fill it up. And if we couldn't succeed with the supplies in these crates, then more supplies weren't really going to help.

Alex and I stacked everything by the entry door, then went to put on our armor. Both Ying and Aoife were already suited up. The smallest armor fit Ying reasonably well. Aoife was in the medium armor and her extra height made the fit a little better than mine.

We suited up and headed out. Ying got the two lightest crates because she was the smallest—and as far as I knew, she didn't have any extra strength. I tried to pass Aoife one of my lighter crates, but she just laughed at me and hoisted both of hers with no apparent effort.

Alex had rigged up a harness and strapped a crate to his

back, so he was the only person with a free hand for a weapon. We all had rifles slung across our backs, but it would take a few seconds to drop our burdens and swing them around. Having someone who could provide covering fire for those seconds was a good idea—one should always hope for the best and plan for the worst.

I'd stowed my smart glasses because the helmet's display worked the same way. We left the bunker and I followed the directions on my display. I'd left *Chaos* in a passive monitoring mode, but with instructions to contact me if any vehicles were detected within fifty kilometers. Cira had also been given a com and instructions to contact us if anything went wrong. Neither of those things had happened, but the forest felt different from inside combat armor.

I moved a little faster.

The return to the ship was uneventful, which only served to make me *more* anxious. We stowed the crates and stripped off our armor in silence. I wasn't the only one feeling uneasy.

"Flight time to the backup command center is about four hours because we'll have to stay low and slow to remain off the sensors and out of cannon range. Eat, sleep, read, do whatever. I'll let you know when we're about an hour out."

Ying nodded. She knew where we were headed. "I'm going to talk to Cira, see if she wants to move out of the medbay."

"Let me know if you need help."

"Thanks. I'll see how she feels," Ying said as she left.

Aoife looked at Alex and then sighed dramatically. "I suppose since you're busy, I'll go offer my services as a pack mule in case Cira's leg is still bothering her." She pinned me with a hard stare. "Let me know if anything changes during our flight."

"I will." After she left, I turned to Alex. "And you? What are you busy doing?"

His slow grin was all heat and temptation. "Being stuck with you."

"I have to fly the ship." If I sounded disappointed, one could hardly blame me.

Alex stalked closer, his presence intense and focused. He leaned in until his cheek brushed mine and whispered in my ear, "I'm happy to watch."

His low voice stroked over my skin and I shivered. The searing desire that I'd been trying to ignore came roaring back. I took a shaky breath and held on to my control by the slenderest of threads. I wanted nothing more than to bury my hand in his hair, lick into his mouth, and spend the next four hours exploring his body.

But duty called.

"I have to get us in the air." He started to pull back, but I wrapped a hand around his upper arm, lightly holding him in place, and tipped my head up to whisper, "Then we'll see what happens." I pressed a fleeting kiss to his lips, then ducked away and beat a hasty retreat to the flight deck.

In another decade or two I might cool off enough so that I wouldn't spontaneously combust.

Maybe.

ALEX DIDN'T JOIN ME ON THE FLIGHT DECK UNTIL *CHAOS* was already in the air. When he appeared, I checked our course and kept an eye out for any other ships or drones in the vicinity, despite the fact that the ship was already doing the same thing.

He slid into the second console and spun the chair around until he faced me. I glanced at him out of the corner of my eye. He sprawled in the chair, a picture of lazy confidence, but heat lurked in his eyes, in the slight curve of his mouth.

I did not mind eyes on me, and indeed, my whole persona

was designed to draw attention, but none of them had made me as restless as Alex's quiet gaze. I fought the urge to squirm, to pace, to go over there and finish what we'd started.

There was no way I could stand four hours of this—there was not enough meditation in the 'verse.

Alex stood and offered me a hand. "You look like you're about to jump out of your skin. Let's burn off some energy."

I slid my hand into his, but froze when I processed the second sentence. I met his gaze with wide eyes. Had he just propositioned me?

He pulled me to my feet and chuckled, a delicious rumble that I wanted to feel pressed against me. "Not *that* way. I thought we'd try some training. Have you ever fought anyone as fast as you?"

I glanced away uneasily. It was one thing to obliquely acknowledge that I was different, but another thing entirely to prove it true. I'd been keeping this secret for so long that I wasn't sure I *could* share it. If I could have, I would have shared it with my siblings ages ago.

Alex touched my arm, pulling my attention back to him. "You are safe with me. I'll never force you to do something you don't want. What would you like to do instead? I play a mean game of rummy."

That pulled a reluctant grin from me. "I'll have you know I'm the family rummy champion three years running."

"Really?"

I laughed. "No, not really. But I do play a decent game of poker. None of my siblings expects the innocent baby of the family to lie and cheat like a fiend, even though they're the ones who taught me how."

Alex shook his head sadly. "Rookie move, giving away your strategy like that. Now I know to watch your hands."

I met his eyes. "If you weren't sick as a child, how did you end up like me?"

"I volunteered," he said quietly, old pain in his voice. "I can't tell you more than that."

I knew about keeping secrets to protect others, so I didn't press, even though I was desperately curious. That knowledge was enough to make me ask, "Will you pull your punches?"

"If you will. You hit like a freighter."

"And you won't tell anyone?"

"No, I won't tell anyone. Not even if you turn purple and sprout five antennae."

I was too anxious to do more than huff out a half-laugh. And that anxiety ramped up higher when Alex stepped back and dropped into a ready stance. The flight deck didn't have a lot of extra room, but if we tried to go anywhere else, I'd lose my nerve for sure.

I moved away from the captain's console and mirrored Alex's stance, except I kept my hands open. Alex nodded and uncurled his fists. I'd learned that even pulled punches could hurt. Taps were less likely to cause damage.

Alex watched me but didn't move. He expected me to attack first. I darted in, not as fast as I could, to tap him on his right arm. Before I could connect, he dodged, fast, and tapped *my* right arm.

He grinned at me and fell back into a ready stance. "You're going to have to do better than that, princess."

I feinted right then came in left. He blocked both blows, but rather than falling back, I pressed forward. I was moving faster, but still not at full speed.

Alex blocked two blows with one arm and used the other to cover a yawn. "Wake me up when you decide to try."

"Baiting me isn't going to work. I'm the youngest of six. I've heard it all."

"If you say so, princess."

The term sounded more like an endearment than antagonism. Still, if he wanted a challenge, I'd give him a challenge. Without any warning, I sped up. I landed two taps before he caught up. "Awake now?"

"I'm getting there." He dodged and deflected two more quick hits. "Damn, you are fast."

"I'm getting there," I parroted with a smile. But Alex was no slouch, either. I'd never fought anyone who could keep up with my speed and I hadn't realized just how much I'd been holding back. It was exhilarating to push myself and find him always there, dodging and blocking. I had to actually work to land hits.

I laughed with the pure joy of it.

And then he changed the game and went on the offensive. He landed a trio of quick taps before I danced out of reach. I'd never defended myself against someone who was as fast as me.

Not only as fast as me, but also better trained than me.

I'd had self-defense tutors, but I'd been sick when I was young. Everyone took it easy on me, and my siblings were quick to rush to my defense and help me on the sly. I'd only passed my training trials because of their help.

Then everything had changed right before I'd turned thirteen. I was suddenly strong, and fast, and healthy, and it was *amazing*. I threw myself into training, fighting harder, practicing longer. I'd felt unstoppable. I could still picture Father's face, glowing with pride, when I'd snapped my training partner's arm.

I faltered in remembered horror, and Alex dropped back with a concerned look.

I refocused and tried to forget the *snap* of breaking bone that haunted my memory. I put Alex on the defensive with a flurry of quick taps. I'd spent so long learning to be slow, and careful, and gentle that it almost felt like a betrayal to use my full speed and strength.

After I'd decided that I wouldn't be Father's pet assassin, I'd been beaten bloody more times than I could count. A few times, only my extreme healing ability had saved my life. But I'd been stubborn even then. The harder Father had pressed, the weaker I'd gotten, until he'd finally given up in disgust.

Would I have chosen a different path if I'd known there were others like me? My siblings loved me, I knew that, but my secrets kept me isolated. Honestly, it was probably for the best that I hadn't known because I would've done almost anything to have a family of people who understood. And Father would have ruthlessly exploited that weakness.

Alex broke through my guard and proved once again exactly how lacking my training had been. It usually wasn't a problem, because I was faster than anyone I fought.

Except Alex.

And he was used to fighting a fast sparring partner, which begged the question: who? Aoife was a skilled shot, but she hadn't shown any other signs that she might be more than she appeared to be. Was she hiding, too?

Alex tapped me again, a light touch on my hip accompanied by a grin. "Am I boring you?"

"You've trained against someone fast. Are there more people like us?"

His face showed his conflict and he pulled back. I stopped attacking and waited. Finally, he shook his head. "I can't tell you." He met my eyes solidly, as if willing me to understand.

And I did.

He wasn't telling me no, which was as good as a yes. There were more of us! I couldn't help the smile that lit up my face. I wanted to interrogate him, but I sealed my lips against the questions. I could respect someone keeping a secret for others. Alex relaxed and nodded, very slightly.

I dropped back into a ready stance. "What am I doing wrong and how do I fix it?"

Alex spent the next hour correcting my stances and offering advice for how to be more effective at hand-to-hand combat. He showed me how to use my speed and strength against someone like him and against the normal opponents I would usually face. I learned more in an hour than I had in years of training.

I was hot and sweaty and incredibly grateful. "Thank you."

"You're welcome. Would you like to grab some lunch?"

My stomach rumbled, not for the first time, and I grinned, then gestured for him to precede me out of the flight deck. "My stomach agrees with that plan. Lead the way."

CHAPTER TWENTY-THREE

The workout and the meal left me feeling pleasantly sated, but with almost two hours to go until landing, I knew it wouldn't last. Ying and Aoife had brought Cira up to the mess hall. Cira's leg was healing, but she wouldn't be storming the command center with us, something she deeply resented.

I shot Ying a sympathetic look then beat a hasty retreat. Her narrowed eyes promised revenge, but there was no way I was getting in the middle of an argument between her and her bodyguard.

Even I wasn't that stupid.

I headed to the flight deck alone. Alex had disappeared, and I missed his comforting presence. In the short time I'd known him, I'd gotten used to having him around.

People tended to float in and out of my life without leaving much of an impression, but I would miss Alex when he was gone. When all of this was over, I would pester Bianca to give him my contact info, to see if he was interested in more. I would open myself up to an older sister inquisition, but it would be worth it.

I was daydreaming of what a date with Alex might look

like when *Chaos* chimed an alarm. A drone had just appeared at the edge of sensor range, but it was on an intercept course. *Chaos* was already correcting to avoid contact, so I watched to see if the drone would also alter course.

It did.

Damn.

I clipped in, then hit the intercom. "Prepare for potential evasive action. We've got a drone on our ass."

There were two options at this point: attempt to run and hide or blow it out of the sky before it got close. Both had drawbacks. Downing the drone would let everyone know that we'd survived the landing and they had enemies on the ground. But *Chaos* was stealthed, which meant the drone was tracking us by some external system. They already knew we were here.

Alex entered the flight deck and slid into the second console as if he belonged there. My heart twisted. It was exactly what I had envisioned when I'd left that console in *Chaos*'s design.

"They're tracking us somehow," I said, getting him up to speed. "We altered course and so did they. We need to down it before it gets close enough for a visual."

"I'm on it." His hands flew over the console, targeting the drone and making minute corrections to the generated coordinates. "Ready to fire on your mark."

"Fire."

Chaos trembled as the large blast cannon engaged. That would light us up on a bunch of ground sensors, so I edged us a little higher and faster. A second later, the drone fell off the sensor grid.

"Direct hit," Alex confirmed.

Now it was a race to see if I could get clear of the area before they scrambled a squadron of fighters after us. *Chaos* could take on a couple of small fighters, but I'd still rather avoid it if I could. And more than one or two would prove dicey.

"How are they tracking us?" Alex asked.

"I don't know. The ship is stealthed and only the passive scans are up. *Chaos* caught the drone because it was transmitting. We should be invisible."

"Can your com be tracked?"

"No. It has a tracker, but I disabled it before I left. Can yours or Aoife's?" He shook his head, so I hit the intercom button. "Ying, Cira, if either of your coms have trackers in them, disable them now. We're being tracked externally."

I heard cursing from down the hall. Ying poked her head in the flight deck. "Sorry, Cat. I didn't even think about it." Her expression tightened. "The tracker is tied directly to House Yamado, encrypted with our strongest encryption. It should be untraceable by anyone other than my family or our director of security. Someone must be looking for me, and now they know I'm on-planet."

"Any chance your House would've sent a friendly drone after you?"

Her mouth tightened. "Not without trying to contact me first."

So if it was Ying's com the attackers were tracking, then they had someone inside House Yamado. My thoughts returned to the looped surveillance video we'd gotten from the Yamado quarter when Ferdinand had disappeared. Had House Yamado not taken care of the traitor then? Or was something else on the ship leaking our location? Neither option was ideal.

"Do you have anything else that can be tracked?"

"No. My backup coms are powered down."

The speed boost had shaved half an hour off our flight

time, but we still had eighty minutes left if we didn't run into anything else. That was a big *if*.

I stayed clipped in and kept an eye on the sensors, watching for the tiniest blip, but despite my hypervigilance, nothing else appeared on the scan. That made me jumpier than if a squadron had attacked.

Someone knew Ying was on-planet. And based on the drone, that person wasn't friendly. All High House members were briefed on the location of the backup command center. If the traitor was high enough in House Yamado's security division, then they likely had been given the information, too, and it would be obvious where we were heading.

Twenty minutes out, I dropped our speed and altitude. We'd headed east, so the local time was well into evening, but it wasn't quite dark enough yet to provide complete visual cover.

Unlike the main command center, the backup location didn't look like a military installation at all. It was hidden underground in the middle of what had once been an ancient, sprawling city. I'd visited a few times. The buildings were long gone, mostly reduced to rubble, but a few stone and metal skeletons remained, hinting at walls.

Because the rubble made it difficult to land and no one wanted to draw attention to the location, the nearest landing point was two and a half kilometers from the base. It was also under surveillance by the command center itself, as was everything close, so we would need to find another spot.

I pulled up the satellite image of the site. The base itself was in a crumbled stone oval that had once been the heart of the city. To the west, a river snaked through the city's ruins. With no remaining bridges, crossing would be tricky.

The main landing point was south, so we needed to stay

north or east. I found a small clearing to the east that would work, but it was nearly five kilometers out.

I kept searching.

There was another option to the northeast, just a kilometer and a half from the base. The open area was small, just big enough for *Chaos*. I couldn't tell how uneven it was from the satellite view, but I didn't notice any large shadows that would indicate big piles of rubble. The site was closer than the main landing site, which meant someone must have decided that it wasn't acceptable for general-purpose ships.

If *Chaos* could land there, then it would save us a lot of time on the ground. But it was close to the main base, almost dangerously so, and it might be under surveillance.

Decisions, decisions.

I turned to Alex. "We have two options. The first is a location five kilometers out that probably won't be under surveillance. The second is one point five kilometers out, but it might be a honeypot, designed to lure in the unwary. Which do you choose?"

"How is the terrain?"

"Old city rubble. Rocky, uneven, and overgrown, but relatively flat."

Alex leaned back and stared at the ceiling. "What kind of defenses do they have?"

"Automated turrets and drones. My com has a beacon that will get us through, unless the rebels have taken the base and revoked my clearance, but it will also broadcast our location, so it's a trade-off. Normally, there is a platoon assigned, but once again, it depends on whether the rebels found the base."

"Wouldn't someone have already brought the gates back up if the RCDF still held the base?"

"Not necessarily. Without the proper authorization, they wouldn't be able to override the main base."

"Do you have the authorization?"

"I have Ferdinand's codes, yes. I wouldn't have come to Earth if I didn't think there was a good chance I could fix the gates."

Alex turned his head toward me. His posture remained relaxed, but his eyes were sharp. "I'm just thinking through the possibilities."

He went back to staring at the ceiling.

I altered course for the closer landing point. If we came in very low and very slow, we might avoid detection. Most sensors were pointed upward, looking for threats from high and fast. We'd come in just over the treetops, set down in that tiny clearing, and run like hell for the base.

I was in the middle of mentally running worst-case scenarios when Alex's voice pulled me from my thoughts. "If it were up to me, I'd pick the closer location."

"I agree. I already changed our course, but I would've let you persuade me the other way if you felt strongly."

He flashed me a grin. "I almost wish I'd picked the other option because I can be very persuasive."

I didn't doubt it for a second.

He sobered. "We should be ready to go when we hit dirt. We need to strike quickly and quietly."

"No combat armor?"

He shook his head. "Not for this, I don't think. The darkness will help cover us, and we need to move lightly. But we'll take all of the weapons and explosives we can each comfortably carry." He stood. "I'm going to go get the others ready. Call me if we run into trouble, otherwise, I'll meet you in the cargo bay."

I nodded my agreement and turned back to my console. I had to get us on the ground in one piece.

OUR APPROACH AND LANDING HAD BEEN EERILY UN-eventful. The backup command center hadn't tried to raise me on coms, but that could be because they hadn't detected us. Or they had, but they were staying quiet to prevent the Syndicate ships from finding them. Or it *was* the Syndicate troops, and they were waiting for us to walk into a trap. It was impossible to tell.

I again wished I could get my siblings' advice. Their love may have felt smothering at times, but it had also been a source of security and comfort. Now that I had to make all of the decisions—and live with all of the consequences—I was afraid I was going to screw it up.

Doubts tried to rise, but I ruthlessly suppressed them. *No.* I might not be as good as my older brothers and sisters, but I was still a von Hasenberg. I was smart and capable and strong as hell. I could do this.

Mini pep talk over, I activated *Chaos*'s ground defense. A ship using a ground defense system usually projected a visible red ring to indicate the area under protection. Since I didn't want to give away our position with a bright red light, I set it to dark mode, which didn't emit any light. If someone wandered into the protected zone, they wouldn't know until they got the audible warning.

If they ignored the warning, *Chaos* would fire on them.

In the cargo bay, Alex, Aoife, and Ying wore lightweight ballistic armor and bristled with weapons. Cira hobbled around with a makeshift crutch, checking Ying's gear and admonishing her to be careful.

I quickly strapped on my own armor, a blaster, a stun pistol, and a combat knife. I slung a blast rifle strap across my body so the rifle hung at my left side. I wore my shielding cuff, now recharged, but I would keep it inactive until I needed it. It was the latest von Hasenberg model that recharged faster and lasted longer, but I had a feeling I'd need every ounce of power before we were done.

"Do you know the entrances and do you have a beacon to get past the defenses?" I asked Ying. When she nodded, I continued, "What about the House Yamado override codes?"

She grimaced. "No."

I looked at her for a long moment. "Can I trust you with Ferdinand's code?" Ying was my best friend, but she was also the daughter of a rival House. I completely trusted her to look out for me, but my family was more of a gray area.

She tilted her head while she considered it. "Yes, but have him change it once everything is back to normal." She grinned. "I don't need the temptation."

I drew her aside and quietly repeated the sixteen-digit alphanumeric code until she had committed it to memory. It took a surprisingly short amount of time, but Ying had always had excellent recall.

When we joined the others, I said, "We should split up and hit two different entrances. If we both get in, then we'll meet in the control room. If not, whoever makes it should bring the gates up."

"I'll go with Ying," Aoife said. "We'll take whichever entrance you think will be more lightly guarded."

"North," Ying and I said at the same time. The northern entrance was in a crumbling, leaking tunnel. It was used more as an emergency exit than a true entrance, but it had a chip reader on the outside to allow entry.

I handed everyone, including Cira, a beacon for the ship's

ground defense and also a tiny earpiece and mic set to the same encrypted channel. Someone at the base might realize we were transmitting, but they shouldn't be able to eavesdrop on what was said.

"Alex and I will take the west entrance. It's a bit farther than the east entrance, but if they caught our landing, they might not expect it. Speed and stealth are paramount. And don't forget, this base could be held by loyal RCDF forces. Try not to kill anyone until we figure out who's in charge."

Everyone nodded.

"*Chaos*, make Cira Zapata a tactical officer," I requested. A chime indicated success. "Cira, you have access to the ship's weapons. Don't leave without a beacon. And keep my ship in one piece."

"I'll do my best." She slanted a sharp glance at Aoife. "Keep Lady Ying safe."

Aoife inclined her head. "Will do."

I looked at the outside temperature and added a hooded cloak over my armor. The dark color would blend into the night and the temperature regulator would provide heat. The others followed suit and then we left the safety of *Chaos* for the unknown.

I could see perfectly well in the dark, but I wore my smart glasses anyway. Not wearing them would've been odd, and I'd spent a lot of time and effort avoiding anything that made me seem odd. The display also showed me the best route to the western entrance, so they were useful for more than night vision.

The tiny clearing where I'd landed *Chaos* was surprisingly flat and level. The rest of our route was not. We split from Aoife and Ying and swept westward. Piles of stones and fragile, rusted metal spikes slowed our progress. Everything was overgrown with plants that had gone dormant for the winter, leaving bare branches and vines to snag our clothes.

A north wind teased the edge of my cloak and whistled through the rubble, making it impossible to hear if anyone followed us. An occasional low stone wall still stood, millennia later. Whoever had built this city had built it to endure.

Beside me, Alex froze in place. I did the same, scanning with my eyes to find what had caught his attention.

A tiny red light blinked on top of the next pile of rubble. "Turret," I murmured. Since it wasn't shooting at us, my security beacon appeared to be working. But we needed to move before that was no longer the case.

Ying's voice whispered across the com. "We're at the door. Entering."

We were still at least two minutes from our door, so we needed to pick up the pace. I wound through the rubble, picking the easiest path I could find and jogging when the ground was level enough to allow it without risking my ankles.

We came to a relatively flat piece of ground, overgrown but not filled with the remnants of old buildings. Ahead, a large pile of stone climbed higher than the surrounding rubble. Here and there, sections of stone walls with arched tops still stood, hinting at the architecture of the massive original structure.

The command center was located underground, hidden by all of the rubble.

I swept wide of the entrance, clearing an arc around it, but no one waited for us. If this was going to be an ambush, it would be inside. We hadn't heard anything from Ying and Aoife, but while their door was closer, they had a longer trek through the tunnels before they hit the main part of the base.

The door was shielded on three sides by strategically placed stone piles. I knew that it opened to a staircase that led down to the underground level. I paused in front of the chip reader disguised as a piece of rusting metal.

Alex, who had been trailing me, stepped up beside me. "Think it's a trap?"

My gut instincts were all over the place, but they all indicated something was weird. "Yes."

He looked at me. "I assume we're going in anyway?"

I grinned. "Of course. I didn't haul these guns all the way over here to turn back now." I sobered. "And Ying and Aoife are already inside."

"Aoife will keep her safe."

I swiped my chip over the reader. If the people inside didn't already know we were here, they did now. I pulled the heavy steel door open.

Alex keyed his mic. "Entering."

The lights in the stairwell were on, illuminating grated stairs leading down and nothing else. I took point since I'd been here before. I drew a stun pistol and eased inside, Alex at my back.

Another locked door waited at the bottom of the steps. I swiped my arm over the chip reader and it unlocked. I wondered how long it would take them to revoke my access. It would require someone high up in either the Consortium or the RCDF.

During the construction of the command center, the crews had found existing tunnels, so they'd incorporated them into the design. Then the base had been expanded several times. Now, it was a maze of hallways, small rooms, and dead ends that made for excellent cover, but the same was true for anyone defending it. We could walk past a squad and never know it because it was impossible to clear every room in the amount of time we had.

The walls were a hodgepodge of ancient stone and modern plastech. I'd brought a tiny camera on a flexible stem that could be bent around corners. The camera streamed video to my smart glasses. I eased it around the first corner, and the video showed an empty hallway.

We weren't exactly in the heart of the base, but I'd expected to encounter a few soldiers or base technicians even out here. Where was everyone?

I keyed the mic. We'd agreed to minimize communication, but I needed to know if the others were seeing the same thing. "Is your side empty?"

"So far," Aoife replied, her voice barely a whisper.

"Be prepared for heavy resistance at the control room," I warned.

"We are."

I led Alex through the maze of hallways, taking a more in-direct route toward the control room. If whoever was in charge planned to ambush us, I wasn't going to make it too easy for them.

"We're approaching the eastern door," Ying said. She, too, had taken a circuitous route.

"We'll be at the south door in sixty seconds."

"See you inside."

I mentally crossed my fingers and prayed for good luck.

The control room was the center of the base, both literally and figuratively. It could be accessed from any side, but each of the entrances consisted of two sets of locked doors, like an airlock. The inner door would not open until the outer door was closed and locked. It was the place we were most likely to be trapped, but we'd brought some surprises for anyone who tried.

I rounded the final corner, Alex on my heels. We had yet to see a single person. Ahead, the first set of double doors waited. I swiped my arm over the chip reader and held my breath.

The doors unlocked and I pulled the right one open, but didn't enter the small, bare chamber beyond. On the far side of the room, a smooth set of heavy sliding doors was set into a reinforced frame. There would be no prying them open and they didn't have any vulnerable hinges. We'd have to go straight through the thick metal with either a plasma cutter or explosives if they didn't open. A chip reader and an overhead light panel were the only other things visible.

This was definitely, definitely a trap. The question was, how bad?

I held the door open with my foot, then transferred my stun pistol to my weaker right hand and drew my blast pistol. I thought about using my rifle, but on the very slim chance that loyal troops were holding command, I needed to be able to stun rather than kill.

Static blasted through my earpiece, but I couldn't catch a single word. The sound cut off abruptly and I tried not to think about what that meant.

"Ready?" I asked Alex.

He nodded, his expression grim. "I will enter first. Find cover fast, then assess the situation. Watch out for Ying and Aoife because they may not be where you expect them, especially Aoife." He met my eyes for a long second. "If anything happens, I will come for you," he vowed.

"I'm not going down without a fight, and I have a shielding cuff. You should let me go first."

He shook his head. "If we provide separate targets, your cuff might be enough to get you to cover. In that case, I'm counting on *you* to rescue *me*."

"I will." I took a deep breath. "Let's do this." I activated my shielding cuff and it vibrated to indicate success. It was fully charged again, so it would protect me from up to eight shots, depending on the range.

Alex stepped through the doorway, and I followed. The room was small, a square roughly three meters per side. The door closed behind us and the bolt slammed home. Alex moved to the left and I swiped an arm over the chip reader on the right wall.

It took a lifetime—in reality, probably half a second—before the door hissed open. I had expected any number of things, but what I *hadn't* expected was to be met with a wall of stun rounds from a line of a dozen soldiers wearing RCDF uniforms.

My cuff vibrated constantly, so I couldn't count the number of shots it deflected, but I managed to take down two soldiers with stun rounds before the shield failed and the first round hit. My armor wasn't designed to deflect stun rounds and lightning arced through my veins.

Fiery pain blossomed bright, but thanks to my unusual physiology, I didn't immediately go down. I bit back the scream that wanted to escape and jerked my arm up, not quite in control. I got off two more shots: one hit, one miss.

Beside me, Alex staggered and dropped to his knees. The soldiers had concentrated their fire on him, and without a shield, he must've taken at least a half dozen rounds. The fact that he was still in control enough to kneel was a testament to his strength.

I dove toward the line of soldiers, a last-ditch attempt to break their line.

It didn't work.

I got a dozen stun rounds for my trouble and the scream I'd been holding back broke free in a grating cry. I slumped to the ground, down, but not out. My muscles were currently outside my control, but I recovered far faster than the soldiers would expect.

Unfortunately, I didn't get to find out.

Two soldiers pinned my shoulders and legs, while a third cuffed my hands behind my back. She couldn't figure out how to remove my shielding cuff, so she added the handcuff below it, tight enough that it dug into my wrist bone. I heard Alex grunt and assumed he, too, was being cuffed, but I couldn't quite get my neck to work long enough to check.

Someone patted me down and removed all of my weapons, my com, and my cloak. They didn't take my smart glasses, possibly because they were styled to look like lightweight vision correction glasses. "Lockdown lima one," I whispered slowly, forcing the words out one at a time. The code wiped away all of my personal data and locked the com in a mode that made it appear dead. The power button wouldn't do anything.

It also turned the com into a microphone that would broadcast audio directly to my glasses as long as we were in range or on the same network, including Earth's satellite array. I could only hope they took it with them when they met up with whoever was in charge.

I used the glasses' eye tracking to mute the audio. It used bone conduction, so no one else should be able to hear it, but better to be safe. I might risk it if someone left with the com, but while we were in the same room, I didn't need the audio. I could hear just fine, even if I still had trouble moving.

Two people picked me up by my arms and dragged me into the middle of the room. They dropped me and my left cheek slammed into the ground. I held back a groan as pain stabbed up into my skull. That was going to leave a mark.

Alex landed next to me with a muffled curse.

"We've got them," a female voice said. She paused, then said, "Understood."

Control slowly returned. I glanced around as much as I could without moving my head, which wasn't much, but I didn't see Ying or Aoife. I did, however, recognize at least two of the people standing guard. They were stationed here, not Syndicate troops wearing RCDF uniforms.

None of them looked at us.

There were also plenty of soldiers wearing plain black fatigues mixed with a few officers in green and red Syndicate uniforms. They were keeping a close eye on the RCDF troops. These weren't trusted traitors, then, but perhaps troops pressed into service under threat.

At least I hoped that was the case.

A few minutes later, one of the inner doors hissed open. It was behind me, so I couldn't see who entered, but Alex growled out another curse.

"Our guests have arrived at last," a male voice said. He didn't have any discernible accent, nothing to give away who it might be. He continued, "High Councillor Yamado will be pleased."

"Ren Yamado is alive?" I asked, surprised.

"No, my dear. That old bastard is dead. High House Yamado now belongs to Ying Yamado. And you let her lead you straight into a trap."

CHAPTER TWENTY-FOUR

Shock and surprise stole my thoughts for a moment, but I *knew* Ying. Yes, she wanted to lead her house. Yes, she hated her oldest brother Hitoshi with a fiery passion, and she would've happily stepped on him on her way to the top, but she loved her Father and she loved her older brother Tae.

She was not responsible.

Doubt tried to slither through, but I pushed it away. Maybe I was naive—many people certainly thought so—but I wasn't going to believe a stranger over my best friend until I had definitive proof.

But that didn't mean I wouldn't play along. Perhaps I could learn something interesting before I escaped. I let icy hauteur slip into my voice. "Where is Lady Ying? I have some choice words for her."

"She was injured in the scuffle with her guard. She is recuperating in the medbay."

The best liars made lies sound like truth, and this man was a very, very good liar. He seemed to know who I was, but the other soldiers in the room might not. It was a thin hope, but it was all I had. "I am Catarina von Hasenberg, daughter of High

House von Hasenberg. With my parents missing and siblings out of communication, I speak for House von Hasenberg. Release us at once."

A moment of silence passed before the man laughed. "You've got your share of arrogance, I'll give you that, but your name means nothing now. Your siblings aren't out of communication—they're dead. House von Hasenberg is no more. Well, it won't be, once we dispose of you."

My breath caught as terror for my siblings sliced through me. He couldn't be right, could he? We were a hardy lot, and even I didn't know where Ferdinand was. Did we have another traitor so high up that they knew Ferdinand's location? Did someone get the drop on all of us?

I shoved the pain down. If I believed the man would lie about Ying, then I also had to believe he would lie about my siblings. I had a lot riding on hope today.

"And what is your role in all of this?" I asked. "Who are you? How did you manage to turn an entire base traitor?"

"Did I forget to introduce myself? Daniel de Silva, at your service." He said it in such a way that I imagined he made a flourishing bow.

That explained the lack of an accent. Most of the Silva family members had the same distinct, lilting accent. But people who rose far enough in the Syndicate hierarchy were adopted into the extended family with the name de Silva—literally "of Silva." The Silva family wanted them to remember exactly where their success came from.

They were a lot like the Consortium that way.

"As for the soldiers, they were all too happy to join me, as is everyone who joins the Syndicate," Daniel said. He moved closer and I got my first look at him. He was in his late twenties or early thirties, with olive skin and dark, wavy hair. He actually looked a lot like the rest of the Silva family. Perhaps he was a distant relation.

"And General Momola?" I asked. "I don't hear her. Was she happy to join you?"

"Regrettably, she had too much stubborn pride to see the benefits of joining us. She and a few others made very compelling examples, though, and the rest wisely decided to enlist in the Syndicate's private army."

An uncomfortable murmur ran through the room as people shifted on their feet. No matter what Daniel said, not everyone was happy to be working for him, but the desire to stay alive was a strong one. I didn't blame them, but I regretted the loss of Lana Momola. She had been genuinely kind and had cared for her troops. I hoped her end had been quick.

Manipulating people was simple: figure out what they wanted and give it to them. Nearly everyone wanted something, even if it wasn't a conscious desire. The real trick was knowing when someone was a lost cause.

Just from our few minutes of conversation, I knew Daniel de Silva was a lost cause. He was a true believer and nothing I could offer him would ever compare to being part of the Silva family, no matter how distant, so I didn't waste my breath trying.

"Take our guests to the brig to await transport," Daniel said. "I want a pair of guards posted on them at all times. We wouldn't want any unfortunate mishaps. The High Councillor has plans for them."

Though I had most of the feeling back in my body, I stayed completely limp as a soldier tried to pick me up. It took two of them to manage it because lifting dead weight was difficult, and I was heavier than I looked.

A shoulder dug into my belly and I had to fight to remain

limp. I wanted to claw and kick and fight, but that wouldn't get me anything except stunned again. I had to pick my battles and this wasn't it. Not quite yet.

Apparently Alex either shared my sentiment or was still down from the stun rounds, because I didn't hear any sounds of a struggle.

The brig was close to the control room. We passed through the two sets of doors, then down a short hall and around the corner. There was only a single cell, designed to hold up to four.

The soldiers dumped us to the ground with zero care. My landing was moderately milder this time, since I had enough control to at least keep my face from smashing into the hard floor, but before I could do more than tense to roll to my feet, someone hit me with a stun stick.

Stun rounds stung, but stun sticks packed a wallop. I grunted and ground my teeth as my muscles spasmed out of control. If I hadn't already been on the floor, I would've been now.

I lost a few seconds. By the time I came back to myself, the soldiers were laughing outside and the cell door was locked tight. I blinked and forced my eyes to work. The cell walls were thick, clear plastech overlaid with blue energy barriers. Attacks would be dispersed by the barriers before touching the physical wall. There was a bare toilet, a tiny sink, and a single bunk bed, bolted down and without either mattress.

Beside me, Alex shifted closer. "Are you okay?" he whispered into my ear.

"Peachy," I muttered. Once again I'd failed. I should be used to it by now, but this time I'd managed to take down Alex, Aoife, and Ying in the process.

"If you're well enough to be sarcastic, then you're fine."

"I've been better."

"Wallow later. We have to figure out how to escape before the transport gets here, and we don't know how long that's going to be."

"I can multitask," I said grumpily. "I'm already working on it."

"Is Ying a traitor?" he asked, his voice flat.

"No."

"Are you sure?"

I hesitated. Was I? Or was I being intentionally blind? Ying was smart and cunning. She absolutely *could* have set up a complicated betrayal without anyone being any the wiser.

But she hadn't. It was a certainty that I couldn't shake, no matter the doubts that assailed me. "I'm sure."

"Okay," he said. "I'm going to break my cuffs and see how the guards react. If they open the door or drop the field, we're golden."

I was so stunned by his easy acceptance of my word, that I almost missed the part about him breaking the cuffs. "You can *do* that?" I asked. I knew he was strong, but these cuffs were solid metal. I could pick my way out, probably, but I'd never tried breaking them. I turned so I could see him, to see if he was joking.

His grin was a touch smug and a lot tender. "Yes, and so can you. It takes a sharp, fast movement, and you can't hold back. It hurts like a sonofabitch, but your wrists will survive. It's better to practice with plastech cuffs, to get the movement right, but you can do it with metal first if you have to. Watch me."

He rolled to his feet in a fluid movement. The guards stopped talking. "You . . . you shouldn't be up yet," one of them stammered. Neither of them wore RCDF uniforms. Were these soldiers de Silva had brought with him?

"But I am," Alex said. He moved his wrists as close together as he could, then his muscles flexed and he jerked his arms apart. The link between the cuffs snapped like it was made of paper instead of metal.

"What the hell?" the second guard asked. "How did he do that?"

"I don't know, man," the first guard said. He backed up a step. "Should we get de Silva?"

"Are you kidding? No." He eyed Alex. "He's loose, but he can't get past the barrier. We'll let one of the RCDF bastards fetch him when it's time."

Alex broke the locks on the metal cuffs like it was nothing, then casually peeled them off his wrists while the guards watched with open mouths. I'd thought we were the same, but now I wasn't so sure. I was strong, but I wasn't *that* strong.

I rolled to my feet and Alex steadied me when the blood rushed out of my head and left me dizzy. My road to badassdom was clearly off to an excellent start.

Alex moved behind me and loosely encircled my cuffed wrists with his hands. He murmured into my ear, his voice whisper soft, "Pull, hard and fast, as explosive as you can. The link has a weakness, but you need a lot of force in a small amount of time. On three." He didn't give me any more time to prepare, just started counting.

On three, I tensed and jerked my arms apart. Or I would have, if the cuffs had broken. Which they did not.

"Try again," Alex encouraged me. "If you don't get it this time, I'll do it for you."

I took a deep breath and focused. Alex wouldn't falsely raise my hopes, I knew that, so he really thought I could do this. All I had to do was prove him right.

I'd spent years and years learning to moderate my strength, to hold back, to be slow and soft and gentle. To pass as normal.

Unlearning that wouldn't happen overnight, and I didn't want it to. I liked my freedom, thank you very much. But for right now, I tried to peel back the layers, to find my true strength.

I moved my wrists together, as Alex had done, to give myself that extra millimeter of room, then jerked my arms apart, putting all of my strength and will into the movement.

The link between the cuffs snapped like a twig and Alex caught my arms before they flew up at the unexpected freedom and gave away the fact that I'd broken my own cuffs.

"Told you," Alex murmured, a smile in his voice.

"Now they're both free," the first guard said, fear in his voice. "Are you sure de Silva doesn't need to know?"

"Do you enjoy being alive?" the second guard asked. "Because taking bad news to de Silva is a good way *not* to be." They continued to argue in low voices.

I couldn't settle on a single emotion. Happiness and awe and disbelief warred for dominance. I *was* a badass. I turned around and threw my arms around Alex. "Thank you."

He squeezed me. "That was all you, princess. I just gave you a nudge."

"I had no idea," I said.

"I know." His voice was gruff with disapproval, but I didn't feel like it was directed at me. "Let me see the cuffs."

I held up my wrist and he pulled the first cuff apart, quietly explaining where to grip and how to do it. He did the second one, too, because it would've been difficult to hide the fact that I did it myself, but he made me talk him through it, to make sure I understood. He gently touched my wrist where the metal had dug into my skin.

"Why are you helping me?" I asked softly.

He looked up from my bruised wrists. "I like knowing

you're able to take care of yourself, and that I helped you realize you could. I like *you*, Cat."

That wasn't the answer I was expecting, so I looked away and deflected. "I hope you ask Bianca for hazard pay after this."

Alex touched my jaw to draw my gaze back to him. "Our deal with Bianca was done as soon as we left House James. It could've been done even earlier if you'd turned out to be an arrogant asshole. Aoife and I are both here because we like and respect you, Cat, not because of Bianca. There's no love lost between me and the Consortium." He grimaced in distaste. "But even they are better than the Syndicate."

"Thanks," I said drily. The weight of the last few hours pressed on me, and I blinked. "Though there may not be much Consortium left after this."

Alex squeezed my shoulders. "I'm sorry, that was thoughtless of me."

I shook my head and tucked my worries away. I would deal with them later, preferably once we were out of this cell. To that end, I broke away from Alex and looked around. I didn't know about any obvious vulnerabilities or weak points, but if there was one, I would find it.

I looked at the guards, who were still arguing about getting backup. "Would one of you be so kind as to open the door?"

They looked at me with identical looks of narrow-eyed suspicion. "No. You are a prisoner," the first one said. He was fair, blond, and young, maybe still in his late teens. The second soldier was older, midthirties, with ruddy cheeks, red hair, and a neatly trimmed beard.

"No, I'm the daughter of a High House, and you are committing treason. Let us out and I'll forget your part in this little charade."

"That's not happening, girlie, so keep your mouth shut," the older soldier said. "You have no power here."

"Maybe, maybe not, but I do have *excellent* visual recall. When I escape—and I will—I'll make sure you two are the most famous traitors in the 'verse and let the Consortium tear you apart. Or you could let us out and we'll peacefully go our separate ways. We'll even give you a lift, if you would rather not be Silva shills any longer."

The younger soldier was on the fence, but the older one was having none of it. "Don't make me come in there."

I smiled and waved an arm in invitation. "By all means."

Unfortunately, he was smarter than that and didn't open the door or lower the energy field. I'd tried. Time for Plan B. I pressed a fingertip to the energy field next to the door. Blue should be safe for touch, and indeed, it didn't shock me.

I pressed as hard as I could, but I couldn't feel the plastech wall just a millimeter away. Energy barriers didn't work well against small, sharp, *fast* projectiles. If I could fashion some sort of spike, I could drive it through the barrier into the wall underneath. Of course, that wouldn't help *me* escape, but I wasn't going to escape without some lateral thinking anyway.

"Keep messing with that and I will turn on deterrent mode," the older soldier said. "Then we'll see how much fun you have trying to escape."

If he changed the setting to deterrent, the barriers would go red and shock anyone who touched them. It would make escaping less fun. It would make being in the cell in general less fun because there would be nothing other than the bed frame to lean against.

I held up my hands in a gesture of peace. "Just remember I gave you a chance, and you didn't take it."

Before he could respond, a grizzled RCDF soldier in his

early fifties stepped into the brig. He had deep brown skin and dark hair sprinkled with gray. Clayton August did not look at me, but he was one of the soldiers I'd recognized—he was Lady Pippa August's uncle, and she adored him.

House August didn't have the clout to influence the RCDF, so I'd called in a couple of favors to get Clayton a month's leave when Pippa had her baby. Hopefully he would still get to enjoy it once everything was said and done.

He addressed the two Silva soldiers. "Your boss wants to know why you haven't reported in yet."

"We did," the younger soldier said.

Clayton shrugged. "I just know what I was told. I'm here to relieve one of you while you report."

The older, red-haired soldier tapped his earpiece but apparently couldn't get a signal out. He turned to his younger companion. "Go report and come straight back. And remember, not a peep about any trouble." He cast a significant glance at Alex and me.

The younger soldier nodded and left. Clayton replaced him, leaning against the wall next to the remaining Silva soldier. "Had trouble, did you?"

"It's no concern of yours."

"Just making conversation, pal. Don't get so worked up."

The Silva soldier sneered, then turned back to watch us. Clayton leaned against the wall like a lazy statue, occasionally scratching his nose or rubbing his arm. Movements, but nonthreatening ones. Slowly, the Silva soldier forgot about him and relaxed.

It was beautiful to watch, but I just hoped it meant help was incoming because Clayton still refused to meet my eyes. I kept moving around the cell, probing at various places, keeping the Silva soldier's attention on me.

Then, with a speed I wouldn't have believed him capable of, Clayton caught the other man by the head from behind, covered his mouth, and drove a knife into his neck, killing him quickly and quietly, albeit in a bloody mess.

Before he'd been stationed here at what was considered a very cushy post, Clayton had been part of the RCDF special forces for over two decades. It was common for extended members of House families to do a military tour, but most chose the officer route. Clayton had not, and he'd reenlisted long after his peers had moved on to private enterprise.

"Lady Catarina, are you all right?" he asked. He disabled the energy field and opened the cell.

I made my escape as soon as the door opened. I didn't think this was a trap, but even if it was, I had a better shot out of the cell than in it. Alex followed me and kept a wary eye on Clayton.

"Yes, thank you, Lord Clayton. Why are you still here?"

He grunted and waved me off, as he always did when I used his honorary title. I smiled. At least some things never changed. I quickly introduced him and Alex.

After nodding a greeting at Alex, Clayton turned back to me. "I thought I might be able to do some good once their backs were turned. Looks like I was right. Plus, there aren't exactly a plethora of ships flying out and I didn't relish months in the bush again."

"What about the other RCDF soldiers?"

"They killed General Momola, as I'm sure you heard. I don't know about the rest. We were questioned individually. For me, they threatened Pippa and her baby if I stepped out of line, but I know the House will look after her. Not everyone is so lucky."

"How many troops does de Silva have?"

"At least a platoon. Somehow they got in without setting off any of the alarms, and they attacked before we heard about the attacks on Serenity. General Momola tried to hold the control room, but we were outgunned."

"Where are they? We didn't see anyone when we came in."

"Half are around central command, the other half are patrolling the outer edges of the base, ensuring no one makes a break for it. They were all ordered into hiding when you entered. You probably walked right by them."

There was no way we could take on a platoon, even with surprise on our side. I'd figured that if the base had fallen, they would leave a squad or two behind to secure it. I'd led us into a trap we would be lucky to escape.

"Do you know where they are holding Ying and Aoife, the two who came in before us?"

Clayton nodded. "They are next door in the general's office. If Lady Ying is colluding with them, then they're treating her poorly. She was stunned and cuffed same as the other."

Relief overwhelmed me. It was *possible* that they'd treated Ying like an enemy so I would continue to trust her, but I didn't think so. They didn't expect us to escape.

"How many guards?" Alex asked. "And how are they being held?"

"Because they're not in cells, there are four guards. They are cuffed, same as you." Clayton glanced at our free arms for the first time. "How did you convince them to remove the cuffs?"

I shrugged. "They dumped us in the cell, hit us with a stunstick, and removed the cuffs. Mentioned something about sending in 'the RCDF bastards' to capture us again."

Clayton growled something under his breath I couldn't quite catch.

"What's the best way out of here?"

"Back through the door the other two came in," Clayton

said. "The north entrance is the least used and the one we're closest to."

"What do we have for weapons?" Alex asked.

"Not a lot. I have a knife, plus whatever this guy had." Clayton jerked his thumb at the dead guard on the ground.

I quickly searched the body and came up with a blast pistol and another knife. I kept the pistol and handed the knife to Alex. It was not a lot to take out four armed soldiers.

"We need to grab Ying and Aoife, then make tracks for the exit. I can listen in on the control room, if my com is still there. Let me check." I unmuted the sound, but only heard indistinct murmurs. "I can't hear anything right now, but I'll keep listening."

"Let's move," Alex said. "We need to get out before they realize we're free."

Clayton nodded and silently led us out of the brig.

CHAPTER TWENTY-FIVE

In the hallway, Clayton turned left and jogged a few meters to the first door. We were so close to the control room that I expected soldiers to pour out any second.

Clayton caught the direction of my gaze. "We looped the video, but it won't hold for long. How do you want to do this?"

Alex swapped his knife for my gun and turned to Clayton. "You distract them, I'll shoot them, and Cat will clean up the rest."

"I'm not great with a blade," I murmured. "Perhaps I should shoot and you should clean up."

Alex grinned. "You'll do fine. Just remember: the pointy end goes in the enemy."

I looked at him with wide eyes. "Oh, so *that's* what I've been doing wrong."

Clayton barked out a laugh. We stacked single file against the wall outside the door and Clayton swiped his chip over the reader. The door opened and Alex dashed inside, the two of us on his heels.

The office was quiet and appeared empty. Two chairs, one

on its side, sat in front of a heavy wooden desk. "It's me, Aoife," Alex said softly.

Her strawberry blond head popped out from behind the desk. She took us in with a glance, then said, "It took you long enough."

"We were in the brig," I said. "Is Ying here?"

"I'm here," she said, her voice coming from under the desk. The chair pushed back and she crawled out.

"Just to be clear, you're not secretly running House Yamado and betraying me right now, are you?"

Her shocked eyes met mine. "No."

"Someone is trying to frame you."

Anger slowly replaced the shock. "Hitoshi." She spat out the name like a curse. To say there was no love lost between her and Hitoshi was a vast understatement. If he had anything to do with the attack and the death of their parents, Ying would kill him or die trying.

"Might be. De Silva tried to convince me that you'd led me here as a trap and you were acting as High Councillor for House Yamado."

The flash of longing that crossed her face was for the position, not the betrayal. "I didn't."

"She's been with me the entire time," Aoife said. "They stunned us as soon as we hit command and then locked us up together. I got free and took out the guards." She said it easily, like taking out four guards was no big deal.

Clayton cleared his throat. "We need to go."

"What's the plan?" Aoife asked as she handed out the weapons she'd confiscated from the guards.

"Out the north door, as fast as we can."

"Okay, let's move," Aoife said. "I've got point."

"I can't let you risk—" Clayton started.

Aoife cut him off. "Save it. I can consistently shoot centimeter groupings at a hundred meters, and I know how to get to the door. If you can do better, you can lead. If not, shut up and follow."

Clayton grinned at her and swept an arm toward the door. "After you."

As soon as we stepped out into the hallway, the indistinct mumbling from my com got a lot louder. I still couldn't make out words, but the timing was too coincidental. "I think they're on to us. Run."

Aoife broke into a sprint without a single question. Ying and Clayton dropped in behind her, and I followed them. Alex brought up the rear. My shielding cuff was dead and I felt entirely too exposed.

A side door just ahead of me swung open, but before I could even shout a warning, Alex was there, knife in hand. The two soldiers inside—thankfully *not* in RCDF uniforms—were dead before they realized they were under attack.

"Get them back!" Daniel shouted, loud enough for my com to pick it up. "Riccardo is going . . ." His voice faded out and no matter how hard I strained, I couldn't catch the end of the sentence.

If Riccardo Silva was here, then that meant the gates weren't entirely down because he'd jumped from Andromeda Prime. Or Silva was using their own private FTL communication system to transfer jump coordinates. We'd long suspected they had the ability, but we'd never found proof.

Aoife rounded the next corner and I heard a controlled burst of blaster fire, three sets of two shots. By the time I turned the same corner a second later, three enemy soldiers were on the ground, dead, and Aoife was still running, apparently unharmed.

"Damn, you weren't kidding," Clayton said appreciatively. He swiped a second gun from a downed soldier and then fell in behind Alex.

We encountered another group of three before we made it to the door. One of them clipped Aoife before she could drop him, but she just switched gun hands and kept running.

My suspicions about her abilities began to harden into certainty, but I had no time to dwell on them, because the door to the northern tunnel was locked tight.

"Seems like a fire hazard," I muttered to myself as I swiped my arm across the chip reader. The console beeped angrily and the door remained locked. Someone had figured out how to remove my access.

Time to bust out the big guns. I tapped the console and entered the House von Hasenberg override. If this didn't work, then we would need to retrieve our explosives in order to breach the door.

I ignored the blaster fire behind me and Ying's pained shout. It had taken me a long time to memorize Ferdinand's code and I had to enter it all at once or I would miss a letter. And if I fucked up the code, the door would go into lockdown for at least five minutes. Heat seared my face as an energy bolt slammed into the wall centimeters away from my unprotected head.

Alex's large form loomed behind me. "I've got your back. Keep going. You have time."

I hesitated and nearly lost my place, but a quick mental repeat got me back on track. My hands shook as I entered the last few digits. Time slowed. Aoife growled out a curse. Alex said something I didn't quite catch. I watched the keypad console with intense focus.

The door unlocked.

I heaved it open, afraid it would lock again. "Door! Go, go, go!"

The others piled through. Aoife came last, still shooting at the soldiers who were stupid enough to appear around the corner. It seemed like most of them had learned their lesson and now just snaked their gun arms around and shot blind. A blaster bolt to the hand was far less fatal than to the head. That bit of caution explained why we hadn't been shot like fish in a barrel.

There was no way to lock the door from this side, so we just had to run for it. We needed to hit the exit before they had time to move soldiers there, so speed was key.

I was glad to see that everyone was well enough to run. Aoife held her left arm tight to her chest and Ying had a visible limp, but overall, we were in much better shape than we could have been.

Just when I thought we might make it, the lights went dead, dropping the tunnel into pitch-black darkness. Clayton cursed and stumbled to a stop. Ying tripped and went down with a short shout. Aoife ran for another few steps before she turned and looked back.

She didn't have glasses on, but it was clear that she could see. She. Could. See. *She was like me!*

I shook myself out of the shock and helped Ying up. "Are you hurt?" I asked.

"Not more than I was," she grumbled. "Those bastards stole my glasses. I should've disguised them like yours."

"I'll lead you," I said.

"What about the others?"

I floundered for a second before Alex came to my rescue. "Aoife and I have ocular implants. Tools of the trade."

Ying nodded gamely, but Clayton looked a little more skeptical. Ocular implants existed, but it was generally pretty obvious at a glance who had them.

Aoife started off again. Alex led Clayton, and I led Ying. She ran beside me, completely blind but trusting me to keep her safe. It was an honor, that trust, and I wondered how I'd ever thought our friendship wasn't real. De Silva had tried to sow doubt, but he didn't know just how close we were. Ying would not betray me, just as I wouldn't betray her.

We made it to the end of the tunnel without any more mishaps. I pulled Ying to a slow stop. "We're at the end."

She nodded and looked around in the dark, blinking like an owl. Aoife opened the door and peered out. Ying squinted as the dim moonlight illuminated our surroundings a little.

Aoife waved us on, and we piled out into the night. The cold air bit at my exposed flesh and I wished I still had my cloak. With no time to waste, we ran straight for the ship, only altering course to avoid the largest obstacles. Alex ran beside me, quiet and quick.

The soldiers had confiscated our beacons, so we couldn't actually get into *Chaos* until I connected to the ship and disabled the ground defense. Or until Cira saw us, which might be faster if she was paying attention.

Aoife topped the next rise then flattened to the ground. She gestured for us to crouch down. "Squad ahead," she said. "They didn't see me, but they're between us and the ship."

"Are they in RCDF uniforms?" Clayton asked.

Aoife shook her head.

Alex touched my shoulder. "You take Ying and Clayton and go around. Aoife and I will distract them and then catch up."

"Or we could *all* go around," I argued. "You don't always have to volunteer for danger, you know. Maybe Aoife is tired of being shot at."

"Not if I get to shoot back," she said with a grin.

I mock-glared at her. "Shush, you."

"I can keep us mostly out of sight," Clayton said, "if I know where we're going."

"My ship is about half a kilometer northeast of here, in a little clearing with flat ground."

"Surprisingly rubble free?" he asked. When I nodded, he continued, "That's the graveyard. I know where you're talking about."

"I didn't see any headstones."

"They're flat and covered by grass, but that's why we don't use that as our own landing zone. It's more convenient, but the graves make it a historic site. Apparently RCDF's request to relocate them was shot down."

I felt bad about landing on people's graves, but they were dead, and I was trying not to be. I figured they'd forgive me.

Clayton led us around the original squad and two more before we made it to the ship. We didn't have much time before the soldiers caught up with us, so I got to work connecting my smart glasses to *Chaos*. It was a multistep process with several levels of validation.

I was still in the middle of it when Alex crossed into the defensive zone and triggered the audible alarm. "What are you doing?" I shouted.

"Getting Cira's attention." He stepped back a millisecond before the ship opened fire.

I tried to force my heart rate back to something close to normal rather than the hummingbird pace where it was currently. Then Alex crossed the line again.

Before I could storm over and murder him myself, the cargo bay ramp lowered and the door opened. "What are you doing?" Cira shouted, sounding almost as disbelieving as I was.

"Getting your attention. Did you disable the defenses?" Alex asked.

"Yes, but I almost didn't get it done before you were skewered."

"I appreciate your haste," Alex said as he ushered us all to the ship. "Cat was going to be all night."

"Those security protocols are there for a reason," I growled. "Otherwise we could've come back to no ship at all."

He grinned at me and bumped my shoulder. "My way was faster."

I rolled my eyes at him and turned to the group. "Anyone with injuries, get to the medbay. I'm going to get us in the air. Try to stay clipped in as much as possible because it might get bumpy if they have ships in the area."

Aoife, Cira, and Ying headed to the medbay. Alex and Clayton followed me to the flight deck. "How bad is it?" I asked as I slid into the captain's chair. Both men remained standing. I worked on getting us into the air as quickly and quietly as possible.

"It's not good," Clayton said. "The Consortium is in chaos and the RCDF doesn't have any clear leadership. We lost a lot of soldiers during the initial attack. House Yamado seems in on it, but I only know that because I overhead de Silva talking about High Councillor Yamado. What are you doing here? I thought you were off-planet."

"I was, but once I heard about the attacks, I came back. I'm here to mount a defense."

"You and what army?" Clayton asked.

"Benedict's, assuming I can get the gates up and Rockhurst to agree to a temporary truce. I'll gather up whoever I can and take back central command. I just have to hold it long enough for Benedict to jump in. He has an entire battle fleet.

He can mop up the rest. And with the gates up, the RCDF ought to be able to send in reinforcements, too."

"I'm not so sure everyone in the RCDF *wants* reinforcements to arrive," Clayton said. When Alex moved protectively closer to me, Clayton laughed. "Not me. I owe Lady Catarina a debt, and my niece is awfully fond of her, though she pretends not to be just to be ornery. Pippa would banish me from the House if I did anything to harm Cat."

That was news to me. I thought Pippa tolerated me at best.

Clayton continued, "Someone told them exactly where to hit and with how many. House Yamado may be involved, but that's not information they would've had. Someone high up in the RCDF chain of command is a traitor."

I agreed. Rooting out all of the traitors was going to be a monumental task.

The engines flared to life and we lifted into the air. There were no other ships showing on *Chaos*'s sensors. I input a roundabout flight path, heading south and east before sweeping back west. The Silvas would expect me to head for Serenity—it was the only other option on-planet. By taking an unexpected path, I hoped to keep them off my tail for as long as possible.

Unfortunately, that gave us nearly seven hours of downtime. I knew I should use it to sleep, but I had a feeling that sleep would be a long time in coming. It might be dark outside, but my body clock thought it was midafternoon. But by the time we arrived in Serenity, it would be close to midnight.

Clayton didn't share my concerns. "Got anywhere I can bunk down? The backup base is not on Universal and I need some sleep before we land."

I shook my head. "Quarters are tight. You'll have to make a pallet in the exercise room downstairs."

"You can use my bunk," Alex said. "Just let Aoife know because you don't want to surprise her."

"I could see that. If only I were a decade or two younger." Clayton grinned ruefully. "I'll let her know. How long until we land?"

"At least six and a half hours."

"See you then."

After Clayton left, Alex settled into the second console, then spun to face me. "What's your plan now?"

The unfamiliar weight of command settled heavily on my shoulders. I kept collecting people who expected me to have answers, but I'd spent most of my life *dodging* responsibility. Shopping trips and charm offensives weren't a matter of life-and-death. This *was*.

I wasn't prepared.

But I also didn't have any other option. If I wanted my friends to live—and I did, desperately—then I had to figure it out, and quickly.

Alex didn't rush me as I thought it through. Slowly, I ticked off points on my fingers. "Make it to Serenity in one piece. Meet with our deputy director of security and see how many people she can round up. Try to find a living Rockhurst and negotiate a temporary truce using my questionable authority as the de facto leader of House von Hasenberg."

"Will they negotiate?"

I sighed. "Lady Rockhurst won't unless she has no other option, and it'll be a cold day in hell before she thinks that. Anne is clever and she'll try to twist any agreement to her advantage rather than agreeing that we have bigger problems. But her status is unknown. Evelyn, her heir, is more likely to listen and agree—if she survived."

"And what of your parents?"

Pain slashed at me. "I haven't heard anything, but Father, like Anne, would not see a truce, however temporary, as a solution. It would be more expedient if he remained out of the picture until it was done." It was the truth, but it felt like treason to admit it aloud. I didn't exactly wish my father ill, but this was a case that would not be helped by his stubborn tenacity.

"After that, I'll find any remaining loyal soldiers and negotiate an alliance of forces with Rockhurst to take back the command center. Maybe we can get some Yamado troops if Ying can contact them, but someone in House Yamado is dirty, probably Hitoshi, so we'll have to be careful. Then I'll have to coordinate the attack, bring up the gates, and get Benedict to jump in with backup forces to drive out the Syndicate. After that, it's clean-up duty."

"That seems like a lot," Alex offered quietly.

My shoulders slumped. He wasn't wrong. Was I crazy to think that I could successfully orchestrate so many moving pieces? Would anyone in House Rockhurst even talk to me? And if they did, would it just be so they could take advantage of the stupidest von Hasenberg?

The doubts were harder to silence when Alex questioned me, too.

I looked away before he could read the expression on my face, but I wasn't fast enough. He stood and crossed to my chair, turned it to face him, then squatted down in front of me so we were eye to eye. "Hey," he said softly, "that wasn't criticism. It was an offer of help. You don't have to do it all alone. You have friends and allies, probably more than you realize. You have me. And we make a badass team."

That pulled a reluctant smile from me. "We do make a badass team."

Then he moved, or I did, and our lips met and it felt like

home. I cradled his face, sliding my palms against the thick stubble adorning his jaw. I licked into his mouth, moaning when he slid his tongue along mine. I pressed closer and he chuckled as he toppled backward onto his butt, pulling me with him.

I ended up straddling his thighs, and when I raised an eyebrow in silent question, he grinned wickedly and leaned in to kiss me again.

Until my stomach made its desire for food known with a loud and persistent growl.

Alex pulled back with a laugh. "You know what this badass team needs? Dinner. Come on, I'll cook for you."

"Well, that's going to be tricky since there's no stove onboard." I didn't cook enough to warrant having the extra space and weight needed for a real kitchen. Synthesizer food wasn't amazing, but it was better than my culinary skills.

Alex shook his head sadly. "I suppose I will have to make do with the synthesizer. Prepare to be amazed."

I reluctantly climbed off his lap and stood. I offered him a hand and helped him stand. With one last look at our flight path, I turned and said, "I *will* be amazed if you can make something delicious come out of that box of mediocrity."

"You just need the right recipes," Alex said.

"I have *all* the recipes. Doesn't matter. Everything is bland." Some unnamed emotion flashed across his face, too fast to identify. "What?"

He grimaced. "I forget who you are sometimes. Of course the daughter of a High House is going to have all of the recipes the rest of the 'verse has to pay through the nose for."

"And then she still has the temerity to complain about it, right? Poor little rich girl should just shut up and be happy." Bitter hurt bled into my tone.

I'd heard some variation of this since I could express emotion. Sad, tired, angry, or upset? Too bad, think of all you have. And it was true. I *was* incredibly privileged. Of course I was, and I knew it.

I tried my very best to use my privilege to improve the lives of the most destitute and vulnerable, as did my siblings, but foundational changes took years of careful negotiations and millions of credits behind the scenes. I'd built armor against the snide remarks and attacks—I knew what we were doing, even if no one else did. But Alex had a way of striking right at my heart.

"That's not what I meant," he said quietly.

I waved a tired hand and dropped back into my chair. "You go on. I'm going to keep an eye on our flight. I'll grab something later."

"Cat—"

"It's okay, really." I blinked and tried to make it true. Instead, I stared at the console without seeing any of it, hurt and hiding.

He moved closer. "It is *not* okay. I hurt your feelings, and I'm sorry."

He crouched down next to me. I could see him out of my peripheral vision, but I kept my eyes firmly glued to the screen in front of me. I swallowed my natural urge to smooth it over, to accept his apology and move on as quickly as possible.

I peeked at him out of the corner of my eye. "If you didn't mean for me to shut up and be happy, what did you mean?"

"Your feelings are always valid and anyone who tells you differently is an asshole," he said fiercely. "*No one* gets to tell you to shut up and be happy. If they do, kick their ass."

He sighed and rubbed the scruff on his jaw. "I have a lot of deep-seated resentment toward the Consortium, and it's still a shock that the woman I care about is part of the very organization I hate. But that's a me problem, not a you problem, and it was completely inappropriate for me to take it out on you. You deserve better." He laughed bitterly. "You certainly deserve better than me."

There was a lot to unpack there, but my mind locked on to one piece in particular. I turned to him and met his eyes. "You care about me?"

Tenderness tinted his smile. "Of course I do, Cat. I don't go to war for just anyone, you know. I figured the kisses would've clued you in. If not, maybe I need to try harder."

"If you try any harder I might combust."

His mouth curved into wicked temptation. "I accept your challenge," he vowed solemnly.

I debated it for a fraction of a second, then tilted my chin up and raised a challenging eyebrow. "Do your worst."

His eyes darkened and his hands fisted on his thighs. "Have dinner with me," he growled, his voice a deep rumble. "Then I will."

I shivered at the promise in his tone. I nodded and he stood and offered me a hand up. I slid my hand into his, then took one last glance at the screen, only to freeze at the radio sensor reading.

When I pulled back, Alex released my hand and leaned over my shoulder. I frowned and tapped into the sensor's details. I wouldn't have noticed anything amiss, except I had kept the ship at maximum stealth. The sensors should not be picking up any transmissions nearby.

Unless someone onboard was transmitting or those bastards had tagged my ship with a tracking beacon.

I hit the ship-wide intercom button. "If anyone is transmitting signals, stop now."

"Not us," Ying said.

"It's not me, either," Clayton said.

"Aoife and I are radio silent," Alex said.

"Looks like they tagged us. We're landing to hunt for the tracker. Meet me in the cargo bay in two." I closed the intercom and turned to Alex. "Dinner and dessert will have to wait."

Alex agreed with a rueful smile. "I'll head down to the cargo bay. Is there anything I should grab?"

"We're going to need coms capable of tracking signals. I have a few spares, but I think my trunk is locked. I'll open it when I get there. Probably some weapons wouldn't be amiss. Grab the drone, too. If we find a tracker, we'll send it off on a new flight."

"Will do."

Alex left, and I focused on finding us a place to land. We were over an endless, sandy desert. I found a relatively flat area tucked between two dunes and brought *Chaos* gently to the ground. As long as we were stopped, we were in danger, especially with a tracker on us. We needed to make this as fast as possible.

With all of us searching, finding the tracker was easy, but removing it was a bit more difficult. It had been shot at the ship, which put it up too high to easily reach from the ground, but too low to reach from on top of the ship.

Finally, Alex lifted me up to stand on his shoulders, and when that wasn't quite enough, he had me step into his hands and he pressed me overhead. The sheer strength required was incredible, but his hold was rock steady.

I pried the tracker off with a combat knife and tossed it to Ying. She and Clayton went back to the cargo bay to work on attaching it to the drone we'd picked up from the supply drop. I sheathed my knife and looked for a safe place to jump down.

"Ready?" Alex asked. "Hop down in front of me and I'll catch you."

I jumped down, and he caught me around the waist and slowed my descent until I touched down softly. His hands lingered for a moment before he pulled away. We were alone, blocked from the others by the bulk of the ship.

I turned to him. "I'm going to steal a kiss."

His eyes lit with his smile. "I don't think it counts as stealing if you warn me first."

I slowly slid my hand up the solid muscles of his chest, around to the back of his head, and into the short, soft strands of his dark hair. "I'm a polite thief."

Then I pulled his head down to mine and the time for thinking was over. I may have started this kiss, but it spiraled out of my control almost immediately. Alex's lips covered mine with slow, intent focus. Desire, hot and heady, turned my blood molten.

I sighed into his mouth and he nipped my bottom lip before sliding his tongue against mine. Lightning crackled through my system, and I pressed up, desperate to get closer. I wanted him to apply that same thorough focus *everywhere*, even if I wasn't sure I would survive the pleasure.

A surprised squeak pulled me back to reality. I glanced to my right to find Ying grinning at me.

"*Sorry*," she mouthed before clearing her throat. "The drone is ready whenever you are."

"We'll be right there."

She dipped her head and turned back toward the cargo bay.

"When we're done saving the world, I'm locking us in a room without distractions," Alex grumbled.

I pressed a quick kiss to his lips and winked at him. "Not if I lock us in first."

CHAPTER TWENTY-SIX

The flight to Serenity stayed surprisingly quiet. Alex brought me a delicious dinner that I ate at my console. Thirty minutes out, I'd risked contacting Marta Stevens, the deputy directory of House security.

It had taken an embarrassingly long time to assure her that, yes, I was the only von Hasenberg available, which meant I was in charge, and yes, I knew exactly what that meant, and yes, I had a plan to ensure someone more capable would be in charge very soon.

We'd worked together during Ferdinand's disappearance, and I'd thought she respected me, so her lack of faith stung. Once again, my reputation preceded me.

After I'd finally convinced her that I *would* be returning to Serenity, like it or not, she had promised to have guards and a transport waiting for us at one of House von Hasenberg's emergency landing zones.

We were closer to the city than I would like, but the transport's range was limited. *Chaos* was tracking a lot of air traffic, and none of it, according to Marta, was friendly. I had the stealth level set to maximum and we were barely skimming over the treetops. Everyone was packed and ready. They were all piled into the flight deck, tense and quiet. Now I just had to put us on the ground in one piece.

Warnings blared as several different systems scanned us. *Chaos* remained silent, giving them nothing. We were thirty seconds out from the landing zone and there wasn't a damn thing I could do except watch the console and pray *Chaos* was up to the challenge.

A small ship, likely a fighter, broke from its standard sweep and headed our way. The ship would cross our landing zone in a minute. It was going to be close.

I broke stealth long enough to send a single encrypted message to the landing zone. The authorization was required to open the roof of the underground hangar and to disable the interior lights. If we were lucky, the hangar door would close before the fighter flew overhead, hiding us from view.

If not, at least we wouldn't be lit up like a star.

Chaos settled into the hangar while the approaching ship came ever closer. The view from the outside camera showed a sliver of night sky still visible when the unknown ship passed directly overhead. I held my breath to see if it would deviate from its course.

It continued on, flying low and fast.

The hangar slid closed, and a few seconds later, the lights came on. The vid screens showed Marta and a handful of security personnel standing next to the stairs and elevators that led outside. I was delighted to find my personal bodyguard Susan and her husband, Matthew, in the group.

We made our way to the cargo bay and loaded up with our packed supplies, including the combat armor we'd pulled from the supply bunker. Before I opened the door, Alex pulled me aside. "Are you sure Marta is on your side? After she didn't want to give up control?"

"Yes." If Marta Stevens was a traitor, I'd eat my blaster. "Her reluctance is my own damn fault," I added bitterly. "I've built my public persona so well that when people look at me, they see the mask. I wouldn't want to give my public self full control of a High House, either." I continued, more quietly, "I'm not even sure the real me should be in control."

"You'll do fine," Alex assured me. "What about the people with Marta?"

I hesitated. "I don't know. Marta is smart and savvy, so I feel like she would've outed any traitors by now. I think Susan and her husband can be trusted, too, but I've only met the others a couple of times."

"Be careful and stay close."

"I will."

By the time the cargo ramp lowered and the door opened, Marta was waiting for me at the bottom of the ramp. She'd left the rest of the group near the exit.

Marta was a tall, stunning woman with jet black hair and deep brown skin. Her eyebrows rose when she caught sight of Ying. I might have left out a few minor details in my initial message.

"Lady Catarina, I'm glad you're in one piece."

"Me, too." I quickly introduced everyone, then we headed for the elevators with the cargo sled following us. "What's the situation? Have you heard from my siblings? Have you found my parents?"

Marta stopped and turned to me, her expression stark. "I have not heard from your siblings. I don't know their statuses. Lord von Hasenberg is in a coma. He's in critical condition, but we have the House's best doctors working on him. They remain hopeful."

"And Mother?"

Her mouth compressed into a bleak line, and I knew, even before she said, "Lady von Hasenberg did not survive the attack. I'm so sorry, my lady."

My breath rushed out and I fought to draw another one. I tried to remember what my last words to Mother were, and I had the sinking feeling that they had been said in anger.

Sorrow and regret mixed with relief and horrible, crushing guilt. I froze, stuck in a maelstrom of conflicting emotions.

Distantly, I saw Alex move toward me, but Ying got there first. She wrapped her arms around me and pulled me close. The others moved away, giving us some space. Ying didn't say anything, didn't offer any platitudes, just gave me silent support, even though I know she had to be hurting with her own loss. My eyes were hot and dry and I wondered what kind of awful person couldn't cry for her mother's death.

My kind, apparently.

Maybe I really was broken.

Ying rubbed my back, and I hugged her in gratitude, then pulled away. She met my eyes. "We will win this," she promised. "Then we'll implement the changes we've talked about."

"Hitoshi might have something to say about that," I said bitterly. In the unlikely event that he wasn't a traitor, he *was* still the head of House Yamado. And he wouldn't give up an iota of power without a fight.

"Hitoshi can fuck off. Tae doesn't want to lead. I'm going to be Lady Yamado. I'll set a new precedent."

Ying had always chafed at the fact that her asshole older brother was heir, especially when it became clear that they had vastly different ideas about how House Yamado should be run. If anyone could set a new precedent, she could. "We'll back you, if it'll help."

She nodded in understanding. If Hitoshi was a traitor, it would be easy for us to throw our support behind Ying. If not, House von Hasenberg butting into another House's business would only hurt Ying's chances.

We joined the others and Alex slipped his hand into mine and gently pressed my fingers. I clung to the quiet support he offered and tried to dig up my public persona. I couldn't quite manage bubbly, but I at least smoothed my face into a neutral expression.

When we arrived at the others, Susan squeezed my shoulder. "I'm glad you're safe, Lady Catarina."

"You, too, and Matthew as well. Thanks for coming."

The transport had to stay low to the ground, which meant the trip back to Serenity took twice as long as it would have in *Chaos*. Marta used the time to bring us all up to speed. There had been no warning about the attacks and current estimated casualties were over four hundred, with a quarter of those civilians. The RCDF command center was completely lost and no one knew what had happened to the soldiers protecting it or exactly how many soldiers the Syndicate had used to secure it.

Marta had let anyone go home who wanted to and she'd also opened the stronghold's doors to the families of House employees. Most of the employees had brought their families back with them, which meant she had about seventy-five security personnel protecting three times as many House employees and civilians. The Syndicate hadn't tried to breach the stronghold yet, but we all agreed that it was only a matter of time.

The transport dropped us in Sector Four of our quarter.

The streets were deserted and the city looked abandoned without the constant flow of transport traffic. Clayton turned to me. "If you don't mind, Cat, I'm going to go check on Pippa."

"Of course. Do you need a lift?"

He glanced around. "If it isn't too much trouble."

"Can we spare this transport?" I asked Marta. When she nodded, I pulled Clayton into a quick hug. "Thank you so much for your help. The transport is all yours. Try to keep it—and yourself—in one piece, okay? And if you need help once you get there, let me know."

"You're welcome. I'll be fine—it's these other bastards who should worry." He grinned at me and raised an arm in farewell. "I'll be in touch." He climbed into the transport and it lifted off. I hoped he would make it to House August without any trouble.

The rest of us quickly made our way into an alley and through a series of interconnected buildings separated by locked doors. In the basement of the final building was a nondescript door with a chip reader. Marta swiped her arm over the reader and the door opened, only to reveal a small, bare room.

Once we were all inside, the door closed and locked behind us. Marta swiped her arm over three unmarked points in order: right, left, middle. A section of wall opened and revealed a staircase going down. This was one of the many hidden entrances to the stronghold under the von Hasenberg main building and only someone with high-level clearance could open it.

We passed through a few more locked checkpoint gates. The one closest to the stronghold was guarded by two people I vaguely recognized from the security team. Marta dismissed the team that had accompanied us, then led us to the office off the main control hub. It would be Father's office, if he were here.

Marta paused in front of the desk and I awkwardly stood

next to her for a beat before I realized she was waiting for me to move *behind* the desk. Alarm prickled down my spine, but I forced myself to slip around the desk. I'd had a lot of practice pretending to be something I wasn't, so I just kept pretending.

I sank into the plush chair and the resulting riot of emotions soured my stomach. I pasted on my social smile and decided to dive right in. "I intend to take back the command center and bring up the gates."

To her credit, Marta didn't *immediately* start yelling. She took a deep breath first, so she had plenty of air to tell me exactly what she thought of my plan.

She was not a fan, to put it mildly.

"And how do you plan to get *inside* the base?" she asked in exasperation. "I've tried contacting every RCDF soldier I know, from the general in charge down to those in the enlisted ranks. None of them answer, so I assume they're dead or as good as. You might be the daughter of a High House, but even you don't have access to the RCDF military command center and those doors can't be cracked with a codebreaker."

"I know someone who can get us in. I just have to persuade her to help us."

"Who is it?"

I shook my head. "I trust you, but I'm keeping it to myself until she agrees. I won't put her life in danger because we have a leak somewhere."

Marta didn't like it, but she reluctantly agreed.

I changed the subject. "Do we know anything about who is on-planet from House Rockhurst? Did Lady Rockhurst survive?"

"I've heard rumors that Lady Rockhurst was badly injured, but we don't have any concrete data. I believe Evelyn is running the House for now."

"Perfect. I need a line to her as soon as possible."

"Communication is proving tricky."

"I have faith in you." As soon as I said it, I grimaced because I'd heard that exact tone from Father more times than I could count. I needed Ferdinand to take over stat, before I slid down the slippery slope into assholedom. And for Ferdinand to be able to get here, I needed Evelyn Rockhurst's help.

I rubbed my eyes. "Sorry, it's been a long day. Please try to get in touch with Evelyn however you can, it's very important. I'm planning to persuade her to accept a truce and throw troops behind a raid on the command center."

Marta blinked at me. "You think she'll end the war, just like that?"

"Just like that," I agreed with a nod. In point of fact, I wasn't sure about any such thing, but I had to try, and if my confidence persuaded Marta, I'd be on my way.

Marta sighed and pinched the bridge of her nose, but she didn't disagree. It was something.

"I'll contact my people," Ying said. "I believe some of them will agree to help, but I may need you to find positions for them if Hitoshi catches wind of it."

"If I agree to take them in, will you give me your word that they won't be spying for House Yamado?"

Ying's grin was quick and sly. "If I must. I'm hoping it will only be temporary until I can take them back, but I will ask them to keep your secrets as if they were my own."

She really was planning to try to take the House from Hitoshi. There hadn't been an internal coup attempt in a High House in at least four generations, and the last one had not ended well for the attempted usurper.

"How many soldiers do you think you can field?"

She tapped her chin and stared into the distance. "Maybe two dozen, depending on what Hitoshi has promised them."

"If you give them the option, the security teams, at least, will choose you over Lord Hitoshi," Cira said. "It's likely true for the rest of the House, too."

Ying's expression slipped into worry. "Until we prove that he is a traitor, Hitoshi is still the head of the House. I'd be asking people to betray their vows."

Cira nodded decisively. "I know. Many will."

I looked at Marta. "How many security troops can we spare for an attack on the command center?"

"Twenty-five, maybe thirty if we push it. But I won't order my people into suicide."

I nodded. "Volunteers only. I don't need people who won't fight. We just have to hold the command center long enough for me to get the gates up. I'll send Benedict a message to be ready to jump as soon as they are up."

Marta shook her head. "All FTL communications are down, even to our properties and ships that don't rely on the gates. Something is jamming the signals."

I pressed my fingers to my forehead. Today was not my day. "I will send a message when the gates come up, as well as a backup jump point, in case we lose them before Benedict arrives. Get me a meeting with Evelyn and start asking for volunteers. Please."

Marta bowed and exited the room. I slumped in my chair and stared at the ceiling. If House Rockhurst came through, I was going to have close to a hundred people counting on me to lead them into a situation where they wouldn't all return.

If not, we'd probably all die here anyway.

Ying came into view, leaning over me. She patted me on the

shoulder. "You're doing well. I'm going to go round us up some help. Do you mind if I leave Cira here?"

"I mind," Cira said. "You can't go alone, and my leg is nearly healed."

I sat up and looked between them. They both wore mutinous expressions. "Cira is welcome to stay, but I agree that it's too dangerous for you to go alone. Check with Marta to see if she can spare a few guards." I sliced my hand through the air when it looked like Cira was going to protest. "If you want to heal, you have to stop moving. Regen gel can only do so much. Heal now, and you can come with us when we take the command center."

Aoife stepped away from the wall where she'd been leaning. "I will accompany Ying. The two of us will make better time than a larger group, and I can protect us both."

"Are you sure?" I asked.

"Yes. Alex can watch your back while I'm gone. Just don't try to raid the command center until I get back."

"Thank you." I turned to Ying. "Does that work for you?"

"I've seen her shoot; it works for me. I'll bring back anyone who is willing to help you storm the compound. I have my com. If we run into trouble, I'll try to let you know, but if we're not back in five hours, assume something happened."

I stood, happy to be out from behind the desk, and pulled Ying into a hug. "Be careful."

She squeezed me, then stepped back and met my eyes. "You, too."

Cira accompanied Aoife and Ying out. She planned to head to the medbay after they left to see if a doctor could patch her up better than the triage we'd given her on the ship.

Only Alex and I remained. I paced while I thought, unable to stand still. I needed to go see my people, to check on everyone and let them know that House von Hasenberg would take care of them whether or not they volunteered to help. I needed to plan my strategy for speaking to Evelyn. I needed to *have* a strategy for attacking the command center.

Instead, all I had was decision paralysis. I was not built for command.

I blew out a breath and leaned a hip against the desk. "If you have any advice, I could use some."

Alex moved closer, until he was all I could see. "You're doing fine."

"Doesn't feel like it. I feel like I'm a second away from becoming my father, and another second away from failing completely."

"Leading isn't easy. If it was, everyone would do it."

That pulled a reluctant grin from me. "I don't know what I'm doing," I confessed to his chest, too scared to meet his gaze and see the judgment in his eyes.

He tipped my chin up with gentle hands. "You don't have to do it alone. What can I do to help? I have experience running military ops. Use me."

"You've already done so much. You shouldn't have to risk yourself again."

"If you think I'm going to let you run off into danger alone, I've got bad news for you. I'll risk myself ten times over if it keeps you safe."

"I can take care of myself."

"I know you can and I don't doubt it, but I *like* taking care of you. Besides that, you're the nicest sparring partner I've ever had. I'm not going to give that up."

I laughed. "That's because I refuse to hit you."

He winked. "Exactly."

"Thank you," I said quietly. "For everything."

He nodded.

Marta peeked in the open doorway. "We lucked out. The hardline communications between here and House Rockhurst are still working. Evelyn is on the line and willing to listen to your proposal. Do you want to take it in here?"

"Yes, please."

She nodded and disappeared, closing the door behind her. I rounded the desk and sank into the high-backed chair with a deep sigh.

Alex flashed me another grin. "You've got this, princess." He settled into the chair in front of the desk so he'd be out of sight of the camera, but he could still hear.

I smiled in gratitude and pulled up the display. Marta transferred the call and I accepted. A second later, Evelyn Rockhurst appeared on the screen. She had the trademark Rockhurst blond hair and blue eyes, and she usually looked like she could take on the world, but today she looked worn.

I imagined I looked the same.

"Hello, Evelyn. Thank you for agreeing to talk."

"I thought you were off-planet." Her tone was cool and suspicious, and her expression gave nothing away.

"I was. I had an emergency jump point in the solar system. Once I heard about the attacks and that the gates were down, I came back."

"Why?"

"I thought I could help. I'm going to get the gates back up. I'd like your help."

She laughed, but it was not a happy sound. Bitterness twisted her mouth. "You think I didn't try that already?"

"What happened?"

"In the first hour after the attack, once I learned the gates were down, I convinced Hitoshi Yamado that an allied assault was our only option. Our troops were slaughtered."

"*Both* of your troops? You have confirmation from someone you trust?"

Evelyn's eyes narrowed. "What game are you playing now?"

"No game." I pressed my lips together as I debated how much I could safely tell her. "I tried to take back the backup command center. I failed, obviously, but the person in charge of the attacking troops, Daniel de Silva, indicated that they were working with House Yamado, and I thought I saw Hitoshi's battle cruiser in orbit with a Silva ship on my way in."

"You're accusing the leader of one of the High Houses of treason?"

"Officially? No. I'm just passing along information you might find valuable."

"My troops went down so fast, there was no time for communication. I only have Hitoshi's word that his faced a similar fate. Just as I only have *your* word that he's a traitor. And I'm surprised you managed to pull yourself away from a party long enough to even notice."

"I know I've given you no reason to believe I'm capable. Mother is dead. Father is in a coma. Our House is in a shambles and somehow, I'm the one in charge, which is laughable. If it were anyone besides the Syndicate, I'd say fuck it and let them have it. But it *is* the Syndicate. I'm not giving up the 'verse to something worse than the Consortium ever was. I'm not letting Hitoshi Yamado become some sort of cruel puppet dictator. You can believe me or not, and you can help or you can hide, but I will make a stand."

A faint smile curved Evelyn's lips. "Well, aren't you full of surprises. I see now why Ferdinand is so fond of you. I always wondered what he saw that I didn't." I couldn't keep the shock off my face and she laughed. "I can't believe Bianca didn't tell you that Ferdinand and I are dating."

"No one tells me anything," I grumbled.

"To be fair, we were keeping it secret, but somehow Bianca found out and questioned me about it when he went missing. Maybe she was waiting for him to tell everyone." She paused and glanced away. "Have you heard anything from him?"

"No. I'm not even sure where he is. But I'm trying to get the gates up so he can come take over because I wasn't meant to lead a House."

"I think perhaps you've fooled yourself, as well as others," she said cryptically. She paused, weighing her words. "I can give you a squad of eight, but that's all I can spare. I'm sorry."

"We'll take what we can get. Once the gates come up, I'm going to ask Benedict to come mop up the Syndicate, but I can't do that if we're at war. I propose a seven-day cease-fire between our Houses."

She stared hard at me, her expression unreadable. Finally, she asked, "Do you have the power to sign such an agreement? What happens if Lord von Hasenberg wakes up in five minutes and decides it's not in his best interest?"

"I do. And if Father wakes up, he'll hate it, but if it's binding, he won't break it. What about you? Where is Lady Rockhurst?"

Pain peeked through Evelyn's mask. "Mother did not survive the initial attack. I am Lady Rockhurst now."

"I'm sorry."

She swallowed and nodded before her mask slipped back into place. "I will agree to the cease-fire. Once the gates are up, I will recall Richard and his battle fleet to help retake Earth.

All other assets will remain in place in Antlia and any attacks or attempts to claim territory will be met with force, cease-fire or no. And if you breach the agreement, you will cede the entire Antlia sector to House Rockhurst in forfeit."

"I may be the youngest von Hasenberg, but I wasn't born yesterday. We will not cede our planets in Antlia because you baited one of our soldiers into breaking the cease-fire and attacking."

"If I were just dealing with you, I would agree, but Lord von Hasenberg will twist any agreement to his advantage unless there are severe penalties. I refuse to have my goodwill abused."

I wondered if this was how the rifts between the High Houses had gone on for so long. Each new generation wanted to make it work, but each was suspicious of the others' motivations. How could I break the cycle?

"What if we signed a peace treaty rather than a temporary cease-fire?" I asked.

"You don't have the authorization to sign it and make it stick. And treaties take weeks to negotiate."

"Treaties take weeks to negotiate when both sides are trying to screw the other. I'm proposing that we try something new. Nothing is going to change if we don't start somewhere. Acting heads of Houses can sign binding agreements in emergencies. I'd say this counts."

Evelyn sighed. "Lord von Hasenberg will just declare war again while our backs are turned. I can't risk it."

"House Rockhurst declared war in the first place," I reminded her.

"And we're winning. Why would I give that up?"

"Are you, though?" I asked with a raised eyebrow. "I've seen the reports. It's a stalemate at best. We're both burning through troops and supplies, but our reserves are deeper than yours. In fact, we have far more to lose by agreeing to peace than you do because we have only one planet to your two."

Respect gleamed in her eyes. "You are not what I expected. You have everyone deceived. How clever." She paused for long enough that I thought our connection had frozen. Finally, she said, "You are correct that change must start somewhere. I agree to your peace, but if your father fucks me over, I'll hold you personally responsible."

"If Father wakes, I'll redirect his wrath to the Syndicate rather than you."

"I hope you can. I'll send you a draft agreement in a few minutes. We will both retain the properties we owned before the war and neither side will pay restitution. Agreed?"

I probably could have pushed for more, but I'd meant it when I said we had to start somewhere. "I agree."

"When are you planning to attack the command center?"

"Soon. Ying Yamado is trying to round up a few people as well."

"Does Lord Yamado know?"

"No, and I'd prefer it if you kept it that way," I said.

Evelyn nodded. "I hope she knows what she's doing."

"I wouldn't bet against her."

"I wouldn't, either. I'll be in touch. You can reach me at this address if something comes up."

I hoped nothing would.

CHAPTER TWENTY-SEVEN

After the call ended, I leaned back in my chair. While I would have loved for Evelyn to commit more soldiers, it wasn't all bad. At least she didn't refuse to help at all, or worse, decide to side with Hitoshi.

"Will Lady Rockhurst really agree to peace so easily?" Alex asked.

"I hope so. If we don't make a change now, then we'll be just as bad as our parents."

"And what if you are?"

I bit back my instinctive protest and really thought about the question. What if we *were* just as bad as the previous generation? Maybe *this* was why nothing ever changed. Each generation thought we were improving things, but really we were just maintaining the status quo.

"I don't know," I said at last. "I need someone from outside the system to keep an eye on us and ensure we're really improving things. Want to volunteer?" I asked lightly, but my pulse beat wildly and my heart was in my throat.

A teasing smile tugged at his mouth. "What do I get in return?"

"The satisfaction of saving the universe?"

His smile heated and morphed into temptation. "I was thinking of something more personal."

"Like what? A statue with your name on it?" I asked innocently.

"While that *is* tempting, how about a kiss?"

"A kiss could be arranged." I stood and circled the desk. Alex remained sprawled in his chair, a predator pretending to be harmless. I approached slowly, aware that he could move far faster than his lazy pose would indicate.

Even with my caution, I wasn't fast enough to dodge the arm that snaked around my waist and tugged me into his lap. I laughed as the world tilted and resettled with me pressed up against the hard muscles of his chest.

"Happy?" he asked quietly.

I heard the question under the question and nodded. "I'm very happy where I am, thank you. But while you make a lovely chair, I believe I was promised a kiss."

Alex's expression remained serious, but his eyes danced. "You're wrong. *I* was promised a kiss."

"So you were." I framed his face with my hands and the stubble of several days' worth of beard growth tickled my palms. I shivered in delight. I loved a man who looked a little rough around the edges. Not that Alex needed any help in the dark and dangerous department.

I slowly drew his face down to mine, until our lips just brushed. I had planned to take this slow, to enjoy a drawn-out tease, but as soon as our lips met, my plans went out the window.

It felt like I'd wanted him forever and the banked desire roared into an inferno of *heat* and *want* and *now*. I moaned and pressed closer, fusing our lips together. I tempted his tongue into my mouth and then sucked on it in a bold imitation of what else I'd like to suck. He groaned and clenched me tighter.

The slow slide of his tongue against mine threatened to send me up in flames. The kisses blended into each other until I was hot and wet and aching. I shifted restlessly, seeking pressure, chasing relief.

Alex's hand found my breast and he palmed the weight of it. I arched into his touch. His thumb stroked my nipple into a hard point. I broke from the kiss with a gasp. Alex trailed kisses down my neck, and the gentle burn of his whiskers made my skin hypersensitive.

The world shifted as he stood and carried me with one arm. He locked the door without setting me down.

"We don't have time," I protested weakly. I didn't want to stop, but without his kisses driving me crazy, all of my pressing worries came back. While I was waiting for Ying, I could be planning with Marta or checking on our people or a million other things.

"Just a few minutes," he coaxed. "I'm not going to take you on a desk—unless you ask very, very nicely—but the world can spare you for a few minutes."

The thought of being spread on a desk while Alex drove us to bliss probably shouldn't have been as enticing as it was, but now that he'd planted the idea, I couldn't get it out of my head. Heat crept into my face until I was sure it had to be scarlet.

Laughter rumbled from deep in his chest. "Thinking of asking nicely, are you?"

"Maybe I was imagining *you* spread out on the desk like a feast and I was just considering where I would taste first."

He groaned and his grip tightened. "Keep talking and I'll forget I wanted to take my time."

I pressed a kiss to his neck, then licked and nibbled my

way to his ear. "We're both strong enough, I bet we could invent some new positions the universe has never seen before," I whispered.

He set me on the edge of the desk, then spread my legs and stepped between them. I could feel him through our clothes, hard as steel. I wrapped my legs around his waist and dragged him closer, until we were practically fused together. I rocked against him and sighed out my pleasure. So close, but still so far.

"I'm not going to fuck you on a desk for our first time," he gritted out. The muscles in his neck were tense as he fought for control.

"Why not?"

"You deserve to be comfortable and I want to have plenty of time to worship every centimeter of you. A desk is not that."

I knew he was probably right, but my tendency toward chaos had taken over and I couldn't help torturing him, just a little. "Okay. I won't ever ask you to do something you're uncomfortable with." I waved toward the chair behind him. "Take a seat. As soon as I've solved this little problem on my own, we'll get back to work. You can worship me later."

His breath hissed out in a rush, as if I'd gut punched him.

I gave him my sweetest smile. "Don't worry, it shouldn't take me long. You can watch if you'd like."

He groaned deep in his chest and closed his eyes for a moment to collect himself. I could see his body was a single line of tense muscle as he tried to maintain his control. His eyes met mine. "Take off your clothes," he demanded.

I shook a finger at him. "Nonparticipants don't get to issue orders." I unclasped my legs and pushed him back a couple of steps. "Sit."

He sat, his expression hot and intense and yearning.

I took a second to consider my path forward. He'd made his preference clear, despite his teasing, and I wasn't going to try to tempt him into sex, as much as I wanted to. So the clothes would stay on.

I laid back across the desk and unbuttoned my pants. I pushed my shirt up, exposing my bare belly and bra. I thumbed a pebbled nipple and moaned at the little jolt of pleasure. It really wouldn't take much to push me over the edge.

Alex's hands were white-knuckled on the arms of his chair.

I slid my left hand down, edging under my underwear. I was swollen and hot and wet and even the lightest touch sent shockwaves arcing through my system. "I wish you could feel how wet I am right now," I told Alex.

I'd always been a bit of a talker during sex and his deep groan told me that he didn't mind at all.

"You could glide home so easily and this empty, achy feeling would go away. You would fill me up, wouldn't you?"

The chair arm snapped.

"Let me touch you," he growled, his voice harsh with need.

I shuddered at the thought of his hands on me. I raised my head to look at him. His eyes burned and his muscles were clenched tight. The fact that he remained sitting despite his obvious desire sent a delicious thrill through me. "Okay," I agreed, "but no sex."

"Deal." The word was barely out of his mouth before he moved. He swept me up and returned to the seat with me straddling his spread legs, my back to his chest. When properly motivated, he could move *fast*.

I could feel him, hot and hard against my ass. I wiggled and he sucked in a breath. Then his right hand slipped under the waistband of my underwear and I went molten. I trembled as his fingers glided past my clit. The fact that I couldn't see what he was doing thanks to my clothes only added to the eroticism.

He dipped one finger into my aching core and my whole body clenched. "More!" I demanded with a moan.

He added another finger, then pressed his palm against my clit. My hips rose and I hovered on the brink of control. I undulated against him, riding his fingers, seeking bliss.

"That's it, take what you need," he rasped into my ear.

The words shattered my control and I moved faster, telling him exactly how good it felt and how much I wanted him. He rocked against me, his breathing rough, and gave me everything I needed.

The world went white and my body bowed into an arch as every muscle clenched and pulsated. Alex's answering groan and shudder pushed my pleasure higher.

I slowly drifted back to Earth, the desire banked but not burned out. It would be so easy to turn around, slide open his pants, and lose myself again. Only honor kept me still. I had already pushed at the boundary Alex had set; I wouldn't cross it.

I turned my head and pressed a gentle kiss to the edge of his jaw. "Thank you."

His chuckle was warm and soft. "Anytime, princess."

He withdrew his hand, causing all sorts of interesting aftershocks, but I held my breath and ordered my body under control. I really did have responsibilities that couldn't wait forever.

I stood on shaky legs and fixed my clothing. I leaned down and pressed a brief kiss to Alex's mouth. "That was hot as fuck," I whispered to him, "but the next time you start something you don't intend to finish, I'm tying you up so all you can do is watch helplessly while I get myself off over . . . and over . . . and over. If you're very, very good I might take pity on you—eventually."

A rumble of pure male pleasure came from deep in his chest. He reached for me but I slipped away. "I'm going to get cleaned up and then go talk to Marta. I want to be ready to go when Ying gets back. I'll meet you in the war room."

MARTA, ALEX, AND I SPENT THE SMALL HOURS OF THE morning discussing various strategies. Alex hadn't lied when he said he had military strategy experience. His guidance shaped our overall plan into something that actually had a chance of succeeding.

Evelyn Rockhurst was also having a late night. When the peace treaty arrived, I opened it with trepidation, but it was short and straightforward. She hadn't tried to screw me, so I signed it, with Marta and another high-level advisor as witnesses. There was no fanfare, no big celebration. This was just the first step on a long road to change. And even though the war was officially over, we couldn't tell the people still fighting.

I had to get the gates up.

While I waited for Ying to return, I sent messages to our allies here on Earth—and those I was trying to charm into being allies. I couldn't ask for troops, no matter how badly we needed them, because I didn't know who might be a traitor. But I checked in, let them know that House von Hasenberg still stood, and that we would help as much as we could.

Lady August responded first, despite the late hour. She didn't ask a single question, but she insisted on sending a squad of eight soldiers in combat armor. I couldn't very well refuse on the grounds of not needing them, not when her uncle had busted me out of a cell in the backup command center, so

I sent Marta to meet them at the same entrance we'd used before.

When they arrived in the main gathering hall, it did not surprise me at all that Clayton was among them. He saw me and raised a hand in greeting. "Pippa and the rest of the family are safe in our bunker with my best soldiers protecting them. Sorry I couldn't bring more."

"We'll take what we can get. Thanks for coming."

He grinned. "Wouldn't miss it." His grin died, and he continued, "They killed General Momola. This won't bring her back, but I hope it gives her some satisfaction on the other side."

I lowered my head in silent agreement. We'd already lost so many, and we were likely to lose so many more. And because this was now my plan, those deaths would be on my shoulders.

After Clayton returned to his soldiers, Alex slipped his hand into mine. "He'll be okay. He's a good soldier."

I could only hope Alex was right.

FOUR AND A HALF HOURS AFTER THEY LEFT, JUST WHEN I was starting to worry, Ying and Aoife returned with forty soldiers, which was far more than I had expected, but also nearly twice as many civilians. Our stronghold was full to bursting, but I couldn't turn them away.

Ying's grim expression told me that it hadn't been easy to get so many out. Several of the soldiers sported blaster wounds and Ying herself had picked up a new limp. With our plan set, I dragged her to the medbay and into a private room. "Let's see it," I demanded.

She bared her teeth at me, but when I just stared her down, she grimaced and dropped her pants. Her right calf was wrapped in a makeshift bandage that was stained with dried blood.

I pointed at the diagnostic table. I didn't trust her not to be concealing something worse, mostly because it's something *I* would do. She lay on the table and I kicked off a scan. While it ran, I gathered supplies to clean and properly bandage her calf.

"You're not leaving me behind," she grumbled. "Or telling Cira. She'll try to get me to stay here."

"I'm going to have to see what the scan says before I can agree," I said. "I know you. You could have internal bleeding and five blaster holes in your torso and you'd still tell me it's just a scrape."

She glared at me. "If so, it's because I learned it from my best friend."

I held up my hands in surrender. "Guilty, which is why I'm on to your tricks."

The scan came back surprisingly good. Ying hadn't been exaggerating. Her calf wound was the worst, and with some re-gen gel and a tight bandage, she should be able to walk on it.

I cleaned and bandaged the wound while she continued to grump at me. When I was done, I asked, "Do you want a pain-killer?"

She shook her head. "No, I need to be clearheaded. There's too much going on for me to be out of it."

I met her eyes. "Was it bad?"

Her shoulders slumped. "Yes. I had to fight people I've known all my life to escape with the ones who wanted to leave. Not everyone made it. Hitoshi has garnered a lot of support from a certain segment. I'm officially being declared a traitor."

I snorted. "That's rich."

She nodded in agreement, but her expression remained

pensive. "I won't let him win, but if we fail tonight, I'm not sure what I'll do."

"We'll regroup and try again. You're not on your own. I'll support you however I can, and I know Ferdinand feels the same way."

"But if your father wakes—"

I sighed. "While I still expect the old bastard to wake at any moment just to bedevil me, he's in bad shape. A wall section fell on him. The doctors don't want to admit just how low his odds are, but I can read a diagnostic scan. His survival chance is less than five percent. The machine is the only thing keeping him alive at this point."

"I'm sorry."

"I'm not, and that makes me feel awful." I looked at her. "Am I a terrible person?"

"Albrecht von Hasenberg is an asshole of the first order. The only people who will mourn his passing are the assholes who benefited from his fight to keep power and control in the upper echelons. You are not a terrible person."

"Sometimes I wonder. What if every generation thinks they're better than the last, but really we're just the same?"

"Would your father send biweekly supplies to a group of street kids on Andromeda Prime?"

"He would if he thought it would benefit him somehow."

"Yet he never did. It didn't even occur to him. We're undoubtedly going to fuck up occasionally, but you can't learn without failing. And if you start down the path of becoming your father, I'll kick your ass until you see reason again."

I hugged her. "Thank you."

"You're welcome, but I don't think you have to worry about it." She slid off the table and her face went so blank that I knew her calf must hurt like hell.

"You don't have to—"

"I'm going. The pain is annoying, not debilitating. I can do it."

I inclined my head. "Then let's do this."

AFTER YING'S RETURN, WE SPENT A FEW MORE HOURS planning, setting the final details, then we all took some downtime. We agreed an attack at night would be best, so we had the day to rest and recuperate.

Ying, Aoife, Alex, and I had been up for over twenty-four hours, so we took over one of the bunk rooms and crashed for six hours. I don't know if the others slept or not, but despite my worries, I slept like the dead. I could've used a few more hours, but I had things to do today.

Deep in the evening, when everyone was busy preparing for the night ahead, Alex and I slipped out of the stronghold and went to get my secret weapon. By the time we returned, the teams were starting to get outfitted for the attack.

Cira's leg was nearly mended and she refused to be left behind again. The on-site doctor cleared her for duty, so although Ying wanted to keep her safe, there was no reason for her to stay behind.

Because we were part of the team that planned to infiltrate deep into the base, Alex, Aoife, Ying, Cira, and I were given ballistic armor and a pair of blast pistols each. I requested another set and the quartermaster didn't even blink. She handed it over with a nod.

I looked around at the large gathering hall brimming with soldiers in various amounts of armor. A precious few were in combat armor, including four of the eight Lady Rockhurst had sent, but we didn't have nearly as many as we needed, even with the extra armor we'd brought with us.

All told, we had seventy-five soldiers to attack a base held by up to ten times that many. It would've been laughably impossible if we'd planned on a frontal assault, but we hadn't.

Our soldiers knew the layout far better than any foreign invaders, even if the attackers had studied the maps. We were going to use hit-and-run tactics to sow mayhem while a small team of six snuck inside. Our group of five would be joined by my secret weapon—Dr. Esteri Kryer, the astrophysicist I'd met at Mother's brunch what felt like a million years ago.

Thanks to her work on the gates, she had clearance to get us into the heart of the base. She had readily agreed to help because her brother was in the RCDF off-planet and she hadn't heard anything from him. She wanted the gates up as badly as the rest of us.

After Alex and I had snuck out to escort her in, I'd hidden her in the main office. With this many people around, I couldn't risk someone leaking her identity because if they locked out her access, then our plan was dead in the water.

At midnight, teams began leaving to take their positions. With limited transports, only squads going to the far side of the base would be able to take them. The rest of us had to walk.

My team met in the main office. Esteri glanced up from her pacing but didn't stop moving. Her hair was pulled back into a severe bun and she wore a high-necked, long-sleeved black shirt and dark gray pants. With her hair pulled back, her cheekbones were even more striking.

"Are you sure about this?" I asked her again.

She nodded once, decisively.

Ying narrowed her eyes. "I know you. You're a doctor, right?"

"I have a doctorate," Esteri agreed, "but I'm an astrophysicist. Esteri Kryer."

"You wrote that incredible paper about the gate algorithm," Ying gushed. "I've wanted to chat with you *forever.*"

That put a smile on Esteri's face. "Most people run away when I start talking about work."

"Ying isn't most people," I said. "Let's get you in your armor before she distracts us for the rest of the night."

"Spoilsport," Ying grumbled good-naturedly.

Esteri had done a rotation in the RCDF science corps before becoming a researcher for them, so while she didn't have combat experience, she at least knew how to put on armor and which end of the blaster to point at the enemy.

Aoife gave her a few more tips and we all discussed some last-minute strategy. Then it was time for us to leave. We had one of the shorter walks, since we were infiltrating the base from the closest edge, but we had a civilian with us.

I checked my gear for the third time. If I'd forgotten anything, it was too late now. We left the stronghold and stayed in the tunnels as long as we could. All of the squads were taking different routes, so if one was picked up, their position hopefully wouldn't compromise the rest.

Everyone wore smart glasses and we were all tied into a local com group. Ying, Alex, Aoife, and I were also tied into the overall group coms, but until the attack started we were running radio silence unless an emergency came up, so there wasn't any chatter.

When we finally emerged into the night, the muggy air made me long for the icy chill of the backup command center. Or at least a breeze to prevent the city from feeling quite so stifling.

Aoife led, with Ying and Cira behind her. Esteri was in the center of the group, so we could form a shield of bodies around her if we were attacked. I was next to last and Alex brought up the rear.

Aoife had her long rifle, as well as two blasters on her hips. I had my shielding cuff and Ying and Esteri had prototype personal shields. Ying's eyes had lit up when I'd handed one to her. When I'd told her that I expected it to be returned, her smile had been angelic, which meant she was already plotting how to keep it.

The small puck-shaped devices were much more powerful versions of my shielding cuff. Marta had argued that I should have one, but my cuff wouldn't work for anyone else, so having both was beyond selfish. Esteri was essential to the plan and Ying already had one injury. If I could save her from another one, I would.

The command center was just outside Serenity between the von Hasenberg and Rockhurst quarters. It should take us about an hour to reach it on foot. We kept to alleys and side streets as much as we could. The streets were deserted. A few lights glowed in building windows, but no one dared to be out.

We were just over halfway to our destination when Aoife peeked around the next corner and froze. A heartbeat later, she waved us back deeper into the alley.

"Patrol," she whispered over the local com. "Too many to take out. We'll go around."

As we got closer to the command center, our fairly straightforward path became snarled because we had to backtrack and find alternate routes to dodge more and more patrols. Most were in groups of four, but some had as many as eight.

But Aoife had uncanny skill at detecting the patrols before they found us, and she led us through them like an expert seamstress threading a needle.

By the time the high wall surrounding the command center came into view, we'd eaten through most of the buffer time we'd built into the schedule. We needed to be in position in the next ten minutes because that's when the fireworks would start.

I just prayed this night would end in victory instead of death.

CHAPTER TWENTY-EIGHT

Anxiety dumped acid into my stomach as we waited for the scheduled start time. We were in position, everyone knew their job, and now we just had to execute the plan. I bounced in place, unable to pace, but needing some sort of movement.

Alex laced his fingers through mine. "You've got this," he murmured. He hadn't activated his com, so the words were just for me.

I took a breath and shared my biggest fear. "People are going to die. If I fail, they're going to die for nothing."

Alex ran his thumb over my knuckles, his expression solemn. "Everyone out here volunteered. They know the risks. They listened to your plan and decided that it was worth it. And you're not going to fail."

I wished I had half his confidence. I was never meant to lead a group. I would have felt so much better going in on my own, because while it probably would have ended in failure, I would bear all of the consequences. Now, friends and strangers were throwing themselves into the line of fire so that I would have a better chance of getting the gates up.

I could not fail them. I *would not* fail them.

I pulled Alex's face down to mine and kissed him, slow and deep, until desire replaced anxiety and my nerves steadied. "Thank you."

He pressed his forehead to mine. "You're welcome. Do what you need to do; I've got your back. *Always.*"

I kissed him again. His support bolstered my own confidence.

We all stood silently watching as the last seconds counted down. When the timer hit zero, I held my breath. Fire bloomed in the distance as something large blew up, then closer as another target was hit.

I could hear distant blaster fire start up as the troops in the base rallied to fight back. And still, we waited.

It felt like two eternities, but I knew from the schedule that it was only five minutes. Finally, Marta's voice came over the com. "Omega team, you're good to go. May the stars shine brightly on you."

I held the blessing close and led the group toward the base. Aoife was behind my right shoulder, her rifle held loosely. She was still the main lookout, but because I knew the base better than she did, I was now in charge of getting us inside. If I fell, the job would go to Ying.

I really hoped it didn't come to that.

We'd decided to save Esteri's access until absolutely required, so we blew the checkpoint's outer door with breaching charges. As soon as the door swung open, we swept inside. One soldier in a black Syndicate uniform was down from the blast and two more fell to our weapons. I hadn't heard them send any warnings, but my ears were still ringing from the blast.

I opened the checkpoint's heavy main gates, then shot the control panel so they couldn't be closed again. Now that our exit was secured, we needed to *move*.

The base had dozens of buildings, both above and belowground, but we'd decided to stay aboveground as long as possible. It was riskier from a someone randomly spotting us standpoint, but the aboveground surveillance wasn't as extensive, and it gave us more room to maneuver. We hoped we'd be able to disappear in the chaos.

And it *was* chaos. Armored soldiers, both in Syndicate black and RCDF camo, ran toward the various attack points. A few lower-ranked Syndicate officers in red and green uniforms were relaying information back to the commanders safely hidden on ships or in the command center.

Our black fatigues and black armor let us both blend in with the night and also with the Syndicate troops around us. We formed two lines and jogged like a squad on a mission, but I kept us to the shadows as much as possible without being obvious about it. A squad moving with purpose was far less interesting than one skulking in the shadows and peeking around corners.

Marta's voice in my ear kept me apprised of the situation. Two squads were falling back under heavy fire. A third had pressed their advantage and taken a guard tower. They were using the heavy tower guns to lay down suppressive fire. Friendly squads were warned to avoid the area. Grenades and explosives were being used to maximize the distraction level.

Our squads were doing their part, now I just had to get us inside.

Because we were moving forward without double-checking every corner, we often ran into enemy squads. Every time we passed close, I waited for someone to recognize that we were part of the invading force. None did because they were all too busy obeying their own orders. But it never got any easier, and by the time we were close to the heart of the base, I was once again a bundle of nerves.

The last major hurdle before we descended to the tunnels came into view. We just had to cross the parade grounds and then we'd be at the science and technology building where Esteri worked. Its basement connected to the tunnels leading to the command center a short distance away.

Unfortunately, the parade grounds were a large, open space, and long enough that going around would add more danger than crossing in the open. A few other squads were crossing, so hopefully we wouldn't stand out too much.

"Activate shields," I murmured quietly. I activated my cuff and heard quiet affirmatives from Ying and Esteri. We would have to watch our distance now, because overlapping shields sometimes behaved in unexpected ways. We'd coached Esteri, but it would be up to me and Ying to keep an eye on it.

We started across the open space at a jog, still in two lines. I tried not to get tunnel vision on the science building, but it was difficult. We were so close.

So, of course, the universe decided to help.

We were most of the way across the parade grounds when a Syndicate officer in red and green stepped out from between the science building and the building next door. Spotting us, he impatiently waved us over.

I had no choice but to comply. We were too exposed here.

I stopped in front of him. This close, I could see he was a second lieutenant, the most junior officer. I snapped a tidy salute and prayed everyone else followed my lead. "Sir?"

"Why are you out of regulation armor?" he demanded. "I should write you up."

The base was under attack and this little man was on a

power trip about uniforms. I kept the distaste off my face and tried to sound young and scared. "Sarge told us to scrounge what we could find, sir, then head for the northeast wall." It was the direction in which we were heading, as well as one of the places we'd hit hardest, just so this excuse would seem believable if needed.

His lip curled. "Who is telling you to disregard orders? What was his name?"

It said something that he automatically assumed the sergeant was a man, but I didn't bother to correct him. I needed him to lose interest, pronto. "I didn't catch his name, sir. But he was in the armory." I hooked a thumb over my shoulder, back the way we'd come and approximately in the armory's location.

"Wait here wh—"

Aoife didn't wait for him to complete the sentence before she struck, quick as lightning. The lieutenant slumped into her arms, his heart shredded by the glistening blade in her hand. She sheathed the knife and easily swung the lieutenant into her arms while I stood frozen. I'd rarely seen death dealt so swiftly up close. When I didn't move, she tilted her head at the science building.

I shook myself out of my shock and led us around the building. Alex kicked in the building's service door. We entered, then propped the door closed with a nearby desk. Aoife disappeared down the hall and returned without the lieutenant's body.

"How do we get to the tunnels from here?" I asked Esteri.

"The back stairs have tunnel access. They are down the hall to the left, but the tunnel door is five-centimeter-thick steel. There will be no kicking it down and even breaching charges might not work."

"How far is the command center from that door?" I knew the answer from the maps, but I wanted to be sure that Esteri's estimate matched what the map showed because she'd actually used the tunnels before.

"Less than a hundred meters. Science and technology employees are often needed down there, so we have our own access tunnel that comes out just a few meters down from the command center door. That's where we'll run into the most resistance, if they're expecting us."

We had a few things to deal with resistance, but it would be best if we could make it all the way *into* the command center before we had to fight. I checked the time. We were running right on schedule. The second wave of attacks would begin in the next five minutes, splitting the attention of whoever held control.

Hopefully.

I led us to the stairway, with direction from Esteri. She'd worked in the building for more than a decade and had spent many nights and weekends exploring its depths, mindlessly walking while she mentally worked on complex problems. She was a far better resource than I'd ever expected and I wondered if Mother knew just how valuable her contributions were. Maybe her presence at the brunch hadn't just been for novelty's sake.

At the bottom of the stairwell, a single steel door without an obvious chip reader sat flush against the wall. Esteri waved her arm at the wall and we all held our breath. The entirety of my plan rested on this door opening. If it didn't, I'd wasted all those lives for nothing.

My heart thundered in my chest, too fast, as I waited to see if everything had been for naught. I balanced on the edge of despair, sure that the door wouldn't open, that my one attempt to lead would fail.

The door opened.

I hardly believed my eyes when the gap around the door became clearer and the heavy metal slab swung inward, revealing an empty hallway.

"Is that an illusion or did my plan really work?" I asked.

"If it is, I'm seeing it, too," Alex said. "Let's move before it vanishes."

Aoife and I started into the tunnel and Ying and Alex dropped back to defend our rear. Cira covered Esteri in the middle of the group. Because Ying, Esteri, and I all had shields, we'd offer a little protection to the person next to us, if we stood close enough.

Esteri didn't know if entry through the science building sounded any sort of alarm, so we'd decided that speed was now more important than stealth. We ran, only slowing to peek around the corners before dashing back into a sprint.

"This is the last corner," Esteri said as we approached. "The command center door is five meters to the left."

This was our last hurrah, our do or die. We ran for the main hallway, counting on surprise and shields to tip the scales in our favor. Aoife fired a fraction of a second after she cleared the corner, and a heartbeat later, I found a target of my own. She went down.

The squad of eight defending the door wasn't dug in and we'd caught them flat-footed. Aoife had hit three before my shield took the first hit. Scattered and shocked, the rest of them fell in a hail of blaster bolts.

We pressed forward. Alex and Aoife tossed smoke grenades in both directions. They would limit our visibility, too, but soldiers couldn't stand at the next corner and pick us off. Now if they got close enough to see us, we could see them, too.

And they didn't have Aoife.

Smoke filled the hallway. Without a breeze, it hovered in

place, creating a little bubble of calm. I looked everyone over. They seemed okay. Aoife had a graze on her arm, but it wasn't deep. I met her eyes. "Ready?"

She nodded and slung her rifle over her shoulder and drew both of her blast pistols. "Let's do this."

She and I would lead the charge into the command center, clearing the way for Ying and Esteri to work on getting the gates up. Alex and Cira would help hold the room and prevent soldiers from flooding in behind us.

It was a solid plan—if everything worked perfectly.

We stacked against the wall by the doors. At my nod, Esteri swept her arm over the reader. The double doors slid apart. Unlike the soldiers in the hall, the soldiers inside weren't caught unaware. Blaster bolts streaked out in a wave of death.

Aoife and I looked at each other across the doorway. My shield would protect us for a few seconds. We would have to use those seconds to find cover and take out as many as we could. She inclined her head, and I dashed through the doorway before my nerve failed.

The room was a wide semicircle arrayed around a flat wall of screens that showed surveillance video from various points around the base. At least fifteen people were in the room, a mix of civilians, officers in Syndicate uniforms, and soldiers in Syndicate black. I didn't see any RCDF uniforms. I also didn't see Riccardo Silva, so I focused on the soldiers first.

I crossed the entrance to the right and continued into the room, faster than they might expect, Aoife on my heels. My cuff vibrated as the shield took hits, but I gave as good as I got. I hit two and Aoife hit four before the shield failed and we were forced to duck behind a console for cover.

"Don't shoot the electronics, you idiots!" a male voice shouted.

Without the need to stick together because of my shield, Aoife and I split up. I went back toward the center of the room while she hugged the outside wall. The civilians were hunkered down. Smart.

I shot at two soldiers and missed both before ducking back into cover.

Ying and Esteri were working their way toward one of the consoles at the edge of the room, using the other consoles as cover. No one was paying them much mind because they weren't shooting.

Alex and Cira *were*.

I joined them. None of us was as good as Aoife, but by and large, we were better than the soldiers in the room.

And *far* better than the officers.

We were down to just a handful of remaining soldiers when searing heat blossomed in my left shoulder. Icy numbness followed and I couldn't feel my left arm. I sank to the floor, stunned.

The ballistic armor I wore was designed in such a way that it protected most of the torso, but a narrow strip at the top of the shoulder was unprotected to allow the garment to lay flush.

A stray blaster bolt had punched straight through the top of my left shoulder. Blood streamed from the wound at an alarming rate. My nanos and natural healing would take care of it, but seeing my life leak out made me lightheaded.

I didn't have time for squeamishness. Hundreds of people were counting on me to get the gates up. And in the rest of the 'verse, billions waited for the supplies and news the gates brought.

I closed my eyes and counted to three, then drew my second blaster with my right hand and lurched to my feet. I wasn't as fast as I had been, but I was still fast enough to shoot the soldier who'd shot me. She went down and I knew she wouldn't be getting back up.

I pushed away the revulsion I always felt at taking a life. Fight now, mourn later.

The last soldiers went down and the civilians remained hidden under their desks. "Everyone up and into the center of the room," I shouted, trying to sound authoritative and not like my shoulder was an inferno of pain. "I'm Lady Catarina von Hasenberg and we're taking back the command center."

"I'm with the RCDF," a woman said.

"That's nice. Get to the center of the room. We're not going to hurt you, but we *are* going to restrain you while we get the gates up and fix the defenses."

She timidly stood. She was in her late fifties, with graying dark hair and pale skin that looked like it hadn't seen the sun in decades. Her clothes were rumpled and tiredness showed in her posture, but her eyes were sharp with intelligence. "You don't have authorization."

I waved her to the center of the room with the blaster in my right hand. "We do."

She shook her head. "They changed the codes. I know what they are. I can fix the orbital system."

Esteri looked up and squinted at the woman. "What's your name?"

"Idoya Bolasti. I usually work in the systems' security department. I had the bad fortune to be tracking down an issue in here when the attack happened. We didn't have time to escape."

Esteri waved her over. When Idoya approached, Ying smiled at her, showing a lot of teeth. "If you are lying to us and you do something to break the system, I will kill you. Slowly."

Idoya swallowed and nodded.

Cira, Alex, and Aoife rounded up the rest of the people who

were still alive and bound their hands behind their backs, then sat them on the floor in the middle of the room. I holstered my weapon and scanned them for bugs and trackers, but they were clean.

We barricaded the doors as best we could, but the room lacked an emergency lockdown that would override the door controls. I wasn't sure if the lack was due to hubris or budget constraints. Either way, it had originally worked in our favor, but now it worked against us.

Cira and Aoife were stationed across from the main door, blasters at the ready. Esteri, Idoya, and Ying stood in front of a console, arguing quietly about timing sequences, tachyons, and a host of other words that sounded scientific but that I had no idea what they meant. I'd known that Ying was interested in science, but I was still impressed by her ability to keep up with an astrophysicist with a doctorate.

Alex came over with a strip of cloth he'd gotten from somewhere and rigged a bandage for my shoulder. It had mostly stopped bleeding but it still stung like a horde of angry bees had taken up residence.

"Are you okay?" he asked quietly.

"I'm still kicking."

He smiled and clasped my right hand. "I'm glad."

I squeezed his hand. "Me, too."

He lingered for a moment longer before going back to patrolling the room. I'd already written the message to Benedict and had an additional message from Evelyn to send to Richard, in case the gate was up for only a short time and she missed the window.

Because the gates had been down for so long, the message backlog would be deep, so I'd tagged both messages as high priority and attached my House seal, which would let them skip to the front of the queue.

I'd copied all of my siblings on the message to Benedict. I wanted to send them all individual messages, but I couldn't risk clogging up the queue any more than absolutely necessary. I'd have to send another message to Benedict with a jump point as soon as I could get one from the gate, but even without that, at least my family would know what had happened and that the war was over.

With nothing else to do, I found a working console and flipped through the various surveillance videos, relaying troop information to Marta.

Our forces were slowly being overwhelmed and falling back. If we were to have any hope of escape, we needed to leave soon.

"Ying, how's it going? We have ten minutes max, and that's pushing it."

"We're almost there," she said without looking up. She and Idoya were standing over Esteri's shoulder, pointing at various things on the screen. Esteri impatiently waved their hands away.

"Can you set it up so that Silva can't use it to jump away?"

"If we had more time, yes," Esteri said. "But as it is, no. Limits require a lot of checks and authorizations because they are meant to be used sparingly."

"Too bad."

She flashed me a smile. "Not usually. It's one of the things that keeps the Consortium from using gate access as a weapon."

I dipped my head in rueful acknowledgment.

True to her word, a couple of minutes later, Ying whooped with victory. "The gate is ours! It'll take sixty seconds or so for the changes to roll out to the other gates, but I can request jump points now. Where do you want Benedict?"

"Put him an hour out. That way he won't jump straight into an ambush. I need at least a pair of points, and it would be best if they were emergency points so they'll be good for longer than the standard two hours."

"On it. We're close on the defensive systems, too."

A moment later, Ying sent a trio of emergency points to my com, all of them an hour away from Earth. I attached them to a quick note to Benedict and sent it high priority and sealed. I started a ninety-minute timer on my com. If Benedict wasn't in com range by the time it went off, then something was wrong.

"We couldn't override the changes to the defensive system," Ying said, "so we deactivated the targeting system. It's a risk if the Syndicate jumps in more ships, but if we leave it up, it'll attack our friendly ships."

"Deactivated is better," I agreed. "Can the backup command center override your changes?"

Esteri shook her head. "No, we locked it down. As long as this command center is still functional, the backup command won't be able to override it, unless they have two High Councillors on site."

"Can someone override it from here?"

"Yes, just like we did. I changed the codes, so it'll take longer, but they can do it."

I looked around. There was no way the six of us could hold this room against an attack, not unless my guardian angel wanted to drop in a six-pack of mechanized armor.

No armor appeared. She must be on a break.

"Will the messages have time to go through before they shut the gates down again?"

Esteri looked thoughtful. "They should. Gate communication takes priority when they come back up, but that should just be five or ten minutes. After that, messages start transferring. The backlog will be steep, but I'm assuming you sent it priority?" At my nod, she continued, "Then I would expect it to be delivered within thirty minutes. If they can defeat my safeguards in that time, I'll resign my position."

I caught movement out of the corner of my eye. The video screen had changed to an internal view of a tunnel. I didn't know where it was, but it was full of soldiers wearing Syndicate black. "Time to go!"

"What about us?" a male voice from the crowd on the floor asked. "You can't just leave us here!"

I could and probably *should*, but my conscience wouldn't allow it. "We'll cut you loose in the hallway, then you're on your own. But if you come back in here and try to override what we've done, I'll find you in a dark alley and make you wish you hadn't. Understand?"

Heads nodded.

"Incoming communication," the computer system intoned. It was too soon for Benedict to be able to contact me, so who was calling?

I moved to a console that faced away from the main door and accepted the link. The console camera's limited field of view wouldn't give the person on the other end of the connection a view of the entire room.

The screen blinked, then Riccardo Silva's handsome face appeared on the screen. If he was surprised to see me, he hid it well. His eyes lit up and he smiled as if all of his holidays had come at once.

"Lady Catarina von Hasenberg, how very good to see you."

CHAPTER TWENTY-NINE

Riccardo Silva was a snake hiding behind a gorgeous face. His dark, curly hair draped over his forehead and set off his blue-green eyes and warm olive complexion. He wielded his smile like a knife—shiny, beguiling, and deadly, without a hint of warmth.

I couldn't see much behind him on the video but it was clear that he was aboard a ship. "Hello, Riccardo. I see you've chosen to hide like a coward while the expendables do your dirty work."

"Oh, that's rich coming from the daughter of a High House. You've been having expendables fight your battles for millennia. Maybe you really are the stupid one. Bianca was far more clever."

I'd have to care about what Riccardo thought of me for that barb to hurt—and I didn't, at all. My older sister *was* clever. I was proud of her. I just wished she'd killed this asshole when she had the chance.

I would not make the same mistake. And I would happily use his assumptions about me to my advantage.

I subtly waved my fingers to tell the others to start evacuating the civilians without taking my eyes off the screen. "Did you call to surrender?" I asked sweetly.

His laugh was not nice. "Hardly. But if you and Evelyn Rockhurst cede control of your Houses to me, then I won't turn Serenity into a smoldering ruin."

Battle cruisers weren't really designed to attack planetary targets but Riccardo had enough weapons onboard to ensure the threat had teeth. The city held nearly a million people and a lot of them were hunkered down in their homes. We didn't have enough shelters for everyone and an evacuation would take too long.

I did the only thing I could: I played dumb. The timer in the corner of my glasses counted down as slowly as stars burned out. I needed to stall to give Benedict time to arrive.

I blinked at Riccardo in confusion. "But if we turned over our Houses, then *you* would run the Consortium."

Riccardo's expression tightened as he tried to determine whether I really was that stupid. But this time, my reputation worked in my favor. His smile was wide and vicious.

"Perhaps we could run it together," he offered, all charm. "As empress, you could buy as many gowns as you like."

I frowned. "I don't think Father would like that."

"I'll deal with your Father." The threat was unmistakable.

Around me, the room fell silent as the last civilians left. A glance at the surveillance video showed that we needed to leave, too, or we'd be trapped.

"Can I think about it?"

"This is a one-time offer. Take it or leave it."

I pouted prettily at him. "That's not fair."

He wavered, but in the end, I wasn't a big enough prize to change his mind. "Sign over your houses or Serenity dies."

I dropped the act. "Your campaign to take over the Consortium will run into some trouble if you kill the very people you're trying to persuade."

His expression twisted. "We don't need your help; we need you *gone.*"

I raised one eyebrow. "You're not exactly convincing me that you'll let the city stand after we sign over our assets. And have you relayed that sentiment to Hitoshi?"

I watched him closely and picked up on the subtle surprise in his expression before he smoothed it behind a slick smile. "I don't know what you mean."

"What did you promise him? Or was murdering his father enough to secure his cooperation? He's too smart to be there with you now, but I think he might find this video enlightening, don't you?"

"Hitoshi knows his place."

Well, now, that was interesting. I almost wished I *was* recording this so I could send it to Hitoshi.

"I will speak to Evelyn and let you know our decision in an hour."

"You have thirty minutes to sign the contract I'm sending. After that, I open fire on the city. And if you made the mistake of calling for reinforcements, I'll be more than happy to shoot them down if the orbital defense doesn't get to them first."

I let my lip curl at the threat, but internally, I was shocked. *He didn't know we'd taken down the defenses.* I wanted to keep it that way, so I responded to the initial statement. "Thirty minutes isn't enough time for me to return and track down Evelyn, much less look over a binding contract."

His smile was not kind. "Then you'd better hurry."

"I guess I will." I disconnected the call without another word and checked the timer. Ten minutes had passed since I'd sent the message to Benedict. He would receive it in twenty minutes, but he wouldn't make it to Earth before Riccardo opened fire.

Despair threatened, but I drowned it with resolve. *Chaos* wouldn't stand a chance against a battle cruiser, but I'd have to try. If I caught a transport and flew straight there, I should be able to get in the air and make myself a target before my thirty minutes were up. Maybe I could buy the city enough time for Benedict to arrive. Riccardo seemed like the type who enjoyed toying with his prey. I would just have to make the game interesting.

"We've got to go now," Alex called from the doorway. The room was empty and I could hear distant shouts from the hallway.

Moving sent fire burning through my shoulder and I hissed out a breath.

Alex noticed my pained expression. "You okay?"

"The hole in my shoulder is reminding me that I'm still alive."

"Come on, I sent the others on ahead, but we're about to have company. Can you run?"

I grinned. "Faster than you."

We dashed into the tunnel leading back to the science building. I wasn't faster than Alex, not with a hole in my shoulder, but I kept up. We came around the final corner and found our way blocked by the door.

The *closed* door.

"Did the others come this way?" I asked.

"Yes. They specifically said they'd leave the door open." Alex cursed harshly. "One of those assholes we freed must've known about this door and didn't want anyone to follow. Ungrateful bastards. Let's go back. There's another exit."

"To the north," I said. We nodded in agreement and ran back.

Only to run into a hail of stun rounds at the corner before the main intersection. Alex grunted as he went down, but I couldn't stop the scream as my shoulder lit up in fiery agony.

A group of six soldiers in Syndicate uniforms laughed and jeered. "That was almost too easy, but you know I'm not going to turn down the bonus," a female voice taunted. The other soldiers agreed, already talking about how they'd spend the promised credits.

They rolled me over and secured my arms behind my back, yanking extra hard on my left arm. I bit my lip hard enough that I tasted the metallic tang of blood, but I didn't give them the satisfaction of another scream.

I used the eye tracking to hard-wipe my smart glasses and lock down my com. I hoped Alex was doing the same thing. A moment later, the soldiers stripped me of both weapons and glasses, but they missed my com.

"Wiped," a male voice said in disgust. "His, too."

Two soldiers hauled me up by my arms. Pain darkened the edges of my vision but I gritted my teeth and willed my body to recover from the stun rounds. Next to me, the soldiers were having trouble lifting Alex's muscular form. I smiled, and based on the way the soldier in front of me stepped away, it was probably bloody and half-crazed.

My fingers tingled. I curled my toes in my boots. *Soon.*

The soldiers finally got Alex up. He met my gaze, eyes clear and cold. He was *furious*. "Remember what I taught you?" he asked, his voice a whisper.

I nodded once.

"On my mark."

The soldiers shook him. "Shut up or we'll gag you."

Progress was slow, but the soldiers didn't seem to mind. They talked and laughed and spent their imaginary credits on alcohol and tech and companions. I remained limp in their grasp even after feeling came back into my limbs.

"Now!" Alex barked.

My arm *ached*, but I poured all of my pain and anger and worry into relentless determination and yanked my arms apart with a shout. My cuffs snapped and I wasted no time in standing and driving a full-force punch into the face of the soldier nearest me.

She crumpled.

Alex snapped his cuffs and rose with a roar, an angry bear out for blood. The soldiers, lulled into a false sense of safety, didn't react fast enough. Without surprise and stun bolts to protect them, we were too fast and too strong and *everywhere*.

By the time we were done, the floor was littered with a half dozen bodies. Alex looked around, then wrapped an arm around my waist and pulled me close, being careful of my arm. "You were amazing. I'm so proud of you." His mouth slanted over mine, hot and fierce, and I pressed up to get closer.

We broke apart far too soon, but we needed to escape before another squad found us. I retrieved my weapons and glasses while Alex did the same. We edged down the hall, taking care to avoid being ambushed again.

The northern door was at the top of a tall stairwell, and it had a working control panel. The door opened on the first try and dumped us into a dim building interior, thankfully empty.

Twenty of my thirty minutes were already gone. If I was lucky, Benedict was about to get my first message, but the jump coordinates would put him an hour out, and there was no way I'd make it to *Chaos* in time to prevent Riccardo from attacking. If we hauled ass and didn't run into any trouble, we might make it back to the tunnels leading to the stronghold before the worst of the attack hit.

And I was just as likely to sprout wings so I could fly there.

I had pulled out my com to let Marta know to expect an attack when it beeped and vibrated with three short pulses, repeated multiple times. The gates were finally processing messages and the emergency ones were coming through first.

Momentarily distracted, I scrolled through the messages, looking for the ones from my siblings, my heart in my throat. When I found the first message from Ada, tears flooded my eyes. She and Loch were okay, as were Rhys and Veronica. They'd been evacuated by Rhys's security staff just before the bombs went off. They'd made it out with only minor injuries from the explosion.

"What is it?"

"Ada is okay. So is your friend Rhys. They escaped just before the blast hit."

I blinked through the tears and kept scrolling. I found Bianca next. She'd been off grid and had only heard about the attacks afterward. She was frantic for news, but she and Ian were unharmed. Ferdinand had also checked in but without any details of where he was or what had happened.

Hannah was alive but injured. She'd lost one of her guards in the attack and had taken a blaster bolt to the stomach, but the private retreat she'd been at had a top-of-the-line medical facility. She was expected to make a full recovery, but she couldn't travel for another day or two, much to her annoyance. She told us not to worry, not that we would listen, and that she'd be home soon.

Which meant the only one I hadn't heard from was Benedict.

It had never occurred to me that my brother might *not* survive the war, not really. He was larger than life, indestructible. He'd *always* been there for me when I needed him. My plan hinged on him because I was so sure he'd be okay—he'd been fine a week ago. Evelyn hadn't mentioned anything when I'd talked to her. Had there been a battle that went unreported?

I swallowed my sorrow and sent Marta a message. I couldn't deal with her on a voice link right now. I hit send and a tiny hiccuping sob worked its way past my control.

Alex pulled me into his chest and wrapped strong arms around me. "Who?"

The dam broke and tears streamed from my eyes, running down the hard planes of the armor Alex still wore. "I haven't heard anything from Benedict since before the attacks."

"I'm sure it's just a communication problem," Alex said soothingly. "He's too cocky to die."

That surprised a shaky laugh out of me because it was entirely too accurate to be a guess. "You know Benedict?"

"I briefly met him when I helped Bianca rescue Ferdinand."

"I'd forgotten about that." I wiped my eyes. "Even if it is a communication problem, it blows up my plan. Riccardo is going to nuke the city in less than ten minutes."

"Then we need to move."

I agreed, even though it felt futile. I'd tried my hand at leading and my failure would cost a million people their lives. The weight of that disaster threatened to crush me. But Alex had risked his life to help me, and I knew he wouldn't leave without me. I might feel like giving up, but I'd never risk his life, too.

We ran.

The base was still in chaos, but it was slowly fading as Marta ordered our troops back to safety. Avoiding patrols slowed us down and we were still hopelessly deep in enemy territory when the sky lit with fire. I stopped and stared, entranced by the beauty of death.

The shots never landed.

They weren't attacks on Earth, they were attacks *in space.*

The com in my hand vibrated and I cried at the name on the display. *Benedict.* Without a word, Alex pulled me into the shadow of a nearby building and sheltered me with his body. My hands shook so much that it took me three tries to answer the voice-only link. I kept it on speaker so Alex could hear. "Benedict?" I croaked out.

"Hey, sis. Sorry I crashed your party early, but I decided to jump in a little closer to home. Thanks for taking down the defenses for me."

"I thought you were dead! Why didn't you message me?"

"I did!"

"You didn't!" I countered.

"The com drone must've gotten lost. But I'm here now. And so is Richard. I may not care for the bastard, but he's fierce in battle." He paused and barked something unintelligible to someone in the background, then came back on the line. "And it looks like Ferdinand's battle cruiser just joined the party. I hope he realizes that Rockhurst is an ally. Get me a line to him!" he snapped at someone.

"Riccardo is threatening to fire on Serenity. If you could prevent that, I'd appreciate it. And Hitoshi's *Vermillion* is up there somewhere. I don't know if he's onboard, but he's not an ally."

"Don't worry, Cat, we've got Riccardo tied up and we're keeping an eye on *Vermillion*. I don't suppose you could take the gate down again so neither of them can jump away?"

I choked out a laugh. "No, you jerk, I almost died getting the gates *up.* I'm not going back until it's firmly under RCDF control again."

"It's good to hear your voice, Cat," he said quietly. "You did well; I always knew we could count on you when the time came."

Emotion clogged my throat. "You, too, Benny." He groaned at the nickname and I knew my job was done. "Stay safe. I expect to see you on the ground soon."

"I'll have this wrapped up in no time at all," he boasted. More seriously, he continued, "My shock troops are loading up now, so you'll see them landing in a few. Tell our people not to shoot them, if you don't mind. See you soon."

"See you soon. Love you."

"Love you, too," he said before he disconnected.

I stared at the com in my hand. When I looked up, Alex was smiling broadly.

"What?"

"You did it."

I waved a hand. "Benedict and Ferdinand and Richard are the ones doing all of the heavy lifting."

Alex shook his head in disbelief. "Are you kidding? You, who persuaded us all to return to Earth to fight, then single-handedly ended a war, plotted how to retake Serenity, executed the plan perfectly, and got the gates back up, despite setback after setback, *you* didn't do any 'heavy lifting'? Do you even hear yourself right now?"

He was right. I'd spent so much time hiding my differences that I often tried to diminish my own successes, to the point that it had become a habit—a *bad* habit. One I was going to work on breaking, starting right now. I smiled at him. "You're right—I'm a badass."

"Fuck yes, you are. It's about time you realized it."

CHAPTER THIRTY

Alex and I moved as fast as we could without looking suspicious, because despite the battle raging in orbit, the enemy troops on the ground did not appear to be surrendering.

If anything, they were getting bolder as the last of our forces pulled back.

Our initial attack had caught the Syndicate soldiers by surprise, but now they were awake and organized. And thanks to the delays, Alex and I were still on the base, behind enemy lines. Avoiding the patrolling soldiers was getting harder and harder.

We were nearly to the outer wall when a blaster bolt sailed by close enough to leave a trail of warmth.

I peeked around Alex. In the distance, indistinct shouts rose from a large group of troops in Syndicate black.

Alex shoved me into the shadows behind an empty supply crate and whispered, "Hide! They haven't seen you. I'll draw them off and meet you at the stronghold."

"No!"

But my cry came too late because he was already crossing into the open space, shooting as he went.

Furious anger mingled with heart-stopping anxiety. Alex moved like nothing I'd seen before, fluid and fast. The Syndicate soldiers couldn't get a bead on him, so despite a handful of near misses, he disappeared around the corner unharmed. The troops followed—deeper into the base.

What was he thinking?

We were going to have a very long, very pointed talk when we met again. And we *would*. I had to believe that or I'd be frozen by sorrow, and I had too many people counting on me to fail now.

Still, I hesitated. The desire to go after him, to ensure he was okay, was nearly irresistible. But if I was caught, then I had handed Riccardo a bargaining chip he would ruthlessly use against my brothers.

I had to trust that Alex knew what he was doing—and that he was strong enough and smart enough to pull it off.

I said a prayer to anyone who would listen and dashed for the wall.

I coiled, using my full strength, and leapt, kicking off from the wall to propel myself higher. I caught the edge of the top with the tips of my fingers, and my left shoulder burned like the sun, but it was enough. I pulled myself up, then paused, looking for Alex, but this part of the base was now eerily quiet.

If he'd gotten himself captured, I would wait to yell at him until after I'd busted him out. *Maybe.* And if he'd been injured, then I would rain hell on whoever thought they could harm what was mine.

With one final look, I dropped over the other side of the wall and headed for the von Hasenberg stronghold.

THE MAIN GATHERING AREA OF THE STRONGHOLD WAS filled with injured soldiers and civilians acting as medics.

Those with major injuries had been squeezed into the too small medbay, but out here, minor injuries waited for regen gel and bandages.

Ying and Aoife caught sight of me first. They both looked over my shoulder and I knew Alex hadn't made it back on his own yet.

Guilt and sorrow stabbed deep. I shouldn't have left him alone. I should've gone after him.

"What happened?" Aoife asked.

"We were almost out when a unit caught sight of us. Alex shoved me into hiding and then took off. I couldn't stop him." My voice cracked and I paused for a deep breath. "I don't know where he is because our glasses were wiped. I had hoped he would beat me back."

When she mutely shook her head, my vision swam. I swallowed the tears. "I need a suit of combat armor, if we have any that's still functioning."

"You can't go back," Ying said, her voice gentle.

"I can, and I will. Someone has to." I turned to stalk off and do just that, but Aoife caught my arm—my *injured* arm. I hissed out a silent curse as the movement pulled on my shoulder.

"You don't need to run off heedlessly; you need medical attention. Trust in Alex. He'll be here. Give him time."

With a new target, my anger rose and I squared up to her and shook off her hand. "What if he's already caught? You're just going to let him suffer? Some partner you are." As soon as I said the words, I regretted them, but Aoife's expression never flickered.

"I *am* his partner. I know him. Have a little faith." Her mouth turned up at the corner. "And don't make me kick your ass in front of all of these people. It would be bad for your reputation."

That pulled a reluctant smile out of me. "It might do my reputation good, assuming you didn't flatten me with the first punch."

Aoife's grin was knowing. "You're tougher than that."

She'd as good as admitted that she knew my secret, but the feeling of panic was more muted this time. Perhaps someday I wouldn't feel it at all. "I'm sorry I took my anger and fear out on you. It wasn't fair, and it wasn't right. I know you care about Alex. I apologize."

She waved me off. "If blowing off some steam gets you to stay put, that's good enough for me. Alex would kick *my* ass if I let you out of here to go look for him."

"She's right," a familiar velvety voice rumbled from behind me.

I spun, caught between yelling and throwing myself at him. Instead, I held myself still and drank him in. His armor was cracked and burned. He was favoring his right side and his right pants leg was soaked with blood. But he was here, and he was standing.

"Medbay, now," I demanded.

He shook his head. "I'm okay. Just clipped my thigh. I can wait for a medic here."

The urge to yell was winning. "There's a first aid kit in the office," I bit out. "I'll patch you up in there."

Ying backed away and mouthed, *Good luck*. She knew me well enough to want to avoid the blast zone.

Aoife looked like she was enjoying herself. "Go," she urged Alex. "Then you can patch up her shoulder."

Alex rounded on her. "Why wasn't it done already?" he growled.

Aoife laughed. "You're perfect for each other."

I silently led Alex to Father's office. The room was empty.

As soon as the door closed behind him, I whirled around. "What were you *think*—"

His lips crashed down on mine.

I nipped him, hard enough to sting, then soothed the bite with my tongue. Alex groaned into my mouth and pressed closer. I poured everything into the kiss, all of my worry and anger and affection.

By the time we broke apart, we were both breathing hard. Desire mixed with all of the other emotions fighting for dominance, and I couldn't decide whether to laugh or cry, so I did both.

Alex rested his forehead against mine and carefully wiped away my tears. "I'm sorry I worried you."

I stepped back so I could see his expression. "You can't just run off and play hero and expect me to be okay with it. We're a *team*. We have to work as a team or I can't . . ." I hid my face and rubbed away more furious tears. "I can't be with someone who doesn't trust me to do my part."

Alex scowled at me. "I led the soldiers away *because* I knew you could do your part. It's easier for one person to get lost in the chaos than two. And I trusted that you could make it back on your own, even though it almost killed me to walk away, to not be there to protect you and watch your back."

"You could've been caught or killed!"

"Taking risks is what I *do*. It's what I was designed for."

"No, it's what you decided on. And you can decide on something different." I stalked to the attached bathroom and retrieved the first aid kit.

By the time I returned, Alex had stripped off his broken armor. He looked thoughtful. I approached cautiously, aware that he could shred my heart with just a few careless words.

Alex pulled the kit from my nerveless fingers. "I'm going to patch up your shoulder. Take off your armor." The stubborn set of his mouth told me arguing that he should go first was pointless.

With his help, I stripped down to my sports bra. My shoulder was a bloody mess, but between my nanos and natural healing, it was already starting to close. Alex carefully cleaned the wound and coated it in regeneration gel.

The gel sped healing, but it burned while doing it. I'd heard the pain described as "white-hot agony," but it had always been more of a gentle burn for me. Tonight was no different.

Once he had finished bandaging my shoulder, Alex's hands lingered on my skin, barely touching. "You're right," he said quietly. "My team is everything to me. I don't have any family—they *are* my family. And I'm bigger and stronger than most of them. So I got used to being the one who'd drag us out of whatever hell we found ourselves in, no matter the risk. If I went down, then at least they would escape."

I slid my arms around his waist and hugged him, careful of his leg. "If you go down, you'll take my heart with you," I murmured. "Please don't break my heart."

He shuddered and clamped me closer. "Never," he vowed.

I enjoyed the comfort of his embrace. This conversation was a starting point. It took a long time to break a bad habit, as I knew all too well. Alex was likely to run in to save the day again in the future, but at least now he knew what he risked when he did. And maybe he would think twice before doing it.

I slowly released him and pushed him back toward the chair behind him. "Sit and let me look at your leg. Can you get your pants off or do I need to cut them?"

We managed to remove his boots and pants without using

a knife, but Alex was grimacing by the time we were done. He settled heavily into the chair and I got my first look at his leg— and his bright blue boxer briefs.

He'd caught a blaster bolt on the outside of his thick thigh, in a gap between the ballistic armor panels. It had punched through, taking a whole lot of skin and a chunk of flesh, but it was far from fatal. He'd been very lucky.

I cleaned the wound, then carefully covered it in regen gel and bandages. Once healing veered dangerously close to caressing, I removed my hands and stood. "Do you want any painkiller?"

He shook his head. "Don't need it."

As if to prove it, he rolled to his feet in one fluid motion. I started to step back, but he caught my waist and pulled me close. "Thank you," he murmured against my temple.

I brushed my mouth against his. "I'm glad you're okay. But next time, you're not getting off so easy."

I could feel his lips tilt up into a smile against my mouth. "Deal."

BY THE TIME ALEX AND I RETURNED TO THE GATHERING area, news was spreading that Benedict and the rest were taking the fight to the Syndicate. We weren't getting as many updates as we'd like, but it seemed like we were winning. Benedict's ground troops swept through the city and into the command center. Two more battle fleets of RCDF ships had flooded in, as well as Ada, Loch, Rhys, and Veronica in one of Rhys's armed and armored smuggling ships.

When Bianca and Hannah arrived it would be a full-on von Hasenberg family reunion.

As the heirs for their respective High Houses, Evelyn and Ferdinand had formally voted to have Hitoshi detained on suspicion of treason. It was a serious charge, but it needed a simple majority to start the investigation. *Vermillion* had surrendered but Hitoshi wasn't onboard. The hunt was on for him.

After the RCDF wrestled control of the command center from the remaining Syndicate troops and deemed it safe, Esteri and Idoya returned to help them with the gates. The Earth gate was put into lockdown mode. Ships could request jump points, but they had to be individually approved.

Riccardo Silva's ship had taken too much damage to jump, so negotiations were under way for his surrender. He vowed to fight to the bitter end, but escape ships were already being launched from his wounded flagship. Some had jumped before the lockdown, but the rest were heading to the uninhabited parts of Earth. It would be a pain in the ass to round them up, but that was a problem for another day.

Just after dawn, with Serenity mostly stabilized, we left the stronghold and went to check on the house. Ada was already there, surveying the pile of stone rubble. This end of the building had held our security offices. It was pure luck that they had been mostly empty when the attack had happened. She looked up, caught sight of me, and rushed over.

I opened my arms and she pulled me into a tight hug. I hugged her just as hard, though it made my shoulder twinge. "I was so worried!" we both said at the same time, then laughed.

"There's someone I want you to meet," I said quietly. "Before the others arrive."

"Would it happen to be Mr. Tall, Dark, and Handsome over there? The one who can't keep his eyes off you?" She tilted her head toward where Alex and Aoife were chatting with Rhys and Loch. Alex stood with his side to the group and every so often, his gaze flickered my way.

Joy spread like warm honey through my veins.

"That would be him. Alexander Sterling." I leaned in and dropped my voice to a whisper. "I'm keeping him, but he doesn't know it yet, so don't scare him off, okay?"

Ada widened her eyes and pressed a hand to her chest. "Me?" she asked innocently.

"I grew up with you. That innocent act doesn't work on me."

Her smile was fond and wistful. "I missed you, Cat."

"I missed you, too. I'm glad you're back." Ada had run for two years, and then, just when I thought I'd get her back, Father had banished her from Earth. I didn't get to visit her in Sedition as often as I would like, and I missed having her near.

Ada's eyes darkened. "Only until Father wakes. Then I was never here."

"I'm not sure Father is going to wake. The machine is the only thing keeping him alive at this point."

"It would be a damn shame if someone tripped over the plug."

I coughed out a strangled laugh. It wasn't as if I hadn't had a similar thought, but I hadn't been brave enough to vocalize it. Trust Ada to cut straight to the chase.

She gave me a wry smile. "Introduce me to your Mr. Sterling before I further contemplate patricide."

We rejoined the others. Ada turned to Alex, her expression unreadable. "What are your intentions toward my sister?"

"Ada," I growled, "you promised!"

She smirked at me. "I didn't, actually. And if you think I'm bad, wait until the others get here. Bianca threatened Loch with a rusty fork. Alex might as well get used to it now. Or get out while he can."

Burning embarrassment spread heat through my face and I wished the ground would open up and swallow me whole. Or maybe swallow *Ada* whole.

Alex wrapped his arms around me from behind, pulling me back into the solid warmth of his chest. "I'm not going anywhere," he said.

I froze in shocked joy, but Ada's expression softened. "Good."

CHAPTER THIRTY-ONE

Late in the evening, Riccardo Silva was captured alive by Benedict's troops. Riccardo refused to confess or admit any wrongdoing, so now the Consortium would have to vote on what to do with him. Killing him as a traitor risked turning him into a martyr, but keeping him alive made him a target for rescue attempts by the Syndicate. Either way, a war with the Syndicate loomed on the horizon.

The thought lingered the next day while I visited our allies, shoring up relationships and gathering support. Pippa August pulled me into a hug and thanked me repeatedly for saving her uncle, even after I explained that *he'd* saved *me*. After months of staying neutral, she pledged House August's support to House von Hasenberg.

It was a bittersweet victory.

Lady Wilma Sollorz and her heir had both survived. Wilma asked several minutes of pointed questions about Ferdinand, and I answered them honestly. She nodded and vowed that she'd ensure the other lower houses fell in line if he had to take over House von Hasenberg. House Sollorz wasn't hugely powerful, but Wilma was old enough to have many allies of her own. I appreciated her help.

Susan and I were sitting at the family table in Macall's Coffee House, taking a much-needed break between visits, when she stiffened beside me. I reluctantly looked up from Skout's report—they had dug up some interesting information.

Speak of the devil. Joseph James approached our table, his expression grim.

Susan tensed to intercept him, but I stopped her with a hand on her arm. "Let's see what he wants," I murmured, but I also drew a blaster under the cover of the table.

Joseph settled into the chair across from me with a flirtatious smile that didn't reach his eyes. "Lady Catarina, what a pleasant surprise."

"Lord Joseph." My voice was cool.

He gestured at the silencer built into the table. "Would you mind?"

I stared at him for a long moment. If I turned on the silencer, I wouldn't be able to call for backup. But nothing in Skout's report had pointed to Joseph, at least not so far.

"Susan, please keep watch by the window." From there, she would be outside the silencer's influence, so she wouldn't be able to hear our conversation *and* she would be able to call reinforcements if we needed them.

With a pointed frown at Joseph, Susan stood and moved away. Once she was in position, I clicked on the silencer. I had no doubt that she was already relaying information to the team outside.

"Have you found new information on the hover bike attack?"

His expression didn't change. "I've come to offer a trade. My family doesn't know I'm here, so if you'd play along . . ." Without waiting for agreement, he clasped my hand and brought it to his mouth for a flamboyant kiss. To anyone watching, it looked like he was being his normal self.

My other hand tightened around the blaster.

"Don't shoot the messenger," he said with a glimmer of real amusement. "At least not until you hear the proposal."

"Talk fast."

"Leave my brother Aaron out of it, and I'll give you the key you need to unlock what you took."

He must be talking about the data file. I'd sent the file to Bianca because I hadn't been able to crack it, but Bianca would—eventually. "And if I don't need your key?"

For the first time, Joseph looked truly worried. "Aaron was at school. He had no part in this."

Aaron was a year younger than Joseph. From what I'd heard, he was gifted but awkward around people. His parents had sent him away to school when he was a child and were perfectly happy for him to stay there.

I raised an eyebrow at the man sitting across from me. "And what about you? What part did you play?"

"I had no part, either, but I should've seen what was happening." He shook his head in disgust.

I tilted my head to the side and considered the truthfulness of his words. "So you're going to fall on your sword for your brother, is that it?"

"Wouldn't you? *Didn't* you? Your attendance at the party couldn't have been a coincidence."

"House James will be no more when this comes to light."

"I have enough money hidden away that Aaron will be okay."

"Will you testify against your family?"

Joseph's smile turned brittle and anguish settled into his eyes. "If I must. As long as Aaron is completely cleared of all association and charges. I want him to be not only free, but free from stigma. My parents are going to try to pin everything on him."

"That's going to be difficult when your sister had several private meetings with Riccardo in Honorius." Skout had been busy since I'd left. I now owed them a pile of credits and a heap of thanks.

Joseph closed his eyes in defeat. "I'd hoped she wasn't that involved."

"Give me the key and I'll do what I can for your brother." *And for you*, I added silently.

He transferred a file to my com, then stood with an elegant bow. "Thank you, Cat," he murmured. "Truly."

"Do not run," I warned.

One corner of his mouth turned up in a wry grin. "I am at your service."

After Joseph left, I sent Bianca the file with a warning that it might be a trap, then went back to Skout's report. Hannah and Bianca were expected back tonight, and I needed all of the information I could get before I had to give them a report.

THE NEXT DAY, FERDINAND CALLED US INTO A PRIVATE family meeting. We met in Bianca's suite. She'd moved back into the main house until her apartment could be repaired.

Tears and hugs and drinks were passed around. I couldn't remember the last time we'd all been in the same place at once. Hannah still moved like she was injured, but she waved off our concern. We kept the conversation light, but a thread of tension ran through the room. We all had a pretty good idea of why Ferdinand had called us together.

A few minutes later, he stood. "Thank you for coming," he said quietly, his voice computer-generated. House doctors were working on a way to replace his missing tongue, but for now, he wore a microphone and tiny speaker on his neck. "Father's condition has not changed. His doctors say they are optimistic, but the diagnostic table tells another story. We must decide what to do."

He moved around the room, handing each person two small, rounded disks, one gray, one red.

"The vote will be anonymous. There is a box in the sitting room. Go in, close the door, make your decision. Gray for death, red for life. There is no right or wrong choice. Because of the seriousness of the situation, the decision to remove his life support must be unanimous." He looked around the room, his expression hard. "There will be no pressure, no persuading. Do not reveal how you voted. Each person gets to make their own decision."

We all nodded. The two disks felt heavy in my hands and nerves made my stomach churn.

Ferdinand went first, then Bianca, Ada, and Benedict. Everyone was taking Ferdinand's words to heart and was in full public mode, expressions guarded. Hannah waved for me to go next. I stood on shaky legs and let myself into the sitting room.

A small black box with a slot in the top sat on the coffee table.

Such an innocent little thing with such big ramifications. I wished Alex was here to hold my hand and tell me I was a bad-ass, because I didn't feel like it right now. I stared at the two disks blindly, weighing my conscience, my future, and my love.

Then I made my choice.

The disk *clinked* softly as it fell into the box. I pocketed the remaining disk and returned to the others. Hannah took her turn, then Ferdinand retrieved the box and sat it on the low table in front of him.

"No matter what happens, I love you all," he said. It was rare for my serious eldest brother to express himself so openly. "And I will continue to do everything I can to protect you, no matter what."

"We love you, too, brother," Benedict said, and the rest of us murmured our agreement.

Every eye focused on the box.

Ferdinand shook it and then turned it over. He lifted the box, so the lid and the disks remained on the table.

Six gray disks gleamed in the soft light.

A collective breath whooshed out of us, and Ada laughed. The tension broke, and we all joined her, wobbly at first, but gaining strength.

The old reign was dead. The future was bright with possibilities.

A FEW HOURS LATER, THE DOCTORS REMOVED FATHER'S life support and he died quietly in his sleep, surrounded by his solemn, dry-eyed children. I felt guilty about my lack of anguish, but mostly I felt relief.

Albrecht and Maria von Hasenberg were cremated, and we gathered to spread their ashes in the family garden in a small, quiet sunset ceremony, filled with only family and those as close as family. Alex stood next to me. I hoped he understood the unspoken significance of the invitation.

Ferdinand had taken on the task himself, and he tipped the urn over Mother's favorite rosebushes. "Rest in peace, Father, Mother."

As the last of the ashes drifted to the ground, the western sky glowed with a stunning mix of red and gold. My tears finally came, tears of regret and hope and peace.

Alex quietly slipped a handkerchief into my hand. I turned to him and buried a sob in his chest. He wrapped his arms around me and let me soak the fine fabric of his shirt with my sorrow.

I took a shuddering breath and wiped my eyes with the soft handkerchief, only for the world to go blurry again. Now that the tears had started, it seemed like they would never stop. "Thank you."

He held me close. "Anytime, princess. I'll always be here for you."

That only caused me to cry harder, but afterward, I felt lighter.

We moved to the outdoor furniture and Benedict cracked open a bottle of Father's best whisky and poured us shots. "To the end of an era," he said, raising the first toast. "And to Ferdinand for beginning a new one."

We all raised our glasses and downed our drinks. The whisky burned a fiery path to my belly. I lost count of the toasts, but we stayed until late in the night, sharing stories of family and love and adventure. If Mother and Father didn't feature in too many of those stories, no one seemed to mind. We had each other. It was enough.

And curled up next to Alex, I dared to dream of more.

CHAPTER THIRTY-TWO

In the following days, I didn't get to see Alex as much as I would like. Fleeting glances, stolen kisses, and lingering caresses were slowly driving me insane, but there was always something that needed doing, and as the members of a High House who wanted to set a new direction for the Royal Consortium, my siblings and I made sure that we were out there doing it.

Alex always gladly pitched in to help, and he was incredibly patient and understanding when I got pulled away, but I kind of wished he'd drag me into a dark alley and have his way with me. However, it looked like the dragging would be up to me.

I started plotting.

I laid my trap with care and baited it with the promise of a delicious dinner. Alex's grin had told me that he knew exactly what I was up to, but he'd agreed to arrive at my suite promptly at six.

It was a quarter till. I smoothed a nervous hand down the fabric of my dress. It was a lacy ivory sheath that hugged my curves and flattered my complexion. The low-cut bodice fastened behind my shoulders, just below the nape of my neck, leaving my back bare. The short skirt was just a few centimeters from being indecent.

It was a dress that left no doubt about the intentions of the person wearing it and tonight I was going to be brave enough to actually let someone see me in it.

If I didn't chicken out in the next ten minutes.

I paced the living room of my suite, as comfortable in heels as I had been in my boots. I took two steps toward the bedroom before checking myself. I was a badass. This dress *killed*. I was going to own it.

At eight minutes till six, the suite doorbell chimed. "Alexander is at the door," the computer said.

Rather than asking the suite to open the door, I crossed to it and opened it manually. Alex stood outside clad in a black suit that showcased the breadth of his shoulders and the thickness of his legs. I tried to remember how to form words. "You're early," I said at last.

A slow, wicked grin tilted up the corner of his mouth. "I couldn't wait any longer."

The banked desire I always felt around him kindled to life. I stepped back and waved him into the suite, then manually locked the door behind him. Tonight we would not be interrupted.

When I turned around, he was there. He crowded me back against the door, and I shivered as the bare skin of my back met the cool metal. Alex's body was hot and hard, encased in designer fabric. The temperature difference made me shiver again. With my heels, we were nearly the same height.

His mouth met mine in a scorching glide of lips and tongue. I buried my hands in his hair with a moan and pulled him more firmly to me. In return, he palmed my breast and tweaked a nipple. When I gasped, he pulled back and gazed down at me, expression hot.

"That dress is the stuff of fantasies," he growled. "*My* fantasies." His lips brushed over my jaw to the sensitive place behind my ear. "I want to unwrap you like a present."

"What about dinner?" I protested weakly. In point of fact, I'd expected to get dinner from the synthesizer—eventually—and hadn't even started on it yet. My plan was going exactly like I'd hoped.

"Dinner can wait. I want dessert first. Hold on." He lifted me with complete ease and I wrapped my legs around his waist. My dress rode up, but not quite high enough for him to get a glimpse of anything interesting. He pulled me closer and groaned into my throat. "Which way to the bedroom?"

I directed him out of the colorful living room and into the quiet oasis of my bedroom. Candles flickered on the nightstands and dresser. A sturdy, straight-backed chair stood alone near the end of the bed, clearly out of place.

"Remember yesterday?" I whispered into his ear.

He nodded, his eyes half-closed in pleasure. Yesterday, he'd pulled me aside and kissed the living daylights out of me, then refused to find a convenient horizontal—or vertical, I wasn't picky—surface.

I shook my head at him. "What did I tell you about starting something you didn't intend to finish?"

The sound of pleasure he made seemed to be pulled from his very soul.

I kissed him, slowly and thoroughly, taking my time, stoking our desire until I burned with need. His hands flexed on my ass, kneading the flesh through my dress, and I moaned into his mouth.

When he took a step toward the bed, I said, "Put me down and sit." When he didn't move fast enough, I gently nipped his earlobe with my teeth.

He put me down, and I removed the gauzy scarf from the back of the chair. Alex sat. I regarded him for a moment before I began unbuttoning his shirt. I let my fingers brush over his skin after every button slid free and his muscles shivered under my hands.

"Take it off," I whispered.

He shrugged out of his shirt and coat, revealing a hard expanse of chest and abs that almost made me forget about my plans. *Almost.* I pressed a kiss to his pec, then moved behind him. I pulled his arms behind the back of the chair and secured his wrists with the scarf. He laced his hands together. It would be laughably easy for him to break free, but this was merely a game. The scarf was a reminder, not truly a restraint.

I moved until I could see his eyes. "Is this okay?" I asked him quietly, seriously.

"*Fuck yes,*" he agreed, his voice gravel rough.

I smiled, happy that he was willing to play along. This dress might be *his* fantasy, but having him bound and helpless was *mine.* "You are going to sit and watch until I tell you otherwise, understand?"

He nodded, expression hot and hungry.

It was impossible to be self-conscious when his eyes burned with desire. My pulse thundered in my ears and I already felt like I was on the edge. It would take so little to push me over.

I slid my skirt up my thighs a millimeter at a time. Alex's gaze was locked on the rising edge of the fabric, and when it cleared the apex of my legs, he groaned like he'd been punched. "Stars have mercy, you're not wearing anything under that dress."

"Not a thing," I agreed. The air was cool on my overheated flesh. I propped my foot on his rock-hard thigh, exposing more of myself. I slid one finger through my heat and it came away glistening.

Alex's pupils were blown and he tracked my finger with intent focus. His muscles tensed as he fought to hold himself still, to not reach for me.

I leaned down, until my lips just brushed his ear, then whispered, "Would you like a taste?"

The groan of agreement rumbled from deep in his chest.

I painted his bottom lip with my finger, then let it linger. He sat stone-still, frozen in agony and ecstasy. "Suck."

When his lips closed around the digit and drew it into the molten cave of his mouth, I moaned and shivered, so, so close to tipping over the edge. Playtime was over. Almost.

I reluctantly pulled away from him and turned. He groaned when I bent to remove my shoes and again when I unfastened the dress and slowly shimmied out of it. I laid back on the bed, bare and open to his gaze.

"Now it's time for your punishment. Do not move until I give you permission. Understand?"

He nodded his agreement, his eyes glued to my body.

I drew it out as long as I could, petting and stroking while telling him exactly what I was doing and how it felt. When I trembled into release, he stood with a growl, the scarf falling away.

"My turn," he said, his voice thick with promise.

His pants vanished and he was *magnificent*. Light brown skin, dark hair, and muscles, so many muscles. My eyes dropped to the impressive erection between his legs. *Oh my.* Followed by, *yes, please.*

"I want that in me," I said boldly.

His grin promised sin and pleasure. "Patience, princess. As I told you, it's my turn now."

He started at my feet, kissing and licking his way up my body—slowly. He skipped the place I wanted him and nuzzled into the soft skin of my belly. I arched with a whine and he pressed a palm to my hip to keep me stationary.

By the time he reached my breasts, I was on fire again, my earlier orgasm forgotten. My hands were buried in his hair, trying to direct him, but he had his own plan. He laved each nipple into a straining point before moving on. I writhed, achy and hot.

I tugged on his hair. "Now, please," I moaned. "I need you."

He shifted and settled between my thighs. Pleasure danced over my skin when his length nudged my clit and my hips lifted, chasing the feeling.

He pulled back and met my eyes. "Yes?" he confirmed.

"Yes! Now!"

He slid home in one glorious stroke that hit every nerve I had and a few I didn't know about. I shouted my rapture to the ceiling and shattered again.

He kept moving, a heady push and pull, give and take, that blended into a long wave of pleasure that crested when he whispered into my ear, "I can feel you're close. Come for me again, princess."

Words had always been my weakness so I sailed into bliss once more.

EVENTUALLY, WE DRAGGED OURSELVES FROM BED TO find food. I threw together a simple plate of meats, cheeses, fruits, and bread—a plate that could be carried back into the bedroom and snacked on over time. I opened a bottle of wine and we feasted in the middle of the bed, naked and unashamed.

It was glorious.

I'd never felt so at ease with someone before, and like dawn breaking, a thought bloomed: I loved Alexander Sterling.

I must have looked as poleaxed as I felt, because Alex stopped eating and asked, "Are you okay?"

"I love you," I blurted out. "You don't have to say anything," I continued in a rush, "I know it's fast and I don't expect—"

"Cat," he interrupted, and from the tone of his voice, I figured it wasn't the first time he'd said it. His slow smile made my heart sing with joy. "I love you, too. I've loved you since the day you set your jaw and decided you'd go to Earth alone if you had to. I love your determination, and your empathy, and your strength."

"But you were so mad at me after that."

"Not mad, terrified. I wanted to wrap you up and keep you safe, but I knew I couldn't."

Happy tears flooded my eyes, even as old fears rose. "I'm not normal," I admitted quietly.

Alex set aside his plate and mine, then pulled me into his arms. "You're better than normal. Do you really not know what they did to you?"

"Nothing specific. I think they altered my genetics somehow. I was too scared to look into it because my father wanted to use me as a weapon. I started faking normal so he'd think whatever they'd done had faded and he'd lose interest."

Alex tensed under me and cursed quietly. "Your father was a real piece of work."

"Don't I know it."

"I will tell you what I know, but you must promise to keep it to yourself. You can discuss it with Bianca and Ada, for reasons that will become obvious, but I need your word that you won't tell anyone else."

"I swear I will keep your secrets safe."

Alex nodded distantly and took a deep breath. "I joined the RCDF at seventeen. I hadn't even been in a year when I heard about a program that promised to turn us into supersoldiers. The people in charge weren't clear about specifics and none of us asked too many questions, blinded by the promised abilities and the pay bump."

He shook his head. "I was young and stupid. We all were. They grouped us into four squads of eight. Loch and Ian were in my squad."

I gasped. "They're like you?"

"Yes. You asked me before what debt I owed to Bianca. When we were rescuing your brother, Ian fell. Bianca jumped out of the ship and went back for him. He's like a brother to me and she saved his life."

"She doesn't get to complain about me going into danger ever again," I said with a grin. Then, very quietly, I added, "Aoife was in your squad, too."

"You're too observant for your own good," he said with a rueful grin. "She was, but you must absolutely keep it a secret."

"I will."

Alex stroked a hand down my arm, but his expression was still distant. I wasn't sure if he even knew he was doing it. "They code-named our experiment the Genesis Project, and the scientists fucked with our DNA," he said. "Soldiers started getting sick almost immediately. That's why I asked about your symptoms, because those were the symptoms we had. Thanks to some genetic fluke, our squad recovered. The others did not."

"But I had those symptoms for *years*," I protested.

"I'm getting there. One story at a time. Like your father, the scientists and the RCDF generals wanted to see what we could do. Our first real mission was to slaughter women and children on Fornax who were starving and rebelling against the price of food. When we refused, our commanders told us that it was us or them. Loch saved us."

"The Devil of Fornax Zero," I whispered, the pieces coming together. "He faked your deaths and sent you into hiding."

"He was our squad leader. We tried to get him to come with us, but he knew the Consortium needed a visible target or they'd keep searching for us. He sacrificed his life for ours, if not literally then figuratively."

"I'm glad he found Ada."

"Me, too. He saved us, and your sister saved him."

I nodded thoughtfully. Ada was blissfully happy, as was Bianca, and they were both with partners who had altered genes. The Consortium as a whole had a very dim view of DNA editing—it was a capital offense—but I doubted my sisters subscribed to the same way of thinking. Maybe now that Father was gone, I could share my secrets with them and they wouldn't find me unlovable.

"So that's me, a military science experiment gone wrong," Alex said lightly.

"Don't say that!"

He smiled. "I've had years to get used to it. I can see the humor now, especially when seeing in the dark is so handy. But now we come to you."

I swallowed nervously. I still wasn't used to talking about myself openly. "What about me?"

"I think you were the first test subject. I think your father tested the changes on you for years before the Genesis Project experiment."

"No. I was born sickly. If anything, the changes cured me."

"Were you, though? You don't have any memories of running and playing? Your older siblings didn't ever mention it?"

They had dubbed me a chaos monster, but I'd thought that was from when I was feeling well enough to play. But I didn't remember a time when they *hadn't* called me that. Had I been completely well at some point?

Had Father stolen my childhood?

I shook my head. "I don't know. I don't want to believe that Father was capable of hurting his own daughter as a child for no reason, but it's possible."

"You should talk to your sisters. If the information exists, Bianca can find it. I've seen her work. It's miraculous."

"She is amazing," I agreed. "After all, she brought me you."

Alex's eyes glowed with happiness, even as wicked desire tugged at the corners of his mouth. "Let me show you just how lucky you are."

I tilted my face up to his. "Please do."

His mouth slanted across mine and the time for words was over.

CHAPTER THIRTY-THREE

I tapped on Bianca's door before I could talk myself out of it. Alex had offered to come with me, but I needed to do this on my own. The door slid open and Bianca called a greeting from inside.

I steeled my spine against the desire to run away. It did not help, but I managed to step across the threshold, and after that, it got easier.

It became easier still once I caught sight of Bianca's radiant face. In the last few months, she'd emerged from the darkness that had shadowed her soul since her marriage to Gregory. She'd gained weight as well and she glowed with health and happiness.

"Coffee or alcohol?" she asked.

"Alcohol. Dealer's choice."

She poured us each a generous glass of sangria from the pitcher in her fridge, then waved me to the sofa. I sat, fidgeting with my glass.

"Did you talk to Alexander?" she asked softly. When I nodded, she continued, "And you have questions about the Genesis Project?"

I started to shake my head, but then I swallowed and blurted out, "I'm like them."

Stone-cold silence settled before Bianca made an anguished sound. "Oh, Cat, I'm so sorry that I didn't see it, that I didn't protect you. You must've felt so alone. No wonder your mask was so strong."

I risked a peek at her. Her face was filled with love, not hate, and deep regret.

"I don't know if you can ever forgive me, but I am so, so sorry," she said, her tone heartbroken.

"It wasn't your fault."

"I should've known when you got sick that something was going on, but the doctors assured us they had it under control. And you were always such a cheerful little tyke, even when you weren't feeling well."

"You don't think I'm an abomination?" I asked, my voice barely a whisper.

She set her glass aside and put her hand on my shoulder so she could squarely meet my eyes. "Never. I would never think that. I think you're amazing. Strong, brave, perfect." She struggled with something for a second, then said, "Gregory experimented on me."

"What? How?"

She breathed out a sigh and wiped her eyes. "Okay, that was harder than I expected. I was right—you are brave and amazing."

"Bianca," I demanded, "what did he *do*?"

"He modified my nanos and gave me a brain implant. I can mentally decode wireless transmissions." Now it was her turn to peek at me. "I haven't told anyone else, except Ian."

"That's why you were so sick," I said. "Gregory was hurting you. That fucker better be glad he's dead because I've recently learned how to use my strength to maximum effect."

"You don't care that I can eavesdrop on wireless messages?" she asked carefully.

"You don't care that I can see in the dark and break bones with my bare hands?"

"You're my sister; I'd love you even if you sprouted horns and a tail. A little extra strength and some night vision isn't anything to get worked up about."

"Exactly. You're my sister. I love you. But I wish you'd told me so I could kick your worthless husband's ass."

"It seems we both kept secrets for too long. Tell me everything."

I told her what I knew and what Alex suspected. She confirmed that I hadn't gotten sick until my fourth birthday, and she promised to look into the House records to see if she could find anything relating to me specifically.

"I think we should tell the others," she said at last. "Both of us."

Blind panic closed my throat.

"It doesn't have to be today, but I think it should be soon. I've hidden long enough. So have you. Father is dead, and Ferdinand will never use us as weapons. Just think about it."

"I will," I promised weakly. I knew she was right, but that didn't stop my instinctive reaction. "Please let me know if you find anything."

She nodded and let me flee.

ALEX MOVED INTO MY SUITE AND IT FELT LIKE HE'D ALways been there. We christened every horizontal surface at least once. I couldn't keep my hands off him, and he, luckily, felt the same.

During the day, we helped rebuild House von Hasenberg or Serenity, but the nights—the nights were ours.

A week passed in a blur, and then, two weeks after the initial attack, the Royal Consortium was set to meet for the first time. Before they did, Bianca, Ying, and I met in Bianca's suite to go over the information we'd uncovered.

Rather, it was *supposed* to be just the three of us, but then Ferdinand showed up with Evelyn Rockhurst. Then the rest of my brothers and sisters just happened to "drop by" along with Ian, Loch, Alex, and Aoife.

Alex grinned at me, then went to stand near the other three he'd come in with. He and Loch were both big and muscled, but I had eyes only for Alex.

Next to me, Ying sighed wistfully. I knew that sigh, so I followed her gaze to the little group around Alex. Aoife grinned and tipped her head in greeting, and a hint of color touched Ying's cheeks.

When Ying noticed my knowing grin, she blushed harder. "You should've seen her in action. It was incredible. Beautiful and deadly. And far too good for me." Before I could comment, Ying shook herself and her mask reappeared, hiding her true feelings. "I thought we agreed this was going to be a small meeting to get our facts straight."

I let her change the subject. "I thought so, too, but this has Bianca's handiwork written all over it. If you're uncomfortable sharing what we've found in front of so many, we can reschedule."

Ying shook her head. "No, it's going to come out sooner or later. Might as well be now, with people I know." She eyed Evelyn, who sat beside Ferdinand. "Are those two . . . ?" She waved her hands together.

I grinned and dipped my head slightly. "They're keeping it quiet."

Ying rolled her eyes. "Not when they look at each other like that."

She had a point. My usually stoic brother did look rather besotted, and Evelyn's cool facade warmed every time she glanced at him.

Bianca stood and the room quieted. "You know why we're all here," she said. She turned to me. "Cat, bring everyone up to speed on what happened with House James." At my questioning look, she nodded. "All of it. We all need to be on the same page."

I stood. No one questioned my ability to deliver a critical report, and my confidence rose. "House James bought Hannah's husband's gambling contracts, then leaned on him to sign over mineral rights in Antlia. Since he couldn't do that unless Hannah was the heir, he took out a contract on Ferdinand's life with the Syndicate."

"So why didn't they kill Ferdinand?" Benedict asked. He flashed Ferdinand an apologetic grimace, but our older brother waved him off.

"Insurance or blackmail potential, most likely. I believe they only planned to keep him around until they got what they wanted. Luckily, Bianca got there before that happened."

I looked down to Ying and she nodded her permission. Hitoshi had vanished in the chaos after the attack, much to Ying's consternation, so in a show of trust, she'd let Bianca into their House network to figure out where he might have gone. Bianca had found a great deal more than that.

Combined with the information from the data chip from House James—which had been unlocked with the key from Joseph—we had a nearly complete time line of treachery.

"Hitoshi Yamado has been working with the Silva family for years. He's also been collecting lower house allies, including House James, by making them grand promises of wealth and power. Once House von Hasenberg and House Rockhurst went to war, Hitoshi seized the moment, especially after he learned what the war was really about. He asked House James to lean on Pierre, and then suggested Silva might solve Pierre's problem."

Hitoshi had been trying to lock down the supply of alcubium, the mineral required for faster FTL travel. He'd nearly succeeded. If not for Bianca's information network and quick thinking, we would be having a very different meeting.

"He expected the attack on Ferdinand to intensify the war. When Bianca found the connection to Riccardo Silva instead, they had to push up their time line. They'd wanted von Hasenberg and Rockhurst to fight longer, so we'd be weaker opponents, but they decided on a more direct approach."

"Attacking Serenity and the rest of the High House heirs," Ferdinand said.

I nodded. "The Silva family wants the Syndicate to run the universe, but they can't do that as long as the Royal Consortium still stands. However, take out two of the High Houses, partner with the third, and suddenly taking over is much easier in the resulting power vacuum. The lower houses who aren't in on it might protest but they'll just get rolled over."

"Hitoshi can't be stupid enough to think the Syndicate will leave him in power," Evelyn said.

"Hitoshi isn't stupid," Ying said. "He's likely got some sort of backup plan or he's working a double-cross. As much as I hate to admit it, he's brilliant, ruthless, and ambitious. He doesn't care who he crushes on his way to the top."

"Where is he?" Evelyn asked.

Ying shook her head. "I don't know. He survived the initial attack, that much I know for sure. But once it looked like the

RCDF was going to take back Serenity, he vanished. His battle cruiser was captured, so he must be on his personal ship. I tried tracking it, with no success."

Evelyn tilted her head, considering Ying. "And how do we know you're not working with him?"

"She's not," Bianca said. "She let me into their network, and she's not good enough to hide information from me." Bianca smiled apologetically at Ying before turning back to the group. "Hitoshi was trying to frame her—clumsily—but as far as I can tell, she is not working with him or Silva. And Hitoshi asked Riccardo Silva to ensure that Ying died along with Cat while they were at House James."

Ying sucked in a quiet breath. She either hadn't known, or hadn't expected Bianca to find that piece of information.

Evelyn sat back, satisfied by Bianca's answer.

"Does anyone have any questions?" I asked. My gaze landed on Alex's handsome face and he smiled in encouragement.

"Many," Benedict said quietly, "but most important: where do we go from here?"

"I think we can all agree that the Syndicate can't be allowed to take over." Every head nodded. "So we need to do everything we can to drive them back into the darkness and ensure that they retain as little power as possible. We also have a unique opportunity to change the universe for the better, so I say we do that, too. I know you all have ideas."

Murmured agreement met my words.

"Let's make those ideas happen. Let's make them *all* happen."

PEOPLE TRICKLED OUT AS THEY LEFT TO GET READY FOR the Royal Consortium meeting. Alex joined me and brushed a soft kiss over my lips. "Nicely done."

"Thank you. I have something for you. And for Aoife."

Alex waved her over. "What's up?" she asked.

While going through the encrypted data chip from House James, Bianca and I had talked about what to do with the three credit chips I'd recovered and the fortune they contained. The money had been meant to ensure that Ying and I did not leave House James alive. Because we had, with the help of Alex, Aoife, and Cira, we'd decided it was best to split the money five ways.

I handed Alex and Aoife each a credit chip. "We recovered three chips from House James. This is your share. Do *not* lose it. And you might not want to carry it around, either."

I'd transferred my share to a secure account and planned to set up a charitable foundation with it, perhaps for children with true genetic issues. Or maybe I'd found a research center to look into genetic research that helped rather than hurt. I hadn't decided, but I knew that I wanted to do something good with this money that had come from a very dark place.

Alex tried to hand his back while Aoife asked, "How much is on here?"

"A lot." I smacked Alex's hands away when he tried to tuck the chip in my clothes after I refused to take it back. "Stop it. You earned it. You helped rescue Ferdinand. You saved me multiple times. You stormed Earth with me despite the fact that you thought my plan was crazy. You earned every credit. If you don't want it, share it with your friends. Set yourself up as a lower house. Buy a ship. Do something with it, but I won't take it back."

Aoife stared at me for a few seconds, then nodded and slipped the chip in an inner pocket. "Thank you."

"You're welcome."

She left with another nod. Alex was not so easy to per-suade. "Take it back."

"Alex, I love you, but I'm not taking it back. It's yours."

When I wouldn't let him get close until he put the chip away, he tucked it into a zippered pocket, and then tugged me against his chest. "What if it was ours?"

I tried to keep my expression serious but a smile kept tug-ging on my lips. "I suppose that would be acceptable."

"I love you. Marry me."

I laughed, delighted. "Well, since you asked so nicely . . ."

He dropped to one knee and gently grasped my left hand. "Catarina von Hasenberg, you are my everything. You are the most amazing woman I've ever met. You are my first thought when I wake and my last thought before I sleep. Will you please do me the honor of becoming my wife?"

I heard a gasp from somewhere behind me, but I could only nod around the lump in my throat. Alex slipped a gorgeous ring on my finger. It fit perfectly. The ring blurred around the edges as I blinked away tears.

Alex stood and I dragged him into a heated kiss. "I love you, you incredible, amazing man, even if you did make me cry."

"I'll make it up to you later," he said, his voice a deep, velvet rumble.

"I'm holding you to that," I promised.

ALEX AND I MANAGED TO ESCAPE FROM FAMILY AND friends—many of whom had returned to Bianca's to wish us well when they heard about the proposal—just long enough to change into clothes appropriate for the Royal Consortium chambers.

Bianca had carefully massaged the data we had on

Hitoshi's betrayal, stripping out the mentions of his allies; we would deal with them later. She'd submitted all of the evidence and now we had to wait for the wheels of justice to turn—slowly.

But today wasn't about Hitoshi, it was about tradition. The long rectangular Royal Consortium chamber slowly filled with representatives of the lower houses. And the RCDF was out in force, ensuring that another attack wouldn't happen on this important day.

House von Hasenberg crowded into our box. The whole family—including Ian, Loch, and Alex—had turned out to show our support, but Ferdinand sat front and center.

To our left, Tae and Ying Yamado sat next to each other in silence. Tae had been injured in the attack and still wore a bandage around his head. Their mother had secluded herself in mourning. Ying's face was a calm ocean.

To our right, Evelyn Rockhurst sat in the front of her box, several of her siblings and her father behind her. On the dais at the head of the room, the three seats for the High Councillors remained empty.

Alex clasped my hand and rubbed a soothing thumb over my knuckles. The ring was an unfamiliar weight that I couldn't stop admiring. Alex caught my gaze and raised my hand to his lips. He pressed a gentle kiss on the back of it and heat licked through me everywhere.

"Behave," I whispered.

He winked. "Never."

The Speaker called the meeting to order, then droned on and on about tradition and honor and I don't know what else. I tuned out until Ferdinand was called to stand. With Father's death, Ferdinand would officially become the High Councillor of House von Hasenberg.

"If anyone has a reason Lord Ferdinand should not be given this position, speak now," the Speaker intoned.

Lord Henderson rose and cleared his throat. "Albrecht promised Ca—"

"Sit down," Wilma Sollorz interrupted. "Before you embarrass yourself."

Henderson rounded on her, but found no sympathy from his fellow Consortium members. Pippa August shot him a withering glare. In fact, half the room glared. I never knew I had so many allies. Henderson found himself facing a wall of opposition.

He dropped back into his seat with a snarl. Next to him, his daughter stared straight ahead.

The chamber fell silent.

Ferdinand took his place on the dais. The Speaker went through the same process again with Evelyn Rockhurst. She took her seat on the dais and smiled at Ferdinand. He smiled back.

The Speaker turned back to the chamber. "As you all know, serious charges have been levied against Lord Hitoshi Yamado. Until the investigation is complete, we will appoint a temporary High Councillor from House Yamado. Tae Yamado, please rise."

Ying's knuckles whitened as she clenched her hands into fists.

"If anyone has a reason Lord Tae should not be given this position, speak now," the Speaker said.

Ying sat serenely, head held high, but I knew what it cost her to stay silent. She loved her brother enough to kill her dreams for his. I wanted so badly to go to her. Alex squeezed my fingers and I realized I had a death grip on his hand. I forced my fingers to go slack.

Then Tae Yamado spoke. "I do," he said simply. "I abdicate. Lady Ying is far better suited to leading House Yamado into a prosperous future than I am. I yield my position to her so that I may focus on my wife and upcoming child."

Murmurs broke out around the room, both at the unexpected abdication and at the announcement that Tae and his wife were expecting a child.

Ying smiled at her brother, her face shining with fierce love. *She'd known.* I'd worried for nothing. Tae and Ying had always been close, so I shouldn't be surprised that they'd talked.

The Speaker pounded his gavel. "This is very unusual," he said at last.

Tae stood straight and proud. "I know. It is an unusual day. But I believe my sister is the best person for the job." He drew Ying up and kissed her on the cheek, then took his seat.

I clapped, too delighted to stick to decorum. My family joined me and soon the whole room thundered with applause. Even those I knew to be traitors clapped, albeit unenthusiastically.

The Speaker pounded his gavel until the room quieted. "Very well. If anyone has a reason that Lady Ying should not be given this *temporary* position, speak now."

I glared at the man for the completely unnecessary reminder that Hitoshi was still out there somewhere. Then I switched my glare to the room, daring anyone to object. No one did.

Ying took her position on the dais, her smile radiant.

The three new High Councillors rose as one and the crowd cheered. The lower houses had no idea what was about to happen, and many of them would not appreciate the changes. Ferdinand, Evelyn, and Ying had their work cut out for them, but for the first time in many years, and hand in hand with the incredible man beside me, I was excited to see what the future would bring.

And maybe I would have that meeting Bianca wanted sooner rather than later. We all deserved to live our lives free of secrets and shadows.

I pulled Alex into a celebratory kiss and he stole my breath. "Congratulations, princess, you did it," he murmured.

"*We* did it," I corrected. "And I can't wait to see what we do next."

Jessie Mihalik returns in 2022 with an exciting new series about a fierce female intergalactic bounty hunter, her motley crew, and a grim former foe who's hiding more than a few secrets.

ABOUT THE AUTHOR

Jessie Mihalik has a degree in computer science and a love of all things geeky. A software engineer by trade, Jessie now writes full-time from her home in Texas. When she's not writing, she can be found playing co-op video games with her husband, trying out new board games, or reading books pulled from her overflowing bookshelves.